Praise for Ilona Andrews and the Kate Daniels series:

Magic Bites

'Splendid . . . an edgy dark fantasy touched with
just the right amount of humor'
New York Times bestselling author Patricia Briggs

'Andrews' edgy series stands apart from similar
fantasies . . . owing to its complex world building and
skilled characterisations'
Library Journal

'Andrews shows a great deal of promise. Readers fond of
Laurell K. Hamilton and Patricia Briggs may find her work a
new source of reading pleasure'
SFRevu

Magic Burns

'With all her problems, secrets and prowess both martial and
magical, Kate is a great kick-ass heroine, a tough girl with a
heart, and her adventures are definitely worth checking out'
Locus

'*Magic Burns* hooked me completely. With a fascinating,
compelling plot, a witty, intelligent heroine, a demonic villain
and clever wry humour throughout, this story has it all'
Fresh Fiction

Magic Strikes

'Andrews' crisp dialogue and layered characterisation
make the gut-wrenching action of this first-person thrill
ride all the more intense. Place your book orders now;
it's worth every penny!'
Romantic Times

Also by Ilona Andrews from Gollancz:

Magic Bites

Magic Burns

Magic Strikes

A Kate Daniels Novel

Magic Strikes

ILONA ANDREWS

First published in Great Britain in 2010 by
Gollancz
An imprint of the Orion Publishing Group
Orion House, 5 Upper St Martin's Lane, London WC2H 9EA
An Hachette UK Company

3 5 7 9 10 8 6 4

A CIP catalogue record for this book is available
from the British Library

ISBN 978 0 575 09395 9

Printed in Great Britain by Clays Ltd, St Ives plc

The Orion Publishing Group's policy is to use papers that are
natural, renewable and recyclable products and made from wood
grown in sustainable forests. The logging and manufacturing
processes are expected to conform to the environmental regulations
of the country of origin.

www.ilona-andrews.com
www.orionbooks.co.uk

To Anastasia and Helen

CHAPTER 1

SOME DAYS MY JOB WAS HARDER THAN OTHERS.

I tapped the ladder with my hand. "See? It's very sturdy, Mrs. McSweeney. You can come down now."

Mrs. McSweeney looked at me from the top of the telephone pole, having obvious doubts about the ladder's and my reliability. Thin, bird-boned, she had to be past seventy. The wind stirred the nimbus of fine white hair around her head and blew open her nightgown, presenting me with sights better left unseen.

"Mrs. McSweeney, I wish you would come down."

She arched her back and sucked in a deep breath. Not again. I sat on the ground and clamped my hands over my ears.

The wail cut through the stillness of the night, sharp like a knife. It hammered the windows of the apartment buildings, wringing a high-pitched hum from the glass. Down the street, dogs yowled as one, matching the cry with unnatural harmony. The lament built, swelling like an avalanche, until I could hear nothing but its complex, layered chorus: the lonely howl of a wolf, the forlorn shriek of a bird, the heart-wrenching cry of a child. She wailed and wailed, as if her heart were being torn out of her chest, filling me with despair.

The magic wave ended. One moment it saturated the world, giving potency to Mrs. McSweeney's cry, and the next it vanished without warning, gone like a line drawn in the sand just before the surf licked it. The technology reasserted itself. The blue feylantern hanging from the top of the pole went dark, as the magic-charged air lost its potency. Electric lights came on in the apartment building.

It was called post-Shift resonance: magic drowned the world in a wave, snuffing out anything complex and technological, smothering car engines, jamming automatic weapons, and eroding tall buildings. Mages fired ice bolts, skyscrapers fell, and wards flared into life, keeping undesirables from my house. And then, just like that, the magic would vanish, leaving monsters in its wake. Nobody could predict when it would reappear and nobody could prevent it. All we could do was cope with an insane tarantella of magic and technology. That was why I carried a sword. It always worked.

The last echoes of the cry bounced from the brick walls and died.

Mrs. McSweeney stared at me with sad eyes. I picked myself off the ground and waved at her. "I'll be right back."

I trotted into the dark entrance to the apartment, where five members of the McSweeney family crouched in the gloom. "Tell me again why you can't come out and help me?"

Robert McSweeney, a middle-aged, dark-eyed man with thinning brown hair, shook his head. "Mom thinks we don't know she's a banshee. Look, Ms. Daniels, can you get her down or not? You're the knight of the Order, for Christ's sake."

First, I wasn't a knight; I just worked for the Order of Knights of Merciful Aid. Second, negotiation wasn't my forte. I killed things. Quickly and with much bloodshed.

Getting elderly banshees in denial off telephone poles wasn't something I did often.

"Can you think of anything that might help me?"

Robert's wife, Melinda, sighed. "I don't . . . I mean, she always kept it so under wraps. We've heard her wail before but she was so discreet about it. This isn't normal for her."

An elderly black woman in a mumu descended the staircase. "Has that girl gotten Margie down yet?"

"I'm working on it," I told her.

"You tell her, she better not miss our bingo tomorrow night."

"Thanks."

I headed to the pole. Part of me sympathized with Mrs. McSweeney. The three law enforcement agencies that regulated life in the United States post-Shift—the Military Supernatural Defense Unit, or MSDU; the Paranormal Activity Division, or PAD; and my illustrious employer, the Order of Knights of Merciful Aid—all certified banshees as harmless. Nobody had yet been able to link their wails to any deaths or natural disasters. But folklore blamed banshees for all sorts of nefarious things. They were rumored to drive people mad with their screams and kill children with a mere look. Plenty of people would be nervous about living next to a banshee, and I could understand why Mrs. McSweeney went to great lengths to hide who she was. She didn't want her friends to shun her or her family.

Unfortunately, no matter how well you hide, sooner or later your big secret will bite you in the behind, and you might find yourself standing on a telephone pole, not sure why or how you got there, while the neighborhood pretends not to hear your piercing screeches.

Yeah. I was one to talk. When it came to hiding one's identity, I was an expert. I burned my bloody bandages, so nobody could identify me by the magic in my blood. I hid my power. I tried very hard not to make friends and mostly succeeded. Because when my secret came to life, I wouldn't end up on top of a telephone pole. I would be dead and all my friends would be dead with me.

I approached the pole and looked at Mrs. McSweeney. "Alright. I'm going to count to three and then you have to come down."

She shook her head.

"Mrs. McSweeney! You're making a spectacle out of yourself. Your family is worried about you and you have bingo tomorrow night. You don't want to miss it, do you?"

She bit her lip.

"We will do it together." I climbed three steps up the ladder. "On three. One, two, three, step!"

I took a step down and watched her do the same. *Thank you, whoever you are upstairs.*

"One more. One, two, three, step."

We took another step, and then she took one by herself. I jumped to the ground. "That's it."

Mrs. McSweeney paused. Oh no.

She looked at me with her sad eyes and asked, "You won't tell anyone, will you?"

I glanced at the windows of the apartment building. She had wailed loudly enough to wake the dead and make them call the cops. But in this day and age, people banded together. One couldn't rely on tech or on magic, only on family and neighbors. They were willing to keep her secret, no matter how absurd it seemed, and so was I.

"I won't tell anyone," I promised.

Two minutes later, she was heading to her apartment, and I was wrestling with the ladder, trying to make it fit back into the space under the stairs, where the super had gotten it from for me.

My day had started at five with a frantic man running through the hallway of the Atlanta chapter of the Order and screaming that a dragon with a cat head had gotten into New Hope School and was about to devour the children. The dragon turned out to be a small tatzelwyrm, which I unfortunately was unable to subdue without cutting its head off. That was the first time I had gotten sprayed with blood today.

Then I had to help Mauro get a two-headed freshwater

serpent out of an artificial pond at the ruins of One Atlantic Center in Buckhead. The day went downhill from there. It was past midnight now. I was dirty, tired, hungry, smeared with four different types of blood, and I wanted to go home. Also my boots stank because the serpent had vomited a half-eaten cat corpse on my feet.

I finally managed to stuff the ladder in its place and left the apartment building for the parking lot, where my female mule, Marigold, was tied to a metal rack set up there for precisely that purpose. I had gotten within ten feet of her when I saw a half-finished swastika drawn on her rump in green paint. The paint stick lay broken on the ground. There was also some blood and what looked like a tooth. I looked closer. Yep, definitely a tooth.

"Had an adventure, did we?"

Marigold didn't say anything, but I knew from experience that approaching her from behind was Not a Good Idea. She kicked like a mule, probably because she was one.

If not for the Order's brand on her other butt cheek, Marigold might have been stolen tonight. Fortunately, the knights of the Order had a nasty habit of magically tracking thieves and coming down on them like a ton of bricks.

I untied her, mounted, and we braved the night.

Typically technology and magic switched at least once every couple of days, usually more often than that. But two months ago we had been hit with a flare, a wave so potent, it drowned the city like a magic tsunami, making impossible things a reality. For three days demons and gods had walked the streets and human monsters had great difficulty controlling themselves. I had spent the flare on the battlefield, helping a handful of shapeshifters butcher a demonic horde.

It had been an epic occurrence all around. I still had vivid dreams about it, not exactly nightmares, but intoxicating, surreal visions of blood and gleaming blades and death.

The flare had burned out, leaving technology firmly in control of the world. For two months, cars started without fail, electricity held the darkness at bay, and air-conditioning made August blissful. We even had TV. On Monday night they had shown a movie, *Terminator 2*, hammering home the point: it could always be worse.

Then, on Wednesday right around noon, the magic hit and Atlanta went to hell.

I wasn't sure if people had deluded themselves into thinking the magic wouldn't come back or if they had been caught unprepared, but we'd never had so many calls for help since I had started with the Order. Unlike the Mercenary Guild, for which I also worked, the knights of the Order of Knights of Merciful Aid helped anyone and everyone regardless of their ability to pay. They charged only what you could afford and a lot of times nothing at all. We had been flooded with pleas. I managed to catch four hours of sleep on Wednesday night and then it was up and running again. Technically it was Friday now, and I was plagued by persistent fantasies of hot showers, food, and soft sheets. I had made an apple pie a couple of days ago, and I still had a slice left for tonight.

"Kate?" Maxine's stern voice echoed through my head, distant but clear.

I didn't jump. After the marathon of the last forty-eight hours, hearing the Order's telepathic secretary in my head seemed perfectly normal. Sad but true.

"I'm sorry, dear, but the pie might have to wait."

What else was new? Maxine didn't read thoughts on purpose, but if I concentrated on something hard enough, she couldn't help but catch a hint of it.

"I have a green seven, called in by a civilian."

Dead shapeshifter. Anything shapeshifter-related was mine. The shapeshifters distrusted outsiders, and I was the only employee of the Atlanta chapter of the Order who enjoyed Friend of the Pack status. "Enjoyed" being a relative term. Mostly my status meant that the shapeshifters might let me say a couple of words before deciding to fillet me. They took paranoid to a new level.

"Where is it?"

"*Corner of Ponce de Leon and Dead Cat.*"

Twenty minutes by mule. Chances were, the Pack already knew the death had taken place. They would be all over the scene, snarling and claiming jurisdiction. Ugh. I turned Marigold and headed north. "I'm on it."

MARIGOLD CHUGGED UP THE STREETS, SLOW BUT steady, and seemingly tireless. The jagged skyline crawled past me, once-proud buildings reduced to crumbling husks. It was as if magic had set a match to Atlanta but extinguished the flames before the scorched city had a chance to burn to the ground.

Here and there random pinpoint dots of electric lights punctured the darkness. A scent of charcoal smoke spiced with the aroma of seared meat drifted from the Alexander on Ponce apartments. Someone was cooking a midnight dinner. The streets lay deserted. Most people with a crumb of sense knew better than to stay out at night.

A high-pitched howl of a wolf rolled through the city, sending shivers down my spine. I could almost picture her standing upon a concrete rib of a fallen skyscraper, pale fur enameled silver by moonlight, her head raised to expose her shaggy throat as she sung a flawless song, tinted with melancholy longing and the promise of a bloody hunt.

A lean shadow skittered from the alley, followed by another. Emaciated, hairless, loping on all fours in a jerky, uncoordinated gait, they crossed the street before me and paused. They had been human at some point but both had been dead for more than a decade. No fat or softness remained on their bodies. No flesh—only steel-wire muscle beneath thick hide. Two vampires on the prowl. And they were out of their territory.

"ID," I said. Most navigators knew me by sight just like they knew every member of the Order in Atlanta.

The forefront bloodsucker unhinged his jaw and the navigator's voice issued forth, distorted slightly. "Journeyman Rodriguez, Journeyman Salvo."

"Your Master?"

"Rowena."

Of all the Masters of the Dead, I detested Rowena the least. "You're a long way from the Casino."

"We . . ."

The second bloodsucker opened his mouth, revealing light fangs against his black maw. "He screwed up and got us lost in the Warren."

"I followed the map."

The second bloodsucker stabbed a clawed finger at the sky. "The map's useless if you can't orient for shit. The moon doesn't rise in the north, you moron."

Two idiots. It would be comical if I didn't feel the blood hunger rising from the vamps. If these two knuckleheads lost control for a moment, the bloodsuckers would rip into me.

"Carry on," I said and nudged Marigold.

The vamps took off, the journeymen riding their minds probably bickering somewhere deep within the Casino. The *Immortuus* pathogen robbed its victims of their egos. Insentient, the vampires obeyed only their hunger for blood, butchering anything with a pulse. The emptiness of a vampiric mind made it a perfect vehicle for necromancers, Masters of the Dead. Most of the Masters served the People. Part cult, part research institute, part corporation, all vomit inducing, the People devoted themselves to the study and care of the undead. They had chapters in most major cities, just like the Order. Here, in Atlanta, they made their den in the Casino.

Among the power brokers of Atlanta, the People ranked pretty high. Only the Pack could match them in the potential for destruction. The People were led by a mysterious legendary figure, who chose to call himself Roland in this day and age. Roland possessed immense power. He was also the man I had been training all my life to kill.

I circled a big pot hole in the old pavement, turned onto Dead Cat, and saw the crime scene under a busted street lamp. Cops and witnesses were nowhere in sight. Gauzy moonlight sifted onto the bodies of seven shapeshifters. None of them was dead.

Two werewolves in animal form swept the scene for scents, carefully padding in widening circles from the narrow mouth of Dead Cat Street. Most shapeshifters in beast form ran larger than their animal counterparts, and these proved no exception: hulking, shaggy beasts taller and thicker than a male Great Dane. Past them, two of their colleagues in human form packed something suspiciously resembling a body into a body bag. Three others walked the perimeter, presumably to keep the onlookers out of the way. As if anyone was dumb enough to linger for a second look.

At my approach, everything stopped. Seven pairs of glowing eyes stared at me: four green, three yellow. Judging by the glow, the shapeshifter crew hovered on the verge of going furry. One of their own was dead and they were out for blood.

I kept my tone light. "You fellows ever thought of hiring out as a Christmas lights crew? You'd make a fortune."

The nearest shapeshifter trotted to me. Bulky with muscle but fit, he was in his early forties. His face wore the trademark expression the Pack presented to the outsiders: polite and hard like the rock of Gibraltar. "Good evening, ma'am. This is a private investigation conducted by the Pack. I'm going to have to ask you to please move on."

Ma'am . . . *Oy.*

I reached into my shirt, pulled out the wallet of transparent plastic I carried on a cord around my neck, and passed it to him. He glanced at my ID, complete with a small square of enchanted silver, and called out, "Order."

Across the street a man congealed from the darkness. One moment there was only a deep night shadow lying like a pool of ink against the wall of the building, and the next there he stood. Six-two, his skin the color of bitter chocolate, and built like a prize fighter. Normally he wore a black cloak, but today he limited himself to black jeans and T-shirt. As he moved toward me, muscles rolled on his chest and arms. His face inspired second thoughts in would-be brawlers. He looked like he broke bones for a living and he loved his job.

"Hello, Jim," I said, keeping my tone friendly. "Fancy meeting you here."

The shapeshifter who had spoken to me took off. Jim came close and patted Marigold's neck.

"Long night?" he asked. His voice was melodious and smooth. He never sang, but you knew he could, and if he decided to do it, women would be hurling themselves into his path.

"You might say that."

Jim was my partner from the days when I worked exclusively for the Mercenary Guild. Some merc gigs required more than one body, and Jim and I tackled them together, mostly because we couldn't stomach working with anybody else. Jim was also alpha of the cat clan and the Pack's chief of security. I'd seen him fight and I would rather take on a nest of pissed-off vipers any day.

"You should go home, Kate." A sheen of faint green rolled over his eyes and vanished, his animal side coming to the surface for a moment.

"What happened here?"

"Pack business."

The wolf on the left let out a short yelp. A female shapeshifter ran over to him and picked up something off the ground. I caught a glimpse of it before she stuffed the object into a bag. A human arm, severed at the elbow, still in a sleeve. We had just gone from code green seven to code green ten. Shapeshifter murder. Accidental deaths rarely resulted in detached limbs strewn across the intersection.

"Like I said, Pack business." Jim glanced at me. "You know the law."

The law said that the shapeshifters were an independent group, much like a Native American tribe, with the authority to govern itself. They made their own laws and they had a right to enforce them, as long as those laws didn't affect nonshapeshifters. If the Pack didn't want my help on this investigation, there wasn't a lot I could do about it. "As an agent of the Order, I extend an offer of assistance to the Pack."

"The Pack appreciates the Order's offer of assistance. As of now, we decline. Go home, Kate," Jim repeated. "You look worn-out."

Translation: shoo, puny human. Big, mighty shapeshifters have no need of your silly investigative skills. "You squared this with the cops?"

Jim nodded.

I sighed, turned Marigold around, and headed home. Someone had died. I wouldn't be the one to find out why. It irked me on some deep professional level. If it was anybody else but Jim, I would've pushed harder to see the body. But when Jim said no, he meant it. My pushing wouldn't accomplish anything except straining relations between the Pack and the Order. Jim didn't half-ass things, so his crew would be competent and efficient.

It still bothered me.

I would call the Paranormal Activity Division in the morning and see if any reports were filed. The paranormal cops wouldn't tell me what was in the report, but at least I'd know if Jim had filed one. Not that I didn't trust Jim, but it never hurt to check.

AN HOUR LATER I LEFT MARIGOLD IN A SMALL stable in the parking lot and climbed the stairs to my apartment. I had inherited the place from Greg, my guardian, who had served as knight-diviner with the Order. He had died six months ago. I missed him so much it hurt.

My front door was a sight like no other. I got in, locked the door, pulled off my noxious shoes, and dropped them in the corner. I would deal with them later. I unbuckled the leather harness that held Slayer, my saber, on my back, pulled the saber out, and put it by my bed. The apple pie beckoned. I dragged myself into the kitchen, opened the fridge, and stared at an empty pie plate.

Had I eaten the pie? I didn't remember finishing it. And if I had, I should've taken the empty plate out of the fridge.

The front door had shown no signs of forced entry. I did a quick inventory of the apartment. Nothing missing. Nothing out of place. Greg's library with his artifacts and books looked completely undisturbed.

I must've finished the pie. Considering the insanity of the last forty-eight hours, I had probably just forgotten. Well, that sucked. I took the pie plate, washed it while murmuring curses under my breath, and put it in its place under the stove. I couldn't have pie, but nobody could deny me my shower. I stripped off my clothes, shedding them on the way to the bathroom, crawled into the shower, and drowned the world in hot spray and rosemary soap.

I had just toweled off my hair when the phone rang.

I kicked the door open and stared at the phone, ringing its head off on the small night table by my bed. Nothing good ever happened to me because of phone calls. There was always somebody dead, dying, or making somebody else dead on the other line.

Ring-ring.

Ring-ring-ring.

Ring?

I sighed and picked it up. "Kate Daniels."

"Hello, Kate," said a familiar velvet voice. "I hope I didn't wake you."

Saiman. Just about the last person I wanted to talk to.

Saiman had an encyclopedic knowledge of magic. He was also a shapeshifter—of sorts. I had done a job for him, back when I worked for the Mercenary Guild full-time, and he found me amusing. Because I entertained him, he offered me his services as a magic expert at a criminal discount. Unfortunately, the last time we had met was in the middle of the flare, atop a high-rise, where Saiman was dancing naked in the snow. With the largest erection I had ever seen on a human being. He didn't want to let me off that roof either. I had to jump to get away from him.

I kept my voice civil. Kate Daniels, master of diplomacy. "I don't want to speak to you. In fact, I don't wish to continue our association at all."

"That's very unfortunate. However, I have something that might belong to you and I would like to return this item to your custody."

What in the world? "Mail it to me."

"I would but he would prove difficult to fit into an envelope."

He? *He* wasn't good.

"He refuses to speak, but perhaps I can describe him to you: about eighteen, dark, short hair, menacing scowl, large brown eyes. Quite attractive in a puppy way. Judging by the way the *tapedum lucidum* behind his retinas catches the light, he's a shapeshifter. I'm guessing a wolf. You brought him with you during our last unfortunate encounter. I'm truly sorry about it, by the way."

Derek. My one-time teenage werewolf sidekick. What the hell was he doing at Saiman's apartment?

"Hold the phone to him, please." I kept my voice even. "Derek, answer me so I know he isn't bluffing. Are you hurt?"

"No." Derek's voice was laced with a growl. "I can handle this. Don't come here. It isn't safe."

"It's remarkable that he has so much concern for your welfare, provided that he's the one sitting in a cage," Saiman murmured. "You keep the most interesting friends, Kate."

"Saiman?"

"Yes?"

"If you hurt him, I'll have twenty shapeshifters in your apartment foaming at the mouth at your scent."

"Don't worry. I have no desire to bring the Pack's wrath on my head. Your friend is unharmed and contained. I will, however, turn him over to proper authorities unless you come and pick him up by sunrise."

"I'll be there."

Saiman's voice held a slight mocking edge. "I'm looking forward to it."

CHAPTER 2

———

I MADE IT BY 3:00 A.M.

Saiman occupied a suite on the fifteenth floor of the only high-rise still standing in Buckhead. Magic hated tall buildings—magic hated anything large and technologically complex, period—and gnawed them down to nubs of concrete and steelwork only four to five stories high. They jutted sadly here and there along Midtown, like decrepit obelisks of some long-forgotten civilization.

Formerly Lenox Pointe and now Champion Heights, Saiman's building, which had been remodeled more times than I could count, was shielded by a complex spell, which tricked the magic into thinking the high-rise was a giant rock. During the magic waves, parts of the high-rise looked like a granite crag. During the flare, parts of it were a granite crag. But today, with the magic down, it looked like a high-rise.

I had taken Betsi, my gasoline-guzzling Subaru, to save time. The magic had just fallen, and considering how weak this wave had been, the tech would likely stay on top for at least a few more hours. I parked Betsi's battered, dented carcass next to slick vehicles that cost twice my year's salary and then some, and headed up the concrete steps to the lobby armored in steel plates and bulletproof glass.

My foot caught on the edge of a step and I nearly took a dive. Great. Saiman was frighteningly intelligent and observant, always a bad combo for an adversary. I needed to be sharp. Instead I was so tired, my eyes required matchsticks to stay open. If I didn't wake up fast, Derek could end the night wading through a sea of hurt.

When a shapeshifter hit puberty, he could go loup or go Code. Going loup meant surrendering yourself to the beast and rolling down the bumpy hill of homicide, cannibalism, and insanity, until you ran into teeth, blades, or a lot of silver bullets at the bottom. Going Code meant discipline, strict conditioning, and an iron will, and subjecting oneself to this lifestyle was the only way a shapeshifter could function in a human society. Going Code also meant joining a pack, where the hierarchy was absolute, with alphas burdened with vast power and heavy responsibility.

Atlanta's Pack was arguably the biggest in the country. Only Alaska's Ice Fury rivaled it for sheer numbers. Atlanta shapeshifters drew a lot of attention. The Pack was big on loyalty, accountability, chain of command, and honor. The Pack members never forgot that society at large perceived them as beasts, and they did everything in their power to project a low-key, law-abiding image. Punishment for unsanctioned criminal activity was immediate and brutal.

Getting caught breaking and entering into Saiman's apartment would land Derek into scalding-hot water. Saiman had connections, and if he chose, he could create a lot of noise. The potential for the Pack to get a huge and very public black eye was significant. The Pack's alphas, collectively known as the Pack Council, would be champing at the bit once they found out about the murder. Right now wasn't a good time to piss them off any further. I needed to get Derek out of that apartment, fast, quiet, and with a minimum of fuss.

I made it to the lobby and knocked on the metal grate. Inside a guard leveled an AK-47 at me from behind his reinforced station in the center of the marble floor. I gave him my name and he buzzed me in—I was expected. How nice of Saiman.

The elevator brought me to the fifteenth floor and spat me out into a luxurious hallway lined with carpet that might have been thicker than my mattress. I crossed it to Saiman's apartment, and the lock clicked open just as I reached out to ring the bell.

The door opened, revealing Saiman. He wore his neutral form, the one he usually put on for my benefit: a bald man of average height and slight build, wearing white sweats. His lightly tanned face was symmetrical, handsome even, strictly speaking, but devoid of any attitude. Being face-to-face with him was similar to looking into an opaque, slightly reflective surface: he enjoyed mimicking the mannerisms of his conversation partners, knowing it unnerved them.

His eyes, on the other hand, were as remarkable as his expression was bland: dark and backlit with an agile intellect. Right now the eyes sparkled with amusement. *Enjoy it while it lasts, Saiman. I brought my sword.*

"Kate, what a pleasure to see you."

Can't say likewise. "Derek?"

"Please, come in."

I entered the apartment, a carefully designed, monochromatic environment of ultramodern lines, curves, and plush white cushions. Even the loup cage, which contained Derek at the far wall, matched the gleaming steel and glass of the coffee table and lamp fixtures.

Derek saw me. He didn't stir, didn't say anything, but his gaze fastened on to me and wouldn't let go.

I walked over to the cage and looked at him. In one piece. "Are you hurt?"

"No. You shouldn't have come. I can handle this."

Obviously I was missing the whole picture. Any minute now he would leap up, wrench the two-inch silver alloy bars apart despite the fact that silver was toxic to shape-shifters, and heroically kick Saiman's ass. Any minute now. Any minute.

I sighed. *Fate, deliver me from the bravery of adolescent idiots.*

"Kate, please sit. Would you like something to drink?" Saiman migrated to the bar.

"Water, please."

I slid Slayer out of its sheath on my back. The saber caught the light of the electric lamps, its pale opaque blade long and slender. Saiman glanced at me from the bar. *Have you met my sword, Saiman? It's to die for.*

I laid Slayer on the coffee table, took a spot on the couch, and studied Derek. At nineteen, the boy wonder was still slightly awkward, with long legs and a lean body that promised to fill out in a few years. His brown hair grew dark, with a rich touch of chrome, and he kept it very short. His face, grim at the moment, possessed the type of fresh, dreamy beauty that made adolescent girls—and probably some moms—melt in his presence. When we first met, he had been pretty. Now he was slowly edging on handsome and promising to develop into a champion heartbreaker. His eyes especially posed danger to anything female: huge, dark, and defined by eyelashes so long they cast shadows onto his cheeks.

It was a wonder he could go out into the daylight at all. I could never understand why the cops didn't arrest him for causing an epidemic of swooning among females eighteen and under.

Saiman would screw anything that moved. With Derek's looks, I'd been afraid I'd find him chained to a bed or worse.

"After our conversation, I recalled where I had seen our young friend." Saiman brought over two crystal glasses, a pale gold wine for himself and water with ice for me. I checked the water. No white powder, no fizzing pill, no other blatantly obvious signs of being spiked. To drink or not to drink? That was the question.

I sipped it. If he'd spiked it, I could still kill him before I passed out.

Saiman sampled his wine and handed a folded newspaper to me. The newspapers had been a dying breed before the Shift, but the magic waves played havoc with the Internet, and the news sheets had returned in all their former glory. This one showed a photograph of a foreboding redbrick building behind a ruined wall. A dragon corpse, little more than a skeleton with shreds of rotting meat clinging to its bones, decomposed in the background among bodies of dead women. The headline proclaimed RED STALKER KILLER DISPATCHED BY BEAST LORD. No mention of me. Just the way I liked it.

A second picture punctuated the article below the first: Derek, carried off by Doolittle, the Pack's physician. The Stalker had broken Derek's legs and kept him chained to prevent the bones from healing.

"He was the boy targeted by the Stalker because of his association with you," Saiman said. "I believe he was blood sworn to protect you."

Saiman had excellent sources and paid well for the information, but Pack members didn't talk to outsiders, period. How the hell did he get hold of that juicy tidbit?

"The oath is no longer in effect." Curran, the Beast Lord of Atlanta, the Leader of the Pack, and Asshole Supreme, who quite literally held Derek's life in his claws, had released Derek from his blood pledge once the Stalker affair was over.

"Magic has an interesting quality, Kate. Once a bond is formed, it affects both people."

I knew Newman's theory of reciprocal magic as well as anyone. Saiman was fishing for information. I was happy to disappoint him. "If you think that I came here out of some residual magical compulsion generated by an old blood oath, you're wrong. He isn't my lover, my secret relative, or a shapeshifter of great importance to the Pack. I'm here because he's a friend. If our roles were reversed, you would be dead by now and he would be using your coffee table as a pry bar to wrench me out of that cage."

I fixed Saiman with my best version of a hard stare. "I don't have many friends, Saiman. If any harm befalls him, I'll take it very personally."

"Are you threatening me?" Saiman's voice held only a mild curiosity.

"I'm simply defining the playing field. If you hurt him, I'll hurt you back, and I won't give a second thought to the consequences."

Saiman nodded gravely. "Please be assured, I'll take your emotional attachment under consideration."

I had no doubt he would. Saiman took everything under consideration. He dealt in information, selling it to the highest bidder. He gathered his commodity bit by bit, piecing together a larger picture from fractured mosaics of individual conversations, and he forgot nothing.

Saiman set his wine down and braided the long fingers of his hands into a single fist. "However, your friend broke into my apartment and attempted to steal my property. I do feel compelled to point out that while I respect your capacity for violence, I'm confident you won't kill me without a reason. I don't intend to give you one, and therefore, I hold the upper hand in our negotiations."

That was true. If this mess got out, Derek would have to deal with Curran. The Beast Lord was an arrogant, powerful sonovabitch who ruled the Pack with a steel hand and three-inch claws. Curran and I mixed about as well as glycerin and nitric acid: put us together, shake a bit, and hit the deck as we exploded. However, despite his many faults, and I would have to borrow Saiman's fingers and toes in addition to my own to count them all, Curran didn't play favorites. Derek would be punished, and his punishment would be severe.

I sipped my water. "Noted. Out of curiosity, what did he try to steal?"

Saiman produced two small rectangles of paper out of

thin air with the buttery grace of a skilled magician. The magic was down, so it had to be sleight of hand. I filed that fact away for future reference: never play cards with Saiman.

"He wanted these." Saiman offered me the papers. I looked at them without touching. They were blood-red. Heavy gold lettering spelled out MIDNIGHT GAMES across the parchment surface.

"What are the Midnight Games?"

"An invitation-only preternatural tournament."

Oh boy. "I take it the tournament is illegal."

"Extremely. In addition, I believe the Beast Lord expressly forbade attendance and participation in the tournament to Pack members."

First, Derek broke into Saiman's apartment. Second, he did it with the intent to steal. Third, he tried to steal tickets to an illegal gladiatorial tournament in direct violation of Pack Law. Curran would skin Derek alive and that might not be just a figure of speech. Was there any possible way this mess could get worse?

"Okay. How can we fix this?"

"I'm prepared to let him go and forget he was ever here," Saiman said. "Provided you accompany me to the Games tomorrow night."

Never ask that question.

"No," Derek said.

I studied the glittering crystal glass in my hand, playing for time. A large crest had been painstakingly cut into the glass, a flame encircled by a serpent. The light of the electric lamp set the cut design aglow, and the crystal scales of the serpent sparkled with fiery colors.

"Lovely, isn't?"

"It is."

"Riedel. Hand-cut. A very limited series, only two made."

"Why do you want my company?"

"My reasons are twofold: first, I require your professional opinion. I find myself in need of a fighter expert."

I arched my eyebrows.

"I would like you to evaluate one of the teams at the Games." Saiman permitted himself a small smile.

Okay. I could do that. "And second?"

Saiman studied the glass in his hand for a long moment and smashed it against the table. It shattered with a pure chime, showering the carpet with a spray of glittering crystal shards. In the cage Derek snarled.

I killed the desire to roll my eyes at all the drama and nodded at the stub of crystal. "If you're planning to cut me with that, you're out of luck. A bottle works much better for this kind of thing."

Delight sparkled in Saiman's eyes. "No, actually, I was planning on making a philosophical point. The glass you now hold in your fingers is the only glass of its kind in existence. It's the ultimate luxury—there is nothing else like it."

The flesh around his wrist swelled, flowing like molten wax. My stomach lurched and tried to crawl sideways. Here we go again. He stored magic like a battery, but I really thought with the technology as strong as it was right now, he wouldn't be able to metamorphose. Live and learn.

Saiman's shoulders widened. His neck, chest, and thighs thickened, straining his sweatshirt. Crisp muscle showed on his forearms. The bones under the skin of his face shivered and I nearly vomited my water.

A new face looked at me: handsome, strong, sensuous, with a square jaw, defined cheekbones, and hooded green eyes under reddish eyebrows. Thick blond hair spilled from his head to fall in a glossy wave onto his newly massive shoulders.

"For most people, I'm the ultimate luxury," he said.

The man collapsed, thinning, flowing, twisting, but the eyes never changed. I stared into those eyes, using them as an anchor. Even when their corners sank, their irises darkened, and a velvet fringe of dark eyelashes sheathed them, I could still tell it was Saiman.

"What I offer is much greater than sex," a Hispanic

woman of startling beauty said. "I offer wish fulfillment. Anything you want. Anyone you want. I can give you your fantasy. And more, I can give you the forbidden."

His face shifted again. Derek. A very reasonable facsimile, good enough to fool me in a bad light. The body still remained female, however. He was getting tired. He must've chugged a gallon of nutrients in anticipation of my arrival to be able to pull this show off.

"I can give you a friend." Saiman-Derek grinned. "Guilt-free. Nobody would ever know. All the secret faces you picture when you pleasure yourself? I can give them to you in the flesh."

Derek just stared, speechless, an expression of utter disgust stamped on his face.

"Is there a point to this demonstration, besides upsetting my stomach?"

Saiman sighed. "You refuse everything I offer, Kate. It hurts my pride."

I crossed my arms. "I refuse because no matter what shape you wear, I know it's you. And you don't really want me for who I am. You want me because I said no."

He considered it. "Perhaps. But the fact remains: by refusing me, you are now my ultimate luxury. That one thing I can't have. You won't see me. You don't return my phone calls. All my attempts to apologize for my behavior during the flare have gone unanswered. It's very difficult to seduce a woman when she refuses to acknowledge your existence. I'm looking forward to having you to myself for an entire night."

"Fucking pervert." Derek finally found adequate words to express his take on the situation.

"I prefer the term 'sexual deviant' myself," Saiman said.

"When I get out . . ."

I raised my hand, halting Derek's promises of very painful and highly illegal things he would have liked to inflict on Saiman. "I'll come with you to the Games." Even if I would rather clean an outhouse. "In return, you acknowledge that Derek never broke into your apartment and you'll surrender all evidence of him ever being present here. Don't plan on a date. There will be no wooing, no seduction, and no sex. That's my best offer and it's not open to negotiation. If you choose to accept it, keep in mind that I'm still a representative of the Order, attending a highly illegal event. Don't put me into the position where I feel compelled to do something about it."

Saiman rose, walked over to the room that served as his lab, and returned with a stack of digital printouts showing Derek in the cage in all his glory. He handed me the pictures, turned on a digital camera, and wiped the memory card clean.

Derek's mask slipped and beyond it I saw guilt. Good. I planned on cashing in on that guilt to get him talking.

Saiman raised a remote, pressed a button, and the cage door fell open. Derek surged up and I stepped between him and Saiman before he could add murder to his list of transgressions.

"I'll pick you up at your apartment at ten," Saiman said.

THE GLASS DOORS OF THE LOBBY SHUT BEHIND US and I let out a breath. The sunrise was still a long way off, and the parking lot lay steeped in darkness, the night breeze cool and cleansing after the perfumed atmosphere of the high-rise.

Derek shook his head, as if clearing fog from his skull. "Thanks."

"Don't mention it."

"I shouldn't have gone through the window." Derek measured the tower with his gaze. "I figured fifteenth floor, sure bet the window would be unprotected. But he's got the whole place booby-trapped."

"He had issues with breaking and entering a few years back. That's why I had to bodyguard him for a while." A vivid image of a man with a pencil through his left eye orbit flashed before me, complete with bloody smudges of my fingerprints on the yellow shaft of the pencil. Thank you, dear memory, for once again attempting to sabotage my conversation. "Saiman takes his security very seriously."

"Yeah."

We reached my car. "There was a shapeshifter death on the corner of Ponce de Leon and Dead Cat. Jim was there and a Pack crew. Know anything about it?"

A dark shadow crossed Derek's face. "No. Who died?"

"I don't know. Jim wouldn't let me get within thirty feet of the body." I looked right into his eyes. "Derek, did you have anything to do with it?"

"No."

"If you did, you need to tell me now."

"I didn't."

I believed him. Derek had many talents, but lying wasn't one of them.

We stood by the car. *Come on, boy wonder. You know you want to tell me what's going on.*

"You shouldn't go with that freak." Derek dragged his fingers through his short hair. "He's dangerous."

"I gave my word. I have to go. Besides, Saiman is a degenerate. He's ruled completely by his appetites. For him, there is no higher goal than to satisfy his urges, and that makes him predictable. I'll be fine."

In the distance a dog erupted in an explosion of hysterical barks. Derek glanced in the direction of the sound. A faint yellow sheen rolled over his irises. He focused, leaning forward, light on his toes, listening to the night, the wolf crouching with hackles raised just beneath his skin.

Derek expected to be jumped any second. Something was seriously wrong.

"Derek?"

He had pulled the calm back on and his face looked inscrutable. But the beast refused to be completely tamed. It clawed and howled behind his eyes.

"Is this Pack or personal?"

"Personal."

"Does Curran know?"

Derek looked at his feet.

I took that as a no. "Anything I can do to help?"

"No."

"I came all this way to bust you out, and you won't even tell me what this is about?"

He shook his head and took off into the night. So much for the guilt.

I watched him fall into that particular wolf gait, long-legged and deceptively easy. He could run like that for days, devouring miles. Derek reached the end of the parking lot, jumped to clear a three-foot concrete wall, and changed his mind in midleap. It was a peculiar thing to see: he shot in the air, unable to stop himself, but instead of going long, he jumped straight up, landed in almost exactly the same spot, turned on one foot, and sprinted to me.

In a breath he halted by my side. "I lied. I need your help."

"Who are we killing?"

"Do you have a pen?"

I got a notepad and a pencil out of my car. He scribbled something on a piece of paper, tore it out, and folded the paper in half. "Promise me you won't read this. This is important. This is the most important thing I've ever done. At the Games there will be a girl. Her name is Livie. She's on the Reaper team. There are only two women on the team and she has long dark hair. Give this to her. Please."

A girl. He risked Curran's rage for a girl.

On the surface, it made sense. He was nineteen and wading through the sea of hormones. But I had never perceived Derek as the type to become blindly infatuated. He took stoic to a new level. More, he worshipped the ground Curran walked on. There had to be more to this. Unfortunately, Derek's face was doing a wonderful impression of a granite wall.

"You tried to steal the tickets to give a note to a girl?"

"Yes."

I scratched my head. "I know you're in trouble. I can feel it. Usually this is the part where I threaten you with terrible bodily harm and promise to dance on your grave unless you tell me everything you know. There's just one slight problem."

Derek grinned and for a moment boy wonder was back in all his glory. "I won't believe your promises of breaking every bone in my body?"

"Precisely."

He barked a short laugh.

"Tell me what this is about. Whatever it is, I will help you."

"I can't, Kate. It's something I have to do on my own. Just please give her the note, okay? Promise me."

I wanted to grab him and shake him until the story fell out. But the only way to stay in this game meant taking the note. "I promise."

"And swear you won't read it?"

Oh, for the love of God. "Give me the damn note. I said I won't read it."

He offered me the paper and I snatched it from his fingers.

"Thank you." A happy little smile curled his lips. He backed away two steps and broke into a run. Before I knew it, he was gone, melting into the darkness of the alley between the decrepit buildings.

I stood in the parking lot holding his note. A nasty chill crawled down my spine. Derek was in trouble. I didn't know how or why, but I had a strong gut feeling that it was bad and it would end even worse. If I'd had a drop of sense, I'd have opened the note and read it.

I sighed, got into the car, and stuck the paper into my glove compartment. Common sense was not among my virtues. I'd promised and I had to stick to it.

My back ached. Even my bones felt tired. I just wanted to lie down somewhere, close my eyes, and forget the world existed. I buckled my seat belt. I needed to know more about the Games and I needed the information before tonight. In the morning I would go to the Order and check their files. And check on that report from PAD. Nothing said the shapeshifter murder and Derek's mess were connected, but I'd feel better if I ruled that possibility out. Even though the Pack was handling the murder. Even if it wasn't my case. And that didn't bother me one bit. Nope, not at all.

I sat in my car, feeling the fatigue wash over me, and thought of Curran. Two months ago I'd found the Beast Lord in my house reading a book. We made some small talk, I threatened him with bodily harm if he didn't leave, and then he moved like he would kiss me. But instead he winked, whispered, "Psych," and took off into the night.

He had made me coffee. I drank every last bit of it that night.

I wasn't sure if he would come back, but if he did, I wanted to be prepared. I had imagined our encounter a dozen times. I had constructed long conversations in my head, full of barbs and witty comebacks.

The bastard didn't show.

The longer his MIA lasted, the surer I became that he would never show up. It was blatantly obvious—he enjoyed screwing with me, and having done so, he got all funned out and moved on. Perfectly fine with me. Best solution possible. I had dreamt of him once or twice, but other than that, everything was peachy.

Wherever this thread of Derek's troubles led, I really didn't cherish the idea of finding Curran on the other end.

It was always good to have a Plan of Action. I started the engine. Item one of the POA: avoid the Beast Lord. Item two: do not fall asleep.

CHAPTER 3

"KATE?"

I have a superior reaction time. That was why although I shot out of my chair, jumped onto my desk, and attempted to stab the intruder into my office in the throat, I stopped the blade two inches before it touched Andrea's neck. Because she was my best friend, and sticking knives into your best friend's windpipe was generally considered to be a social faux pas.

Andrea stared at the black blade of the throwing dagger. "That was great," she said. "What will you do for a dollar?"

I scowled.

"Scary but not worth a buck." Andrea perched on the corner of my desk. Short, blond, and deadly. A full knight of the Order, Andrea had one of those nice-girl faces that instantly put people at ease and made them fall over themselves in a rush to disclose their problems. I once went shopping with her, and we heard no fewer than three life stories from total strangers. People never wanted to tell me their life stories. They usually scooted out of my way and said things like, "Take whatever you want; just go."

Of course, if the total strangers had known Andrea could shoot dots off dominoes at twenty yards, they might have decided to keep their issues to themselves.

Andrea eyed the file on my desk. "I thought you were off today."

"I am." I jumped down. I had caught three hours of sleep, dragged myself to the office in search of background information on the Midnight Games, and promptly passed out at my desk facedown on the open file despite the near-critical amount of coffee in my system. Which explained why I had failed to hear Andrea enter the office. Typically I didn't go zero to sixty out of dead sleep unless I was startled.

I rubbed my face, trying to wipe away the layer of fatigue. Somebody had poured lead into my head while I was sleeping, and now it rolled around in my skull, creating a racket. "I'm looking for some info on the Midnight Games."

Unfortunately, the file on the Games proved to be anorexic. Three pages of shallow overview on structure, no specifics. This meant there was another file, a big fat one, with a nice CLASSIFIED stamp on the cover, which put it squarely out of my reach. As security clearances went, mine was bare minimum. This was one of the rare moments when I regretted not being a full-fledged knight. As it was, getting my hands on the secret file would prove slightly harder than getting an ice cream cone in Christian hell.

"I don't know much about it," Andrea said. "But one of my instructors was in it, before the tournament was outlawed. I can tell you a little bit about how it worked back then. Over lunch."

"Lunch?"

"It's Friday."

That's right. Andrea and I always had lunch on Fridays. Typically she just waylaid me in the office and didn't give me any choice about it. In Andrea's book, lunch was something friends did. I was still getting used to the idea of friends. Steady relationships were a luxury I wasn't allowed to have for most of my life. Friends shielded and protected you, but they also made you vulnerable, because you sought to return the favor.

Andrea and I had worked closely during the flare. I had saved her life; she had saved my kid, Julie, who had started the flare as a street rat with a missing mom and ended it a killer of demons, who lost her mother permanently but gained crazy Aunt Kate. After the flare, I had expected Andrea and me to quietly drift apart, but Andrea had other plans. She became my best friend.

My stomach growled, informing me that I was ravenous. Food and sleep—you could do without one, but not without both. I put Slayer into the back sheath where it belonged, returned the throwing knife to its sheath on my belt, and grabbed my bag. Andrea checked the two SIG-Sauer P226s she carried in hip holsters, patted down her hunting knife and a smaller backup firearm on her ankle, and we were ready to go.

I STARED AT THE HUGE PLATE OF GYROS. "I'VE died and gone to Heaven."

"You have gone to Parthenon." Andrea took a seat opposite me.

"True." The only way I could get into Heaven would be by blowing up the pearly gates.

We sat on the second floor, in the garden section of a small Greek joint called Parthenon. The garden consisted of an open-air patio, and from our table I could see the busy street beyond an iron rail. The only drawback to this place was the furniture. The tables were wooden and decent enough, but they were flanked by uncomfortable metal chairs bolted to the floor, which meant I couldn't really watch the door.

I scooped the meat with my pita. My brain kept returning to Derek with a small smile in the night-soaked parking lot. A big, heavy ball of worry had accreted in my stomach over the past few hours.

I was stuck. Aside from Derek, who wasn't talking, the only people who could shed light onto this situation were Pack members. There might have been a way to broach the subject with them without giving away the facts of Derek's spectacular escapade, but I was too stupid to think of any. And considering the recent death, they would want full disclosure. If I said anything about Saiman or the Games, Derek would be punished. If I said nothing, he might risk his hide doing something idiotic.

Combined with my headache, all this rumination put me into a foul mood. For all I knew, Derek's little note said, "Meet me at the Knights Inn. I bought the rainbow-colored condoms." Of course, it could also say, "Tonight I kill your brother. Get the stew pot ready."

I should have just read the damn note. Except I'd given my word I wouldn't. In the world of magic, your word had weight. When I gave mine, I kept it.

Besides, going back on my word would betray Derek's trust. Actually, any action on my part would betray Derek's trust: I couldn't read the note, I couldn't ask anybody about the note, and I couldn't refuse to deliver the damn note. I would've really liked to kick him in the head right about now.

To top it off, my calls to PAD cops produced no useful information whatsoever. A dismembered body of a woman was found on the corner of Dead Cat and Ponce de Leon. She was identified as a member of the Pack and the matter was turned over to the shapeshifters. End of story.

I looked at Andrea. "The Midnight Games."

Andrea nodded. "One of my mentors was in it. The Games are held in the Arena, a bunker of some kind. It's run by the House, which always consists of seven members. They make most of their money off betting on fighters. There are individual bouts, but the big banana is their team tournament. It's held once a year. Fourteen teams participate. Each team consists of seven fighters, all with specific roles."

"They enjoy the number seven, don't they?" I chewed

my food. Seven had some mystic significance. Not quite as much as the number three, but plenty: seven wise men of Greece, seven wonders of the world, seven days of the week, seven-league boots, seven poets of Moallakat . . . No clue as to what it meant, if anything. Perhaps the creators of the tournament simply wanted to ground it in numerology.

"My mentor fought as a shoote . . ." Andrea glanced at the street and fell silent. Her eyes narrowed. She looked completely focused, like a hawk sighting a plump pigeon. If she'd had a rifle in her hands, I'd have been worried she was about to snipe somebody.

"Can you believe it?"

I looked in the direction of her stare and saw Raphael. The werehyena loitered across the street, a tall man with coal-black hair, dressed in jeans and a black T-shirt. His hands were thrust in his pockets and he shouldered a backpack. He saw us looking at him and froze. *That's right— you're so busted.*

"I think he's stalking me." Andrea glared.

I waved at Raphael and motioned him over.

"What are you doing?" Andrea ground out through clenched teeth. Her face went pale, and I could almost see the faint outlines of spots on her arms.

Raphael attempted a weak smile and headed toward us, zeroing in on Parthenon's doors.

"I want to find out if he knows anything about the Midnight Games. He'll tell me anything if you let him sit with us. I think he really likes you."

An understatement of the year. Raphael carried a huge torch for Andrea. During the flare, when she nearly died, he had bent over backward to take care of her.

"Yeah." Andrea loaded so much scorn into one word, I actually paused.

This was one of those thin-ice areas of friendship, which had a great potential for dumping me into freezing water. "You really don't like him?"

A shadow crossed Andrea's face. "I don't want to be his TWT-IHFB."

"What does that mean?"

"That Weird Thing I Haven't Fucked Before."

I choked on a bite of gyro.

Raphael chose that moment to emerge from the door. Pissed or not pissed, Andrea watched him as he walked toward us and so did I. I practically dislocated my shoulder twisting in my seat so I could catch a glimpse. He moved with an easy shapeshifter grace, a kind of inborn elegance usually reserved for highly trained dancers and martial artists. His black hair, worn down to his shoulders, moved as he walked, absorbing the sunlight. His skin was tan, and his face . . . There was something so interesting about him. Taken by themselves, his features were unremarkable, but put together they somehow combined into an intensely attractive face. He wasn't handsome, but he drew your gaze like a magnet, and his eyes, deep, piercing blue, were positively smoldering.

You looked at Raphael and thought sex. He wasn't even my type and I couldn't help it.

Raphael stopped a few feet from our table, not sure what to do next. "Hello. Andrea. Kate. Didn't expect to see you here."

I turned back to the table and heard my back pop. That would teach me.

"Sit down," Andrea hissed.

Raphael gently lowered his backpack with one hand, took the only remaining free chair, and sat, looking a bit on edge. Andrea stared at the street. Together they looked like complete opposites: Andrea was five-two tops, with short blond hair and lightly tanned skin, while Raphael was about six feet tall, with skin the color of coffee with lots of cream, black hair, and intense eyes.

"So what's in the backpack?" I asked. Small talker. That's me.

"Portable m-scanner," Raphael said. "Picked it up from the shop. Been in there ever since the flare—they couldn't test to see if it worked until a magic wave hit."

When it came to m-scanners, "portable" was a relative

word. The smallest weighed about eighty pounds. It was good to be a werehyena.

Andrea got up. "I'm going to get some dessert. Kate, you want anything?"

"No," I said.

"You?"

"No, thank you," Raphael said.

She marched away.

Raphael looked at me. "What am I doing wrong?"

I paused with a piece of pita bread in my hand. "You're asking me?"

"I don't have anybody else to ask. You know her. You're friends."

"Raphael, I've never had a steady boyfriend in my entire life. It's been over a year since I've had sex. And you know how well my last attempt at a love life turned out. I think you were there, weren't you?"

"Yeah. I was the one with the shotgun."

I nodded. "I think we can agree that I'm the worst person you could ask about how to fix a romantic relationship. I don't know what to tell you."

"You know Andrea."

"Not that well."

Raphael looked crestfallen. "It's never taken me this long," he said quietly.

I sympathized. He had pined after Andrea for two months now. For a werehyena, or bouda as they were called, a courtship that long was unheard of. Boudas were adventurous. They enjoyed sex, a lot of it and with a variety of partners. Women dominated the bouda pack, and from what I understood, Raphael was rather popular, both because of his patience and his status as the son of Aunt B, the boudas' alpha. And his looks guaranteed that he wouldn't have to chase nonshapeshifter women for too long before they took him for a test-drive.

Unfortunately, Andrea was not a nonshapeshifter woman, nor was she a bouda. Lyc-V, the virus responsible for the shapeshifter phenomenon, affected animals as well as humans. In very rare cases, the resulting creature was an animal-were, a being who started its life as an animal and gained the ability to turn into a human. Most animal-weres turned out to be sterile, mentally retarded, and violent, but occasionally one could function in a human society well enough not to be killed outright. And even more occasionally they could procreate.

Andrea was a beastkin, a child of a hyenawere and a bouda. She hid it from everyone: from the shapeshifters, because some would kill her owing to an ancient deepseated prejudice, and from the Order, because the moment they realized she was a shapeshifter, they would jettison her from the ranks. Technically, as a shapeshifter, Andrea was subject to Curran's power, and the Order demanded absolute loyalty. So far Curran hadn't pressed the issue, but he could change his mind any moment.

As far as I knew, only the bouda clan within the Pack, Curran, Jim, Derek, Doolittle, and I knew what Andrea was. And we all quietly conspired to keep it that way without ever actually discussing the subject.

"You really want some advice?" I asked.

"Yes."

"Try to think less like a bouda and more like a man."

He bristled. "What the hell is that supposed to mean? Bouda is what I am."

I wiped the last smudge of tzatziki off my plate with my bread. "She's a knight of the Order. Only one in eight who enroll into the Order's Academy makes it to graduation. She's worked very hard at being a human. Be her friend. Talk to her. Find out what books she reads, what guns she likes . . . Speaking of books, I can tell you something specific about Andrea, but it will cost you."

"What do you need?"

"The Midnight Games. Everything you know."

"Easy enough." Raphael grinned. "You go first."

"How do I know you'll pay up?"

"Andrea's coming up the stairs. I can hear her. Please, Kate." He did his version of puppy eyes, and I almost fell out of my chair.

"Fine." Kate Daniels, trained negotiator. When in possession of some valuable information, give it away to the first sexy man you see with no guarantee of return. "Lorna Sterling. She writes paranormal romances. Andrea loves her with unholy love. She has a stack of her books under her desk at work. She's missing numbers four and six."

Raphael pulled a pen out of his backpack and scribbled on his forearm. "Lorna?"

"Sterling. Books four and six. Andrea's been haunting that bookstore on the corner for weeks looking for them."

Andrea emerged from the door, carrying a milk shake and a plate of sliced peaches. The pen vanished into Raphael's backpack.

I leveled my hard stare at Raphael. "Give."

"The Midnight Games are forbidden," he said. "By the direct order of the Beast Lord, no member of the Pack may participate, aid, or bet on the Midnight Games."

"That's it? That's all you got?"

He shrugged. There was more to it; I could tell by his face. He was holding out on me. Bastard. I looked at Andrea. *Help me.*

She took a peach, bit a tiny piece from it, and licked her lips slowly. Raphael did a stunning impression of a pointer sighting a pheasant.

"How come they're forbidden? Is there a story behind it?" Andrea bit another piece of peach and licked her lips again.

"Yes, there is," Raphael murmured. I almost felt sorry for him. *I wonder if that would work with . . .* I grabbed that thought and stomped on it before it had a chance to infect my head with nonsense.

Andrea smiled. "That sounds interesting. I'd like to hear it."

Raphael caught himself. "It's not something we explain to outsiders."

"Too bad." Andrea shrugged and glanced at me. "Are you ready to go?"

"I was born ready." I reached for my bag.

"I guess there wouldn't be any harm in telling it this once," Raphael said.

I let go of the bag.

"In two thousand twenty-four, the tournament was still legal, and the championship came down to a fight between the Necro Lords and Andorf's Seven. Andorf was a huge were-Kodiak, twenty-five hundred and eighty pounds in beast form. Had paws bigger than my head." Raphael spread his hands, indicating a paw the size of a large watermelon. "Big, mean, vicious bastard. Loved to fight. He put together a good team, but by that point there were only four of them left: Andorf, a wolf, a rat, and my aunt Minny."

CHAPTER 4

ANDREA'S MOUTH HUNG OPEN IN A DECIDEDLY unseductive manner.

"Aunt, huh?" I said to say something.

Raphael nodded. "That's how the bouda clan used to make its money. We'd bet on ourselves. It was different back then. Now we have the Pack, which provides us with operating funds. We draft a budget. We have an investment plan and own shares in businesses. But back then there was no such thing as a 'Pack.' There were isolated clans and we pretty much sank or swam on our own."

The bouda clan counted less than twenty people. Sixteen years ago, it must've been even smaller. They couldn't have had an easy time of surviving. "Who was on the other team in the championship?"

"Four navigators from the People." Raphael counted off on fingers. "Ryo Montoya, Sam Hardy, Marina Buryatova-Hardy, and Sang. As much as I hate the fuckers, it was a deadly team."

Of that, I had no doubt.

"Why would the People involve themselves in the fight?" Andrea frowned.

"They were just building the Casino. There was some talk of money gone missing and repercussions coming down their chain of command if it wasn't found fast. They bet a lot and needed to win."

"So what happened?" I leaned forward.

Raphael grimaced. "The People had an edge. The bloodsuckers tore the rat in half and my aunt's guts were all over the Pit. Looked like curtains for Andorf's Seven."

"And?"

"Andorf went nuts. Nobody knows if he went loup or just berserk—bears do that sometimes. He shifted into full beast form, ripped the vamps to shreds, crushed the wolf's skull, then broke through the fence around the Pit, and went after the navigators. They ran, and he chased them through the crowd. Mauled whoever got in his way. Killed all four and over a hundred spectators. Then he rammed the wall and took off."

"Holy crap." Andrea drained a third of her milk shake.

"Yeah. Not the best way to end the night."

An enormous were-Kodiak gone mad on the streets of Atlanta. A Kodiak trained as a fighter, smart as a human, stronger and bigger and badder than the average bear. It would have been the ultimate nightmare for the shapeshifters.

"There was a massive manhunt," Raphael said. "Andorf hid in Unicorn Lane."

An area of deep, wild magic, Unicorn Lane sliced across Downtown like a scar. Treacherous magic swirled and pooled there even during tech. Even the Military's Supernatural Defense Unit didn't dare to stay too long.

"An assembly of clans was called to try to figure out how we would deal with that mess, because all sorts of shit had broken out. The People were calling for the expulsion of all shapeshifters; the zealots came out in force with that Sign of the Beast crap again. It couldn't have gotten more screwed up. This clusterfuck needed to be fixed and fast. The wolf clan was the largest."

"Of course." Andrea snorted.

"Francois Ambler headed the wolf clan at the time, and people called for him to go and take Andorf down. He wouldn't do it. The way my mother tells it, he got up and just walked away. Abandoned the clan, gave up being an alpha, and took a ley line out of town." Raphael smiled. "What happened next only the alphas know. But I can tell you the facts: three days later Andorf's head showed up on the Capitol's steps. And two days after that, Curran became Beast Lord. The first law he made forbade Pack members from participating in or betting on the Games."

I counted in my head. Two thousand twenty-four, I was nine. Curran was only a few years older than me . . . "How old was he?"

"Fifteen."

"Shit."

Raphael nodded. "Yeah."

We sat in silence for a long minute, digesting the story. What meager hopes I had of finding a sympathetic ear within the Pack in regard to Derek's problem had just evaporated into thin air. This was one law on which there wouldn't be any leeway. What should I do now?

Andrea stirred her milk shake with a spoon. "So, how are things with you and Curran?"

There were times in life when I wished for supreme mental powers. Like telekinesis. Mostly, I wanted them to crush my opponents. But right now I wanted them so I could pull the chair out from under Andrea and make her fall on her butt.

I settled for spitting three times over my left shoulder.

"Are you warding off evil?" Raphael's eyes widened.

"Well, the two of you did say the forbidden name. I have to take precautions. I need something wooden. Lean forward, Andrea, so I can knock on your head."

Andrea cracked a smile.

"To answer your question, we're great. Never better. I

haven't seen His Fussiness in two months, and I couldn't be happier. If my luck holds, he's lost interest and found himself somebody else to hound for his amusement."

During the flare Curran had finally found a way to pay me back for all those times I'd nearly brought him to apoplexy. He had told me I would sleep with him sooner or later and thank him for his services in bed. Hell would sprout roses first.

"He hasn't found anyone, as far as I know," Raphael said. "Nobody has seen him with a woman since the flare. That's not terribly unusual for him, but it's not common either."

I rolled my eyes. "And that means what?"

Raphael leaned forward and lowered his voice. "Have you ever seen a lion hunt a herd?"

"No."

"They are very single-minded. When a lion stalks a herd, he sneaks in close, lies down, and surveys them to choose his victim. He takes his time. The deer or buffalo have no idea he's near. He finds his prey and then he explodes from his hiding place and grabs it. Even if another, perfectly serviceable animal ends up within his reach, he isn't going to alter his course. He has chosen, and he would rather go hungry than change his mind. A dumb way to live, if you ask me, but that's their nature. Me, I don't ignore opportunities."

"Yeah." Andrea's voice dripped with sarcasm.

Raphael gave her a hurt look. "I am what I am."

"You're a man first. You sit here in a human shape, wearing human clothes, making human noises. Pretty obvious which part of you is in control. But when someone points out your excesses, you wave your hands around and start crying, 'Oh no, it's the beast! I can't help it!'" Andrea caught herself and clamped her mouth shut.

I did my best to change the subject. "I think you give our relationship too much credit. I irritate the hell out of Curran and he found a way to pester me. It's nothing."

"You may be right," Raphael said.

"His Majesty needs a can-I girl anyway. And I'm not it."

"A can-I girl?" Andrea frowned.

I leaned back. " 'Can I fetch you your food, Your Majesty? Can I tell you how strong and mighty you are, Your Majesty? Can I pick out your fleas, Your Majesty? Can I kiss your ass, Your Majesty? Can I . . .' "

It dawned on me that Raphael was sitting very still. Frozen, like a statue, his gaze fixed on the point above my head.

"He's standing behind me, isn't he?"

Andrea nodded slowly.

"Technically it should be 'may I,' " Curran said, his voice deeper than I remembered. "Since you're asking permission."

He stepped into my view, reached for a chair at a table next to us, and found it bolted to the floor. He gripped the chair and plucked it from the concrete with one hand, leaving four screws sticking out of the floor. He put the chair next to me, back first, and saddled it like a horse, crossing his arms on the top of the back to show off carved biceps.

Why me?

"To answer your question, yes, you may kiss my ass. Normally I prefer to maintain my personal space, but you're a Friend of the Pack and your services have proven useful once or twice. I strive to accommodate the wishes of persons friendly to my people. My only question is, would your kissing my ass be obeisance, grooming, or foreplay?"

Raphael went a shade paler and bowed his head. "By your leave, m'lord."

Curran nodded.

Raphael grabbed Andrea by the hand.

Andrea blinked. "But . . ."

"We have to go now." Raphael's smile had a bit of an edge to it. He fled and dragged Andrea with him, leaving me and Curran alone. Traitors.

CHAPTER 5

"YOU DIDN'T ANSWER MY QUESTION," CURRAN
said. "What will it be?"

"No," I said.

Curran grinned and my heart made a little jump. I didn't
expect that.

"That's it? That's your witty comeback?"

"Yep." Eloquence 'R' Us. When in trouble, keep it
monosyllabic—safer that way.

Curran rested his chin on his crossed arms. Really, he
wasn't anything special. Today he wore faded jeans and a
grayish-blue polo shirt of all things. It's hard to look lethal
in a polo shirt, but he managed. Perhaps because it did
nothing to hide the definition on his chest or the hard lines
of his shoulders. In fact, if he flexed, he'd probably rip it. I
knew that under that shirt his body was hard like a suit of
armor.

Perhaps it wasn't his body, but the air about him. When
he wanted to, Curran literally emanated menace. I had seen
him roar in fury and display an icy, determined anger, sharp
like a dagger, and I wasn't sure which was more terrifying.

The gold fire in his eyes triggered some sort of primordial fear in me, a feeling born ages ago by the light of the young fire, before reason, before logic, when human existence was ruled by the fear of things with claws and teeth and of being eaten. That fear shackled me. I couldn't rationalize it away. I had to fight it with pure will and so far I had held my own, but I had no guarantee I would resist it the next time he decided to treat me to his alpha stare.

Curran looked me over slowly. I did the same, matching him smirk for smirk. Blond hair cut too short to grab. Nose that looked like it had been broken and never healed right, an odd thing for any shapeshifter, and especially for one of Curran's caliber. Gray eyes . . . I looked into those eyes and saw tiny gold sparks dancing in their depths. And my heart made another little jump.

I'm in so much trouble.

"I like the hair," he said.

In the spirit of an off-duty Friday, I wore my hair down. I mostly braided it or curled it into a bun to keep it out of the way, but today it just sort of hung there, a long dark brown wall shifting in the breeze on both sides of my face.

I flexed my wrist, popping a long silver needle into my palm from the leather wrist guard, grabbed my hair, twisted it into a bun, stuck the needle into it to hold it in place, and showed him my teeth in a little smile. There.

He laughed. "Cute. You ever get tired of pretending to be a hard-ass?"

Cute. I think I would prefer to be stabbed in the eye rather than be called cute. "To what do I owe the pleasure of Your Majesty's company?" And the ruination of my lunch.

"I just wanted some peaches." He smiled.

Since when did a death in the Pack result in such good cheer?

"Is there any particular reason you were asking about the Midnight Games?" he asked.

"I have a passing interest in history." I was on shaky

ground. I had no clue if he knew about Derek or not. I needed to cut this conversation short. "Does the Pack require my services as an employee of the Order?"

"Not at the moment." He leaned back, picked up the plate with Andrea's peaches, and offered it to me. "Peach?"

My smile got sharper. During the flare, Curran offered me some soup and I ate it. Later the boudas' alpha, Aunt B, explained the facts of life to me: shapeshifters offered food to their prospective mates. He was at once declaring himself my protector, implying that I was weaker than him, and propositioning me. And I took it. It had amused him to no end. Had I known what the soup meant, I would've eaten it anyway—I was half-dead at the time.

I crossed my arms on my chest. "No, thanks. I'm not accepting any more food from you."

"Ah." He took a slice, broke the fruit in half, and tossed it into his mouth. "Who clued you in? Raphael?"

"Does it matter?"

His eyes flashed with gold sparks. "No."

Liar. The last thing I wanted was to cause Raphael difficulties because he'd ruined Curran's private joke. "I read it in Greg's notes." I took a couple of bucks out of my pocket, folded them, and stuck the bills between the salt and pepper shakers.

"Leaving?" he asked.

Your powers of deduction are truly marvelous, Mr. Holmes. "Since you have no need of my professional persona, I'm going to return to my duties."

"You're off today."

And how did he know that?

He ate another peach. "The Order has a sixteen-hour shift limit when the magic is down. One of our rats saw you late last night getting an old lady off of a telephone pole. Apparently it was a hilarious affair all around."

"I live to amuse." I rose.

Curran struck at my wrist. His fingers were cat-quick, but I had spent my life honing my reflexes, and he missed.

"Well, look at that." I studied my free wrist. "Denied.

Good-bye, Your Majesty. Please pass my condolences to the family."

I headed to the door.

"Kate?" His sudden change of tone made me turn. All humor had drained from Curran's face. "Whose family?"

CHAPTER 6

BEFORE THE SHIFT, THE STREET OF PONCE DE LEON
had channeled the massive flow of traffic from Stone
Mountain through Decatur and Druid Hills past City Hall
East all the way to the skyscrapers of Midtown. The Bell-
South Tower, Bank of America, and the Renaissance Hotel
were little more than heaps of rubble now, but City Hall
East still stood. It might have held on because it wasn't all
that tall—only nine stories high. Its age probably played a
part. Steeped in history, the building had evolved through
the years, from the 1926 Sears depot to a government hub
to a community of condos, shops, and restaurants sheltering
a couple of acres of green. But there was a third, much
more compelling reason for its continued existence. About
twenty years ago Atlanta's University of Arcane Arts had
purchased the massive two-million-square-foot monster. It
now housed faculty, students, libraries, laboratories, research facilities . . . If anybody could keep a building standing, four hundred mages ought to be it.

The presence of mages—and mage students who, like all
college students, were rather impulsive in their purchases—

had revived Ponce de Leon. It was a bustling street now, full of shops, stalls, and eateries.

Dead Cat Street was a sorry narrow affair by comparison. It wound its way between the newly rebuilt two- and three-story apartment buildings to a small plaza containing a convenience store and a grocery. Curran and I stood on the edge of the narrow sidewalk, looking at Dead Cat Street, as the horse carts and passersby traversed Ponce de Leon to our right. The body had been found a couple dozen yards from the corner. The scene was clean. No smudges of blood on the pavement. No signs of struggle. No nothing. If I hadn't come through here last night, I wouldn't have known anything untoward had taken place.

Curran stood very still, breathing deeply. Minutes stretched into the past. Suddenly his upper lip rose, baring his teeth. A precursor of a growl shivered just beneath his teeth. His eyes flashed with gold.

"Curran?"

A lion glared at me though gray human eyes and vanished, replaced by Curran's neutral face. "Nice, thorough job."

I arched my eyebrows at him.

"They salted the scene with wolfsbane. The stems are dried out, ground into powder, and mixed with some base. Dry detergent works well. Borax. Baking soda. Not as effective as a wolfsbane paste, but enough of it will overwhelm the scent trail. Jim's crew dumped about a gallon of it here."

I filed that tidbit away for future reference. "So the sniff test is a bust?"

Curran smiled. "You can't salt the air. Even here, with all the traffic and draft, the scents linger above the ground. Tell me what you saw and we'll compare notes."

I hesitated. Talking to Curran was like walking through a minefield. You never knew when something would set him off, and Jim, screwed-up asshole though he might be, was my former partner. "Why don't you ask Jim instead? He would probably want a chance to tell you himself."

Curran shook his head. His face was grim. "When one of ours dies, I get a call. No matter the hour. I was in the Keep last night and didn't get one. I saw Jim this morning and he said nothing to me about this."

"He must have a compelling reason for withholding the information."

"Kate, did you extend an offer of cooperation to the Pack on behalf of the Order?"

Oh, bite me. "Yes, I did. It was declined."

"As Beast Lord, I now accept your offer."

Damn it. The Mutual Aid Agreement bound me to disclose all knowledge of the incident.

I stared at him helplessly. "How do you always do that? How do you always maneuver me into doing something I don't want to do?"

Curran's face lightened a little. "I've had a lot of practice. The Pack contains thirty-two species in seven tribes, each with their own hang-up. Jackals and coyotes pick fights with wolves, because they have an inferiority complex and think they've got something to prove. Wolves believe themselves to be superior, marry the wrong people, and then refuse to divorce them because they cling to their 'mating for life' idiocy. Hyenas listen to nobody, screw everything, and break out in berserk rages at some perceived slight against one of their own. Cats randomly refuse to follow orders to prove they can. That's my life. I've been at this for fifteen years now. You're easy by comparison."

And here I thought I was a challenge. "Pardon me while my ego recovers."

He grinned. "It's a benefit of having principles. Boxed into a corner, you will always strive to do what you think is right, especially when you don't like it. Like right now."

"I suppose you have me all figured out."

"I understand why you do things, Kate. It's how you do them that occasionally pisses me off."

Occasionally? "I want to assure you, Your Majesty, that I spend long nights lying awake in my bed worrying about your feelings."

"As well you should." A half-laugh, half-growl reverberated in his throat. "Provoking me won't work. Tell
me what you saw. Or should I make a formal request in
writing?"

This was apparently a "let's teach Kate humility" day.
He had me by the throat.

I thought back to the scene, reconstructing it in my head.
"I came in by mule from Ponce de Leon. There were seven
shapeshifters. Two in wolf form, scanning the scene for
scents. One was here." I walked over to indicate the right
spot. "Male. Looked like a typical European wolf, *Canis
lupus lupus*, coarse dark gray fur streaked with sandy
brown, especially on the nose. The second one was here." I
crossed the street to approximate location. "Might have
been a female, but I'm not sure. Brown, almost cinnamon
fur, black or very dark chocolate muzzle and dark ears.
Light yellow eyes. Looked like Cascade Mountain wolf to
me."

"George and Brenna," Curran supplied. He was watching me with intense interest. "Jim's best trackers. Go on."

I crossed the street to the other side of Dead Cat. "Two
shapeshifters here, sliding a corpse into a bag. Both female.
The one on the right was average size, lightly built, ash-
blond hair cut in a bob. Never saw her face." I took a wide
step to my left. "Native American, slightly plump, dark
skin, early forties, long hair in a braid. Pretty."

Curran said nothing.

"Perimeter guard here." I pointed to my left. "And here."
I turned to indicate the second spot. "And one right there." I
stabbed my finger where the guard had stopped me. "The
two in the back looked similar, dark-haired, Latino with
a touch of Indian, possibly Mexican, young, male, short,
compact, very quick, trouble in a fight. The guy who
stopped me was in his midthirties, maybe early forties.
Military haircut, light brown hair, hazel eyes, muscle heavy,
a dedicated bodybuilder. Not as quick as the other two but I
got the impression he could carry me and my mule both.
Spoke with a touch of an accent, Aussie or New Zealand.

Favored his left arm a bit. Might have been hurt recently. You want me to describe the clothes?"

Curran shook his head. "How long were you here?"

"About a minute and a half, maybe two." I crossed the street over to where I saw Brenna yelp. "Brenna found an arm right here. I think perhaps a female arm, because the sleeve was pale and shimmered a bit. Some kind of metallic fabric, an evening gown or blouse, not the type a man would typically wear unless he was very flamboyant."

"Tell me about Jim."

"He materialized out of thin air right here. Very dramatic." I raised my head. "Ah. Probably jumped off this balcony." I recounted the conversation. "That's all I got. Didn't see the body. Didn't get any details."

Curran's face took on this odd look. It looked almost like admiration. "Not bad. Natural recall or something the Order taught you?"

I shrugged. "Not the Order. My father. And it's not perfect. I typically forget the most important item on my shopping list. But I'm trained to evaluate the situation for possible dangers, and seven shapeshifters packing away a dead body in the middle of the night on a deserted road is a lot of danger. Your turn to share."

"A deal is a deal." Curran stepped into the road with me. "She wasn't killed here. The scent of blood is faint and the ground isn't stained, but still dirty so nobody rinsed the pavement off. The body had been cut into at least six pieces. This is a dump site, chosen because one of our offices is only eight blocks away. That's the closest they could get to our territory without being stopped by a patrol. There were at least three of them, and they don't smell human. I don't know what they are, but I don't like their scent."

Better and better.

"Can't tell you much more than that, except that Jim had his best cleanup crew with him. I know every person you described. They're very good at what they do."

And none of them had said anything to him about it. The million-dollar question was why?

"Once accepted, the assistance of the Order can't be declined," I told him. "I'm now part of this investigation. That means I'll have to come into your territory and ask uncomfortable questions."

"I have some questions to ask as well." Liquid gold drowned Curran's eyes. The tiny hairs on the back of my neck stood on their ends. I really didn't want to be Jim right now.

"I'll contact you to schedule time for the interviews." He turned and walked away, leaving me in the middle of the street. Beast Lord, a man beyond mundane niceties like good-bye and thank you.

As I walked back to civilization, I realized that for the first time in the six months I had known Curran, we had managed to have a conversation and part ways without wanting to kill each other. I found that fact deeply troubling.

CHAPTER 7

———◆———

A SMALL BROWN-PAPER PARCEL WAITED FOR ME
by the door of my apartment. I stopped and pondered why
in the world it hadn't been stolen. The apartment, which I
had inherited from Greg, wasn't in the worst part of town
but not in the best one either. My guardian hadn't been
concerned with security; he'd bought the apartment because
it was close to the Order.

I frowned at the parcel. It lay on the grimy landing before my new door—the old one had to be replaced when a
demon burst through it. I'd built a bit of a reputation in the
neighborhood as that crazy bitch with a sword who lives in
32B, an image I carefully cultivated, but even so, an unat-
tended parcel should have been pilfered within seconds of
hitting the ground.

Maybe it was booby-trapped.

I pulled out Slayer. The light filtering through the grimy
window above me caught the opaque, nearly white metal of
the saber, layering a nacre sheen along the blade. I nudged
the package with the saber's tip and dodged just in case.

Nothing.

The package lay quietly. Yes, yes, and as soon as I picked it up, it would sprout blades and slice my hands to ribbons.

I crouched, cut across the cord securing the paper, and carefully slid the paper aside, revealing green silk and a little card. I picked up the card. *Please call me. Saiman.*

I swore under my breath and took the parcel inside the apartment. My answering machine indicated no messages. Nothing from Derek.

I tore the paper and dumped the contents of the parcel onto my bed. A pair of wide silk pants, light magenta in color, green slippers, and an ao dai: a long, flowing Vietnamese garment, half-tunic, half-dress. The clothes were exquisite, especially the ao dai, made of fern-green silk and embroidered with lighter green and tiny flecks of magenta.

I got the phone and dialed Saiman's number.

"Hello, Kate."

"What part of 'no date' did you not understand?"

A barely audible sigh filtered through the phone. "Unless you've been to the Games, it's hard to describe the atmosphere. It's a remarkably violent, brutal place. The normal boundaries of common sense don't apply. Cooler heads do not prevail, and everyone's burning to prove their physical prowess. You're an attractive woman. If you come dressed as you were last night, we'll be inundated with challengers. I think we'll both agree that calling that much attention to ourselves is unnecessary."

He had a point.

"I've chosen these items with great care," he said. "They permit full freedom of movement. If you wear them, you'll look less like a bodyguard and more like—"

"Arm candy?"

"A companion. Please, be reasonable, Kate. Play Emma Peel to my John Steed for one night."

I had no clue who Emma Peel or John Steed was.

Saiman's voice softened, gaining a warm velvet quality. "If you are uncomfortable, I understand. We can always renegotiate the terms of our bargain."

He sank enough innuendo into "renegotiate" to make a professional call girl blush.

"A bargain is a bargain," I said. Better to pay up here and now. Being in debt to Saiman didn't appeal to me in the least, and he knew it. Outmaneuvered yet again.

"Green is your color," Saiman said in a conciliatory way. "I had the ao dai tailored to you. It should fit."

I had no doubt it would. He'd probably turned into me and tried it on. "I'll give it a shot."

"I'll pick you up at ten. And, Kate, perhaps a touch of makeup . . ."

"Would you like to assist me with my choice of underwear as well?"

My sarcasm whistled right over his head. "I would be delighted. While I'd love to see you in a balconette bra, I'm afraid for this particular occasion I would have to go with a foam-lined seamless due to the tight fit of the garment across your breasts . . . Perhaps I could come over and review what you have available . . ."

I hung up. A panty party with Saiman. Not in his wildest dreams.

EIGHT HOURS LATER, AS I STEPPED OUT OF SAI-man's car into the parking lot of the Arena, I reflected on the fact that he had proved right. Although the green silk hugged my chest, leaving absolutely no doubt that I was female, the dress widened below. Two slits sliced the ao dai on the sides, reaching an inch past the high waistband of the pants. The sleeves flared at the wrist, wide enough to mask my wrist guards, which I had filled with silver needles.

Unfortunately, there was nowhere to put my sword. That was okay. I didn't mind carrying it.

Saiman held on to my passenger door. He chose to be tall and middle-aged tonight, a man past his prime but still trim and dapper in a sleek dark suit and a black turtleneck. His features were large and well-defined, with a patrician nose, powerful chin, wide forehead, and pale hazel eyes under forceful white eyebrows. Platinum-gray hair framed his face in a carefully trimmed mane. In his right hand he held a long black cane tipped by a silver dragon head.

An aura of wealth radiated from him, enhancing his looks like a layer of polish. He smelled of money and prestige. His voice was the auditory equivalent of expensive coffee, rich, smooth, and slightly bitter. "Kate, I'm afraid the sword has to stay."

"No."

"Weapons are forbidden everywhere but the Pit level. You won't get through the door."

Shit.

I sighed and put Slayer between the front seats. "Stay here. Guard the car."

Saiman shut the door. "Is the sword sentient?"

"No. But I like to pretend it is."

A remote clicked in Saiman's hand. The car answered with an odd chime.

"What was that?"

"My security system. I wouldn't recommend touching the vehicle. Shall we?" He offered me his elbow. I rested my fingers on his arm. A deal was a deal. I was his arm candy for the night.

At least I looked the part. I had twisted my hair up and stuck a couple of reinforced wooden sticks into the knot to keep it put. I'd even brushed on some makeup to match the ao dai. The dress already added a touch of exotic, and mascara and dark eye shadow took me into intriguing territory. Pretty was forever out of my league, but striking I could manage.

A large building sat before us in the middle of a huge parking lot. Brick and oval in shape, it rose three stories tall, stretching into the night for what seemed like forever. Buildings of this size were rare in Atlanta.

Something about the location tugged on me. "Wasn't there something else here?"

"The Cooler. This used to be Atlanta's ice-skating rink. Obviously, we've made some modifications."

I chewed on that "we." "Are you a member of the House, Saiman?"

"No. But Thomas Durand is." He indicated his new face with an elegant sweep of his hand.

Not only I was going to an underground tournament dressed like a bimbo, but my escort owned a chunk of it. Great. Since I had gambling and illegal combat covered, maybe afterward I could score some drugs and high-class hookers for an encore. I sighed and tried to look as though I didn't kill things for a living.

"Are those blades in your hair?" Saiman asked.

"No. Putting sharp-bladed things into your hair isn't a good idea."

"Why not?"

"First, someone could hit you in the head, driving the blades into your scalp. Second, eventually you have to pull the blades out. I have no desire to dramatically unsheathe my hair weapons and end up with half of my hair sliced off and a giant bald spot."

A wooden tower clawed at the sky about a hundred yards from the Arena, close enough to cover the entire roof with the fire of the machine guns and cheiroballistae mounted on the platform at its top. The people manning the tower wore distinctive black-and-red uniforms.

"Red Guard?"

"Yes."

"I guess blood sport pays." Otherwise the hosts of this little shindig wouldn't be able to hire the most expensive guard unit in the city. I knew a few Red Guardsmen, and they deserved their pay. A few years ago I had considered joining them for the steady paycheck, but the work was dull as hell.

"The Coliseum, the pride and joy of Rome, could seat fifty thousand people." Saiman permitted himself a smile. "Fifty thousand spectators at a time when the horse was the most efficient method of transportation. Blood sport pays, indeed. It also attracts rule breakers, which is why the Guardsmen patrol both the outer perimeter and the inside, especially the ground floor, which surrounds the Pit, where the fights take place. The fighters' rooms are located there and the House doesn't tolerate any squabbles outside the Pit."

My evening had just gotten a lot more complicated. Tag along with Saiman, give him the slip using the ninja skills I didn't have, get past the best guards in Atlanta, penetrate the ground floor full of gladiators, find the girl with dark hair, hand her the note, and get back before Saiman suspected anything amiss. Piece of cake. Could do it in my sleep. Once again, I felt a distinct urge to punch Derek in the mouth.

We crossed a two-foot-wide, fluorescent white line painted on the pavement.

"Why the line?"

"We are now under the protection of the Guards," Saiman answered. "Inside the line they take an interest in our welfare—up to a point. Outside the line, we're on our own."

"Ever had deaths in the parking lot?"

"If you weren't an agent of the Order, I'd tell you we had two in the last month. But since you are, I have to claim ignorance." Saiman gave me a coy smile. Spare me.

We headed toward the brightly lit entrance, flanked by four Red Guards, two armed with automatic weapons and the other two carrying Chinese spears decorated with crimson silk standards. Odd choice of weapons but they looked pretty.

Saiman and I passed between them and stepped through the narrow arched entrance into a hallway. A woman stood in our way, sandwiched between two male Red Guards who looked as though they lived for a chance to run into the woods with a fifty-pound rucksack so they could blow up a loup compound. Their boss was slightly taller than me, a shade leaner, cinched into a light brown leather vest and armed with a rapier. Her right hand was bare, but a thick leather glove shielded her left. A sheen of emerald green coated the rapier's blade as if it were made of green bottle glass. Ten to one, enchanted.

I gave the woman a once-over. Short red hair. Clear gray eyes. I looked into the eyes and saw a hard-ass looking back.

"Rene. As always, a pleasure." Saiman did his ticket trick again and handed the two rectangles to Rene.

Rene favored the tickets with a glance, returned them to Durand, and fixed me with a territorial stare making it obvious the ao dai hadn't fooled her for a second. "Don't kill anybody in my building."

"Do your job right and I won't have to."

I let Saiman lead me away, down the hallway. He bent to me and said in a confidential voice, "Rene is—"

"The head of security."

"Her sword—"

"Is enchanted, probably poison, and she is preternaturally fast with it."

"Have you met her before?"

I grimaced. "The rapier is a duelist's weapon, best in a one-on-one fight. It relies on precision: you're trying to puncture vital organs and blood vessels with an inch-wide blade. A normal rapier wouldn't stop an enraged shapeshifter, for example. The damage area is simply too small, which means for Rene to be effective, she has to bank on poison or magic and she has to strike very quickly to give it a chance to work. I suspect poison, because Rene wears a left glove, which means she doesn't want to touch the blade with bare skin, even though the tech is up. Am I correct?"

"Yes." Saiman seemed a bit taken aback.

Rene's rapier probably functioned similarly to Slayer. My saber smoked in the presence of undead and liquefied undead tissue. If I left it in the undead body, it also absorbed the liquefied flesh. Unfortunately, I rarely had a chance to leave it in the body long enough, and as a result, Slayer turned thin and brittle after too much fighting, and I had to feed it. I would bet a good portion of my salary that Rene had to replenish her rapier as well.

We rounded the bend, climbed a narrow staircase, and

stepped into a different world. The floor was Italian tile, rust and sand, laid in an elaborate pattern of small and large checkers. Light peach walls offered narrow niches on the right, filled with spires of bamboo in heavy ceramic pots. On the left, tall arches cut the wall, each blocked by a heavy rust curtain. Ornate feylanterns, now dull in the absence of magic, decorated the space between each arch. A dozen fans slowly rotated on the ceiling, their lamps spilling soothing light onto the hallway.

The steady hum of a gathering crowd filtered through the curtains. We were on the third floor.

The magic hit, choking the electricity. The lamps died a blinking death. The fans slowed to a lazy stop and the twisted glass tubes of feylanterns ignited along the wall, tinting the hallway with their pale blue radiance.

A deep, throaty bellow ripped through the white noise of the crowd, a hoarse, inhuman sound of fear, rage, and pain rolled into one. The tiny hairs on the back of my neck rose. Saiman watched me for a reaction. His expression had a smug look to it.

I ignored the noise. "Where are we going?"

"To the VIP observation deck. If you recall, I mentioned my need for your professional opinion. The members of the team you are to evaluate typically loiter there before the fight."

"Which team would that be?" I asked, recalling Derek's note tucked away in my left wrist guard. Give the note to Livie of the Reaper team . . .

"The Reapers."

Figured.

CHAPTER 8

———◦———

THE SEMICIRCULAR OBSERVATION DECK WAS BARE-
ly a third full. Most of the light came from the clusters of
candles burning on the small, round tables. Beyond the
tables, a crescent-shaped floor-to-ceiling window offered a
view of the parking lot and the city steeped in darkness.

As I strode next to Saiman to the table by the window, I
catalogued the patrons. Sixteen people total, three bodyguards, four women, two dark-haired, but none looked like
a fighter.

My gaze slid to a man two tables over, and I felt a light
jolt, like a live wire shocking my arm. He was large, probably close to six feet, and dressed in supple gray leather,
most of it hidden by a coarse plain cloak. Long dark hair
fell down his shoulders.

His gaze fastened on me and wouldn't let go. Power
coursed through his light blue eyes. He sat easy, his manner
relaxed and cordial. If you accidentally stepped on his foot,
he might be gracious and apologize for getting in your way.
But there was something about him that communicated
power and the potential for incredible violence. He knew

with absolute certainty that he could kill every person in the room in seconds, and that knowledge far surpassed the need to prove it.

The liquid in his glass was clear. Vodka or water? Water meant somebody who wished to remain sober, and therefore posed a bigger threat.

Saiman held out a chair, expecting me to sit in it, which would put my back to the man. "The other chair," I murmured. The man still stared at me.

"I'm sorry?"

"The other chair."

Saiman smoothly switched to the opposite side of the table and pulled out the other chair. I sat. Saiman sat, too.

A waiter glided up, obscuring my view. Saiman ordered cognac. "And the lady?" the waiter inquired. Saiman opened his mouth.

"Water, no ice," I said.

Saiman clamped his mouth shut. The waiter flittered away, revealing the dark-haired man, who had pivoted subtly so he could watch us. He looked at me as if he was searching for something in my face. I broadcasted "bodyguard" loud and clear. *That's right—looking is free; touch Saiman and I'll crush your windpipe.*

"There's no need to play my bodyguard," Saiman assured me.

"There's no need to play my date." It was a matter of principle. If somebody sniped Saiman while I sat two feet away, I would have to pack up my knives and take up farming instead.

"I can't help it. You're simply stunning."

"Is this the part where I swoon?"

The man rose and headed toward us. Six-two at least. I didn't like the way he moved, smooth, gliding easily on liquid joints. A swordsman. An exceptional swordsman, to move with such grace considering his size. Tall, supple, deadly.

Saiman sighed. "At the risk of sounding crude, wooing

you is like playing basketball with a porcupine. No compliment goes unpunished."

"Then stop complimenting."

A young red-haired man entered the observation deck and briskly crossed the floor. The swordsman halted in midstep. The young man approached, said something softly, and stepped to the side, treating the man with the deference given to a senior officer. The swordsman glanced at me one last time and walked away.

Saiman chuckled.

"I don't see the humor in it."

The waiter delivered our drinks: my water in a flute and Saiman's cognac in a heavy cut-crystal glass. Saiman cupped the bowl of his glass in his palm to warm the dark amber liquid, and held it close, letting the aroma rise to his face.

"Male attention is to be expected. You're a captivating woman. Edgy. Fascinating. And there are certain advantages to being seen in my company. I'm attractive, successful, and respected. And very rich. My reputation in this particular venue is beyond reproach. Your beauty and my position create an air of allure. I think you'll discover that men here will find you very desirable. We could be a devastating duo . . ."

I flexed my wrist, popped a silver needle into my palm, and offered it to him.

"What's this?"

"A needle."

"What should I do with it?"

He'd walked right into it. Too easy. "Please use it to pop your head. It's obscuring my view of the room."

The doors of the observation deck opened and two men entered. The one on the left towered over his buddy. Tall, large, his hair cropped so close it was merely stubble on his large scalp, he held himself ramrod straight. He wore black pants, huge combat boots, and nothing else. Twisted swirls of tribal tattoos, precise and coal black as if painted in pitch, spiraled up his arms, stained his chest, and climbed up his back over his neck. A lot of elaborate ink. Interesting that it would all be the same color.

Beside him walked a man with hair so blond, it resembled a lemon. Cut even with the corner of his jaw, it flared around his narrow face in a disorganized mess. It was an odd haircut for a man but he somehow pulled it off without looking too feminine.

"And here they are." Saiman leaned back casually.

"Reapers?" I murmured.

"Yes. The dark brute uses the stage name 'Cesare.' The blond is Mart."

"What are their real names?" If anyone knew, Saiman would.

"I have no idea." Saiman sipped his cognac. "And that bothers me."

The Reapers zeroed in on our table.

"Anything in particular I'm looking for?"

"I want to know if they're human."

I watched Mart. Lean, bordering on thin, he wore a long gray trench coat he left hanging open. Under it was what could only be described as a cat burglar suit: black and skin-tight over his chest, it hugged his legs before disappearing into soft black boots. If it wasn't for the tightness of the suit, I would've missed the minute tensing of his leg muscles. He leapt and landed in a light crouch on our table.

Excellent balance—didn't slide at all when he jumped, landed on his toes, the table barely moved.

Mart looked straight ahead, presenting me with a carved profile. Very light eyes, blue, rimmed in darker gray, but undeniably human. Good bone structure, masculine, without obvious weakness. Compact frame, narrow, corded with lean muscle. Long limbs, providing for good reach. No odd scent. Looked human to me, but I'd never known Saiman to be wrong. Something had to have given him pause, but what?

When in doubt, poke the beehive with a stick to see if anything interesting flies out. I clapped my hands. "I had no idea Pit teams had such pretty cheerleaders. Can you do it again, but with more spirit this time?"

Mart turned to me and stared, unblinking. It was like looking into the eyes of a hawk: distance and the promise of sudden death.

I pretended to think and snapped my fingers. "I know what's missing. The pom-poms!"

No reaction. He knew I had insulted him, but he wasn't sure exactly how.

Saiman chuckled.

Mart still stared at me. His skin was perfect. Too perfect. No scratches. No cuts. No imperfections, no pimples, no blackheads. Like alabaster polished to light gloss.

"What brings you to our table, gentlemen?" Saiman's voice was relaxed. Not a shadow of anxiety. I had to give it to him—Saiman had balls.

The tattooed man crossed his arms. His frame was lanky, his limbs very long in proportion to his body. Definition showed on his arms, but his muscle was long rather than thick. He fixed Saiman with an unblinking stare.

"You will lose." He pronounced the words very distinctly, his deep voice tinted with an accent I couldn't place.

I reached over slowly to touch Mart's face. He grabbed my hand. I barely saw his hand move and then my fingers were clamped in his. Grip like a steel vise. Fast, too. Possibly faster than me. This should be interesting. I kept my fingers limp. "Oh, you're strong." He was strong. He also left himself wide open. I wondered if he would be fast enough to block a champagne glass if I broke it and shoved it into his throat. That would be a very tempting theory to test.

"Mart!" Saiman's voice snapped like a whip. "You break her, you buy her."

Mart swiveled his head toward him. It was a very odd gesture: only his head turned. Like an owl. Or possibly a cat. He released my fingers. He had probably discounted me because I was a woman in a brightly colored dress.

A dark-haired woman entered the deck. She was young,

barely eighteen if that. Her features would've made her at home on the streets of Delhi: deep dark eyes, round, full face, sensuous lips, dark hair that streamed behind her. She wore plain jeans and a dark long-sleeved shirt, but the way she walked, rolling her hips slightly, shoulders held back a little to showcase her breasts, made me want to picture her in a sari. An exotic Indian princess. Men watched her move. Three to one, this was Livie, the intended recipient of Derek's note. I had no trouble seeing how she would inspire a young male werewolf to lose all common sense.

She reached our table and halted a couple of feet away, keeping her gaze down. "Asaan," she murmured to Mart. "Mistress wants you."

The tattooed man bared his teeth. She had interrupted their intimidation routine.

The woman bowed her head in submission.

In a moment the Reapers would leave and my chance to pass Derek's note would leave with them. What to do?

Across from me two women excused themselves and headed to the corner of the room, where a small sign pointed toward bathrooms.

"I need to go to the ladies' room!" I announced a bit too loudly, got up, and stared at the dark-haired woman. "Come with me. I don't want to go by myself."

She looked at me as if I were speaking Chinese. You stupid idiot girl.

"I don't want to go by myself," I repeated. "There might be weirdoes in there."

The tattooed man jerked his head toward the bathroom and she sighed. "Okay."

As we departed, I heard the tattooed man's voice. "When you die, your woman will scream."

"Is that a threat?" Saiman chuckled.

"A promise."

We stepped into the bathroom. The moment the heavy door closed behind us, she turned around. "There you go, all set. Unless you want me to hold your hand until you sit on the toilet, I've got to go."

"Are you Livie?"

She blinked. "Yes."

"I'm Derek's friend," I said.

The name hit her like a punch. She reeled back. "You know Derek?"

I pulled the note from the wrist guard. "For you."

She snatched it from my hand and read it. Her eyes widened. She crumpled the note and dropped it into the circular hole in the marble counter.

"Are you in trouble?"

"I have to go. I'll be punished if I stay too long."

"Wait." I grabbed her by the forearm. "I can help. Tell me what's going on."

"You can do nothing! You're just a slut." Livie jerked her arm out of my hand, ripping her sleeve, punched the door open, and took off.

There are times when strenuous mental conditioning comes in handy. It helps you to keep going when you're wading through the sewers up to your thighs in human excrement hacking at an endlessly regenerating Impala worm. It also keeps you from screaming when two young idiots intend to commit suicide by Reapers and resist all attempts to be saved.

The note. She'd thrown the note away. I gave my word I wouldn't read the note before giving it to her, but since she had read it and tossed it into the garbage, the note was now the property of the public. I was Jane Public, so technically I could read the note.

The two women I had seen enter the bathroom earlier exited the stalls, carrying on a conversation about somebody's biceps. They walked past me and proceeded to touch up their already perfect makeup before the mirror.

I ran through my reasoning in my head. It was a bit thin, but I was past the point of caring.

I stepped up to the counter and stuck my arm into the hole. My fingers grazed clumps of wet paper towels.

The ladies stared at me as if I had sprouted a chandelier on my head.

I gave them a nice smile, withdrew my hand, and looked into the hole. A short, wide trash can full of discarded tissue. I could fish all day and not get the note. The counter was marble, but the cabinet under it was metal. A small door allowed access to the trash can. I grabbed the handle. Locked.

The ladies determined that ignoring me was the most prudent course of action and resumed their biceps-related discussion.

I looked at the lock. Lock picking wasn't my forte. Busting things, on the other hand, was right up my alley.

I backed up to give myself a bit of room. It was good that the counter was relatively high. Hard to place a low kick with enough power. I stepped forward and hammered a side kick to the door. Metal boomed like a drum. The door buckled under my foot but held.

The women froze.

I sank a front kick into the dent. *Boom.*

Good door. *Boom.*

The door shuddered, slid down, and crashed to the floor with a thud. I smiled at the horrified ladies. "Dropped my engagement ring down there. You know how it is. A girl will do anything for a diamond."

They fled.

I pulled the trash can out and dug through it. Paper towel, paper towel, used tampon . . . Ugh. Who put used tampons into the paper towel wastebasket? There it was.

I unrolled the crumpled note. "By the Red Roof Inn, same time, tonight."

Pieces began to line up in my head. A breathtakingly beautiful girl, seemingly the property of a team of lethal, possibly not human, gladiators. A young male werewolf with an overdeveloped protective instinct. Derek was in love—nothing less would cause him to break Curran's laws—and he was planning to rescue her. He was also in the fast lane to getting his balls chopped off.

Okay, so what possible time could it be and where was the Red Roof Inn? The Red Roof Inn was about the only hotel franchise actively remaining in business. Any shack's roof could be painted red, instantly identifying it as a place to purchase a room for the night. Problem was, I hadn't the foggiest idea where there might be a Red Roof Inn in this area of Atlanta.

The Reapers struck me as a paranoid sort, the kind who would leave and arrive together. If I were them, I would depart shortly after their last fight of the day was over. They also kept Livie on a short leash. Her absence wouldn't go unnoticed for long. Derek was an idiot, but a bright idiot. He would realize this. He would meet her someplace close to their exit route. Best-case scenario, they would talk and she would go back. Worst-case scenario, he had some sort of getaway vehicle ready for their joint escape. Which would end in disaster.

I kicked the wastebasket back under the counter, leaned the door to cover up the hole, straightened my dress, and emerged from the bathroom.

Saiman sat alone. He raised one eyebrow at my appearance. A gesture copied from me—Saiman was annoyed. But not enough not to rise at my approach.

"Another minute and I would have had to request a rescue party from the management," he said.

"You are the management."

"No, I'm an owner."

Touché. "What's your beef with the Reapers?"

"I think you misunderstood the nature of our agreement." He offered me his elbow. "I bartered for your evaluation of a team. You're the one under obligation to disclose the information, and be assured I'm overcome with the desire to hear your report. I'm positively aquiver."

"Aquiver?"

"Indeed. Shall we walk to our seats?"

I sighed and let myself be led from the deck. I was very tired of being kept out of the loop.

CHAPTER 9

WE WALKED DOWN TO THE FIRST FLOOR, TO AN-
other luxurious hallway pierced with arches. Saiman picked
one of the arches seemingly at random and held the heavy
rust curtain aside. Beyond the curtain lay a small balcony.
Circular and encased by a solid steel railing that came mid-
way to my hip, the balcony offered four chairs upholstered
in soft rust fabric and positioned movie-theater close.

I stepped past the curtain to the railing. A huge hall
greeted me, too large to be called a room. Oblong and vast,
it stretched for at least a hundred and fifty yards. Its walls
were honeycombed with arched balconies arranged in three
rows. Each balcony held six to eight people and offered its
own exit door, which, if our particular door was any indication, opened to the wide corridor. The management was
trying to minimize the chances of a stampede if things went
sour.

The walls plunged lower than the ground level. Sunken
underground, the bottom floor had no balconies or seats.
Bare concrete sloped gently to the center, where an oval
arena of sand lay. A heavy-duty chain link fence defined it,

anchored by numerous steel posts. The Pit. Our balcony protruded from the wall much farther than the rest, and if I took a running start, I could have jumped to the fence.

The sand inside the fence drew my gaze. I looked away. "Special seats?"

"The best in the house. Despite our proximity to the Pit, we're quite safe." Saiman pointed above us. A metal portcullis waited above us, obscured by a velvet curtain. "I can drop it with a pull of the lever. And then of course, there are additional precautions." He pointed to the bottom floor.

To the left of us on the concrete sat an E-50, an enhanced heavy machine gun, mounted on a swivel base and manned by two Red Guards. Guns weren't my thing, but I knew this one: it was the Military Supernatural Defense Unit's weapon of choice when facing a loose vampire.

The E-50 fired .50-caliber ammo at more than three thousand feet per second. At two thousand feet, a round from this gun was deadly. At a hundred yards, it would rip through solid steel like tissue paper. At a maximum rate of fire, an E-50 spat out half a thousand bullets a minute. Of course, at a maximum rate of fire, it also melted the barrel after a few thousand rounds, but if you didn't take down a vampire within the first few seconds, you were dead anyway.

An identical gun waited across from us at the far right. Whatever was caught between them would be dead instantly. Unfortunately, even the best gun was only as strong as the guys manning it. If I wanted to cause trouble, I'd take the gunners out.

Just in case the tech failed, two additional teams of Guardsmen bided their time in the opposite corners: one with an arrow thrower and the other with an assortment of weapons.

"I see you don't want a repeat of the Andorf accident."

If Saiman was surprised at my knowledge of Games-related trivia, he didn't show it.

"We don't. But I assure you, we still get plenty of shapeshifter participation."

"How? Didn't the Beast Lord veto it?"

"We import shapeshifters from outside the Pack's boundaries. They fight and we pull them out before the requisite three days are up."

All visiting shapeshifters had three days to approach the Pack for permission to stay within its territory, or it would approach them and they wouldn't like it. "Sounds expensive."

Saiman smiled. "It's well worth it. The price of tickets alone covers most fighter-related expenses. The real money comes from betting. On a good fight the House takes in anywhere from half to three quarters of a million. The highest intake on a championship fight was over two million."

With hazard pay, I made just above thirty grand a year.

I stared at the sand of the Pit. In my head, the building vanished. The fence, the concrete, the guns, Saiman, all dissolved into the blazing sun, blindingly bright and merciless. I heard the noise of the crowd in the wooden stands, the quick staccato of Spanish, the high-pitched laughter of women, and the hoarse cries of the bookies calling out numbers. I felt my father's presence behind me, calm and steady. The reassuring weight of the sword tugged on my hand. I smelled my skin, scorched by the sun, and blood fumes rising from the sand.

"Shall we sit down?" Saiman's voice intruded upon my reverie. Just as well.

We took our seats. Huge rust curtains slid aside on the far left and right of the chamber, revealing two entrances: the one on the right painted garish gold and its twin on the left in a cheery shade of solid black.

Saiman leaned to me. "The fighters enter through the Gold Gate. Corpses leave through the Midnight one. If you 'walk out gold,' you've won the match."

A long, deep bellow of a huge gong tolled through the Arena, calling the spectators to silence. A slim woman in a silver dress stepped out of the Gold Gate.

"Welcome! Welcome to the house of combat where

death and life dance on the edge of the blade." Her voice was deep for a female and it carried through the Arena. "Let the Games begin!"

"Sophia," Saiman said. "The producer."

The woman disappeared back into the Gold Gate.

A huge scoreboard suspended on chains slid down from the ceiling and stopped just above the Midnight Gate. Two names written on white paper in beautiful calligraphy sat in twin wooden frames: RODRIGUEZ VS. CALLISTO. The odds beneath it said -175+200. Rodriguez was a slight favorite to win. If you bet on him as the winner, you would have to put in $175 to get back an extra $100. If you bet on Callisto and she won, for every $100, you'd get your money and $200 back.

"Both human. Mildly interesting." Saiman dismissed the scoreboard with a wave of his hand. "The Reapers, Kate? I'm eager to hear your assessment."

"Both Mart and Cesare are fighters?"

Saiman nodded.

"Have you ever seen them bleed?"

"Cesare. During a bout with a werejaguar, he suffered several deep gashes across the chest and back. Mart so far has been untouched."

I nodded. "Have you noticed how perfect Mart's skin is?"

Saiman frowned. "Its tone is quite even, but I don't see your point."

Not surprising. Someone who treated skin like clay he could mold and mash at will wouldn't realize the significance of a perfect complexion. "Pimple" was simply not in Saiman's vocabulary.

"Ordinary people have blemishes. Acne, bruises, blackheads, clogged pores, small scars. Mart has none. His skin is completely uniform and unnaturally perfect."

"Perhaps he has accelerated healing."

"I've seen shapeshifters with scars, and they regenerate broken limbs in a couple of weeks. A normal human's history is written in their skin, Saiman. We have training scars from before we got good enough. But he has none. How long since you first met him?"

"Two months."

"So he has been in Georgia since late summer. Have you ever seen him sunburned?"

"No."

"A man with skin that shade should develop a nice crispy crust after half an hour under Atlanta's sun. Why is he paler than a flowering dogwood? And have you ever seen him with a different hairstyle?"

I could almost feel wheels turning in Saiman's head. "No," he said slowly.

"Hair always at the same length?"

"Yes."

I nodded. "Let's talk about his buddy Cesare. Tattooed from head to toe?"

"Yes."

"Did you notice that all of his ink looks perfectly fresh? First, most people get tattooed over a period of years. A complicated design takes time. The process is ritualistic for many people and as important as the result. Ink fades over time, faster if exposed to the sun. All of his tattoos—at least everything I could see—were the same color, bright black. As if he never goes outside."

"Perhaps he simply planned his tattooing ahead of time and used sunblock."

"I doubt very much that a man could walk into the tattoo parlor and unroll a full body plan of tribal designs. In any case, you said he bled. Deep wounds would cause distortions in his designs, especially considering how intricate his are. A thickening here and there, smudged, broken lines. I saw none."

A troubled expression disturbed the handsome symmetry of Saiman's face.

Once blood, fluid, or any other tissue was removed from the body, the owner could no longer mask its magic. An m-scanner picked up traces of that magic and registered it in different colors: purple for vampire, green for shapeshifter, blue or gray for human. I didn't see the problem: take a blood sample, run an m-scan, anything not blue or silver meant nonhuman. An m-scan was foolproof.

"Have you m-scanned them?"

"Several times. Both register blue. Pure human."

Odd. "The m-scanner is a hell of a thing to rebut," I said. "But the fact remains: you have two China dolls, one almost albino and the other painted with pretty black swirls. And they really don't like you. I'd get a bodyguard, Saiman. And I would warn him to expect unusual things from your attackers."

Two humans walked out onto the field. Rodriguez was in his forties. Short and wiry, he had chosen a short, curved kukri blade. Front heavy, it was designed to sink into flesh almost on its own. Callisto topped him by a foot and outweighed him by about thirty pounds. Her olive-skinned limbs were disproportionately long. She carried an axe. A silver chain wound about her right arm.

The gong tolled. Callisto swung her axe. Had she caught Rodriguez, the blow would've cleaved the smaller fighter open, but Rodriguez danced away, nimble like a cat. Callisto struck again, a diagonal blow that exposed her left side. Rodriguez refused to commit and dodged instead. The crowd jeered.

I leaned on the railing, tracking Rodriguez across the field. He had both experience and skill. But a dangerous ferocity tinted the sneer on Callisto's face.

"Who will win, Rodriguez or Callisto?" Saiman asked.

"Callisto."

"Why?"

"A hunch. She wants it more."

Rodriguez lunged. His blade hacked Callisto's thigh. Vermillion drenched her leg. I smelled blood.

Callisto snapped her arm. The chain swung in a pale metal arch and wound itself about Rodriguez's neck with unnatural precision. The end of the chain reared above the fighter's shoulder and at its end I saw a small, triangular head. Metal jaws came unhinged. Small metal fangs bit the air. Callisto pulled. The links of the chain melded into a serpentine body in a shimmer of steel.

The metal snake clenched its coils. Rodriguez chopped at it in a desperate frenzy, but his kukri slid off the steel body. He was done. The crowd roared in delight.

Rodriguez's face turned purple. He went down to his knees. The sword slid from his fingers and plunged into the sand. He clawed at the metal noose constricting his throat.

She just watched him. She could've stopped it at any point. She could've killed him with her axe. But instead Callisto simply stood there and watched him suffocate.

It took fully four minutes for Rodriguez to die. Finally when his legs stopped drumming the ground, Callisto retrieved her chain, its links once again mere metal, and shook it at the crowd. The spectators howled.

I unclenched my fists. It had taken every ounce of my will not to jump into the Pit and pull that thing off Rodriguez's neck.

I hadn't believed I could think less of Saiman. He proved me wrong.

Four men in gray scrubs emerged from the Midnight Gate, loaded the corpse onto a stretcher, and took it away.

Saiman leaned back in his seat. "As I said, mildly interesting."

"I find it horrific."

"Why? I've seen you kill before, Kate. Granted, you do it with considerably greater skill."

"I kill because I have to. I kill to protect myself or others. I won't take a life to titillate a crowd. Nor would I torture a man for the pleasure of it."

Saiman shrugged. "You kill to survive and to appease your own misguided conscience. Those in the Pit kill for money and the gratification of knowing they are better than the corpse at their feet. At the core, our motives are always self-serving, Kate. Altruism is a fog created by sly minds seeking to benefit from the energy and skill of others. Nothing more."

"You're like a god from a Greek myth, Saiman. You

have no empathy. You have no concept of the world beyond your ego. Wanting something gives you an automatic right to obtain it by whatever means necessary with no regard to the damage it may do. I would be careful if I were you. Friends and objects of deities' desires dropped like flies. In the end the gods always ended up miserable and alone."

Saiman gave me a stunned look and fell silent.

CHAPTER 10

———◆———

FIGHTS CAME ONE AFTER ANOTHER, ENDING IN death far more often than necessary. Too much blood, too much gore, too much show. Too much amateur enthusiasm cut short by icy experience. Once in a while Saiman asked me who would win. I answered, keeping it short. I was ready to go home.

The gong tolled once again. The scoreboard descended carrying two names: ARSEN VS. MART. -1200+900. Arsen was a heavy favorite to win.

"I would like to offer you a job," Saiman said.

I was too sickened to muster any disbelief. "No."

"It's not of a sexual nature."

"No."

"Out of six fights, you have picked a winner every time. I want to employ you as a consultant. Members of the House evaluate the fighters prior to the event to determine the odds the House will give for each fight . . ."

"No."

Mart walked out onto the sand. He had lost the trench coat, and his black suit clung to his slender frame. He moved quietly, a dark, lean shadow, his blond hair the only spot of color. He carried two swords like two sunbeams trapped in steel, one long, one short, a classic katana and a wakizashi.

"Three grand per evaluation."

I turned to Saiman and looked at him. "No."

A deep bellow rolled through the Arena. It started low, a long, heavy roar produced by an inhuman throat, grew to a thunder, and broke into a cacophony of snorts and rapid, sharp cries. The crowd went completely silent. My hand went above my shoulder, but my saber wasn't there.

"*What* is that?"

Saiman's face shone with smug delight. "That's Arsen."

A huge shape appeared in the dim depth of the Gold Gate. Slowly, ponderously, it moved just to the edge of the light. Shadows clung to the contours of vast shoulders and a thick, muscled torso, obscuring a large helmet.

The Red Guard holding open the wire fence door to the Pit looked as though he wanted to be anywhere but there.

Arsen bellowed again and burst into the light, galloping into the Pit. The Red Guard slammed the door closed and took off.

Arsen charged to the center of the Arena, put on the brakes, raising a spray of sand in the air, and roared. The silent audience stared in shock.

He was seven feet tall and layered with slabs of hard, carved muscle that stretched his coal-black hide. His short fur flared into a shaggy mess on his chest and ran down his stomach in a narrow line to widen at his crotch, striving but not quite succeeding in masking his generous endowment. A fringe of hair climbed his thighs and the backs of his arms to droop in a long mane off his massive neck. Two pale horns protruded from his skull. His face was a meld of human and bull: a bovine nose and a bovine mouth, but human eyes peered out under the coarse ridges of his eyebrows. A braided beard dangled from his bottom jaw. His legs terminated in hooves. His arms ended in hands that could enclose my face with their thick, blunt fingers, only two per hand and a thumb. The spear in his right hand was the size of a two-by-two.

I remembered to close my mouth. "A werebull?"

"No. Something much more exotic," Saiman said. "He was born this way and he doesn't shapeshift into a human. He's a minotaur."

Arsen dug the sand with his left hoof, kicking it up, and shook his head. Gold loops of earrings glittered in his left ear. He was power, strength, and rage, bound in flesh and straining to be unleashed.

Mart didn't move. He stood, the two swords in his hands pointing down and apart.

"Arsen is my personal fighter." Saiman's voice vibrated with pride.

"Where did you find him?"

"Greece. Where else?"

"You brought him over from Greece?" By boat. With sea serpents and storms. It must have cost a fortune.

Saiman nodded. "It was worth it. I have no resources to waste on cheap things. I would sacrifice a considerable sum to have the Reapers humiliated. This was a mere pittance."

Arsen bellowed. His eyes locked on Mart. He lowered his head.

Mart simply stood, unmoving and silent.

Moist air puffed from the minotaur's nostrils. Arsen hunched his shoulders and charged.

He came roaring down, impossible to stop, like a battering ram.

Mart made no move to evade.

Twenty feet. Fifteen. Twelve.

Mart leapt into the air, unnaturally high, like a piece of black silk suddenly jerked out of sight. He sailed over the minotaur and landed on its shoulders. For a moment he actually rode on Arsen's back, balancing with laughable ease, and hopped off, light as a feather, into the sand.

Arsen wheeled about and lunged, thrusting his spear in a classic Greek move. Mart dove under the thrust, deflecting the arm with his shorter blade. His katana kissed the inside of Arsen's right thigh. In a split second, Mart reversed the strike, sliced Arsen's left thigh, and twisted away from the minotaur's reach.

It was blindingly fast. "He's dead."

"What?" Saiman glared at me.

"Arsen's dead. Both femoral veins are cut."

Thick gushes of red stained the minotaur's thighs. Mart turned on his toes, faced our box, and bowed with a flourish, bloody swords held wide.

Rage twisted Saiman's features into an unrecognizable mask.

Mart walked away to the Gold Gate.

Arsen let out a weak moan, more of his lifeblood spilling with every palpitation of his heart. His knees hit the sand. With a shudder he toppled forward and fell facedown.

The crowd exploded in a rabid crescendo of cheers. Saiman surged to his feet and took off through the balcony door. I waited about thirty seconds to put some distance between us and ran out of there as if my hair were on fire. As far as I was concerned, the night was over. It was time to go and track down the Red Roof Inn.

CHAPTER 11

———◦◦◦———

EVEN THE BEST PLANS HAVE A FLAW. MINE HAD two: first, I had no clue where the Red Roof Inn was, and second, I had no transportation. The first problem I resolved with relative ease: I grabbed the first Red Guard I came across and interrogated him. The only Red Roof Inn in the area lay to the west, on the way to the South-West ley line, twenty minutes by horse or a good hour on foot. Forty-five minutes if I jogged. It was close to 2:00 a.m., and with the magic up, the odds of finding a horse to commandeer were nil. Anybody sensible enough to ride a horse wouldn't be out at this hour, and if they were, they could defend themselves and would take a rather dim view of losing their mount. I should've brought my running shoes.

I emerged into the night. The magic had robbed the entrance to the Arena of its electric illumination. Instead runes and arcane symbols glowed red and yellow along its walls, their intricate patterns weaving the solid wall of a ward. One hell of a ward, too—the whole building shimmered in a translucent cocoon of defensive magic, sealed tighter than a bank vault.

I inhaled deeply and let the air out, exhaling anxiety with it. The Arena behind me loomed, emanating malice. Greed and bloodlust mixed there into a miasma that tainted all who entered.

A stone building filled with men and women in evening wear or a sand arena enclosed by crumbling wooden stands filled with people in rags, it made no difference. I had never forgotten fighting on the sand, but I hadn't realized that my memories lay so close to the surface.

The sand marked a number of firsts for me. The first time I fought without any guarantee of my father rescuing me. The first time I killed a woman. The first time I killed in public, and the first time I was deified for it by a bloodthirsty crowd.

My father judged it to be an experience I had to endure and so I had done it. It must've left a scar, because I had only to look at the sand and my arms itched, as if dusted with its grit. I brushed off the phantom powder, shedding the memories with it. I wanted to take a shower.

Right now Derek was probably lying in wait for Livie at the rendezvous point. He was a careful wolf. He'd get there hours in advance. I needed to get my ass to the Red Roof Inn.

First order of business: retrieve Slayer. I headed to Saiman's car.

"Kate?"

Out of the corner of my eye I saw Saiman exit the building. Crap.

"Kate!"

I stopped and looked at him. "The fights are over. We're done."

He caught up to me. "Apologies for my hurried exit . . ."

"I don't want an apology, Saiman. I want my sword out of your car. I fulfilled my obligation; now I have to go."

He opened his mouth to speak but he must have seen something in my face that gave him pause, because he clamped his mouth shut, nodded, and said, "Very well."

We strode to the car.

"How would you have gotten your sword out without my help?" he asked.

"I'd break the window." We stepped over the white line.

"You would vandalize my vehicle?"

"Yep."

"You do realize that the car is heavily warded?"

I felt someone's gaze hit me in the back like a brick. I glanced over my shoulder. The tattooed Reaper, Cesare, stood just behind the white line, over which we had stepped a moment ago. Backlit by the floodlight, he stood very straight, his face wrapped in darkness. His eyes glowed red.

"Company."

Saiman saw Cesare. "Hilarious. I had no idea I'd given them the impression of being susceptible to childish intimidation tactics."

"I think they have more than intimidation in mind." I accelerated. The sleek black bullet of Saiman's vehicle with my saber in the front seat waited a good twenty-five yards away.

A man leapt over the row of cars and landed in front of us in a crouch, blocking the way. Dark hair dripped from his head. He glanced up. His eyes glowed like two red-hot coals. His mouth opened. An unnaturally long tongue spilled out, lashing at the air. His lips drew back, showing rows of curved fangs.

Alrighty, then.

Out of the corner of my eye I saw Cesare, still waiting behind the white line, his arms crossed on his chest.

The man with the snake tongue shifted along the ground in a crouch. Long strands of drool stretched from between his fangs and dripped on the pavement, sending a heady scent of jasmine to swirl through the air. Perfumed monster spit. What was the world coming to?

Saiman went pale. His hand gripped his cane.

The man's glowing eyes stared at Saiman. He raised his hands and showed him two daggers, narrow and sharp like a snake's fangs.

I wasn't even in the picture. Perfect.

Saiman grasped the shaft of his cane with his left hand, edging the handle up with his right. I caught a glimpse of metal between the handle and the dark wood. The cane hid a dagger and he was planning to use it in a heroic fashion.

The man made an odd hooting sound that raised the tiny hairs on the back of my neck, tensed, and sprung.

It was a great, preternaturally high leap, designed to clear the twenty feet between us in a single bound. Saiman took a step, drawing the dagger in a quick jerk, and leaned forward, preparing to meet his attacker.

The first rule of bodyguard detail: keep your "body" out of harm's way.

I swept Saiman's right foot from under him, hitting him in the chest with my left hand. He was so committed to his impending strike that his position placed him ridiculously off balance. He went down on his back like a log. I snatched the cane-sheath from his hand as he fell and thrust it up.

The cane caught the snake-tongued man just under the breastbone. The air burst out of his mouth in a startled gasp. I turned, whipping the sheath around, and smashed it on his temple. The hollow wood broke, leaving me with a shard. The blow would've taken down a normal human. He should've been done then and there.

The man staggered a bit, shook his head, and lunged at me, stabbing with his daggers. I dodged and backed away, drawing him farther from Saiman to the car.

A searchlight swept over us, lingered for a second, and moved on. The guards had to have seen us.

The snake boy kept cutting the air, his swipes enthusiastic but a bit off the mark. Still catching his breath. If he ever got his wind, we'd be in deep shit. Almost to the car. Step. Another step.

Saiman staggered to his feet.

"Stay away!" I barked.

The snake man glanced back, slashing at me with his right to cover up. I grabbed his wrist with my left hand, pulled him forward and down, and stabbed the splintered cane under his ribs, into his kidney. He screeched. I hurled him past me straight into Saiman's car.

His body collided with the passenger door. The defensive spell rippled with a flash of bright yellow and clutched at the body. Orange sparks flew. The snake man flailed in the ward, stuck to the car as if glued, his body jerking in a spasmodic, obscene dance. The stench of burning flesh rose from his chest. His arms flexed. His hands—still clutching the daggers—braced against the car. He was trying to push free. The ward wouldn't be enough. God damn it, he just refused to die.

I pulled the sticks out of my hair and clenched them in my fist.

With a sound of torn paper, the ward split, exhausted. The snake man broke free and lunged at me. I kicked his knee. It was a good, solid blow. He went down and I grasped his head by the hair and plunged the hair sticks into his left eye, once, again, and again, four times. He screamed. I flipped my hold and buried the sticks in his socket as far as they would go.

The daggers fell from his hands. I swiped one and sliced his throat. The razor-sharp blade nearly took his head off. Blood fountained, drenching me. I whirled to check on Cesare, but found only empty space. The Reaper had vanished.

The snake-tongued corpse lay limp and pale in a puddle of its own blood. I looked at Saiman and raised one red-stained finger. "Definitely not human."

Saiman's face shook with fury. "This is an outrage. I own a seventh of the House."

The ward on Saiman's car had been broken. "You mind popping the locks?"

He found the remote with a trembling hand and pushed the button. Nothing happened.

"The magic's up," I told him.

He swore, produced the keys, and unlocked the door. I grasped Slayer's hilt and instantly felt better.

Saiman dragged his hand through his hair. "I need you to come back to the Arena with me."

"No. I have a prior engagement."

"You're my witness!"

I tried to speak slowly and clearly. "I have somewhere to be."

"We're in the middle of nowhere. You have no vehicle."

"I have two legs."

"If you come with me and tell the House what happened, I'll drive you anywhere you want."

I shook my head. It would take too long before he was done.

"I'll get you a horse!"

I stopped in midstep. A horse would cut my traveling time by a third. I turned. "A quick statement, Saiman. Very quick. Then you give me a horse, and I leave."

"Done!"

As we marched back to the Arena, he said, "I thought you said those weren't blades in your hair."

"They aren't. They're spikes. Breathe deep, Saiman. Your hands are still shaking."

RENE'S EYES WERE CLEAR AND COLD LIKE THE crystalline depths of a mountain lake. Saiman's indignant outbursts shattered against her glacial composure.

"How long does it take to retrieve one corpse?"

"The body will be here in a moment."

I perched against a desk. We stood in one of security's rooms. Precious seconds ticked by. There was nothing I could do about it. Rene was doing her job and I had to let her do it.

Rene glanced at me. "Did you cut out the heart?"

I shook my head. "Didn't see the need. I scrambled the brain and cut his head off. I never had one regenerate a head on me."

"True." Rene nodded in agreement.

Saiman picked up a coffee mug, stared at it, and hurled it against the wall. It shattered into a dozen pieces. We looked at him.

"Your date appears to be hysterical," Rene told me.

"You think I should slap some man into him?"

Saiman stared at me, speechless. I had to give it to Rene—she didn't laugh. But she really wanted to.

A squad of Red Guards came through, carrying the snake man on a stretcher. Two guards and an older man followed. The man handed Rene a large book bound in leather and spoke softly. She gave him a crisp nod.

"We take the safety of our guests and especially of our House members very seriously. However." She raised her hand and counted off on her fingers. "First, this incident took place outside of our jurisdiction. Our responsibility for you ends at the white line. Second, this creature isn't registered as a part of the Reaper team or their crew. Nobody recognizes him. The fact that a member of the Reaper team watched the incident doesn't indicate the team's complicity in the assault. He's under no obligation to assist you and he may have simply enjoyed the spectacle. Third, the entire Reaper crew and team, with the exception of Mart and two crew members, left the premises as soon as the first bout began, nearly three hours ago . . ."

A shot of cold pulsed through me. "Is that normal?"

Rene started at the interruption.

"Is that normal?" I insisted.

"No," she said slowly. "Typically they stay to watch."

Derek never did anything without preparation. He would arrive at the rendezvous point hours in advance. The Reapers would have had a three-hour window to interact with him, while I was busy playing scorekeeper for Saiman's amusement. I spun to him. "I need that horse *now*."

Saiman hesitated.

"A horse, Saiman! Or I swear I'll finish what he started."

THE RED ROOF INN LOOMED ON THE EDGE OF A ruined plaza, flanked on both sides by heaps of rubble that had been buildings in their previous life. Two stories tall, its top floor sagging to the side under a crooked roof painted a garish crimson, the inn resembled a stooped old man in a red ball cap huddling under a blanket of kudzu.

I stopped on the edge of the plaza. Under me a pale gelding snorted, breathing hard after the fifteen-minute canter through the dark streets.

Blood smears stained the crumbling asphalt. In the silver gauze of moonlight, they looked thick, black, and glossy, like molten tar.

I dismounted and walked into the plaza. The magic had fallen while I rode. Technology once again gained an upper hand and I sensed nothing. No residual magic, no trace of a spell, no enchanted observer. Just dusty asphalt and blood. So much blood. It was everywhere, spread in long, feathered smudges and cast about in a fine spray of splatter.

I crouched by one of the puddles and dipped my fingers into it. Cooled. Whatever happened here had finished a while ago.

A fist clamped my heart and squeezed it tight into a painful ball. Dread choked me. Suddenly there wasn't enough air. I should have read the note sooner.

I took the ball of guilt and fear that threatened to engulf me and stuffed it away, deep into the recesses of my mind. The task at hand required only my brain. I would deal with the pain later, but now I had to concentrate on the scene and think.

Violence had occurred here, but the plaza didn't look as though combat with a werewolf had taken place. All shapeshifters had two forms: human and animal. Gifted shapeshifters could maintain a warrior form, an in-between beast man, huge, humanoid, and armed with a monster's claws and nightmarish fangs. Most had trouble maintaining it, and few could speak in it, but despite these drawbacks, the warrior form was the most effective weapon in a werewolf's arsenal. Derek's was one of the best. He would have assumed it the moment the fight began.

If Derek had fought in this plaza, there would be scratches on the asphalt. A few clumps of wolf fur here and

there. Shredded flesh—he tended to rip into his targets. I
saw none. Maybe he didn't fight here after all. Maybe he
came upon it and took off . . . I stuffed the hope into the
same place I had packed the guilt. *Later.*

A fine spray of pale, smooth droplets stained the asphalt
to the left. I moved over, carefully stepping between the
blood smears, and knelt. What meager hope I had shattered.
I would've recognized the color of those pale patches anywhere. They were drops of melted silver, cooled into glob-
ules by the night. I pried a couple from the asphalt and slid
them into my pocket. There was no way to melt silver in
the middle of the parking lot without some sorcerous
means. Either the Reapers had a strong magic user with
them or . . .

A sharp growl made me turn. Two wolves hovered on
the edge of the plaza, their eyes glowing pale yellow like
twin fiery moons. George and Brenna.

George's muzzle wrinkled. He planted his legs wide
apart. His black lips parted, revealing a huge maw and pale
fangs. A snarl ripped from his mouth.

I rose very slowly and held my hands up. "I'm not a
threat."

Brenna snapped at the air, flinging spit. Her shackles
rose like a dense coat of needles.

"I didn't cause the bloodbath. You know me. I'm a
Friend of the Pack. Take me to Jim." As long as I didn't
touch Slayer, I had a chance at a peaceful resolution. If they
jumped me while I held my saber, I would damage them. I
was trained to kill, I was good at it, and in the adrenaline
rush of a fight with two 200-pound animals, I would kill
and then regret it for the rest of my life.

Two growls drowned out my voice. They leaned forward, emanating bloodlust, exuding it like a lethal perfume.
My sword arm itched.

"Don't do this. I don't want to hurt you."

A high-pitched coyote yowl cut through the snarls. The
night parted and a lean shadow sailed over the wolves. A

tall, shaggy body charged me—a shapeshifter in a warrior form, flying over the asphalt, tree-trunk legs pumping, huge, muscular arms spread wide. I caught a flash of grotesque jaws armed with two-inch fangs that would rip my face off my skull in a single bite.

The wolves charged. Shit.

I ducked under the swipe of the shapeshifter's sickle claws and rammed my elbow into the monster's solar plexus. He jerked forward from the force of the blow and I sank two silver needles into his neck, behind the ear. He screamed and clawed at his head.

Behind him the night belched two more nightmares.

The wolves were almost on me.

I rammed a quick kick to the shapeshifter's knee. Bone crunched. Good-bye walking. I kicked him into George, popping another needle into my hand, spun about, and slammed right into Brenna. Damn. Teeth clamped onto my wrist guard, her mouth swallowing my arm, and I dropped a needle into her throat. Brenna dropped my arm and yelped, spinning in a circle, trying to spit out the silver burning her tongue.

Fire raked my back. I whirled, rammed the attacker's furry orange arm, exposing the armpit, and forced a needle into the shoulder joint. The shapeshifter howled. The arm went limp.

They swarmed me. Claws clamped my shoulders. Teeth bit my left thigh. I kicked and punched and stabbed, popping silver needles from my wrist guard and sinking them into furry bodies. Bones snapped under my kick. I twisted, snapped a quick punch, crunching someone's muzzle, and then my room to move shrank to nonexistent. A furry ginger-red arm crushed my windpipe and pressed the side of my neck, cutting the blood flow to the brain. Classic choke hold. I leaned back and kicked with both legs, but there wasn't enough space. I couldn't breathe. My chest constricted as if a red-hot iron band had caught my lungs and squeezed and squeezed until the light shrank. Huge fangs closed over my face, bathing my skin in a cloud of fetid breath. A stray thought dashed through my head—what sort of animal makes an orange shapeshifter? The world went dark and I slipped under.

CHAPTER 12

MY THROAT HURT. MY THIGH BURNED—EITHER
someone had scalded me with boiling grease while I was
out or a werewolf had bitten me. The rest of me felt broken,
like I'd been passed through a laundry wringer. I opened
my eyes and saw Jim sitting in a chair.

"Fuck you," I said and sat up.

Jim rubbed his face with his hand, as if trying to wipe
away what bothered him.

My whole body ached, but nothing seemed permanently
out of commission. My mouth tasted of blood. I ran my
tongue along my teeth. All there.

"Did I kill anybody?"

"No. But two of my people are out until their bones
heal."

We looked at each other.

"I stood there with my hands up, Jim. Like this." I raised
my hands. "I didn't pull my sword. I didn't make any
threats. I just stood there like a submissive bitch and asked
them to please let me speak to you. And this is what I got?"

Jim said nothing. Asshole.

"Show me an Atlanta shapeshifter who doesn't know me. Your crew, they recognized me. They know who I am, they know what I do, and they still fucked me up. You've worked with me for four years, Jim. I fought with the Pack and for the Pack. I fought with you. I'm an ally, who should have earned the trust by now. And you and yours treat me like an enemy."

Jim's eyes went ice-cold. "Here you have trust when you grow fur."

"I see. So if a loup bites me tomorrow, it will mean more to you than everything I've done up to this point." I rose. Fire laced my thigh. "Is Derek okay?"

Stone wall.

"God fucking damn it, Jim, is the kid okay?"

Nothing. After all the shit we'd gone through together, he shut me out. Just like that. The loyalty that bound me to Derek meant nothing. The years I'd spent looking out for Jim while he looked out for me as we teamed up on Guild gigs meant nothing. With one executive decision, Jim had cast aside the slender standing I had clawed and fought for with the Pack for the last six months. He just sat there, silent and cold, a complete stranger.

The words dropped from Jim's lips like a brick. "You should go."

I had had just about enough. "Fine. You won't tell me why your crew worked me over. You won't let me see Derek. That's your prerogative. We'll do it your way. James Damael Shrapshire, in your capacity as the Pack's chief security officer, you have permitted Pack members under your command to deliberately injure an employee of the Order. At least three individuals involved in the assault wore the shapeshifter warrior form. Under the Georgia Code, a shapeshifter in a warrior form is equivalent to being armed with a deadly weapon. Therefore, your actions fall under O.C.G.A. Section 16-5-21(c), aggravated assault on a peace officer engaged in the performance of her duties, which is punishable by mandatory imprisonment of no less than five and no more than twenty years. A formal complaint will be filed with the Order within twenty-four hours. I advise you to seek the assistance of counsel."

Jim stared at me. The hardness drained from his eyes, and in their depths I saw astonishment.

I held his stare for a long moment. "Don't call; don't stop by. You need something done, go through official channels. And the next time you meet me, mind your p's and q's, because I'll fuck you over in a heartbeat the second you step over the line. Now return my sword, because I'm walking out of here, and I dare any of your idiots to try and stop me."

I went to the door.

Jim stood up. "On behalf of the Pack, I extend an apology . . ."

"No. The Pack didn't do that. *You* did that." I reached for the door. "I'm so mad at you, I can't even speak."

"Kate . . . wait."

Jim walked to me, took the door, and held it open. Outside three shapeshifters sat on the floor in a hallway: a petite woman with short dark hair, one of the Latino men, and the older bodybuilder who had stopped me at the first murder scene. A short, dark gray line marked the woman's neck, where Lyc-V had died from the contact with silver. Hello, Brenna. They probably had to cut her throat to get the needle out. The cut had sealed but it would take the body a couple of days to absorb the gray discoloration—the evidence of dead virus. Shapeshifters had trouble with all coinage metals—that was why most of their jewelry was steel or platinum—but when it came to toxicity to Lyc-V, silver beat out gold and copper by a mile.

The shapeshifters looked at Jim.

Muscles played along his jaw. His shoulders tensed under the black T-shirt. He was pushing against a wall only he could see. "My bad."

"My bad?" That was all he had? That was it?

He thought about it for a second and nodded. "My bad. I owe you one."

"Your attempt at damage control is duly noted." I shook my head and headed out.

"Kate, I'm sorry. I fucked up. It didn't go down right."

He finally sounded like he meant it. Part of me wanted to kick him in the head, walk away, and just keep walking until I got the hell out of there. I considered the situation: Jim had apologized in front of his crew. That was all I would get. He wouldn't get down on his knees and beg my forgiveness. In the end it wasn't about Jim and me. It was about the kid.

Jim must've sensed what I was thinking. "I'll take you to him."

That cinched it. As we walked past the shapeshifters, he paused, looked at them, and said, "She's in."

I followed him along the gloomy hallway and down a rickety flight of stairs. The air smelled musty. The stairs accepted our weight with shrill creaks of protest. This wasn't one of the Pack's regular offices, or at least I didn't recognize it. It was hard to forget a place plastered with panda wallpaper. Jim's face grew grimmer with each step.

I was still pissed. "What kind of shapeshifter has orange fur anyway?"

"Weredingo."

Now I'd seen everything. Well, at least he didn't steal my baby.

The stairs terminated in a heavy door. Jim halted. His gaze bored into the door with hate reserved for mortal enemies.

"They broke him," Jim said suddenly, a barely contained growl clawing at his words. "They broke the boy. Even if he survives, he'll never be the same."

THE ROOM WAS DIM. A SMALL FLOOR LAMP spilled light onto the rectangular glass box filled with swamp-green fluid. The box was shallow—only two feet tall, and at first, I mistook it for a casket.

I'd seen it before. The shapeshifters called it the tank. A restorative device, invented by Dr. Doolittle, self-proclaimed physician to all things Pack and wild.

A nude body rested in the green liquid, connected to life-support equipment by thin capillaries of IV tubes.

In all my twenty-five years I had never seen a shapeshifter on life support.

I knelt by the box. Breath caught in my throat.

Derek lay encaged in wire. An angry band of magenta swelling marked the flesh over his broken bones, where the abused muscle refused to heal. His right leg was shattered beneath the knee, the shin one continuous misshapen mess of purple ringed with bands of dark gray. Another purple stain marked his left thigh—the femur, the toughest bone in the body, broken right in the middle, snapped like a toothpick.

Two fractures scarred Derek's right arm, above the elbow and at the wrist. Identical breaks marked his left arm. The inhuman precision of the mind that would conceive the need for breaking both arms in exactly the same places made me grind my teeth.

My heartbeat slowed. My head grew hot, my fingertips cold. Breath rolled around my lungs like a clump of ice. This wasn't just a beating. This was an exhibition. A purposeful demonstration of cruelty and hate. They had mangled him, broken him so completely, as if they sought to obliterate what he was. It made me furious and I clenched my hands until my nails dug into my palms.

Deep purple streaked with gray stained Derek's chest, outlining his rib cage and creeping up to his throat, where gray pooled at the base of the neck caught in a brace. An open gash sliced across his torso from his left side up onto his chest, to his right shoulder. The wound was black. Not gray, not bloody—black.

I looked at his face. He no longer had one. A mishmash of broken bones stared back at me, the flesh raw and seeded with gray, as if someone had attempted to sculpt a face out of ground beef and left it in the open air to rot.

Rage shook me. *I'll find you. I'll find you, you fucker, and I'll make you pay. I'll rip you apart with my bare hands.*

All rational thought fled from my head. The room shrank, as though I'd gone blind, while inside me fury built and howled. I wanted to scream, to kick, to punch something, but my body refused to move. I felt helpless. It was a most terrible feeling.

Minutes stretched by, long and viscous like honey dripping from a spoon. Derek still lay there, dying quietly in the vat of green liquid. His chest rose ever so slightly, but aside from that small movement, he might as well have been dead already. If he were a normal human, he would've departed long before his beating had been finished. Sometimes greater regeneration just meant greater suffering.

Someone's hand came to rest on my shoulder. I looked up. Doolittle's kind face greeted me.

"Come on now," he murmured and pulled me up. "Come on up. Let's have some tea."

CHAPTER 13

WE WERE IN A SMALL KITCHEN. DOOLITTLE TOOK
a plastic ice tray from the freezer, twisted it with his dark
hands, and sent the cubes clattering into a glass. He poured
iced tea from a pitcher and set the glass in front of me.

"Tea will help," he said.

I drank out of respect for him. It was shockingly sweet,
more syrup than drink. Ice crunched between my teeth.

"Why isn't he healing?" My voice came out flat, a one-
note gathering of words with no inflection.

Doolittle sat opposite me. He had a genteel manner
about him that instantly put one at ease. Usually I found
myself relaxing slowly in his company. Merely being in the
presence of the Pack's physician proved soothing. Not today. I searched his eyes for reassurance of Derek's survival,
but they offered me no comfort: dark and mournful, they
contained none of the humor I was accustomed to seeing.
Today he just seemed tired, an old black man bent over his
glass of iced tea.

"Lyc-V can do many miraculous things," Doolittle said.
"But it has its limits. The gray color on his body shows the

places where the virus died in great numbers. There isn't enough Lyc-V left in his tissues to heal him. What little remains is keeping him alive, but for how long nobody can say." He looked into his cup. "They beat him very badly. The bones are shattered and crushed in so many places, I can't remember them all. And when they were done breaking him, they poured molten silver onto his body. Into his chest."

I clenched my hands.

"And on his face. And then they dumped him to die in the middle of the street from a moving cart, four blocks from our southern office."

Doolittle reached behind him and handed me a cotton kitchen towel.

I took it and looked at him.

He gave me a small, kind smile. "It helps to wipe them off," he said.

I touched my cheek and realized it was wet. I pressed the towel against my face.

"It's good to cry. No shame in it."

"Can he be helped?" My voice sounded normal. I just couldn't stop crying. The pain kept leaking out of my eyes.

Doolittle shook his head.

My brain started slowly, like an old clock after years of disrepair. The Reapers had discovered Derek at the Red Roof Inn, beaten him, and dumped him by the Pack's office. Jim's crew found him and tracked the scent back to the location where the beating had taken place.

"He hasn't turned," I said.

Doolittle's face voiced a silent question.

"There were no signs of a wolf at the scene. Pints of blood, too many for one person, so he had to have fought and injured them, but no fur. No claw scratches. He killed a vamp in a warrior form. He should've shifted forms the moment they jumped him, but he didn't. How is that possible?"

"We don't know," Jim said.

He leaned against the doorframe like a bleak shadow knitted from anger. I hadn't heard him approach.

"Regeneration and change of shape are irrevocably linked." Doolittle drank his tea. "There are things that can be done to induce a change in one of us. We've tried them all, trying to break him from the coma. Something is blocking him."

They were so calm about it. "Why aren't you surprised?"

Doolittle sighed.

"He isn't the first," Jim said.

THE FIRST PICTURE SHOWED A CORPSE OF A MAN. His face was crushed, the skull indented with such tremendous force, his head resembled a shovel. His chest bone had been cut out of his body. His ribs jutted from the wet mush, the pale cage of bone slick with dark blood.

The black-and-white photograph looked absurdly out of place on a red-and-white-plaid tablecloth. Like a hole into some horrific gray world.

Jim drank a bit of his tea. "Doc, this stuff is pure honey."

"A little sweet never hurt nobody." Doolittle looked offended and poured more syrup into my glass.

Jim shook his head. "The Midnight Games. Sixteen years ago a championship fight went all to shit. A big dumb sonovabitch of a bear lost his way and went wild. Killed a crowd of civilians."

I didn't interrupt. He was talking and I didn't want to do anything to make him stop.

"A lot of people should've stepped up to bring the bear down and didn't. Curran took ownership of it and got it done. That's what an alpha does. It was damn clear after that who was in charge."

Jim leaned forward, his arms on the table. "An alpha's first law must be solid. It shows what the alpha stands for. No matter what other shit happens, the alpha has got to uphold that law, because once he lets somebody question it, his whole rule comes into doubt. Curran's first law is 'Don't touch the Games.'"

"It's a good law," Jim continued. "We don't need to be messing around with a place that's interested in making us dead in a pretty way. Even the People stay the hell away from it since it's gone underground."

He fell silent. Like Curran, Jim mostly hid his emotions, but his eyes betrayed him this time. Dark and troubled, they brimmed with anxiety. He was keeping it in check, but I could sense it. Jim was uneasy. Haunted.

"So what made you mess with the Games, Jim?" I prompted.

"They're importing shapeshifters. Some are on the level. They brought a mountain cat out from Missouri a few months ago. A decent female. But some are scum. They come in to scope our territory. They're a threat. That's a security issue, and that makes it mine."

Pieces clicked together in my head. "You put a mole into the Games. And you didn't tell Curran because you didn't think he would be reasonable about it." Jim took it upon himself to make a decision only the Beast Lord could've made. It wasn't just a Bad Idea. It was a Sure to Get You Killed in a Hurry Idea.

Jim pushed the photograph toward me. "Garabed. Good, strong cat. Armenian. Found him like this a block from the Northern Office."

Now I saw it. Jim had a dead shapeshifter and he couldn't tell Curran about it. Knowing Curran, he would shut down the whole operation at the root. The Beast Lord had to uphold his laws. But now that one of his people was lost, Jim couldn't let it go. He had to find and punish the guilty. First, to avenge the death, and second, because his crew would abandon him if he didn't. The first duty of an alpha was to protect his clan, and Jim's crew was his clan for the time being.

"Garabed showed no signs of shifting shape?" I asked.

"None."

If I were Jim, I'd put somebody back into the Games.

Somebody vicious, smart, and skilled. Somebody hard to take down . . .

"You brought Derek in."

Jim nodded. "He's the best covert agent I have. He looks"—words caught in his throat—"*looked* like a brainless pretty boy. Nobody pays him any mind. But he misses nothing."

"What happened?"

Jim grimaced. "He went there for a month and came back with this weird-ass story about the Reapers. It's the name of a team. They came out of nowhere a few weeks ago and landed with a lot of noise. Half of them m-scanned as human, but Derek said they weren't. Didn't smell right. He thought they had some sort of beef with us. Not just with the Pack but with our whole kind. Something about us being a meld of humans and animals, and those guys hate both. He told me there was a human girl in the Reaper crew and spun this long story about how she wanted to switch sides and would tell us all about the Reapers and Gar's murder if we got her out."

"And you told him no."

Jim drained a third of his glass. "I told him it was too risky. The Reapers travel together, fifteen, twenty, sometimes thirty per group, always armed."

"As if they know they're going in and out of enemy territory."

Jim nodded.

"And they can't be tracked by scent? They have to have a base of some sort."

Jim looked like he'd just bitten a lime. "The problem isn't tracking. The problem is the location of their base."

"Where is it?" Why did I have a feeling this wouldn't be good? With my luck, the next thing to come out of his mouth would be something crazy, like Unicorn Lane . . .

"In Unicorn—"

I held my hand out. "Got it."

Unicorn Lane gave no quarter. Savage magic roiled there, streaming through the gutted corpses of skyscrapers, too powerful to harness, too dangerous to fight. Ordinary objects became suffused with lethal power. Horrible things that shunned the light hid in Unicorn, feeding on lesser monsters and spinning foul magics of their own. Lunatic cultists with secret power, deranged loups, cast-out Masters of the Dead, when they had nowhere to go, when every friend and every family member turned them away, when the apprehension directive on their profiles became "Shoot on sight" and desperation muddled their minds, only then did they try to enter Unicorn Lane. Most became nourishment for abominations. The rare few who survived went mad, if they weren't already.

There was a reason why Andorf the Bear who had rampaged at the last legal Games chose Unicorn Lane as his refuge. There was a reason why Curran had set our first meeting on the outskirts of Unicorn, just deep enough to weed out the scared and kill the stupid.

To follow thirty monsters in human skin into Unicorn Lane in the middle of the night was a cruel and unusual way to commit suicide.

"Scouting their base is right out," Jim said. "But suppose we did somehow spring the girl before they hit Unicorn Lane. We just kidnapped one of their own. Guilty or not, human or not, they would go to war with us after that. We can't afford another damn war."

"Not without cause," Doolittle put in.

"All he had were some funny smells and a girl with a big mouth. I told the kid to stop chasing tail and bring me some proof. He went there one more time, but I could tell the girl made an impression."

"I've seen her," I told him. "I can't blame him."

Jim started. "How?"

"You finish first, then I'll tell you my side."

Jim shrugged. "Derek clammed up. I saw reason wasn't getting through—he would try to rescue her one way or another, and I pulled him out of it. The tickets to the Games are hard to get and go for three grand apiece. I knew he didn't have three grand lying around, and even if he managed, the type of ticket he could get wouldn't let him into the lower level. I put a tail on him, told him to chill, and thought that was the end of it."

Ahh, but Derek had seen Saiman at the Games and recognized him by scent. He knew Saiman in his Durand persona owned part of the House and had "go anywhere" tickets.

"While Derek was cooling off, I put Linna into the Games in his place." Jim placed a second photograph in front of me. A corpse of a woman lay on the surgical table. The outline of her body was distorted, uneven. I studied the photo and realized she was in pieces. The body had been severed into sections and reassembled bit by bit.

"They carved her into twelve pieces," Doolittle said. "Each piece exactly six inches long. She was probably alive while they did it. And no, she didn't change shapes either. Her clothes were still on her."

"I was picking her off the pavement when you came by." Jim clenched his teeth. "Then my tail returned. The kid lost him. And then we found Derek."

I didn't need further explanation. Jim's crew had chased the scent, retracing the trail of Derek's assailants, and found me dipping my fingertips into his blood.

"What do you have?" Jim asked.

I told him. When I came to the part where I led Curran to Linna's dump site, Jim closed his eyes and looked as if he wanted to strangle me. I kept going until the whole story was out on the table. Jim decided he needed more tea. He probably needed something a lot stronger, but he'd have to fight Doolittle for it. The Pack doctor took a dim view of alcohol consumption.

"Did you tell Curran?"

"No."

"Does he know about this office?" *Please say yes.*

"No. This is one of my private places."

"So as far as he knows, you and your crew went AWOL?"

He nodded.

"Rogue," Doolittle said. "The correct term is 'rogue.' What the cat isn't telling you is that right now Curran thinks a good chunk of his security force split from the Pack. He's turning the city upside down looking for Jim. There is an order out for Jim to contact Curran."

"I'll call him in the morning," Jim said.

"Which will only make things worse, because the Beast Lord will give the order to return to the Keep, and, you see, this young man here will decline."

Jim growled low in his throat. It bounced from Doolittle like dry peas from a hard wall.

"Now why would you do that?" I stared at Jim.

"I have my reasons," he said.

"To refuse a direct order is a breach of Pack Law," Doolittle said. "By tradition, Jim will have three days to change his mind. And if he doesn't, Curran will have to do what the alpha does when he is defied." Doolittle shook his head. "It's a hard thing to contemplate, killing your friend. Bound to make a man crazy."

Crazy Curran ranked right up there with monsoons, tornadoes, earthquakes, and other natural disasters.

I turned to Doolittle. "And you? How did he get you into this mess?"

"We kidnapped him," Jim said. "In broad daylight with much noise. He's safe from Curran."

"And right after I got Derek into the tank, I had to treat my kidnappers for injuries." Doolittle shook his head. "I didn't take kindly to being shoved into a cart and sat upon."

Since Jim had gone through all this trouble to set Doolittle up as an innocent victim, Jim must've expected a shit storm of hurricane proportions when Curran found them.

"I was kidnapped." Doolittle smiled. "I have little to worry about. But someone who helps Jim hide from his alpha of her own free will, well, that is a completely different story."

"Don't you have someplace to be?" Jim's eyes flashed green.

Doolittle got up and rested a heavy hand on my shoulder. "Think before you sign your death warrant."

He left the room. It was me and Jim.

In a fight, Curran was death. He'd never liked me. He'd warned me to stay away from the Pack's power struggles. I'd get no leeway this time.

"Jim?"

He looked at me and I saw it, right there, shining clear through all his mental shields: fear. Jim was terrified. Not for himself—I'd known him for a long time and threats to his personal well-being didn't inspire terror in him. He was off balance, as if he'd been knocked down in the dark and had sprung to his feet, not sure where the next blow would come from.

He had "his reasons," and I needed to know them. "Tell me why I shouldn't call Curran right now and blow this whole thing out of the water."

Jim looked into his glass. Muscles clenched on his arms. A brutal internal battle was taking place inside him, and I wasn't sure which side was winning.

"Seven years ago, a string of loup infestations hit the Appalachians," he said. "I had just started with the Pack. They brought me along as an enforcer. Tennessee let us in right away, but it took North Carolina two years to decide they couldn't handle that shit on their own. We went in. It's all mountains. Old Scotch-Irish families, separatists, religious nuts, they all run there and squat on their own personal mountaintops and then they breed, and their kids set up trailers and cabins right there, a spit away. People come there to be by themselves. Everybody minds their own business. Nobody talked to us. Families had gone loup, entire clans, and nobody knew. And sometimes they knew and didn't do anything about it. You've been to the Buchanan compound. You know what we found."

Death. They found death and kiddie pools full of blood and half-eaten children. Women and men, raped, torn to pieces, and raped again, after they were dead. People flayed alive. They found loups.

"We were combing through Jackson County when the local cops called us. A house had caught on fire on Caney Fork Road, but none of them wanted to go up there. Claimed Seth Hayes owned the house and he shot trespassers on sight. Since we were close and would get there faster, could we please swing by."

Bullshit. The cops knew Hayes had gone loup. Probably known it for a while. Otherwise why call shapeshifters about a house fire?

"The place sat on the edge of a damn cliff. Took us an hour to come up on the house. The building was a ruin by that point. Nothing but charred coal and greasy smoke and that stink. The loup stink."

I knew that smell. Thick, musky, sour, it overlaid your tongue with a harsh, bitter patina and made you choke. The scent of a human body gone spiraling out of control into the depths of Lyc-V's delirium. I had smelled it before. Once it stained you, you never forgot it.

Jim kept on, his voice flat. "The kid sat in the ash. He'd dragged two bodies out, what was left of his sisters, and just sat there, waiting for us to finish him off. Filthy, skinny, starved kid covered in his dad's blood. He stank like a loup. I thought we should kill him. I looked at him and thought 'loup kid' and said so. Curran said no. Said we'll take the kid with us. I thought the man was crazy. The shit that kid had been through, he wasn't even human anymore. I looked at him and saw nothing left. But Curran went and sat with the kid, and talked him into following us. The kid didn't speak. I didn't think he knew how."

Jim drew his hand over his hair. "We didn't even know his name, for fuck's sake. He just followed Curran everywhere like a tail: to the gym, to the Keep, to the fights. He'd sit by the door while the council meetings ran, like a dog. Curran would read books to him. He'd sit and read to the kid and then ask his opinion. He did this for a month until one day the kid answered."

Jim's eyes blazed. "Now the kid has a half-form better

than mine. Taught himself to speak in it. Might be the wolf-alpha one day. I can't do it to him."

"Do what?"

"I have to fix it, Kate. Give me a chance to fix it."

"Jim, you're not making sense."

Doolittle walked back inside, a platter of hush puppies in his hand. "She doesn't have your frame of reference, James. Let me take over." He sat and pushed the hush puppies my way. "When a shapeshifter suffers a great deal of stress, be it physical or psychological, it stimulates the production of Lyc-V. The virus saturates our bodies in great numbers. The higher the virus swells and the faster it spikes, the greater are the chances of the shapeshifter going loup."

"That's why the greatest risk of loupism coincides with the onset of puberty." I nodded.

"Indeed. Derek is under a great deal of stress. Something is blocking him, and if we manage to successfully remove the block, the virus will bloom inside him in huge numbers very quickly. It will be a biological explosion."

His words sank in. "Derek might go loup."

Doolittle nodded. "It is a definite possibility."

"How definite?"

"I'd estimate a seventy-five percent chance of loupism."

I rested my elbow on the table and put my forehead on my fist.

"If Curran becomes aware of the situation, and if Derek becomes a loup, Curran will have to kill him," Doolittle said. "It will be his duty as the Beast Lord. The rules of the Pack dictate that when a member of the Pack becomes a loup, it's the duty of the highest alpha present to destroy them."

God. For Curran, killing Derek would be like killing a son or a brother. He'd worked so hard to bring him out after Derek had teetered on the edge of loupism. To have him fall into insanity now would . . . He'd have to kill him. He'd do it himself too, because it was his duty. It would be like me having to kill Julie.

Doolittle cleared his throat. "Curran has no family. He's

a survivor of a massacre. Mahon raised him, saving him in much the same way he saved Derek. Killing Derek will inflict severe psychological damage," Doolittle said. "He will do it. He has never shunned his responsibilities and he wouldn't want anyone else to bear the weight. He has been under a lot of pressure in this last year. He's a Beast Lord, but in the end he's only a man."

In my head, I pictured Curran standing by Derek's body. It was in my power to spare him that. Not for Jim's sake, but for his own. You should never have to kill children you saved.

He would be furious. He'd rip Jim to pieces.

"He gave us three days," I said. "If we don't resolve this by the end of those three days, I'll go to him. I'll tell him. If Derek goes loup before that, I will kill him." *Please, God, whoever you are, please don't make me do this.*

"That's my responsibility," Jim said.

"No. Curran accepted an offer of assistance from the Order. That means that in the matters of this investigation, I outrank you. It's my responsibility and I'll take care of it." I had three days. I could do a lot in three days.

Jim's eyes flashed.

"Deal with it," I told him and looked at Doolittle. "What would keep a shapeshifter from shifting?"

"Magic," he said. "Very powerful magic."

"Feeding comes first, mating second, and shape-changing is third. Hard to override it," Jim ground out.

"But the Reapers did override it. They held the key to it. And they damn near obliterated Derek." I clenched my teeth.

"Your sword's smoking," Doolittle murmured.

Thin tendrils of smoke snaked from Slayer in my sheath, the saber feeding on my anger.

"Nothing to worry about." I drummed my fingertips on the table. "I could possibly manage to take the Reapers into custody. But I have no reason to hold them. First, we have no proof they took out Derek."

"They would smell of his blood," Jim said.

"So do I. There was enough of his blood in that plaza to stain anyone who came into contact with it. That's not enough. Did you m-scan the scene?"

"Blue and green across the board." Jim shrugged in disgust.

The m-scan recorded the colors of residual magic. Blue stood for human and green stood for shapeshifter. It told us absolutely nothing. Maybe if I prayed to Miss Marple, she'd hook me up with a clue . . .

"Another problem with bringing them in," I said, "is the Games themselves. Let's say I bring them in. I'll have to ask questions like 'What were you doing in that plaza?' If they admitted to being a team in the Games, I'd have to follow up on it. I can't just ignore the existence of an underground gladiatorial tournament. The cops, Order, and MSDU have to know the Games are going on. The fact that they take place at all means a lot of money and influence are backing them up."

Jim nodded. "You'd get shut down before the investigation ever hits the ground."

And that was why I liked working with Jim. He didn't waste any time on calling me a coward, on baiting me, and suggesting I was afraid of the pressure. He understood that if the powers that be came to bear on me, the investigation would become difficult and my progress would be slower than molasses in January. He simply acknowledged it and moved on to the next possible avenue. No angst, no bullshit, no drama.

"So officially, we both can do nothing," I said.

"Yeah."

Doolittle just shook his head and ate his hush puppies.

"I take it we'll have to fight in the Games to get to the Reapers."

"Yeah."

"How come you never invite me to the easy jobs?" I asked him.

"I like to challenge you," he said. "Keeps you on your toes."

I leaned forward and drew a line across the tablecloth with my finger. "Unicorn Lane. Thirty-two blocks long and ten blocks wide. Long and narrow." It used to be thirty blocks long and eight blocks wide, but the flare boosted it and Unicorn grew, swallowing more of the city. "As I understand it, the Reapers go in there and vanish. And your guys can't track them down."

"Your point?"

"You remember the firebird capture from the summer two years ago? Half of Chatham County was burning and the bird smelled like smoke. You couldn't track it and it burned through every trap we had." And he had been pissed off as hell about it, too.

Jim frowned. "I remember. We baited it with a dead possum that had a tracker in it."

"Can you get your hands on a tracker like the one we stuck into the possum?"

"It can be done."

"What's the maximum range of the tracker?"

"Twenty-five miles, if the tech is strong."

I smiled. More than enough to cover Unicorn Lane.

CHAPTER 14

———◉———

JIM SCOWLED AT SAIMAN'S DOOR. "THE PERVERT,"
he said.

"He prefers to think of himself as a sexual deviant."

"Semantics."

We'd talked our plan over on the way through the city. It
wasn't a great plan, but it was a slight improvement over
my usual "go and annoy everyone involved until somebody
tries to kill you." Now I just had to sell my snake oil to
Saiman.

Saiman opened the door. He wore a tall, thin platinum
blonde, long of leg and decorated with a sneer. Jim bristled.
If he had been furry, his hackles would've risen.

Most people confronted with two armed thugs on their
doorstep would pause to assess the situation. Especially if
one of those two had threatened to kill you five hours
earlier if you didn't give her a horse, and the other was a
six-foot-tall man with glowing green eyes who wore a fur-
edged cloak, carried a shotgun, and looked as if he lived to
grind people's faces into brick walls. But Saiman merely
nodded and stepped aside. "Come in."

We came in. I sat on his sofa. Jim assumed a standing position behind and slightly to the left of me, with his arms crossed on his chest. Soft music layered with a techno beat played in the background. Saiman made no offer to turn it off.

"I've returned your horse," I told him. "It's downstairs with the guards." Jim had brought a spare mount for me.

"Keep it. I have no need of one. Would you like something to drink?"

And risk another ultimate luxury lecture? Let me think . . . "No, thank you."

"Anything for you?" Saiman glanced at Jim, saw the Stare of Doom, and decided safety had its advantages over courtesy. "Pardon me while I get something for myself. I think better with a glass in my hand."

He made a martini and came to sit on the love seat, crossing one impossibly long leg over the other and flashing me with his cleavage. *Yes, yes, your boobies are nice. Settle down.*

"How did it go with the Reapers?" I asked.

Saiman glanced at Jim. "Less than satisfactory."

"The Order has a certain interest in the Reapers." Technically that was true. I was an agent of the Order and I had an interest in the Reapers. I had an interest in killing every last one of them in an inventive and painful way.

"Oh?" Saiman arched an eyebrow, once again copying me.

"More to the point, I have a personal stake in this matter. I want the Reapers eliminated."

Saiman's gaze probed me. "Why? Does it have anything to do with your young friend?"

I saw no point in lying. "Yes, it does."

Saiman saluted me with his glass. "I find personal motives to be best."

He would, the selfish bastard.

"So what do you need from me?" he asked.

"I propose a partnership." I was getting better at this game. I didn't quite throw up in my mouth as I said that.

One small victory at a time. "You want the Reapers out. So does the Pack, and so do I. We join forces. You provide access to the Games. We provide the muscle."

"I'm to be an opportunity while you will be the means?"

I nodded. "We share information and resources to accomplish a common goal. Think of it as a business arrangement." The business angle would appeal to him.

Saiman leaned forward, very intent. "Why should I work with you? Just how badly do you want this, Kate?"

A low warning growl reverberated in Jim's throat.

I leaned back and swung one leg over the other, mimicking his pose. "You need us more than we need you. I can flash my ID, walk into the Midnight Games, and make myself a giant pain in the ass. I'm very good at that."

"I have no doubt," Saiman murmured.

"I'll shine a big searchlight onto the Games and the Reapers in particular. Sooner or later they'll develop a burning desire to kill me, and Jim here will help me slaughter them one by one. He has a big axe to grind. Meanwhile, the attendance to the Games drops, House profits plummet, and you lose money."

I gave him a smile. I was aiming for sweet, but he turned a shade paler and scooted a bit farther from me. Note to self: work more on sweet and less on psycho-killer.

"Since you don't wish to work with us, you'll have to hire some muscle to assist you with the Reaper issue. As the parking lot incident showed, they're all about loading you on the first available train to the afterlife. You require protection, which will cost you a lot of trouble and money—judging by Mart, you must employ top talent if you wish to keep breathing. After the Reapers help a couple of your bodyguards find their wings and halos, you'll have to hire replacements, only now you'll enjoy the reputation of a man whose bodyguards die. Prices will shoot up into the stratosphere and the quality of employees will drop. Despite popular misconceptions, most bodyguards aren't suicidal. So you see, you need us more than we need you. We'll kill the Reapers one way or the other. We don't really care. We work for revenge, not for money."

Saiman studied me as if he saw me for the first time. "This is a side of you I'm unfamiliar with."

It was the side of me I used to settle disputes between the Guild and the Order, which was technically my job. I rose. "Think about it. You know my number."

"Is there a method to your madness?" Saiman asked.

"You'll have to shake on it to find out." Since I trusted him about as far as I could throw him, I would've preferred to have his signature in blood on a magically binding contract, but I'd take a shake. Provided he didn't spit into his hand first.

I took exactly three steps toward the door before he said, "We have a deal."

"HERE IS WHAT I KNOW," I SAID. SOME OF IT CAME from Jim and some of it I had put together. "The Reapers entered the picture approximately two months ago. Most of them are certified as human and have passed the m-scan with flying colors."

"Blue across the board." Saiman's face dripped distaste.

"But the Reapers aren't exactly human. We've established that. However, because they fight as 'normals,' initially the House gave long odds in their favor. They were an unproven commodity and most humans fighting against a shapeshifter or a vamp will typically lose. The Reapers cost the House a great deal of money, correct?"

Saiman confirmed it with a short nod. "Yes. There are also other reasons for their 'humanity.' You see, to participate in the tournament, the team must consist of seven members, at least three of whom have to be human or a human derivative, such as a shapeshifter. Without three humans, they wouldn't be able to enter the tournament."

"So to sum up: you don't know what they are, how they're tricking the m-scanner, or where they go when they leave the Games?"

"No." Saiman wrinkled his nose in distaste, a distinctly female gesture that fit the blonde to a T.

"Not very useful, are you?" Jim said.

Thank you for your help, Mr. Diplomacy.

Saiman glanced at him. "Twenty-one years ago, on April twenty-third, you killed the man who murdered your father while they had been incarcerated. You nailed your father's killer to the floor with a crowbar through his stomach, and then you dismembered him. The coroner estimated he took over three hours to die. His name was David Stiles. You were never charged with the crime."

Oh boy.

"I disclose this fact to prevent any appearance of incompetence on my part. I deal in information. I'm expert at it. When I say that I don't know what the Reapers are, I say it with all the weight of my professional expertise behind it."

Jim laughed softly, displaying his white teeth in a wide smile.

Saiman inclined his head in an amicable bow. He may have gathered information about Jim, but he didn't know him. Jim was a jaguar. He showed his teeth only to people he intended to kill. He wouldn't kill him just yet, because we needed him, but one day when Saiman least expected it, he would find himself stalked by death from above.

And I would have absolutely nothing to do with any of it. "Back to the Reapers," I said. "Do you know what they want?"

"That I can answer. They want the Wolf Diamond," Saiman said.

I waited for him to elaborate but he just sipped his martini. He wanted to be prompted. Fine. I obliged. "What is the Wolf Diamond?"

"It's a very large yellow topaz."

"Why the name?" Jim asked.

Saiman pondered his martini. "It's the precise shade of a wolf's eye. The stone is bigger than my fist."

A flashy prize. The topaz itself would be very valuable owing to its uniqueness, and the presence of the stone gave the tournament a nearly legendary flair: a contest between the mightiest warriors for a fabled gemstone and glory. In reality, it was a sick game, where lives were thrown away for the sake of soft bills. Glory? There was no glory in dying for somebody else's money and glee.

"How did you acquire the stone?" Jim asked.

"It was bought by one of the House members and donated to reward the winner of the upcoming tournament. It's an extravagant prize, in line with our current style. People who patronize our venue expect exotic."

A topaz bigger than a man's fist was certainly exotic. I searched my brain for any rudimentary gem lore. Topaz was one of the twelve apocalyptic stones protecting the New Jerusalem. Naturally yellow and expensive, it was rumored to have a cooling influence on one's temper and to protect the wearer from nightmares. The generic "protection" property was the default setting for all precious stones—that was what people said when they had no clue what the stone did or when it had no mystic properties whatsoever. I made a mental note to find a gemology book and look up topaz.

"I've traced the history of the stone three owners back to a German family," Saiman said. "It doesn't appear to have exhibited any supernatural properties. There are a number of legends attached to it, a completely normal occurrence for a precious stone of this size. The predominant belief seems to be that the stone possesses virtue and can't be sold or taken by force, but must be gifted or won, or it will bring death to the one who stole it. I've been unable to determine if that's rubbish. The Reapers seem to feel the curse is true. They approached the House shortly after acquisition asking how they could obtain the stone. Given their propensity for violence, I expected them to attempt theft or burglary, but they have done neither."

I frowned. "Since we know very little, identifying them would be the first step."

"And how do you propose we do that?" Saiman arched an eyebrow and gave me a seductive smile. It failed both because he was Saiman and because he looked like a woman.

"Simple. We kill one."

Saiman pondered this.

Talking through it was a piece of cake. Doing it would be a completely different matter.

"We know that the Reapers travel in packs, which makes them difficult to follow. We also know that they disappear into Unicorn Lane, which makes them difficult to track by scent and magic. However, we're in possession of a tracking unit whose range covers the entire Lane. We kill a Reaper and plant a bug into his body. Once they leave, we track them to the exact spot in Unicorn and approach it at our leisure. We observe their headquarters. There are all sorts of interesting questions that can be answered. How many of them are there? How are they organized? Do they have guards? Are these guards human? How do they get food? What do they eat? Is there a crew that goes out to forage? Can we apprehend the foragers and"—*tear them apart a shred at a time until the damn bastards tell me how to fix Derek*—"and question them?"

"You seem sure you can kill a Reaper." Saiman stared into his empty glass, seemingly amazed by the disappearance of his martini.

I thought of Derek dying slowly in the tub of green liquid. His bones broken, his face gone, his body hurting . . .

Saiman shifted in his love seat. "Kate, your sword seems to be emitting a vapor."

I put a leash on myself. "Get me into the Pit. I'll take care of the rest."

"I would love to, but I can't." Saiman waved his arm in disgust. "The Reapers are scheduled for one final bout before the tournament, which is a team event. The bout has been advertised as Stone class. You don't qualify."

"I can do it," Jim said.

Saiman shook his head. "As much as I would love to have the Pack's chief of security in the Pit, you wouldn't qualify either. Stone class means an extra-large fighter."

True. Jim was never a heavyweight. Even in his half-form, he was lean, quick, and lethal, but not bulky.

"I do have a Stone fighter available." Saiman smiled. "Me."

That beating I had taken from the Pack must've done permanent damage to my hearing. "Me who?"

"Me as in myself."

I squeezed my eyes shut.

"What are you doing?" Saiman asked.

"I'm counting to ten in my head." It worked for Curran; surely it would work for me . . . Nope, not feeling any better.

I opened my eyes. "I kill on a regular basis. So please understand that I say this with the full weight of my professional expertise behind it: you've gone off the deep end. You're enthusiastic but unskilled, and you lack the physical strength and reflexes needed to kill a Reaper. If you enter the Pit, you will die horribly and in great pain and I won't be able to jump in there and pull you out."

"You've never seen me fight in my original form."

A vision of golden-haired Adonis dancing through the snow flashed before me. "Yes, but I saw you dance. Your original form, while devastating to horny women and gay men, isn't likely to slay any Reapers. You'll get your head bashed in and we'll lose an opportunity to plant the bug."

Saiman smiled, a thin stretching of lips without any humor. "That was *not* my original form."

Touché. "In that case, I hope your original form is a two-headed dragon spitting fire."

"Give me an opportunity to fail," Saiman said. "I promise that my corpse won't interrupt your 'I told you so' speech. The bout is tonight. May I count on the two of you to act as my crew?"

What choice did we have? "Fine."

Saiman rose. "I'll have to make a formal appearance for the first part of the evening. After the fight, provided we accomplish the actual kill, the Reapers will be grounded by the Red Guards for one hour to allow us a head start. The

House doesn't wish any friction between fighters outside the ring. That will give the two of you ample time to arrive in Unicorn and make the necessary preparations. I'll stay the night in the Arena, in my private rooms, to recuperate."

Or he would stay the night in the morgue. The thought hung in the air like a funeral shroud. None of us mentioned it.

CHAPTER 15

AFTER JIM AND I WERE FINISHED WITH SAIMAN, Jim dropped me and the Pack horse at my apartment. I wanted to go back with him. I wanted to be there in case Derek woke up. I had this irrational idea that my staying close would somehow fix him.

But it wouldn't. If I had gone back with Jim, I wouldn't have slept, and I needed sleep and food badly. The Reapers wouldn't take kindly to having one of their own knocked out of their lineup. If Saiman managed to deliver on his promise, they might come after us. I needed to be rested and sharp. So I took a shower, scrubbing every square inch of my skin and hair with scented soap to kill the smell of Jim's posse, ate cold beef with black bread, tomato, and a little cheese, took a much-prized and expensive aspirin, and passed out.

I awoke at eight because my phone rang. I raised my head off my pillow and stared at it. It rang and rang, filling my head with noise. The answering machine came on and a familiar voice made me sit straight up.

"Kate."

Curran. *Oy*. Two hours of sleep wasn't sufficient to deal with him.

"Call me as soon as you can."

I picked up the phone. "I'm here."

"You're screening your calls?"

"Why not? It saves me from conversation with idiots."

"Is that an insult?" His voice dropped into a deep growl.

"You're not an idiot," I told him. "You're just a deadly psychopath with a god complex. What is it you want?"

"Have you seen Jim?"

"Nope."

"He didn't call you?"

"Nope." But his goons beat the daylights out of me.

"What about Derek?"

"Nope. Haven't seen him either."

There was a momentary pause. "You're lying."

Shit. "Now what would make you think that?"

"You didn't ask me if Derek is okay, Kate."

That will teach me to have delicate diplomatic conversations first thing in the morning.

"That's because I don't care. You told me you'd bring me in on the investigation. You promised me full cooperation and interviews. That was Friday morning. It's Sunday now. Forty-eight hours have passed. You blew me off, Curran. Just like always. Because you expect me to trip over my feet in a rush to help you, but the precious Pack can't cooperate with outsiders. What you hear in my voice is apathy." And bullshit. Lots and lots of bullshit.

"You're rambling."

Curran two, Kate zero.

"This is very important, Kate. Jim defied me. He's refused a direct order to pull his crew in. I can't let it stand. He has seventy-two hours to decide what to do. Then I'll have to find him."

"You've known Jim for years. Doesn't he get the benefit of the doubt?"

"Not for this." The hard shell on Curran's voice broke. The alpha vanished for a moment, leaving a man in his place. "I don't want to have to find him."

I swallowed. "I'd imagine he doesn't want you to find him either."

"Then help me. Tell me what you know."

"No."

He sighed. "For one moment, forget it's me. Put aside your ego. I'm the Beast Lord. You're a member of the Order. You're subordinate to me in this investigation. I order you to disclose the information. Do your job."

It stung. I was doing my job to the best of my ability. "You're mistaken. I'm not subordinate to you. You and I are on equal footing."

"I see. Is Jim with you now?"

"Yes, he is. We're having rough sex. You're interrupting."

I hung up.

The phone rang again.

Answering machine. ". . . not helping, Ka . . ."

I picked up the phone, held it for a second, and hung up. I didn't want to lie to Curran. Even if it was for his own sake. Making shit up and trading witty barbs just wasn't in me at the moment.

My bedroom was full of comfortable gloom, except for a narrow slash of light, which snuck through the gap between my curtains to fall right on my face. I stuck a pillow on my head.

I was drifting off into dreamland, the pillow on my head blocking the annoyingly persistent ray of light, when I heard a key turn in my lock. My door swung open.

The only person with a key to my place was the super, and he would never enter unannounced.

I forced myself to lie still, my limbs loose. Some picture I presented: my butt in white cotton panties sticking out, my head under the pillow. Not the most advantageous fighting stance.

I lay, hyperaware, all my senses straining. Very soft footsteps approached the bed. Closer. Closer.

Now!

I whipped about, launching a sweeping kick. It caught the intruder in the midsection, eliciting a distinctly male groan, and he went down. I leapt off the bed and lunged for Slayer, but it wasn't where I'd left it. I dropped and saw it far under the bed. He'd kicked it on his way down.

A steel hand grasped my ankle. I flipped on my back and hammered a kick into his shoulder that had the entire force of my body behind it.

He groaned and I saw his face. "Curran!" I would've preferred a homicidal lunatic. Oh, wait . . .

That second of amazement cost me: he lunged at me, knocked my arm aside as if it were nothing, and pinned me to the floor. His legs clamped mine. He held my right arm above my head, my left between our bodies, and leaned, his face only inches from mine, my side touching his chest.

He wrapped me up like a package. I couldn't move an inch.

"I thought you were some sort of maniac!" I growled.

"I am."

"What are you doing here?"

"Looking for Jim in your bed."

"He isn't here."

"I see that."

Little golden sparks danced in his dark gray eyes. He looked terribly pleased with himself and slightly hungry.

I squirmed away from him, but he just clamped me tighter. It felt like fighting in a straitjacket made of heated steel. There was absolutely no give in him. Pinned by his Beastly Majesty. I'd never live that down.

"You can let me go now," I told him.

"Do I have your permission?"

"Yes, you do. I promise not to hurt you."

A hint of a grin curved his mouth. He had no plans to let me go. And I couldn't outmuscle him. Crap.

"You're enjoying this, aren't you?"

He bobbed his head up and down, the smile like a smudge of white paint across his face.

"How did you get in?"

"I have my ways."

The light dawned on me. He was the one who had replaced my door two months ago, because I was rather busy trying not to die. "You kept a key to my apartment. You bastard. How often do you come here?"

"Once in a while."

"Why?"

"To check on you. Saves me the trouble of sitting by the phone waiting for your 'come and rescue me' calls."

"You don't have to be troubled: there won't be any more calls. I'd rather die than call you."

"That's what worries me," he said.

His legs pinned mine, his thighs hard like they were carved of wood. His chest pressed against my breasts. If I could turn a little to the right, my butt would slide against his groin. A little to the left and my face would end up in his neck.

"I'm not one of your subjects," I told him. He was entirely too close, too warm, and too real. "I don't follow your orders and I sure as hell don't need your protection."

"Mmhm," he said. He apparently found my face incredibly fascinating, because he kept looking at me, at my eyes, at my mouth . . .

"Do you ever come here when I'm here?"

"Occasionally."

"I would've heard you."

"You put in twelve hours and get wiped out, and I'm very quiet." His hold eased a little. I lay limp. That was it—lure him into a false sense of security. We weren't that far from the night table, and under the table on the bottom shelf was a dagger.

"The Beast Lord—my own personal stalker. Gee, every girl's dream."

"I don't engage in stalking."

I stared at him in disbelief. "And what do you call this?"

"This I call controlling my opponent so she doesn't injure me."

"What else do you do while you're here? Read my mail? Look through my underwear?"

"No. I don't go through your things. I just come once in a while to make sure you're in one piece. I like knowing you're safe, asleep in your bed. I haven't stolen anything . . ."

I ripped my left arm out of his hand and slammed my elbow into his solar plexus. He exhaled in a gasp. I lunged for the dagger and sat on top of him, my knees pinning his arms, my dagger on his throat.

He lay still. "I give up," he said and smiled. "Your move."

Er. I was sitting atop the Beast Lord in my underwear, holding a knife to his throat. What the hell was my next move?

Curran's gaze fixed on a point on my shoulder. "That's a claw mark," he said, his voice gaining a hard edge. "Wolf. Who?"

"Nobody!" Oh, now there was a brilliant answer. He would believe that.

"One of mine?" Gold flashed in his eyes like lightning.

Well, since every shapeshifter in Atlanta was one of his, that kind of answered itself, didn't it? "Since when do you give a crap about my welfare anyway? I think you're confused as to the nature of our relationship. You and I, we don't get along. You're a psychopathic control freak. You order me around and I want to kill you. I'm a pigheaded insubordinate ass. I drive you mad and you want to strangle me."

"Once! I did it once!"

"Once was plenty. The point is, we don't play nice. We—"

He jerked his arms out from under my knees, pulled me to him, oblivious to the dagger, and kissed me.

His tongue brushed my lips. Heat rolled through me. His

hand caught in my hair. Suddenly I wanted to know how he tasted. He'd kissed me before, just before we'd fought the Red Stalker. I'd been remembering that kiss for four months now. It couldn't have been as good as my memory made it out to be. I should kiss him and exorcise that phantom kiss so I would never think of it again. I opened my mouth and let him in.

Oh. My. God. The Universe exploded.

He tasted intoxicating, like wild wine.

I sank against him, drunk on his taste and his scent, seduced by the feel of his hard body wrapped around mine. My head swam.

Kiss me more. Kiss me again. Kiss me, Curran.

What the hell was wrong with me?

"No!" I struggled against the stone wall of his chest. He held on a moment too long and released me with a low, hungry growl. I jumped off him and backed away, unsteady on my feet. "Are you out of your mind?"

"What's the matter? Forgot that 'not if you're the last man on earth' bit?"

"Get out!"

He just lay there on my carpet, lounging like a lazy cat with a smug smile. "How was it?"

"It was flat," I lied. "No spark. Nothing. Like kissing a brother."

My head was still spinning. I wanted to touch him, to run my hands up his T-shirt, to slide my fingers along his rock-hard arms . . . I wanted to feel his mouth on mine.

No! No touching. No kissing. No. Just *no*.

"Really? Is that why you put your arms around my neck?"

Sonovabitch. "That was temporary insanity." I pointed to the door.

"You sure you don't want me to stay? I'll make you coffee and ask you about your day."

"Out. Now."

He gave an exaggerated sigh and leapt to his feet without the help of his hands. Bloody show-off.

He offered me my dagger, hilt first. "Do you want this back?"

He'd made me *drop* the dagger. I never dropped my weapons unless it was on purpose.

I swiped the weapon from his fingers and chased him to the door, keeping a blade between us. Curran opened the door and paused in the doorway. "Seventy-two hours, Kate. That's all Jim gets. He knows it and he knows I'm looking for him. Now you know it, too."

"Got it," I snarled.

"You sure you don't want to kiss me good-bye, *baby*?"

"How about a good-bye kick to the throat?"

I slammed the door closed, leaned against it, and slid down to the floor to review the situation. The Beast Lord. Lion of Atlanta. Sir My Way or the Highway. A frustrating, infuriating, dangerous bastard who scared me into blind panic until all the brakes on my mouth malfunctioned.

He kissed me. No, he admitted to breaking into my apartment to watch me sleep, he pinned me down on the floor, and then he kissed me. I should have broken his nose. Instead I kissed him back. And I wanted more.

I tried to put it into perspective. I had told him I'd never sleep with him. He told me I would. For him it was a game and he was simply trying to win. Someone once explained to me that if you lined up all of Curran's former lovers, you could have a parade. He was sizing me up for another notch on his bedpost. If I gave in, I'd be a footnote in his procession of girlfriends: Kate Daniels, Investigator for the Order, whom his Furry Majesty had banged briefly until he got bored and moved on to bigger and better things, leaving her street cred in tatters.

An open relationship with Curran meant professional suicide. The agents of the Order were impartial by definition. Nobody would deal with me after I slept with the head of the shapeshifters. More important than that, when Curran lost interest in what I had to offer, he'd take my heart, smash it with a hammer into bloody mush, hand me the ruin, and walk away untroubled.

I understood all this and still I wanted him. He drew me like a damn magnet. I wanted him more than I'd ever wanted anybody before in my life. For those few moments, he'd made me feel safe, wanted, needed, desirable, but it was an illusion. I had to get a grip.

The more I thought about it, the more pissed off I got. He thought he had me bagged. His Majesty was long overdue for a rude awakening.

I growled and went to dress.

BY SEVEN I REACHED THE OFFICE. THE ORDER OCcupied a plain box of a building, crude, brick, sturdy, and warded so heavily when the magic was up that an entire division of the Military Supernatural Defense Unit could batter it for days. There had to be another facility in the city, a state-of-the-art headquarters, but I didn't rank high enough to know its location.

I climbed to the second floor, opened the door, and stepped into the hallway. Long and gray, it stretched into the distance like a narrow, drab tunnel at the end of which loomed a black door. A heraldic lion of polished steel reared in the center of the door, identifying it as the office of the knight-protector, the head of the chapter and my immediate supervisor.

"Good morning, dear," Maxine's voice said in my head.

"Good morning, Maxine," I said. Technically I could have just thought it, if I'd concentrated hard enough for Maxine to pick it up, but talking worked better for me. I could grasp an undead mind with mine and crush it like lice, but telepathically I was a complete dud. I ducked into my office, expecting a two-foot-tall stack of paperwork. My desk was clean. Pristine. Stack-less.

"Maxine? What happened to my files?"

"The knight-protector decided to clear your schedule."

"Is that a good thing or a bad thing?"

"The Order appreciates your services. Particularly when it comes to your late-night work."

The light dawned. Ted was giving me unofficial approval to screw with the Midnight Games. There would be no investigation. Ted already knew as much about the Games as could be humanly known. He simply lacked the means or an excuse to do anything about them. Now I presented him with a golden opportunity. He was throwing me at the Games like a stick into a wheel. I was capable and completely expendable. Any public problems I caused would be excused by my half-assed status. I wasn't a knight. I wasn't properly trained. The Order would disavow any knowledge of my activities, paint me as an overeager incompetent, and toss me out on my behind.

Andrea manifested in my doorway, walked in, and closed the door. "Raphael called. Apparently an order just went down the chain of command. Any member of the Pack who attacks you is going to have a long, unpleasant meeting with Curran."

I raised my pen in a mock salute. "Yippee. I had no idea I was a fragile flower in need of His Majesty's protection."

"Have you been attacked?"

"Yep. I was good and didn't kill anybody."

Andrea sat down in my client chair. "What's going on?"

I got up and activated the ward. Dim orange glyphs ignited in the floor, intertwining in twisted patterns. A wall of orange surged up to seal the door. It was the spell my guardian had used to secure the room. People told knight diviners secret things, the kinds of things a confessor or psychiatrist might hear. Greg's defensive ward was soundproof, sight-proof and magic-proof. Not even Maxine's telepathy could penetrate it. It had taken me a month of painstakingly retracing the glyphs on the floor to figure out how he had done it.

I unlocked my top drawer, pulled out the file, and put it on the desk. "Do the hand."

Andrea raised her hand. "I will not disclose the information I am about to receive, unless authorized by the person who surrenders this information to my discretion. I will not use this information for personal gain even under duress, coercion, or to save myself or others from imminent physical harm. I do so swear by my honor as a knight of the Order."

It was a hell of an oath. More people flunked out of the Academy on oath breaking than any other test of will. When you've been beaten, drowned, whipped, and then branded with a hot iron, most people will say anything just to make the torture stop. There was a narrow band of pale skin on my back, the reminder of where a hot iron had kissed me. It proved I'd passed. I knew Andrea had an identical scar. We both would remember the secrets we had to keep for our test oaths to the end of our days and never reveal them. Not even through a stray thought.

I handed her the file. She read through the pages and looked at me. I filled in the holes, including Curran's visit.

Andrea blinked a couple of times. "Shit. Fuck shit."

"'Shit fuck' would also have been accepted."

"The head of Pack's security has gone rogue, Derek is near death, and you're mated to the Beast Lord."

"Jim hasn't gone rogue; he's just not following orders at the moment."

"That's what going rogue is!"

Okay, I had to give her that one. "And for the record, I'm not mated to Curran."

Andrea shook her head. "What planet are you from? He's slipping into your apartment to tuck your blanket in at night. That's the protective urge at work. He *thinks* you're mated."

"He can think whatever he wants. That doesn't make it true."

Andrea's eyes widened. "I just realized: he's treating you like a shapeshifter alpha. You're playing by the rules of not-quite-human courtship here. Has he asked you to make him a dinner yet? Dinner is a big deal."

"No, he hasn't." Hell would freeze over before I cooked for Curran. "Look, I'm not a shapeshifter and he's dated humans before."

"That's just it." Andrea tapped her nails on the table. "A direct come-on like that is a challenge. That's how an alpha male would approach an alpha female. They are all about power struggles and the hunt, and they don't do subtle well. I realize this sounds twisted, but it's a backhanded compliment on his part."

"He can take his compliment and shove it where the sun don't shine."

"Can I quote you on that?"

"Be my guest. I've worked too hard to be his passing fancy."

I reached to put the folder back into my drawer and my fingers grazed an old paperback. *The Princess Bride.* That night in Savannah, when he had almost kissed me, he'd been reading it, and when I told him to leave, he'd said, "As you wish."

A frown crossed Andrea's face. "So where does all this leave you? Are you going to disappear for a while?"

I nodded. "I have to see this through, and I can't do it with Curran breathing down my neck."

"Need any help?"

"Yes. I'm putting in a request to analyze some silver samples to the computer database. It might take a day or two to process. If you could pick it up . . ."

Andrea waved her arms. "Of course I'll do it. I meant shoot-somebody type of help."

"Oh. Not at the moment. But I'll call you if I need a bullet through somebody's head."

"You do that. Try not to get killed."

"Will do."

We looked at each other.

"So how was it?" she asked. "Kissing Curran?"

"I can't let him kiss me again, because if he does, I'll sleep with him."

Andrea blinked. "Well," she said finally. "At least you know where you stand."

I CALLED JIM AND LEFT THE OFFICE. I WOVE BACK and forth through the morning traffic. Nobody followed me. Finally I stopped at a small fried chicken joint.

Glenda smiled at me. A plump woman with honey-colored hair, she'd once spent her nights tormented by phantom snakes. It took a week, but I finally found the cause hiding out in her attic and killed it. Now I got a smile with my chicken wings.

I held up ten bucks.

"You want a five-piece?" Glenda asked.

"Nope. I want to use the phone." This was a conversation best had out of the office.

Glenda put a phone on the counter, checked it for the dial tone, and grabbed my ten bucks.

I called the Keep, introduced myself to the disembodied female voice on the phone, and asked for the Beast Lord. In less than fifteen seconds Curran came on the line.

"I'm going into hiding with Jim."

The silence on the other side of the phone had a distinctly sinister undertone. Perhaps he thought that his kissing super-powers had derailed me. Fat chance. I would keep him from having to kill Derek. That was a burden he didn't need.

"I thought about this morning," I said, doing my best to sound calm and reasonable. "I've instructed the super to change the locks. If I ever catch you in my apartment again, I will file a formal complaint. I've taken your food, under duress, but I did take it. You rescued me once or twice, and you've seen me near naked. I realize that you're judging this situation by shapeshifter standards, and you expect me to fall on my back with my legs spread."

"Not necessarily." His voice matched mine in calmness. "You can fall on your hands and knees if you prefer. Or against the wall. Or on the kitchen counter. I suppose I might let you be on top, if you make it worth my while."

I didn't grind my teeth—he would've heard it. I had to be calm and reasonable. "My point is this: no."

"No?"

"There will be no falling, no sex, no you and me."

"I wanted to kiss you when we were in your house. In Savannah."

Why the hell was my heart pounding? "And?"

"You looked afraid. That wasn't the reaction I was hoping for."

Be calm and reasonable. "You flatter yourself. You're not that scary."

"After I kissed you this morning, you were afraid again. Right after you looked like you were about to melt."

Melt?

"You're scared there might be something there, between you and me."

Wow. I struggled to swallow that little tidbit. "Every time I think you've reached the limits of arrogance, you show me new heights. Truly, your egotism is like the Universe—ever expanding."

"You thought about dragging me into your bed this morning."

"I thought about stabbing you and running away screaming. You broke into my house without permission and slobbered all over me. You're a damn lunatic! And don't give me that line about smelling my desire; I know it's bullshit."

"I didn't need to smell you. I could tell by the dreamy look in your eyes and the way your tongue licked the inside of my mouth."

"Enjoy the memory," I ground out. "That's the last time it will ever happen."

"Go play your games with Jim. I'll find you both when I need you."

Arrogant asshole. "I tell you what, if you find us before those three days run out, I'll cook you a damn dinner and serve it to you naked."

"Is that a promise?"

"Yes. Go fuck yourself."

I slammed the phone down. Well, then. That was perfectly reasonable.

On the other side of the counter an older, heavyset man stared at me like I had sprouted horns.

Glenda handed me the money I'd given her. "That was some conversation. It was worth ten bucks."

I got up just in time to see Brenna ride up, leading an extra horse.

CHAPTER 16

I VISITED DEREK. I STAYED FOR HALF AN HOUR and then Doolittle came in, took a look at my face, and decided I needed another lovely glass of tea. I followed him into the kitchen. It smelled like food: a rich, savory aroma of gently spiced meat and fresh pastry. The scent grabbed me and I practically floated to the table, just in time to see Jim slide a golden brown loaf onto the cutting board. He carefully sliced an inch-wide section from it, revealing a beautifully cooked medium-rare sirloin.

I nearly fainted. "Beef Wellington?"

Jim scowled. "Just because you never have any decent food in your refrigerator . . ."

"It's because you or Derek or Julie eat it all."

Brenna came in and got a bowl of salad out of the fridge.

"Plates are in the cabinet," Jim said.

I got out four plates, found silverware, and set the table. Doolittle put a glass of iced tea in front of me. I tasted it. It had so much sugar, if you put a spoon into it, it would stand up all by itself.

Jim placed a slice on my plate. When I made Beef Wellington, it looked good. His looked perfect.

Brenna sat next to me. "Sorry about the thigh."

It took me a second to connect the stinging bite on my leg to the quiet woman next to me. "No problem. Sorry about the needle."

The scar on her throat had faded, but a thin gray line was still there. "It's okay," she said. "I've had silver in me before."

"Where is everybody else?" I asked.

Nobody answered. Chatty Cathys, the shapeshifters.

I cut into my Beef Wellington and put a small piece in my mouth. It tasted like heaven. Jim cut his meat with the precision of a surgeon.

"Curran called."

The three shapeshifters around me stopped breathing for a moment.

"I thought I'd mention it before you started eating. I didn't want you to choke."

"He say anything?" Jim asked.

"You have three days to turn yourself in." I imitated Curran's voice. "After that he'll have to find you. And he doesn't want to find you."

"Anything else?"

"He mostly cussed after that. I told him you and I were having a hot roll in the hay and he was interrupting."

Tea came out of Brenna's nose.

Jim struggled with it for a long moment. "I wish you hadn't done that."

"He didn't believe it." I left it at that. Mentioning my morning exercise and naked dinner promise was bound to give Jim apoplexy. "He can't find us here, can he?"

"Never underestimate our lord," Doolittle said.

"It's hard to say," Jim said. "Curran's persistent. He'll find us eventually. But not for a while."

I hoped he was right. If not, both of us would have some explaining to do.

•   •   •

WE WAITED FOR SAIMAIN IN THE PARKING LOT OF the Games.

Jim's black, fur-trimmed cloak flared behind him as he walked, revealing a black leather vest, black pants, and black steel-toed boots. His body was toned to the point of absurd: he looked like a prizefighter in his prime, his thick muscle crisply defined, his stride loose, his bearing broadcasting bad-ass. An ugly scowl sat on his face. He looked as if he wanted to punch somebody.

"You need a pair of shades," I told him. "Someone might mistake you for a yuppie."

"Never happen."

Saiman's sleek ride slid into the parking lot. He got out, dapper and urbane in his Thomas Durand persona, popped the trunk, and took out an oblong object bundled in canvas and wrapped with a cord. He swung it onto his shoulder, which proved to be a difficult feat—the thing was about four and a half feet long and two feet wide.

We headed to the door. Saiman caught up with us and passed the bundle to Jim. Jim showed no strain as he took the bundle. It might have been light as a feather, but by the way Saiman's stride eased, I could tell it had to be heavy.

"Your crew passes." Saiman handed me two yellow tickets and slowed down, putting some distance between us and himself.

We reached the doors and I presented the crew passes to the outside guards. They waved us on to Rene's welcoming arms. Recognition sparked in her eyes. She surveyed Jim and turned to me.

"Congratulations, love. You traded up. Does he treat you well?"

"He's a teddy bear," I said.

Teddy bear looked like he was suffering from murder withdrawal. Rene grinned. "He certainly is. First room on the right, get yourself logged in." Rene glanced at the doors, where Saiman was making his grand entrance. "Hurry now.

Your ex is coming through. We don't want him getting hysterical again."

THE FIGHTER LEVEL WAS BASICALLY A LONG hallway forming a ring. Red Guards were thick in the hallway like flies on a dead horse. Big deadly flies, armed with Tasers, chains, and nets. No fights would break out there. Inside the ring lay a large exercise room located directly under the Pit. Outside the ring branched off fighter quarters: sets of rooms where the fighters waited for their bouts.

Jim leaned against the doorframe of our room, like some dark sentinel. The patrolmen gave him a wide berth.

I sat at a bench. I had inspected our quarters: the front room where we waited now was long and narrow, a bottleneck. No door separated us from the hallway. In case of trouble, a couple of Guards could easily contain a dozen people or more within the room.

On the left a door led to a narrow locker room with a bench and three showers and off it was a small bathroom with three toilets, separated by partitions. Behind me another door led to a large bedroom housing eight double bunks. The Order's files said the teams were sequestered once the tournament began and for three days they lived in their fighting quarters.

Above us the crowd roared, enthused by someone's death.

Guilt gnawed on me. It haunted and stalked me, just waiting to pounce when I had a dull moment. I should have kept Derek from being hurt. As they had beat him, in the parking lot, he had been utterly alone. He knew no help would be coming. That was his last memory: the molten silver being poured on his face.

My heart clenched. I tried to make some words come out, anything to keep thoughts out of my head. "My father would've approved of this place. Of all the arenas he took me to, this is the best equipped and best secured."

Jim's gaze was still firmly fixed on the hallway and the patrols. "What kind of father would take a kid to the slaughter?"

"The kind who wanted his daughter to get used to death. I guess you could say I turned out according to his plan."

"Yeah. He teach you to talk a lot of shit, too?"

"Nope. Picked it up from you."

We sat in silence.

"My dad hated killing," Jim said. "Couldn't do it, even when he had to."

"Not everybody grows up to be a monster."

Another thump. The noise of the spectators died down to a hum. I got out my throwing knives and began polishing them with a cloth.

"He was human," Jim said.

"The Pack never turned him?"

"No."

Jim was half. Could've fooled me by the way he treated outsiders. Usually mates of shapeshifters became shapeshifters themselves.

"How did it go over with the cat clan?"

Jim gave a barely perceptible shrug. "We're cats. We mind our own business. He was welcome, because he was a doctor. Not many physicians in the Pack. Doolittle and he were friends. Graduated together."

I remembered Saiman's words. He said Jim killed the man who had murdered his father while they were both incarcerated. "How did he end up in prison?"

"One of the lynx children went loup. A little girl. She was ten. The alpha was out and the parents brought her to him to be put down. Humane death and all that shit."

Once a shapeshifter went loup, there was no return.

"He couldn't do it," Jim said. "He gave her an injection and she went to sleep. He told the family he wanted the body to see if he could autopsy it and find out what caused loupism. They believed him. He hid her in a cage in the basement. Took tissue samples to try and find the cure. She broke out and killed two people before we caught her and put her down. One of them was a pregnant woman. There was a trial. He got twenty-five to life."

Jim still wasn't looking at me. "His second day in prison a lowlife called David Stiles stabbed him in the liver. Later I found David, and I asked him why. He wasn't in the position to lie. You know what he said?" Jim turned to me. "He said he felt like it. No reason."

I didn't know what to say.

"My father helped people. He treated a loup kid like she was normal. I treated a normal kid like he was loup and six years later sent him to have his face beaten off his head. Doolittle tells me he's fading. He doesn't have long. If my dad was alive, he'd spit in my face."

It was an old wound and he'd ripped the scab off and left it raw for me to see. I had no salve to put on it, but I could show him my own scar. "If my father knew that I deliberately put myself here, in this situation, for the sake of another person, he would consider himself a failure."

Jim looked at me. "Why?"

"Because ever since I could walk, he taught me to rely only on myself. To never build a relationship or to attach myself to a human being, even to him. He used to send me out to the woods for several days with nothing except a knife. When I was twelve, he dumped me in the Warren. I ran with the Breakers for a month. Was beaten several times, almost raped twice." I braided my fingers into the Breaker gang sign. "Still remember how."

Jim just stared at me.

"Friends are a dangerous thing," I told him. "You feel responsibility for them. You want to keep them safe. You want to help and they throw you off balance, and the next thing you know you're sitting there crying, because you didn't make it in time. They make you feel helpless. That's why my father wanted to make me into a sociopath. A sociopath has no empathy. She just focuses on her purpose."

"Didn't quite work out that way," Jim said quietly.

"No. His training had a fatal flaw: he cared. He asked me what I wanted to eat for dinner. He knew I liked green, and if he had a choice between a blue sweater and a green one, he'd buy the green one for me even if it cost more. I like swimming, and when we traveled, he made it a point to lay our route so it would go past a lake or a river. He let me speak my mind. My opinion mattered. I was a person to him and I was important. I saw him treat others as if they were important. For all of his supposed indifference, there is a town in Oklahoma that worships him and a little village in Guatemala that put a wooden statue of him at the gates to protect them from evil spirits. He helped people, when he thought it was right."

I shook my head. "I have this picture of what my dad wanted me to be, and I can never measure up. And I don't want to. I have my rules. I stick to them. That's hard enough as it is. If that means my dad would spit in my face, so be it."

ALMOST TWO HOURS HAD PASSED BEFORE SAIman made it to the room. He strode briskly inside, his face flushed.

"The bug?"

Jim held out a small, flesh-colored disk the size of a quarter. "A transmitter," he said. "The deeper into the body you shove it, the better. Make him swallow it. We don't want it found."

Saiman accepted the transmitter and crossed the floor to the door in the opposite wall, swiping the bundle of canvas on the way. He entered and shut the door behind him.

Minutes stretched by. Behind the closed door something thumped.

"Think he can do it?" Jim asked.

"Nope. But we don't have a choice."

We sat some more. Above us something howled in the Pit, sending a dull hum of resonance through the ceiling.

"Cold," Jim said.

A moment later I felt it too, a dry, intense cold emanating from the door that hid Saiman. I rose. "I'll go check on him."

I knocked. The wood of the door burned my fingers with ice. "Saiman?"

No answer.

I pushed the door and it swung open, admitting me inside. The room curved to the right and I saw only a small section of it, illuminated by the bluish glow of the feylanterns: a shower stall, its curtain pulled aside. A long icicle dripped from the metal showerhead.

"Anybody home?"

A layer of frost slicked the floor under my feet. I turned to the right, moving slowly. My shoes slid a little. I caught myself on the wall and saw him.

He sat slumped on the bench, his enormous back knotted with hard clumps of muscle beneath skin so white and smooth, it seemed completely bloodless. Coarse hair fell down his back in a long blue-green mane. A fringe of hair trailed the vertebrae of his spine, disappearing into ragged pants of wolf fur. Sitting, he was taller than me, too huge to be a man.

"Saiman?"

The being turned his head. Piercing eyes stared at me, distant, pale blue, yet lit from within with power like two chunks of ice that somehow stole the fire of a diamond. He had the face of a fighter carved with exacting precision by a master sculptor: terrifying, forceful, arrogant, and touched with cruelty. His eyes sat sunken deep into their orbits, guarded by a thick ridge of blue eyebrows. His cheekbones were pronounced, his nose wide, and the line of his jaw so strong he could have bitten through bones with little effort. Gone was the philosopher, the urbane erudite, who pontificated on the meaning of luxury. Only a primitive remained, hard, cold, and ancient as the ice that hugged the bench on which he sat.

I wanted to raise my hands to shield myself from that gaze. Instead, I made myself walk to the bench and sit by

him. He made no movement. Next to him, I looked like a
toddler.

"This is the original form?" I said softly.

"This is the form of my birth." His voice was a deep,
contained bellow.

"And the golden dancer on the roof?"

"He's what I could have been. What I should have been.
There is enough of him in my blood to let me assume his
shape with infinite ease, but I don't delude myself. This is
the true me. One can't deny blood."

On that we were in agreement.

Above us something thumped. The noise of the spectators swelled. Saiman raised his monstrous head to the
ceiling. "I'm frightened. I find it richly ironic. What a
ridiculous notion."

He raised his massive arm, the forearm sheathed in
silver-blue hair. His fingers shook.

"It's natural," I said. "Only the insane aren't scared before the fight. They can't imagine dying."

"Do you feel fear, Kate?"

"Always."

"Why do you do it, then?"

I sighed. "Fear is pain. It hurts. I sink into it and use it
like a sharpening stone gliding against a sword. It makes
me better, more aware. But I can't be scared for too long, or
it will wear me out."

"How do you make it stop?"

"I kill."

The blue eyes regarded me with a strange look, half-
terror, half-surprise. "That's it? No noble purpose?"

"There isn't always a noble purpose. There is usually a
reason. The need to save someone or something. Your
friend, your lover, an innocent who doesn't deserve to be
hurt. Sometimes it's a purely selfish reason. One might
fight for their body, their good name, or their sanity. Sometimes it's just a job. But deciding to fight and doing it are
two different things."

"How can you live like that? It seems unbearable."

I shrugged. "Like you, I harbor no illusions. I was conceived, born, raised, and trained with one purpose in mind: to become the best killer I could be. It's what I do." *So eventually I can kill Roland, the most powerful man on Earth.*

"It's time," Jim's voice said from beyond the door.

A long, deep sigh issued from Saiman. He rose. His head nearly brushed the ceiling. Eight and a half feet tall. Wow.

"Do you prefer the Aesir?"

The word hit me like a bolt of lightning. Pieces fell into place in my head: Saiman, golden and high on magic, dancing on the roof and celebrating "the time of the gods," his fluid changes of shape, his self-interest, his ego, and him now, an enormous monster, a giant of a man. I gaped at him. He wasn't supposed to exist.

"My other shape, Kate. Do you like it?"

"Yes," I said, managing to make my voice even. "So are you all god or did one of your divine relatives get fresh with a human?"

For the first time Saiman smiled, displaying white teeth that would've been at home in the mouth of a polar bear. "A quarter. It's enough. The rest is frost and human."

He scooped the canvas bundle off the floor. The fabric fluttered down, revealing a four-foot-long club studded with metal spikes thicker than my fingers. Saiman bent and stepped through the doorway. I heard a startled growl from Jim.

Saiman kept going, out of the room, into the hallway, each step like two of mine. Jim's teeth were bared in a snarl.

"Come on." I swiped Slayer and chased Saiman into the hallway. The Red Guards hugged the walls as he passed by.

Jim caught up with me. "What the fuck is he?"

"Vikings," I managed, breaking into an outright run.

"What about Vikings?"

"Vikings called their gods Aesir."

"That tells me nothing."

The Gold Gate loomed before us, and through its lit rectangle I saw the Pit and the sea of spectators. Saiman paused in the gloom, his club resting on his shoulder.

"He said he is a quarter Aesir, which probably means his grandmother was a Viking god. But there is only one Norse deity who can change shape the way he does and he wasn't Aesir. He was Loki, the trickster, a giant who became a god. Saiman is the grandson of two Norse deities, Jim."

Saiman swung the club off his shoulder with the ease of a child with a toy baseball bat and stepped through the gate into the light. The crowd fell silent. The silence stretched as the audience tried to come to terms with an eight-and-a-half-foot-tall humanoid. Saiman didn't wait for them. His club in hand, he strode to the Pit.

CHAPTER 17

THE REAPER WAITED AT THE FAR END OF THE sand. Inhumanly tall and packed with thick muscle, he had the build of a champion weight lifter, his body so overdeveloped it resembled an action figure. If I went up against him, I'd have to strike at a joint—if he clenched up, the sword might not penetrate all that muscle.

The Reaper wore black boots, and nothing else. Swirls of henna designs covered every inch of his pale body. He carried two heavy bearded axes, sharpened to razor gleam, each three feet tall. They were meant to be used two-handed.

Saiman entered the ring, his long legs moving slowly. He towered over the Reaper by a foot or so, which made the axe fighter just over seven and a half feet. Despite the height difference, they probably weighed the same. You could see Saiman's ribs, and the Reaper would have trouble picking up coins from the ground without crouching.

A Red Guard closed the fence door and scurried away to the protection of the wall.

As the gate clanged shut, the resolve drained from Saiman. A light trembling began in his arms. He hunched his shoulders. I could taste his terror from where I stood. The Reaper sensed it too and grinned, baring his teeth. They were filed to points, like the teeth of a shark.

The smell of blood and hot sand invaded my nostrils. I squinted against the bright glow of huge feylanterns and took a step to the Pit . . . and almost bumped into a guard barring my way.

"No further. If you exit the gate, your fighter forfeits the match."

It wasn't my fight.

I leaned against the golden arch. Jim halted next to me. It was up to Saiman now.

The Reaper tossed one of his axes in the air. It spun, the bluish blade shining as it captured the torch light, and he caught it with deft quickness. The crowd loved it.

A gong tolled through the chamber. As its deep ring died, Saiman glanced back at us.

"Come." The Reaper's voice was a raspy growl, touched with that same accent I couldn't quite place. He motioned with his axe. "Come! I cut you down to size."

Saiman hesitated.

"Come!"

Saiman turned halfway, facing me. His eyes brimmed with fear. We should've never put him into the damn Pit. He wasn't a fighter. No matter how big he was, unless he had courage enough to kill for his survival, he would be simply cut down.

"Move," I whispered. That first step was the hardest. Once he broke the dread chaining him and struck the first blow, he would be fine. But he had to move.

The Reaper raised his arms wide as if asking the audience for an explanation. Boos and jeers erupted, at first isolated, then gaining strength, until they swelled into a wall of sound.

The Reaper held up his axe. The noise died down. "I cut you now," he announced.

He advanced, flexing, hefting his axes. Saiman took a

step back. The Reaper smirked and kept coming. An ugly
grimace skewed his face. He raised the axes and charged.

Saiman dodged, but the edge of the left axe caught his
thigh. Blood drenched the frost-white skin. Shock slapped
Saiman's monstrous face. The axe fighter paused to soak in
the applause.

Saiman stared at the blood. His lips trembled. His eyebrows came together. A wild light danced in his deep eyes.

Pain, I realized. Pain was his trigger. Saiman was afraid
of pain, and once it lashed him, he would do anything to
keep it from hurting him again.

With a terrible bellow, Saiman swung his club. The
Reaper leapt aside and the club smashed the ground, sending a spray of sand into the air. Without a pause, Saiman
swiped the club up and charged. The Reaper jumped back.
The club's steel spikes fanned his face. The Reaper ducked
left, right, but Saiman whipped the club at him as if it
weighed nothing. The axe fighter ran.

All thought vanished from Saiman's glassy eyes. He
roared and chased the Reaper back and forth through the
Pit, his face terrible to behold, his mind lost to fury. I wasn't
sure he knew where he was or what he was doing here, but
he knew he had to kill the fleeing Reaper.

"Ice him," Jim murmured. "*Ice* him."

Our stares met and he shook his head. Like the Norse
warriors of old odes, Saiman was lost to his berserker rage,
too far gone to remember he had magic.

The Reaper stopped. As the club whistled past his chest,
a hair short of ripping him open, he pivoted and struck at
the club's handle with his right axe, trying to knock Saiman
off balance. It was a good move. Saiman's momentum,
aided by the Reaper's strike, would drive the club forward,
leaving the Reaper free to cleave at Saiman's right arm and
side.

The axe connected to the club. Ice swallowed the blue
axe blade, shot up the handle to the Reaper's arm, and
caught his fist. The Reaper screamed. Desperate, he
chopped at Saiman's elbow, but the giant let go of the club,

hurtling it and the Reaper into the wire fence. The Reaper's back hit the wire right in front of me. He barely had a chance to bounce off. Saiman loomed above him, his face deranged, locked his hands into one enormous fist, and brought them down onto the Reaper's skull like a hammer.

The Reaper dodged at the last moment and the blow landed on his right shoulder. Bones crunched. The Reaper howled. Saiman reached for the Reaper's shoulders. His enormous hands gripped his opponent's flesh, and Saiman jerked him off his feet as if he were a child, and smashed his head into the Reaper's face. Blood flew, staining Saiman's features. He threw the Reaper against the fence and pummeled him with his fists, breaking into a rabid frenzy of blows.

The fence shuddered and quaked. With each crushing punch, wire cut into the Reaper's overmuscled back, leaving bloody, diamond-shaped gouges. His head lolled. Saiman struck and struck, growling, oblivious to the red mess of blood and bone that stained his hands. The wire cut deeper and deeper.

"He's going to push him through that fence like a sieve," Jim growled.

The crowd had gone silent, stunned by the ferocity of his onslaught. Only Saiman's labored breathing, laced with furious grunts, echoed through the Pit.

I turned to the guard. "The Reaper's dead; pull him off."

The guard gave me a look reserved for the mentally ill. "Are you out of your mind? Nobody's going to get into the Pit with him. You step in there, you're his target."

A group of patrolmen gathered behind us. "Jesus," one of them murmured.

There was nothing left to do. We stood and watched Saiman vent his rage and terror on a battered piece of Reaper meat.

Four minutes later, the magic drained from the world in an abrupt gush and Saiman finally stepped away from the corpse. The thing that slid to the floor of the Pit no longer bore any resemblance to a man. Wet, red, soft, it was just a heavy mess of tissue, stuffed into black boots.

Saiman retrieved his club. The trance dissipated from his face. He looked around, shook his head as if surprised to find himself there, and raised his weapon.

A lonely male voice from the left screamed, "Yeaa-aaaahhhhh!"

The audience exploded in an avalanche of cheering.

Saiman turned, buoyed by the applause, and stumbled, favoring his blood-drenched leg. He was about to make history as the first man with regeneration to bleed to death.

"This way!" I jumped and waved my arms. "Come this way!"

Saiman shambled about in a bewildered daze.

"Here!" Jim's roar momentarily overwhelmed the noise of the crowd, punching my eardrum. I stuck my finger into my left ear and wiggled it a bit.

Saiman jerked and pivoted toward us. Recognition ignited in his eyes and he limped to us, dragging his club behind him. The guard swung open the fence door and took off like a frightened rabbit. Saiman paused at the fence. Oh, for God's sake.

"Come on, this way." I waved my arms at him. "Come on!"

He limped through the gate, using his club like a crutch, sagged, and would've fallen but Jim slid his shoulder under him. Suddenly the hallway was full of Red Guards. They closed about us like a wall of black and red.

"Blood loss." Saiman's voice came in a gasp.

"Next time, remember to heal," Jim grunted, keeping him upright.

"I won."

"Yes, you did," I agreed. "Very well-done."

Saiman dropped his bloodied club. I picked it up and fought not to bend double under the weight. Sixty pounds at least. I maneuvered it over my shoulder.

We moved down the hallway, shielded by the guards on all sides.

"You plant the bug?" Jim murmured.

"Yes. Pushed it into his chest. I need to sit down."

"Keep it together, almost to the room." Jim's face showed no strain, but the muscles on his arms bulged with effort.

"It's over," Saiman gasped. "I'm so glad it's over."

"ALL RIGHT, GENTLEMEN."

I thought to point out that I wasn't a gentleman, but Rene's voice had that "shut up, I'm working" tone that left no room for discussion.

She surveyed us. Saiman sat on the floor, with his back against the wall. He had drunk almost a gallon of water before the bleeding finally stopped. The wound sealed and now his eyes were closed. Jim stood next to him, making everyone feel unwelcome in the close vicinity of his personal space. Behind Rene four Red Guards blocked the entrance to our room. Two more stood inside, watching us as though we were thieves in a jewelry store.

"The Reapers are a new team. This is their first loss."

Second, technically, if you counted the fellow in the parking lot.

"We're going to do this by the book. The Reapers are grounded. You have one hour to clear the premises and be on your way, which will give you a reasonable head start. I strongly urge you not to linger. We want to avoid unpleasantries outside the Pit."

There was a slight commotion outside.

"The Reapers are here to congratulate you."

"Are you out of your mind?" I stepped between the door and Saiman. Slayer was in my hand. I didn't recall drawing it.

"It's a twenty-year tradition," Rene said.

The guards parted, and Mart and the tattooed Reaper stepped into the room. Rene and the Red Guards looked like dogs who had just sighted a deer.

Mart leveled his thousand-yard stare at me.

"We congratulate you on your victory," Cesare boomed.

"Very nice. They heard your congratulations," Rene said softly. "Be on your way now."

Mart was still staring at me.

"On your way," Rene repeated with a bit of force.

He turned toward the door and hurled a narrow stick at me. I dodged but I didn't have to. The Red Guard next to me slashed at it with his short blade, cutting it in midflight. Two halves of my hair stick fell to the floor. A little souvenir someone had plucked from the body of the snake man in the parking lot and delivered to Mart.

Rene's rapier pointed at Mart's throat. "One more and you and your team are permanently disqualified."

Mart smiled at me: a charming smile full of genuine joy.

I showed him my teeth. *Bring it.*

He bowed slightly, unconcerned by the point of the poisonous rapier an inch from his neck, turned on his toes, and left.

Rene followed him out.

CHAPTER 18

WE DELIVERED THE GIANT TO DURAND'S ROOMS under the pretext of Durand wanting to meet him. Inside Saiman sank onto the opulent bed. His body shuddered and assumed the shape of Thomas Durand. He closed his eyes and fell asleep. I covered him with a blanket and we were off.

We left the Arena without any incidents, mounted, and headed back to Downtown.

Jim rode as if he were wrapped in barbed wire: stiff, shoulders rigid, keeping as straight and immobile as he could.

"That horse deserves a medal for not throwing you."

A torrent of obscenities washed over me. Having spent a considerable amount of time in Jim's company before, I was able to distill the gist of his displeasure from his filthy tirade: if he had known the tech was going to hit, he would've brought a gas-guzzling vehicle instead of two pieces of meat with skinny legs and a hysterical disposition.

We veered south and circled Downtown, aiming for the south end of Unicorn. The Reapers always headed north in a straight line. Chances were, they might have caught a whiff of our scent, but would suspect nothing when it turned right, away from their route.

We made it there a few minutes after four. The sunrise was still a long way off. Ahead Unicorn lay, a blighted scar on the urban surface. Crumbling office towers, twisted and gutted, sprawled on their sides among the rubble, like sterns of damaged ships about to sink into the stormy sea of mangled asphalt. Moonlight glittered on the piles of shattered glass, the remnants of a thousand broken windows. Yellow hairs of toxic Lane moss dripped from abandoned power lines, feeding on metal.

Several blocks from Unicorn the terrain grew too rugged for horses. Unlike the northern end, where streets sometimes ran almost right up to Unicorn, here debris choked the passageways, making islands of gravel in the rivers of sewage. The stench brought tears to my eyes. I'd never had a burning desire to wear a used diaper on my face, but I'd imagine the effect on my nose would have been very similar.

At our approach a man stepped from the shadows. I recognized the weredingo. He passed Jim a set of car keys. "They beat you here," he said in a raspy voice. "'Bout half an hour ago. Came in from the north, rode for a mile or so, and stopped."

Jim nodded and the dingo took the horses and melted into the night. Jim ducked into a ruined building and I followed. Inside, a Pack Jeep waited. Jim got in and tapped a small digital display affixed to the dashboard. A green grid ignited on the screen, and I recognized the faint outline of Unicorn. A small green dot blinked near the center.

Jim frowned. "Fast fuckers."

The Reapers had beaten us here despite an hour's lead. True, we took a long way around, but still, that was inhumanly fast.

Jim shed his cape and passed me a small rectangular box. I popped it open. Camo paint, three different colors, each in its own little section. Even a small mirror. Most camo came in a stick that was hard as a rock. You had to rub the damn thing between your palms to warm it up or your face ended up feeling scraped with steel wool.

"Fancy. You went all out."

"I've got connections." Jim grinned without showing his teeth.

I smeared a thin layer of brown on my face and blobbed a few irregular blotches of green and gray here and there, trying to break up my features. Jim applied his with easy quickness. He hadn't glanced in the mirror at all.

The dot hadn't moved.

I checked my belt: bandages, tape, herbs. No R-kit. The regeneration kits misfired about ten percent of the time. There was no telling what Unicorn Lane would do to it. It might sprout teeth and take a chunk out of my hide. I'd have to tend to my wounds the old-fashioned way.

We left the vehicle and took off parallel to the Lane.

Half an hour later we went to ground under the twisted plastic carcass of an enormous sign advertising long-forgotten cosmetics. We were about a half mile south of the dot's location. Any closer and we were likely to run into the Reaper sentries. Nothing said the Reapers stationed sentries, but nothing said they didn't either. We had to brave Unicorn Lane. At least the magic was still down.

"Want to go first?" I offered.

Jim shook his head. "You lead; I follow."

In Unicorn, my sense of magic was better than his. "I never thought I'd live to see the day."

"You may not see the end of it."

He just had to rain on my parade.

Ahead a barricade of boulders blocked our way, wet and shiny with otherworldly perspiration. I slipped between them.

Touch nothing.

Don't think.

Trust your senses.

I knew behind me Jim would step where I stepped. He'd freeze when I halted.

We slunk into the narrow street, skirting the rubble. Above us Lane moss shivered on the tangle of power lines, dripping corrosive slime.

A pair of eyes ignited in the second floor of the ruin to our right. Long, narrow, and flooded with scarlet unmarred by an iris, they tracked our progress but made no move to follow.

We skirted a filthy heap and I saw a metal cage lying to the left. Large enough to enclose a human, it looked brand new. No rust. No scratches. I kept moving, watching it out of the corner of my eye. The narrow path would take us close to it.

Ten feet.

Eight.

Seven.

It didn't feel right. I halted.

The cage snapped upright, unfolding like a flower. The bars flexed. Metal flowed like water, turning into insectoid legs armed with razor-sharp claws. A dark body sheathed in black bristle burst from the refuse and leapt at us, bar-legs outstretched, claws poised for the kill.

I ducked into its leap and thrust my sword into its dark gut.

I CROUCHED IN THE SHADOWY ENTRANCE TO THE underbelly of a ruined building. Behind me Jim stood wrapped in the gloom like a cloak. He fished a small vial from his pocket. I reached behind me, grabbed my shirt, and pulled it up to expose my back. Wetness brushed the aching cut on my spine and singed me with the sharp burn of disinfectant. I heard the faint hiss of medical tape being torn. Jim slapped the gauze on my cut and taped it up. The last thing I needed was to bleed all over Unicorn Lane. Considering my screwed-up heritage, my blood would probably blow up.

In the half hour since we'd entered Unicorn, we'd been attacked four times, all by things for which I had no names.

Jim's shirt hung in shreds. His body had repaired the damage, but the blood on the tatters of his shirt testified that the integrity of his mighty form had been sorely compromised.

I dropped my shirt and looked up. Directly ahead of us stood a wide building. Not a hotel or an office—those tended to stretch up, and when they fell, they either toppled like logs or crumbled from the top down, story by story chewed to dust by magic. No, this structure was long and relatively squat. A mall maybe? One of those giant department stores, which no longer survived, like Sears or Belks?

The building, still showing tan stucco, sat right in the middle of the block. Its roof and upper story were missing, eaten away by magic. Twisted steel beams jutted from the drywall like the bones of some half-rotten carcass. Green shimmered through the gaps in the building's framework. I looked to Jim. He nodded. The Reaper base. Had to be.

We squatted down.

Five minutes.

Another five. The night had brightened to a muted gray glow that usually signified the sun rising. In the predawn light the green shroud behind the building gained crystal clarity: trees. To my knowledge, there were no parks in the middle of Unicorn Lane. Where did the trees come from?

Going into the trees with the Reapers waiting on the other side would be reaching for new heights of stupidity. I wasn't that ambitious. The wall was a far better bet. Climb, gain high ground, survey the playing field.

We sat. Listening. Watching. Waiting.

No movement. No noise. I touched my nose. Jim shook his head. No useful scents either.

The magic hit us in a choking tide. Violent power roiled through Unicorn. It spiked, stealing my breath, and settled into deceptive placidity. Not so good.

A low thunder boomed through the silence.

Jim hissed.

Another blast erupted from the building, as if an enormous trumpet attempted to play a fanfare but succeeded in belching only a single powerful note, so charged with magic, it slid along my skin like a physical touch. The sound of a muted tornado rolled through the stillness of predawn. I had heard this sound a dozen times in my life—all from a movie screen. It was the sound of a plane engine.

I dashed across the street. Jim sprinted past me, leapt up on the wall, and scrambled up like a gecko. It's good to be a werejaguar. I hit the wall and began climbing, finding holds on the crumbling stucco and exposed steel framework.

Jim reached the top of the building, where the wall had crumbled, and cried out in a short, pain-charged snarl. His arms jerked back, his spine arched, and his feet left the ground. He hung in midair, convulsing.

I scrambled up. My fingers hooked the top of the wall. Stucco fell apart under the pressure of my hands. I slid, caught an iron rod, and pulled myself back up and onto the building.

An eerie nipping sensation rolled across my skin, as if a rough, sandpaper tongue had scraped a layer of cells from every single inch of my body. It peeled a little from my face, from my body hidden under my clothes, from between my toes, from the inside of my ears, from my nostrils, from my eyes.

A ward. The Reapers had booby-trapped the top of the building. Cleverly done. I hadn't sensed its presence, and we had blundered straight into it.

Pain lanced through me, setting every millimeter of my skin on fire and lifting me off the ground. I cried out, then clamped my mouth shut as the fire scorched the inside of my mouth. The thudding of my heart filled my ears with a freakishly loud, rapid beat. I felt myself unraveling, consumed cell by cell. Unable to do anything but jerk and thrash, I rotated on an invisible spit. Beside me, Jim's clothes tore and a werejaguar spilled forth.

Desperate times called for desperate measures. I spat a power word. *"Dair." Release.*

The magic tore from me in a blinding burst of agony as

if I'd thrust my hand into my stomach and ripped a clump of entrails out. I saw black and tasted blood.

The ward split and vanished. My feet hit the solid reality of the wall and I froze, blind and afraid to move. The after-shocks rocked through me. During the flare, using power words had been easy. Now, with the magic so low, if I used one more without resting, I risked passing out.

Something landed next to me. Hard hands grasped me, steadying me, the tips of claws scratching my skin. Jim.

The darkness blocking my vision dissolved and I saw two green eyes peering into mine. Jim turned and pointed away to the trees. I looked in the direction of his claw and gasped.

A wide, wooded valley gently sloped down before rolling to the blue peaks of mountains beyond. Moss-tinted rocks punctured the greenery with their gray spines. Between them, towering spires of trees rose to dizzying heights, their branches tinseled with vines that dripped cream and yellow blossoms. Birds perched among the foliage like glittering jewels. The wind smelled of flowers and water.

I looked back over my shoulder. Urban graveyard. Looked to the front: fairy-tale jungle. You could pack three Atlantas into that valley.

I crouched on the wall. Was this some sort of alternate dimension, a pocket of magic-infused reality? Was this a portal to someplace far away? If the Reapers felt the need to protect it with a magical trap that would snare and kill any intruders, it must be valuable to them. Perhaps it was their home.

Next to me, Jim stretched his neck and inhaled the breeze, the way shapeshifters did when they wanted to sample the scents. An imperceptible change came over him. The lines of his body shifted, flowing, subtly reshaped by the breath of the jungle. Usually awkward in warrior form, he became sleek and elegant, like a finely wrought dagger, his human and beast sides in perfect balance. His coat gained a vivid golden tint, against which coils of rosettes stood out like black velvet. He opened his mouth and a soft, coughing roar spilled forth, almost like a purr—if great cats could have made such a sound.

It was silenced by a peal of thunder.

A gleaming golden structure punctured the jungle in the east, rising slowly through the trees. Square in shape, its corners punctuated by stocky towers tipped with silver cupolas, it resembled a palace. The first floor was solid wall, a wealth of sculpture and textures shiny with metallic luster. Atop the wall sat a pillared hall: huge, airy arches, defined by slender columns and guarded by a low latticed rail. Above it, on the roof of the building, a garden bloomed, an exotic riot that made even the verdant jungle barren in comparison. Bizarre trees spread their branches, tinseled with blood-red garlands of vines. Thousands of flowers bloomed, interrupted by ornate ponds.

The hum swelled. The metal palace rumbled and crept up, higher and higher above the treetops, above us, into the sky. A cloud of steam billowed from its fundament and coalesced into a dense curtain of fog. In a moment the palace disappeared from view and the sky gained a small cloud.

I blinked a couple of times and held my arm to Jim. "Pinch me."

Claws sliced my flesh. *Ow.*

I stared at a couple of red dots on my forearm and licked them, tasting the sharp bite of magic on my tongue. Yep. Real. I did just see a golden palace fly off.

A small clearing marked the spot where the palace had rested. Sand-colored structures interrupted the greenery: terraced roofs, an overgrown gateway, and in the distance a tall stone spire.

"Home, sweet home?" I murmured.

"We should visit. I feel hungry."

I nearly fell off the roof. Jim couldn't speak in a half-form. Until now, that was. His grotesque jaws had shredded the words into rags, but I still recognized the meaning. "The jungle has been good to you," I said.

"My kind of place."

"If we go down there, there's no guarantee we'll make it out."

Jim shrugged.

"As long as you're game." I looked around for a foothold.

A muscled arm swiped me by my waist. Jim pushed off and suddenly we were airborne, flying above the ground very far below. My heart tried to jump into my throat. We punched through the canopy and landed on a thick branch. I remembered to breathe. "A little warning next time."

Jim made a raspy sound that suspiciously resembled a laugh. "Welcome to the jungle."

THE BRUSH WAS DENSE. SLENDER TREES WITH oval leaves and vast crowns mixed with teak choked by ficus. Here and there unfamiliar shrubs dripped pink and purple flowers reminiscent of orchids. Acacias, their bark dark on crooked stems, sifted mimosa-scented pollen from long yellow blossoms. Tall, twisted trees offered clusters of orange-red flowers, so vivid their branches looked on fire. Vines bound it all, perfuming the air with a faint scent reminiscent of jasmine.

I did my best to move quietly, but Jim flashed his teeth at me twice. He glided through the brush on soft paws like a phantom, sleek and deadly.

We climbed atop a low hill and went to ground at its apex. An ancient city lay below us. Crumbling structures sat strewn across a wide clearing amid sand-colored granite boulders. Ruined houses and square pavilions jutted like islands of granite from the sea of green grass. An overgrown street, paved with smooth square slabs, ran diagonally to the left of us, terminating in an ancient marketplace. At the far end of the clearing, a husk of a tower stabbed the sky: a tall, square base, upon which smaller and smaller square stories were stacked. It looked like a Dravidian temple to me, but I was far from an expert on India.

I looked to Jim. He slipped away, leapt up on the roof of the nearest structure, and slunk into the depths of the old city. I sank deeper into the brush and settled for a wait.

Around me birds sang a dozen melodies. I studied the jungle. No sign of animals. No snakes slithering along tree limbs, no paw prints, no scratches on the trunks. You'd think there would be monkeys, foxes, maybe wolves. Nothing. Aside from distant bird songs, the jungle might as well have been dead.

Jim leapt into the grass next to me. "One building in the back, several Reapers: three, maybe more."

"Hunters?"

"Could be. A lot of animal smells and blood."

It made sense—flying away in a magical palace was all good and well, but the Reapers still had to eat. In their place I'd leave small hunting parties in the jungle and park by them once in a while to pick up the meat.

"Human blood, too," Jim said.

Human blood was never good.

We headed into the ruin, Jim along the rooftops and on the ground, hugging the ancient walls. Unfamiliar flowers, orange, lemon-yellow, and scarlet, bloomed among the husks of the buildings. Heady fragrances floated in the air, spicing the breeze. I smelled sandalwood, vanilla, cinnamon, jasmine, some sort of citrus . . . Maybe the Reapers made perfume on the side.

We reached a wide square punctuated by a statue of a large stone chariot. Four winged elephants drew the chariot, all carved with precise detail, from the wrinkled tusks to the tassels on their gear. Each elephant was about the size of a Saint Bernard. The chariot itself, resting on ornate stone wheels that looked like they could actually turn, resembled a smaller, more opulent version of the flying palace.

An unreasonably large stone man sat on the roof of the chariot; he was at least as big as the elephants. Numerous arms fanned from his shoulders like feathers of a male peacock's tail. His shoulders supported several heads. I couldn't see the other side, but if the statue was symmetrical, there were at least ten. The front face was that of a beautiful man; the others were monstrous.

Jim's lean form paused on the roof of a structure directly opposite the chariot. He crouched and looked at me.

I knelt by the chariot's wheels. The building on which he perched was long, with solid walls and narrow windows. And in good repair. Dark, unfamiliar, and full of Reapers. How nice.

Jim pointed his thumb back over his shoulder. *Go to the back.*

I dashed to the side and jogged through the ruins, doubling back to the rear of the building. I pulled Slayer out and snuck along the wall until I could see the square and the chariot.

Jim dropped from the roof, glanced at me, and planted his feet. His maw opened. A long, rolling roar tumbled out, ending in a pissed-off feline snarl.

A challenge.

A dull thud resonated through the square. Two shapes walked out into the open, their backs to me. Both male, broad-shouldered, heavily built, and wearing identical T-shirts and pants. Jim spat and growled, making a ruckus. Neither heard me moving in behind them.

The forefront man tore off his T-shirt. The skin of his back split down the middle. Shaggy black fur spilled through the gap. The creature ripped the human flesh off its left shoulder, revealing a deformed clavicle.

His hands clutched at the remainder of the human skin and jerked it off his body like a paper hospital gown. He kicked the shreds aside, swelling in size, until he stood seven feet tall. Dense black fur striped with orange sheathed his frame in a reversal of a tiger pelt. He raised his arms to the side and I realized what was wrong with his clavicle: a second set of shoulders branched from his spine, set parallel, side by side with the first. Four muscular arms flexed, clawing the air.

His buddy gave out a long, hoarse sigh and shed his own skin suit. He was shaped like a human, with the appropriate set of limbs—thank God for small favors—but his skin was blood-red and layered with a pattern of tiny scales.

I had expected a welcoming committee, but nobody had mentioned a free striptease.

Jim snarled. The four-armed freak took a deep breath and leaned forward. A deafening roar washed over me, the deep, primeval sound of a huge predator hunting for its prey in darkness. It drowned Jim's snarls and he took a small step back.

The creature roared louder, taking Jim's retreat as his due and promising no mercy. He was larger than Jim and at least a hundred pounds heavier. Jim hissed. The four arms motioned to him: *come.*

Jim leapt onto the four-armed creature. The moment they clashed in a whirlwind of teeth and claws, I sank Slayer into the back of its red-scaled friend. The blade bit deep, severed the spinal column, and came out in a small spray of crimson. The Reaper whipped around, but his legs failed him. As he went down, I saw his face: human and impossibly beautiful.

Wood groaned. A lean shape sailed over me and landed in a crouch on the stones. A female creature. Her mint-green body was furry on the stomach and chest and studded with foot-long needles like a porcupine's on her back. Black claws the length of my hand tipped her fingers. She glared at me with yellow eyes and charged.

Her clawed hand swiped at me, too fast. I dodged left, but she caught me. Pain sliced down my side. She dashed, trying to get behind me. I let her, reversed my blade, and stabbed backward into the soft green gut just under her rib cage. Slayer sliced into flesh, meeting elastic resistance, and I withdrew.

The creature raked at me with its left hand, oblivious to the blood gushing from its stomach. I spun and threw myself back, dancing away. Claws whistled past my face. I kept dodging. Strike, strike, strike. No finesse, no special training. Like a cat fighting: clawing straight ahead. Just like the fellow in the parking lot.

I dropped under the claws and sliced across her inner thigh. It cost me another singe of pain along my back, and I rolled clear.

Strike, strike, strike. Keep dancing with me, baby.

Red stained the creature's fur with her every step. Her strikes lost their lethal speed. Her chest heaved. She stumbled, swayed forward, and I caught her and pulled her onto my sword. Slayer sliced into her chest and emerged from her back, bright with arterial blood.

Across the clearing, the four-armed freak tore away from Jim, sprinted to the trees, leaping to an inhuman height, and fled into the branches. With a snarl, Jim chased him and vanished into the jungle. Going after them would be a waste of time. I couldn't match Jim's speed, and a jaguar needed no help hunting through the trees.

I slid the inert body off my saber.

The red-scaled man lay prone on the ground, swallowing air in rapid, shallow gulps. Beyond him, the door to the building gaped, a rectangle of solid black. I flicked my blade, flinging the blood from it, and walked into the house.

It took me less than a minute to clear the three vast, gloomy rooms. Empty.

I went back outside and crouched by the scaled man. The wound in his back was deep. I had removed a section of his spine with my strike, and even with accelerated regeneration, he wouldn't be walking anytime soon.

"A week ago a young werewolf tried to take a girl from you," I said. "You beat him, tortured him, and dumped him by the shapeshifters' house, but you let him live. Why?" Here's hoping he understood English.

The scaled lips stretched in a grimace that could've been a smile, revealing snake fangs. "To send . . . a message."

"What's the message?"

"We are stronger. We shall triumph over half-breeds."

Alrighty, then. "Who are the half-breeds? Are they shapeshifters?"

"Half-man, half-animal . . . Two base races become one. Scum of the world . . . We shall overtake. Overcome. We shall . . ." He coughed.

"Any hope for peace?"

The creature strained to raise its head off the ground. Diamond pupils gazed at me. "We . . . don't do peace," he said in a hoarse voice. "We don't make . . . treaties. We kill. Kill and burn. Eat the meat. Celebrate. Rule in half-breeds' stand . . ."

"So you want the Pack's territory?"

He strained to say something else. I leaned toward him. He focused on me. "Rape," he promised. "Many, many times. Until you bleed . . ."

"I'm so flattered."

He raised his hand and traced a short line over my chest. "Carve out your heart . . . won't cook it in the fire . . . eat it raw when all half-breeds are dead."

We weren't getting anywhere. "What are you?"

"Warriors . . . supreme."

Hard to be supreme with your spine cut. "What are you called? Do you have a name?"

He rolled his eyes to the sky. "Glorious . . . army . . . blood like a red flower blooming . . . Soon. Very soon. We shall have the jewel. We shall honor the promise to the Sultan of Death and destroy the half-breeds . . . We shall take their place, grow stronger, and when our time comes . . . we shall . . . teach the Sultan of Death humility."

"Who is the Sultan of Death?"

The Reaper's eyes glinted with stubborn denial.

I reached into my belt and pulled out a canteen of lighter fluid and matches. "This liquid likes fire. It burns very hot for a long time. Tell me how to reverse the magic you put on the shapeshifter, and I won't pour it on your chest and set you on fire."

"Human . . . I'm beyond . . . you."

"You're not beyond pain." I twisted the cap off the canteen.

He smiled at me and gulped. No words came out. His

eyes rolled into his skull. Short, abrupt moans erupted from him as if he suddenly went dumb. He shuddered, clawed at his throat . . .

He was choking.

I thrust Slayer between his teeth.

CHAPTER 19

———◦◦———

TWENTY MINUTES LATER, GUTTURAL COUGHS AN-
nounced Jim's return. I waited for him by the scaled man's
corpse. He leapt off the tree and dropped a limp body onto
the grass. Bulging dead eyes glared at me from a face that
wasn't even remotely human. A cross between a tiger and a
Chinese temple dog might have looked like that.

"Shapeshifter?" I asked.

"No. Doesn't smell right."

The werejaguar glanced at the two prone forms and
prodded the red-skinned creature. He didn't respond and
Jim gave a small snort.

"Swallowed his own tongue," I explained.

Jim sighed, a purely feline fatalism twisting his monstrous face. "You get anything before he croaked?"

"They dumped Derek as a declaration of war. According
to the recently departed, you are scum, a mix of base races
of human and animal, and no peace is possible. They hate
the Pack and plan on killing you all in a glorious slaughter
with much bloodshed and much feasting on your flesh, as
soon as they get the jewel. They've allied themselves with

the Sultan of Death, who will help them nuke you, after which they're hoping to double-cross him. Oh, and I'm to be raped many, many times."

It was hard to roll your eyes in a half-shape. Jim gave it a good college try. "Who is the Sultan of Death?"

"Beats me."

Roland would certainly fit the bill. I didn't say it out loud. Roland was the center of my existence. As long as I'd been aware of myself, I knew that I had to kill him and that if he ever found out about me, he would sacrifice every resource at his disposal to kill me. His power was incredible. Legends of him floated through the ages, and almost every ancient civilization had a record of his reign. Hunting him would be akin to assassinating a god. I needed more experience and more power, before I could even contemplate that confrontation. Until my abilities grew, I had to hide, living every moment with the awareness of being discovered. My paranoia ran so deep it was a wonder I didn't check for Roland's agents under my bed.

Any mysterious threat, any unknown danger, any mention of a magically powerful being automatically brought Roland to the front of my mind. Yes, the Sultan of Death fit him perfectly—he had brought undeath into the world. But the title could refer to someone completely different. Just because I had fixated on him didn't mean the rest of the world had.

"This keeps coming back to the Wolf Diamond. I have a feeling they plan to use it as a weapon. It was how he said it, Jim. He said, 'We shall have the jewel' the way MSDU might say, 'We shall have air support.' "

Jim swore.

I led him inside, into the first room. A long stone table ran the length of the room. On the table Saiman's victim, still in his human body, lay spread-eagled on his stomach. Strips of flesh had been carved from his back and buttocks down to the bone and stacked aside like meat cuts in a butchery shop. I walked over to a huge stainless steel chest freezer sitting by the table. It was unplugged—there wasn't a single outlet in the ruins—and filled with ice and raw meat. Steaks, ground patties, slabs of ribs, pork chops, venison roasts layered atop one another, some in plastic, some in paper, some simply sitting, wedged, dripping frozen blood. I pointed to the left, where several long hunks of meat sat crammed into a corner. The skin on the meat was the color of coffee with cream.

Jim sniffed and recoiled.

"Human?"

"Yes." He snarled and spat to the side. I'd had much the same reaction when I first realized what it was. These bastards caught some person, chopped him up, and stuffed him into a freezer to be eaten. We'd never know his name. Or his sex for that matter. Somewhere a person simply didn't come home and nobody would ever find out why. It made me sick.

Jim glanced at the table, where slabs of flesh, carved from the body of Saiman's victim, lay in a stack. "Cannibals."

"Equal opportunity carnivores: any flesh is meat. They don't discriminate. There is more."

He followed me into the second room. Empty and dusty, it offered several straw sleeping mats tossed haphazardly into a corner. A mural stretched on the wall, painted on a long sheet of plain brown paper, pinned to the stones with tape. Bright with garish red and green and gold, the mural began with a hellish forge. A waterfall of molten metal fell into a wide basin in its center. Anvils stood by the walls, lightning bolts and twisted metal tools hung from the hooks in the ceiling, and dark smoke billowed, obscuring the edges of the picture and twisting to form a frame around the forge. A demonic man hefted a huge hammer, critically surveying a half-forged sword in his hand. Monstrously muscled, he wore a leather apron and nothing else. A dark beard protruded from his face, and his eyes glowed red.

The next panel of the mural showed a room strewn with pillows. A beautiful man reclined in the center, clad in gauzy robes and surrounded by nude women bearing fruit and garlands of flowers. The man's delicate face bore little resemblance to the dark inhabitant of the forge, but the dark beard gave him away. The metalsmith cleaned up rather nice.

The third part of the mural was unfinished. A pale gold wash had been applied through the faint pencil outline. The graceful man from the center of the mural had become a god: he had grown three additional heads and six arms. One face looked straight at me, two faces showed in profile, and an outline of the back of his head pointed to a fourth face turned away from me. North, east, south, and west.

Two enormous wings protruded from his shoulders, and between the wings shimmered a mirage of a city: a sea of elegant towers and domes guarded by a wall. The style of the mural didn't point to any mythology in particular; it reminded me more of a comic book than anything else. The poses were stylized, the man's musculature seemed greatly exaggerated, and all women came equipped with tiny asses, disproportionately long legs, and perfectly round, udder-sized breasts.

"Ring any bells?" I looked at Jim.

Jim shook his head.

"Yeah, me neither."

I pulled the mural off the wall and rolled it into a tube.

Jim took the corpse from the table, slung it over his shoulder, and took it outside.

I went back to the freezer. I would've liked to bury the human remains, but we had neither the time nor the means to do it. I pulled a leather pouch from my belt, untied the cord securing it, and sprinkled dark green dust over the meat, careful not to inhale or touch the powder.

"Spicing it up?" Jim asked from the doorway.

"Water hemlock. Also called cowbane." I put the pouch away. "Thirty minutes and then projectile vomiting, violent convulsions, and death or permanent nervous system damage. A little present from me for their table."

Jim stepped outside, grasped the four-armed freak, swung it onto his shoulders, and stared pointedly at the

other three bodies sprawled on the grass. They were our
evidence. I would have to carry one. A seven-foot-tall
scaled monstrosity, a green creature covered in foot-long
needles, or the guy missing most of his flesh from his ass
and legs. Hmmm, let me think . . .

CHAPTER 20

CARRYING CORPSES IN PLAIN DAYLIGHT, ESPE-
cially corpses with four arms, pretty much takes the whole
notion of "not drawing attention" out back and explodes it
with fireworks. Especially since the people doing the carrying are covered in blood and look like they've been dragged
through a hedge backward. Not to mention that one of them
is a werejaguar in a warrior form and the other a woman
hauling a human corpse with his ass cut off.

Fortunately, the outskirts of Unicorn were deserted. One
would have to be some sort of special breed of idiot to approach that street in the first place. Apparently, Atlanta was
experiencing a moron shortage, and today Jim and I were
the only idiots of this caliber.

Even without his butt and thighs, Saiman's unfortunate
victim weighed a ton. We passed out of the jungle into the
city with no problems, but carrying him through Unicorn
Lane and out to the vehicle proved to be near my limits. I
had slid into a kind of fog where taking the next step was
all that mattered. I dimly recalled reaching the spot where
we had left the vehicle and finding a cart hitched to a pair

of horses instead. The dingo must've come back with the horses once the magic wave had hit the city. Unfortunately, he didn't stick around.

I also remembered packing the corpses into the cart under some canvas and sliding into the seat to steer, because Jim, being the top man on Curran's Most-Wanted List, had to stay out of sight. Then there was the trek across the city, through the morning traffic. The glow of pain along my side and back nicely kept me awake. A layer of jungle dirt had mixed with Reaper blood on my skin, and the fall sun baked it into a crust over my face and hair. At least I had no trouble with traffic jams. The rival drivers took one look at my blood-encrusted persona and scrambled to get out of the way.

I drove and thought of Roland.

I had no mother. Instead I had Voron, whom I called my father. Tall, his dark blond hair cropped short, Voron had led me through my childhood with his quiet strength. Voron could kill anything. He could solve anything. He could fix anything. I would do anything for one of his rare smiles. He was my father, one of the two constants in my life.

Roland had been the other.

He entered my life as a fairy tale that Voron would tell me before bed. There once was a man who had lived through the ages. He had been a builder, an artisan, a healer, a priest, a prophet, a warrior, and a sorcerer. At times he had been a slave. At others he was a tyrant. Magic fell and technology reigned, and then magic rose again, and still he persevered, ancient like the sand itself, driven through the years by his obsession for a perfect world.

He had many names, although he called himself Roland now. He had been master to many men and lover to many women, but he had not loved anyone as much as he loved my mother. She was kind and smart and generous and she filled Roland with life. My mother wanted a baby. It had been millennia since Roland had sired a child, because his child would inherit all the power of Roland's ancient blood and all of his ambition, and Roland had fought too many wars to kill children who had risen against him.

But he loved my mother too much and he decided to give her a child because it would make her happy. She was only two months along when he started to have second thoughts. He became obsessed that the child would oppose him, and he decided to kill the child in the womb.

But my mother loved the baby. The more obsessed Roland became, the farther she pulled away from him.

Roland had a Warlord. His name was Voron, which meant *raven* in Russian. They called him that because death followed him. And Voron loved my mother as well.

When Roland was away, my mother ran and Voron ran with her. He was there when she gave birth to me. For a few blissful months on the run they were happy. But Roland chased them, and my mother, knowing that Voron was the stronger of the two, stayed behind to delay Roland so he and I could escape. She sank her dagger into Roland's eye and then he killed her.

And that was where the fairy tale ended and we would check for a knife under my bed and then I would go to sleep, hoping to kill my natural father one day.

Wherever we went, whatever we did, Roland's presence followed me. He was my target and the reason for my existence. He gave me life and I would take his.

I knew him intimately. Voron had been his Warlord for half a century, and would've served him through the ages, kept young and virile by Roland's magic, if my mother hadn't come along. He taught me everything he learned about his former master. I knew what Roland looked like. Voron had shown me his photo and I had committed it to memory before we burned it. I recognized his face on the statues in old history books and found it once in a Renaissance painting of a battle. I read the Bible passages about him, what little there was. I knew his lieutenants, his weapons, his powers. And Roland's age had given him vast power. He could control hundreds of undead at once. He wielded his blood like a weapon, solidifying it at will to create devastating weapons and impenetrable blood armor. It was his fucked-up blood that accounted for my power.

Voron had been a supreme warrior. He took every crumb of his knowledge and he poured it into me, tempering me like a blade. *Grow stronger. Survive. Kill Roland. End it forever. Until then, hide.*

Four months ago I made a conscious decision to stop hiding. I had questioned it ever since. I lacked the strength and experience to face Roland, but now I was playing out in the open, and our eventual confrontation was inevitable.

An instinct told me he was the Sultan of Death. Which meant that if I kept tugging at this tangled mess of a problem, I might end up running across someone from his inner circle. The idea filled me with dread.

I was afraid of Roland. But I was scared for Derek even more. And I was scared for Curran.

When I finally drew up to the shapeshifter safe house, the morning was in full swing. I pulled back the tarp. Jim slept atop the corpses. He'd reverted back to his human form and was naked as a jaybird. I shook him a few times, but he seemed to have gone into a Sleeping Beauty–like stupor and I wasn't going to kiss him to wake him up.

I knocked on the door. No answer. I tried the handle— and the door swung open. I stuck my head in and called a few times but nobody materialized to assist me.

Brenna was supposed to have watched the door. The only thing that could've drawn her from it was . . . *Please don't let Derek be dead.*

At the thought of going down to the basement, my legs nearly gave out. I wasn't sure I could take seeing him dead.

I needed to go down there but I couldn't make myself move. I swallowed and stared at the doorway.

The bodies. I better go get the bodies. That's a good idea.

It proved surprisingly difficult to maneuver a four-armed corpse through the door. I tried it for a full three minutes before my patience ran dry. But by the time Brenna appeared at the top of the gloomy staircase, I had matters well in hand.

"Is Derek dead?"

"Not yet."

Relief rolled though me. I needed a nice place to sit down. "I thought you were guarding the entrance," I said, sliding Slayer under my arm.

"I was. I had to let someone in." She stared at the corpse at my feet.

"It's not Curran, is it?" I asked.

"No."

"Great." I gathered up the four severed arms and nodded at the stub of the body. "Would you mind getting the bigger piece?"

DOOLITTLE HAD TAKEN ONE LOOK AT ME AND prescribed an immediate shower. Half an hour later, showered, patched up, and given a mug of coffee by Brenna, I felt almost human. Doolittle had disappeared into the depths of the house to continue his constant vigil on Derek. It was just me and two corpses. At about half a mug, Jim wandered into the room, looking mean and hungover. He favored me with an ugly scowl and flopped into a chair.

"Now what?"

"We wait."

"What for?"

"My expert. She's with Derek now."

We sat for a while. I was still out of it. Doolittle was the best medmage in the business, hands down. My back almost didn't hurt and the pain in my side was a distant echo. But I was so tired I could barely see straight.

I had to check with Andrea on the results of the silver analysis. I tried the phone. No dial tone.

A young woman strode into the room. She was barely five feet tall and very slender. Her skin was almond dark, her face wide and round. She looked at the world through thick glasses and her eyes behind the Coke-bottle lenses were very brown, almost black, with a touch of Asian ancestry to their cut. She stepped into the apartment and peered at me as I closed the door.

"Indonesian," she announced, shifting a tote bag on her shoulder.

"What?"

"You were trying to figure out what kind of 'nese I am. Indonesian."

"I'm Kate."

"Dali."

She looked to where Jim sat. As she swept past me, I caught a glimpse of a book in her tote bag: a long, lean blond man brandishing an improbably enormous sword posing with three girls strategically arranged at his feet. One of the girls had cat ears.

Dali fixed Jim with her disconcerting stare. "You owe me. If he finds out I'm here, I'll be dead meat."

He who? *He* better not be Curran.

"I take responsibility," Jim said.

"Where are the corpses?" Dali asked.

"Behind you."

Dali turned and stumbled over the four-armed freak's legs, and would've executed a beautiful nosedive if she were an ordinary human. As it was, she managed to jump away and land with perfect balance if not perfect grace. Shapeshifter reflexes to the rescue.

Dali adjusted her glasses and shot me an irate look. "I'm not that blind," she said. "I'm absentminded."

Perhaps she was also telepathic.

"No," she said. "I'm just not stupid."

Okay.

Dali surveyed the four-armed corpse. "Oh boy. Polymelic symmetry. Any other supernumerary body parts? And did you have to hack his arms off?"

"Yes, I did. He wouldn't go through the door."

"You say it like you're proud of it."

I was proud of it. It was an example of quick thinking in a difficult situation.

Dali shrugged her tote to the floor, knelt by the corpse, and stared into the gaping hole where the creature's heart used to reside. Jim had really done a number on it. "Tell me everything."

I described the ward, the jungle, the flying palace, the ruins, the stone chariot with multiheaded driver, and the fight, with an occasional comment from Jim. She nodded, raised the corpse's front left arm to take a look at the back set, frowned . . .

"So who isn't supposed to know you're here?" I asked. *Please don't be Curran, please don't be Curran . . .*

"The Beast Lord," Jim said.

Damn it.

"Technically she's under house arrest."

"What for?"

"I went for a drive." Dali picked up the corpse's foot and studied the claws. "Nice and pliant. No rigor mortis at all."

"He put you under house arrest because you went for a drive?"

"She slipped a roofie to her bodyguard, hot-wired a car, and went drag racing on Buzzard's Highway. In the dark." Jim's face held all the warmth of an iceberg.

"You're just upset that I made Theo look stupid." Dali dropped the hand. "It's not my fault that your lethal killing machine was so excited by the prospect of getting his hands on my tiny boy-breasts, he forgot to watch his drink. Quite frankly, I don't see what the big deal is."

"You're legally blind, you can't pass the exam to get a license, and you drive like shit." Jim's lip wrinkled in a silent snarl. "You're a menace."

"Drivers on Buzzard don't come there to be safe. They come there for thrills. If they knew I was legally blind, it would just make things more interesting for them. It's my body. I can do whatever I want with it. If I want to get in a wreck, then I should be able to do so."

"Yes, but you drove to Buzzard's Highway," I said. I really needed more coffee. "What if you wrecked on the way and hurt yourself, or worse, hurt somebody else, another driver or a pedestrian, a kid crossing the street?"

Dali blinked. "You know, that is precisely what Curran said. Almost word for word." She sighed. "Let's agree that, in retrospect, it wasn't one of my brightest moments. Do you have anything else besides the corpses?"

Jim handed her the rolled-up mural. She pulled the paper open and frowned. "Here, you hold this end, and, Jim, you hold this end. Okay, separate."

She actually wanted me to move. She must've been out of her mind. We walked apart until the paper was unrolled. She glanced at it for a second, nodded, and waved her hand. "You may let go. So, do you have any ideas as to what corner of mythology your friend belongs?"

I took a wild stab in the dark. "Hindu. First, we have a jungle, the ruins of what looked like a Dravidian temple to me, then a stone chariot drawn by elephants, and a humanoid with many arms and heads. We also have a tiger monster and he has four arms. Not that many mythologies feature extra sets of arms or that many extra heads in a humanoid. Several heads on dragons or giants, yes. Extra limbs and heads on a humanoid, no. Also, the girl called one of the Reapers 'Asaan.' I looked it up and it's a term for a guru or practitioner of Dravidian martial arts."

Dali looked at me for a long moment. "You're not stupid either."

"Yes, but that's all I got."

"I believe this is a rakshasa." She nudged the four-armed corpse with her toes. "And if I'm right, the two of you are in deep shit."

"AT FIRST THERE WAS VISHNU, EXCEPT AT THAT point he was Narayana, the embodiment of Supreme Divinity."

Dali sat on the floor next to the corpse.

"Narayana floated in endless waters, wrapped in a great albino serpent and having a marvelous time, until a lotus grew from his navel. Within the lotus, god Brahma, the creator of worlds, was reborn. Brahma looked around, saw Narayana being content to float, and for no apparent reason became obsessed that his water would get stolen. So he made four guardians, two couples. The first couple promised to worship the water, and they were yakshasas. The second couple promised to protect the water, and they were rakshasas."

"Talk strengths and weaknesses," Jim said.

"Rakshasas are born warriors. They were created for this purpose. According to legend, they are conceived and carried to term in a single day, and upon birth, they instantly grow to the age of their mother. They are carnivores and have no qualms about consuming human meat. They come in a vast variety of shapes and sizes. They're excellent illusionists and magicians."

I sighed. This just got better and better. "For some reason I thought rakshasas were humanoid tigers, like a shapeshifter in a warrior form but with a tiger's head."

Dali nodded. "They are most often depicted as monsters resembling tigers, because a tiger is the scariest thing an Indian sculptor or artist could reasonably picture. Elephants are larger, but they are vegetarians and mostly keep to themselves, while tigers are silent, deadly, and actively hunt people."

A humanoid tiger, equipped with extra arms and human intelligence, would be the stuff of anyone's nightmares.

"Rakshasas realize that tigers are frightening and often adopt this form; however, legends say that they can be ugly or beautiful. Out of three rakshasa brothers, one could be lovely beyond description, one could be a giant, and one could sprout ten heads. It really varies. Some sources insist that one can never know the true form of a rakshasa; only the form they favor most at the moment."

"Anything else?" Jim asked softly.

"They can fly."

Delightful. "Ours didn't fly. They mostly jumped unnaturally high."

"That could be due to low magic, incorrect information, or an insufficient number of people believing in the myth. Or all three. Take your pick."

"Can these rakshasas do something that would stop you from shifting?" I asked.

Dali thought about it. "They're shapeshifters but not in the same way we are. They deal in illusion. You said they pulled their human skins off. Where are the skins? You brought his ripped clothes. I find it very hard to believe that between the two of you, you forgot to pick up torn human hide."

I concentrated, recalling the scene as we left the house. "The skins disappeared."

Dali nodded. "That's because technically there were no skins. Magic or no magic, you couldn't physically pack that"—she kicked the four-armed corpse again—"into a human hide. Rakshasas don't actually flay a human and pull on his skin. They consume a human in some way, physically, mentally, or spiritually, or all of the above, and then they assume the shape."

Light dawned in my head. "The skin ripping was an illusion. An intimidation tactic."

"Exactly. They pretended to cast off human skins because they wanted to disturb you. Rakshasas are exceedingly arrogant and cunning but not too bright. Their mythical king, Ravana, is a prime example: ten heads but very little brain. The flying palace you saw, assuming both of you haven't gone insane, is most likely Pushpaka Vimana, an ancient flying machine. Ravana appropriated it from its original owner and was flying around on it to and fro when he came upon Shiva the Destroyer during his rest." Dali paused for dramatic effect.

Hindu mythology wasn't my strongest suit, but even I knew about Shiva. Any god titled Destroyer of Worlds wasn't to be taken lightly. When not enjoying his home life with his loving wife and two sons, he ran around the woods wrapped in cobras and wearing a torn tiger skin still dripping blood. He stripped pelts from fearsome beasts with a touch of his pinkie. His wrath was likened to Rudra, a roaring storm. In his malignant aspect, he was absolutely terrifying. In his benign aspect, he was easily amused. His forehead hid a third eye, which, when directed outward, burned everything in his path and periodically destroyed the universe. Anything associated with Shiva had to be treated with kid gloves while wearing a Level IV biohazard suit and preferably a tank.

Dali smiled. "Ravana managed to annoy Shiva, and the Destroyer of Worlds put him into a cage of stone bars. Ravana had to sit there and sing until Shiva got tired of listening to him and let him go. Ravana was the ultimate rakshasa: arrogant, flashy, and ruled completely by his impulses. He was what they would aspire to be. You're dealing with terrible show-offs, convinced of their own superiority. To them you're amusing food slash adoring audience. They'll milk everything they got for dramatic effect and they get off on playing to the crowd."

Jim and I exchanged glances. If you got your jollies by getting the herd high, the Midnight Games was the place to do it.

I turned my cup upside down, looking for more coffee. None came out. Still, the crowd-pleasing factor had to be just a bonus. They were after the gem. Why? I was swimming in a sea of random information and it refused to make itself into anything logical. I opened my mouth to ask Dali about the topaz, but Jim jumped ahead of me.

"Can you explain the jungle?"

She made a face. "I have no idea. It could be some sort of pocket of deep magic. Or a portal into a magic jungle land. I'd need more information to answer this question. By the way, I'm so thirsty, my tongue feels like paper."

Dali licked her lips and Jim went into the kitchen and came back with a glass of water, which he handed to her. She drained half of it. "So, the rakshasas hate us."

"'Us' as in shapeshifters or 'us' as in normal humans?" I asked.

"Both. This takes us back to Ravana. Ravana was an

upward-climbing type of individual. He had ten heads, and every century he sacrificed one of his heads by hacking it off. Finally he had only one head and the gods could stand it no longer, came down in all their heavenly glory, and asked him what the hell did he want to stop doing that. He asked for immunity from every race except that of men and animals. He thought us to be too puny and lowly to harm him. Once he got his immunity, he set about conquering Heaven, burned the city of the gods, killed all the dancing girls . . . And then Vishnu decided he had just about enough of that, went to Earth to be reborn as a human, Rama, marshaled together an army of animals, and nuked him."

If rakshasas were as arrogant as she said, they would hate humans and animals with the passion of a thousand suns. And shapeshifters were both. Bonus genocide. Now the Reapers' half-breed revulsion made sense.

"Is there anything in the legends about a topaz called the Wolf Diamond? A large yellow gem maybe?" I asked.

Dali wrinkled her forehead. "Topaz is associated with Brihaspati—Jupiter."

"The Roman god?" Jim frowned.

"No, the planet. Honestly, Jim, the world doesn't revolve around the Greco-Roman pantheon. Rudra Mani, Shiva's gem, is also gold in color. He carries it on his neck. By the way, Shiva was the one who gave the rakshasas the gift of flying."

"This one would be large," I said. "A powerful stone."

"Rudra Mani is pretty large. The size of a baby's head."

Saiman had described the Wolf Diamond as being the size of a man's fist . . . Either a big fist or a very small baby . . . Unless he meant an ice giant's fist. "What do you know about it?"

Dali rolled her eyes. "It's supposed to be a stone of virtue. It also belongs to Shiva, if you catch my drift. With Shiva, you never know what you're going to get. He might find a rakshasa baby, think it was cute, and give it the power of flight and the ability to grow to adulthood in one day. Or he might start stomping demons for fun."

Jim crossed his massive arms on his chest. "So we have a rock that belongs to a bipolar god with a warped sense of humor."

"Pretty much. Not a lot is known about Rudra Mani. I'll look it up. We don't even know if your topaz is Rudra Mani or some other chunk of yellow stone." Dali waved her hands. "It's too vague. It could be anything or nothing."

I wouldn't be at all surprised if the Wolf Diamond was Rudra Mani in disguise. Mythological elements tended to occur in bunches. We had rakshasas who were firmly associated with Shiva in the Hindu myths. Shiva had a large yellow rock. The rakshasas planned to enter a tournament to win a large yellow rock. It would be foolhardy to assume that the two rocks weren't one and the same.

At least we'd get no Shiva. The flare had come and gone, so he couldn't manifest. No Shiva was good, whichever way you looked at it.

I looked at the bloodied stump that once had been the axe fighter facing Saiman. Next to the four-armed monstrosity, he looked almost fragile. "Why is he still in the human skin?"

"What?" Dali wrinkled her nose at me.

"This fellow ripped off his skin and started roaring and waving his four arms around the first chance he got. The axe fighter remained in his human form. Why?"

Dali put her cup down. "Well, you're assuming the axe fighter isn't human. But even if he is a rakshasa, he might not have wanted to change shape. You said they are posing as humans. He would blow his cover."

"He was beaten to a pulp," Jim said. "Trust me, he would've changed. It's the matter of the survival instinct taking over."

All these facts tried to coalesce in my head. I could almost grasp it. "Perhaps he couldn't change shape. Maybe something kept him from changing. Kind of like something is keeping Derek from shifting. An object. A spell. Something that suppresses the magic."

Jim caught on. "Something that would also fool the m-scanner into reading them as human."

Dali kicked off her shoes and began pulling off her shirt. "I'll have to shift. I'm more sensitive to magic in my animal shape and my sense of smell is better."

I looked to the floor. The shapeshifters mostly fell into two camps: some were very modest, and some would strip in the middle of the Market Highway without a moment's thought. Apparently Dali was of the second category.

A deep, low rumble of a large cat rolled through my apartment, a cascade of sound bouncing off my skin. I looked up.

A white tiger stood in my living room. Glowing as if sculpted of fresh snow, she looked at me with ice-blue eyes, enormous, otherworldly, like some eternal spirit of the North, taiga, and winter hunt. Long stripes outlined her fluid shape with coal black. More than a mere animal, more than a lycanthrope in the beast form, she was majestic. I couldn't even breathe.

And then she sneezed. And sneezed again, blinking, and when she raised her head again, I realized that only one glacial eye looked straight at me. The other stared off to the side. The tiger spirit went cross-eyed like a Siamese cat.

The tigress raised one paw, looked quizzically at it, put it down, and rumbled low in the throat, a befuddled expression on her big face.

"Yes, those are your paws," Jim said patiently.

At the sound of his voice, the tigress backpedaled, stumbled over the four-armed body, and sat on it in the most undignified manner.

"You're sitting on the evidence," Jim said.

The tigress leapt up and spun around, nearly taking me off my feet with her butt. A snarl ripped from her mouth.

"Yes, there is a dead creature in the room. Lie down, Dali, and relax. It will come to you."

The tigress settled on the floor, peering at the bodies with open suspicion.

"She has short-term memory loss after the shift," Jim murmured. "It will wear off in a minute. The cross-eyed thing will go away, too. Some cats react that way to stress."

"Does she get aggressive?" The last thing I needed was to get raked over hot coals because I used excessive force to subdue a raging cross-eyed weretigress with temporary amnesia.

Jim's face took on an odd expression, so unusual on his hard mug that it took me a moment to diagnose it as embarrassment. "No. She gags on raw meat and blood."

"What?"

"She won't bite or scratch or she'll vomit. She's a vegetarian."

Oh boy. "But when she's in beast form . . ."

He shook his head. "She eats grass. Don't ask."

Dali rose and sniffed the four-armed body. She began at his feet, her flat feline muzzle trailing a mere quarter inch above the skin. The dark nose scanned the long toes of the left foot, tipped with sharp claws, and slid up, along the shin to the knee. Dali paused there, licked the hard pane of the kneecap, and moved up along the thigh. She stopped at the crotch, shifted to the right, and repeated the same thorough scent search with the right leg.

It took her a full five minutes to complete her survey.

"Anything?" I asked.

Dali shook her magnificent head. Damn it. We were back to dying Derek lying in a vat of liquid.

"Alright." Jim nodded. "Change back. I thought of something else to ask."

The tigress nodded. Her white pelt stretched, quivered, but remained on her body.

"Dali?" Jim's voice was calm and measured.

The white fur crawled and snapped back into a tiger. Glacial-blue eyes stared at me, and in their crystal depth, I saw panic.

The tigress ran.

She dashed around the room, trampling the bodies. Her furry shoulder brushed the tall, tulip-shaped lamp. The lamp went flying and exploded against the floor in a shower of glass. Dali rampaged over the shards and collided with the LCD display on the wall. The large metal frame slid off its hook and thundered down, landing on Dali's skull. I winced.

Dali whipped about, her eyes completely wild, and met Jim. He stepped in her way and stared.

Dali shivered. The fur rose on her haunches. She snarled.

Jim simply stood. His eyes were pure emerald.

With a heavy sigh, Dali hugged the ground and lay down.

Alpha of the cats in action.

Jim knelt by Dali. "Can you change shape?"

The tigress whined low. I took it as a no.

Small streaks of blood seeped from Dali's huge paws, vivid against her white fur. Given her aversion to blood, she probably wouldn't even lick her injuries. I fetched the med kit Doolittle had used to patch me up, fished out a pair of tweezers, and settled down by her feet. She offered me one enormous paw. I opened the bottle of antiseptic, poured some on a piece of gauze, and wiped the blood from the huge pads. Three glass shards sat embedded in the flesh, trophies of her glorious battle with the lamp.

"I want you to keep trying to revert to human shape," Jim said. "Don't strain yourself, but keep a steady pressure."

I hooked the first shard with the tweezers and plucked it from her paw. Blood gushed. Dali jerked, pulling me with her. Fire laced my side. I winced. There went Doolittle's patching.

"Hold still, please."

Dali whined and let me have her paw. The cut didn't seal. I swiped at it with gauze. Still open. Shit. She and Derek now exhibited the same symptoms: an inability to shift and retarded regeneration. I deposited the bloody piece of frosted-white glass onto the lid of the first aid kit.

"Let's talk scents." Jim's voice was smooth, soothing. "Did you smell anything odd off the bodies?"

Dali rocked her head side to side.

I plucked another shard from her paw. "Aside from shape, do you feel any different?"

Dali whined. That was the trouble with shapeshifters in animal form: they couldn't vocalize and most couldn't write. Yes and no questions were our only option.

I hooked the third shard, but the tweezers slipped. The sucker was deep in there. "Dali, spread your fingers for me if you can."

Huge claws shot out from her paw as she spread her toes.

"Thank you." I pinched the shard and pulled it out.

The tiger flesh boiled under my fingers and I found myself holding a human hand.

"Oh my God." Dali's voice hit a trembling high note. "Oh my God."

"What did you do?" Jim leaned forward, focused as if he sighted prey.

Tears swelled in Dali's eyes. "I thought I would be stuck in animal form forever." She looked around the room. "I wrecked the place. And your wound . . . I'm so sorry."

"Don't worry about it," I mumbled, focused on the shard. It looked yellow to me. The tulip lamp had been frosted white. "Happens all the time."

I grabbed the first aid kit, held it under the tweezers in case I dropped the shard on the way, got up, and carried the sliver of glass to the window. The shard sparkled, casting a faint yellow shade onto the white first aid box. Hello, Mr. Clue.

Jim frowned at the shard. "Topaz?"

"I think so. What do you want to bet this is a piece of the Wolf Diamond?" It made sense. The Reapers wanted the Wolf Diamond so they could use it as a weapon against shapeshifters. Two plus two equaled a bloody chunk of silicate in my hand. "Do you think it prevents transformation?"

Jim swiped it from the tweezers and sliced the flesh of his palm with a quick flick of his nails. He slid the shard into the cut.

Green rolled over his eyes. His lips trembled. A shiver ran through his body, raising the hair on the back of his arms. His gaze had gone jaguar-wild, but his shape remained human.

Without a word, he extracted the shard and dropped it into the lid as if it were red-hot.

This was it. This was the weapon the rakshasas needed to destroy the Pack. The gem couldn't be stolen; it had to be won or it would bring a curse upon its thief. They entered the Midnight Games so they could get the gem, and once they got it, they would carve it into a thousand pieces and use the shards to prevent shapeshifters from assuming their animal or warrior form. Without shapeshifting and regeneration, the Pack would become filling for the rakshasa meat grinder.

"I must've stepped onto the shard when I touched the body," Dali murmured.

"You mean, when you stomped all over it." Jim shook once, as if flinging water from himself. "The kid has one inside him somewhere. But the m-scanner isn't picking it up."

Dali touched the shard with her fingertip. "It's so small. The scanner might not be sensitive enough to detect it with low magic."

"I don't want to slice him to ribbons looking for it. He might not make it. There has to be another way," Jim said.

The plan shaped up in my head. "I'm going to Macon."

Jim blinked and a light sparked in his eyes. "Julie, your ward. She is in school near Macon. And she's a hell of a sensate."

Julie, the kid whom I met during the flare, had a one-in-a-million talent. She was a sensate and she could read the colors of magic better than any m-scanner. She was studying in the best boarding school I could get her into, only two hours away by ley line.

I nodded. "If anybody can find the shard in Derek's body, she will."

CHAPTER 21

I TAPPED MY FINGERS ON THE COUNTER, THE phone to my ear, and checked the gauze I pressed against my ribs. Still bleeding.

The line clicked and a soothing female voice greeted me. "Ms. Daniels?"

"Hello."

"My name is Citlalli. I'm Julie's counselor."

"I remember. We've met." Memory thrust an image before me, a small dark woman with Madonna eyes. A very strong empath. Like surfers, the empaths rode the waves of people's emotions, feeling the grief or joy of others as if it were their own. They made excellent psychiatrists and sometimes their patients drove them insane.

I frowned. Something was up. I didn't ask to speak to the counselor.

"Ms. Daniels . . ."

"Kate."

"Are you precognizant, Kate?"

"Not that I know of. Why do you ask?"

"I'm drafting a letter to you regarding Julie, and I wondered if my concentration may have triggered your phone call."

Oh no. "What did she do?"

"Julie has developed some issues."

Julie was an issue riding on an issue and using a third issue for a whip. But she was mine, and despite the kind quality of Citlalli's voice, all my needles stood up defensively. I tried to keep the hostility out of my answer. "Go on."

"Due to the gap in her education, she has to take remedial classes."

"We discussed that prior to her admittance."

"Academically she's progressing ahead of schedule. I have no doubt that she will catch up with her peers by the end of the year," Citlalli assured me. "But she's experiencing problems adjusting socially."

She had practically lived on the streets for the last two years, hiding from gangs and being brainwashed by her scumbag boyfriend. What did they expect from her?

On the other end of the line, Citlalli cleared her throat softly. My irritation must've been intense enough for her to pick up. I took a deep breath and cleared the baggage. Emotions receded, still present but held deep below the surface. It was a meditation technique I had learned in childhood. I rarely used it because I liked to ride the edge of my emotions. Fear, anger, outrage, love, courage, I utilized them for a boost in the fight. But I knew how to suppress them, and the older I got, the easier suppression came to me.

"I'm sorry. I didn't mean to cause you discomfort. You were describing Julie's problems?"

"Thank you. Children can be cruel at Julie's age. They struggle for personal identity. Establishing pecking order becomes very important. Julie finds herself at a disadvantage. Academically she's behind, so she can't use her accomplishments in that area to gain popularity. She's not very good at sports, partially due to malnourishment and partially because she doesn't have remarkable talents in that arena. We have some outstanding athletes and she realizes she will never be a star. She doesn't excel at combat, and while those with knowledge find her magical sensitivity impressive, children appreciate flashier magics more."

"In other words, she isn't a jock, she isn't a warrior, she's taking remedial lessons, and her magic is lackluster because she can't breathe fire or melt metals with a blink."

"Essentially. Some of the children in the same position reach for their family history to establish their cred with other kids."

"Julie doesn't have any remarkable family members." No heroes. No great mages.

"She has you."

"Oh."

"She's been telling stories. Beautiful, terrifying stories of demons and goddesses and witches. I know they are true recollections because I feel her sincerity. But the kids . . ."

"They're picking on her because they think she's lying."

"Yes. We're monitoring the situation very closely. She has not suffered any abuse. However, Julie's an emotional child . . ."

"She's a chunk of plastic explosive with a fuse armed."

"Aptly put. She has a knife."

I closed my eyes and counted to three. I had taken away all her knives and searched her twice before I dropped her off.

"She refuses to part with it. We can take the knife away physically. But it would greatly reinforce the damage already done to her ego. It would be much better if she gave it up voluntarily and I'm afraid you're the only person who could compel her to do so at this stage."

I glanced at the clock. Eleven. Felt like 6:00 p.m. "What's Julie's schedule for the rest of the day?"

There was a pause. "Remedial algebra until one, second shift lunch until one thirty, instruction in the remedial arcane until three, social studies until four, and archery until five . . ."

"Does she take archery with the other children?"

"Yes. It's an outside activity."

If I hurried, I could get there before five. "Could you do me a favor? Please tell Julie at lunch, so the other children will hear, that her aunt is coming to pick her up during archery practice?"

"Absolutely."

"Thank you."

I hung up and saw Jim leaning against the doorframe. "Kid okay?"

"Yeah. I'm leaving to pick her up."

"I'll send someone with you."

"I don't need an escort."

Jim leaned his hands on the table and stared at me. "I assume the worst. If it was me, I'd have a way to track my dead. I'd track them here and watch the house. I'd follow you when you left and hit you when you're at your weakest—when you had the kid with you. You die. Julie dies. Derek dies. I don't tell you how to swing your sword. That's your thing. Security's my thing. Take someone with you."

My side had finally stopped bleeding. The magic of Doolittle's med-spell must've caught up and repaired the damage.

"Kerosene?" I asked.

He reached into the cabinet and handed me a bottle of lighter fluid and a box of matches. I went to the sink, dropped the gauze, sloshed fluid on it, and set it on fire. "Fair enough. Let me take Raphael."

"The bouda?" Jim's face wrinkled in distaste. "You want to bring a bouda into this?"

"None of you can go. In case you missed it, there is a Pack-wide APB out on you and your crew. But Curran would never give an order to apprehend me."

"You seem very sure of that."

I knew the way Curran's mind worked. Having me brought to him would not be as satisfying as catching me himself. He wouldn't give up that chance. Of course, saying that to Jim would lead to explaining the "not only will you sleep with me, but you'll say please before and thank you after" conversation Curran and I had had. And the insane morning antics. And the naked dinner promise. What the hell was I thinking kissing him anyway?

"I'm not under Curran's jurisdiction." I chose my words carefully. Hopefully he'd buy it. "He has no authority. Ordering the Pack to detain me would be sanctioning the kidnapping of a law enforcement official." Which wouldn't stop Curran for a second. "Let me take the bouda."

"What makes you think he won't turn us over to Curran?"

"He's in love with my best friend. I'll ask him to help me pick up Julie and that's all. Technically, he won't be aware he's helping you and your lot in any way."

Jim shook his head, dialed the number, and handed me the receiver. "You talk to him."

I listened to the ringtone. "Can you have horses waiting for us at the ley point in Macon? Something flashy that I wouldn't normally ride in a million years?"

Jim gave a fatalistic shrug. "Sure."

"Hello?" Raphael's smooth voice murmured into the phone.

"Raphael? I need a favor."

RAPHAEL WAITED FOR ME BY THE LEY LINE, LEANing against a Jeep. The Jeep had been modified to run on enchanted water and it looked like it had tried to vomit its engine through its hood.

Raphael looked ... There were no words. I had explained my plan on the phone and he had arrived wearing leather: black, shiny boots up to his knees, black leather pants that showed off his legs, and a black leather cuirass that molded to him like a second skin. A shotgun hung over his shoulder. An oversized sword, three feet long and nearly six inches wide, rested at his waist in a short sheath, completing his ensemble. The sword was too heavy for any normal human and covered with black runes etched into the upper portion of the blade. Coupled with the rich waterfall of Raphael's black hair and his smoky blue eyes, the effect was devastating. I wasn't sure what I needed more: a cardiac surgeon to restart my heart or a plastic one to reattach my jaw.

Two teamster ladies waited for their shipment on the ley line platform. They watched Raphael and did their best not to drool. As I neared, one of them, a redhead, nudged the other with an elbow, and said, "We're expecting a load of plug nickels from Macon."

Ammo. Bullets were an expensive commodity. Some merchants took slugs in lieu of money; that was how the term "plug nickels" had come about.

Raphael dazzled them with a smile. "Not a highwayman."

"Too bad," the redhead said. "Because you can hold up my shipment anytime."

Raphael bowed. The ladies looked close to fainting.

I marched over and stood next to him before the teamsters threw caution to the wind and jumped him right there on the platform. The redhead eyed me. "Killjoy."

I turned and gave her my hard stare. The teamsters moved to the other end of the platform. I didn't blame them. I was decked out. Unlike Raphael, who was shiny, I had gone for the solid, light-gulping black of treated leather, from the tips of my soft boots to the shoulders hidden by the dramatic cloak I had to borrow from Jim. I looked like a piece of darkness in the shape of a woman. Jim wasn't happy about letting me have the cloak either, but I had no clothes that would adequately serve my plan and no time or place to get them. All of us were living on a timer we'd borrowed from Derek, and his time was running out.

The cloak coupled with a black leather vest made me suitably menacing. All that was missing was a giant neon sign with rotating sparklers proclaiming HARD CASE. LINE TO GET YOUR ASS KICKED FORMS TO THE RIGHT.

A wide smile stretched Raphael's lips.

"If you laugh, I'll kill you," I told him.

"Why the rifle? Everybody knows you can't shoot."

Who were these everybodies and would they like to stand in front of me, preferably within ten feet, so I could discuss this issue in greater detail? "I can shoot just fine." I just missed eighty percent of the time. With the gun anyway. I did better with a crossbow and even better with the knife. "Do you know the runes on your sword are nonsense?"

"Yes, but they look mysterious."

Before us the ley line shimmered. Some poetic descriptions likened it to the rise of warm air above the heated asphalt. In reality the effect was more pronounced: a short, controlled spasm, as if an invisible vent slid open, belching a distorting blast, and abruptly closed. The ley current was no joke. The magic itself flowed about a foot and a half off the ground. It grabbed you and pulled you with it at speeds ranging from sixty to roughly a hundred miles per hour. Anything living dumb enough to step into the current had to wave bye-bye to the bloody stumps of its legs severed just below the knee. Most people used ley taxis, rough, wooden platforms cobbled together, but anything sturdy enough to support a body would do in a pinch. A vehicle. A surfboard. A piece of an old roof. I'd seen a guy ride on a ladder once. Not something I would try.

Raphael put the car in neutral. We rolled the vehicle across the platform to the ley line. The current jerked before us. I hopped into the cab and Raphael joined me a second later. The car slid into the ley line.

The magic jaws of the current snapped at us. My heart skipped a beat. The Jeep became utterly still, as if it were held immobile and the planet merrily rotated under it, speeding on its way.

Raphael pulled out a paperback and handed it to me. The cover, done back in the time when computer-aided image manipulation had risen to the level of art, featured an impossibly handsome man, leaning forward, one foot in a huge black boot resting on the carcass of some monstrous sea creature. His hair flowed down to his shoulders in a mane of white gold, in stark contrast to his tanned skin and the rakish black patch hiding his left eye. His white, translucent shirt hung open, revealing abs of steel and a massive, perfectly carved chest, graced by erect nipples. His muscled thighs strained the fabric of his pants, which were unbuttoned and sat loosely on his narrow hips, a touch of a strategically positioned shadow hinting at the world's biggest boner.

The cover proclaimed in loud golden letters: *The Privateer's Virgin Mistress*, by Lorna Sterling.

"Novel number four for Andrea's collection?" I guessed.

Raphael nodded and took the book from my hands. "I've got the other one Andrea wanted, too. Can you explain something to me?"

Oh boy. "I can try."

He tapped the book on his leather-covered knee. "The pirate actually holds this chick's brother for ransom, so she'll sleep with him. These men, they aren't real men. They're pseudo–bad guys just waiting for the love of a 'good' woman."

"You actually read the books?"

He gave me a chiding glance. "Of course I read the books. It's all pirates and the women they steal, apparently so they can enjoy lots of sex and have somebody to run their lives."

Wow. He must've had to hide under his blanket with a flashlight so nobody would question his manliness. Either he really was in love with Andrea or he had a terminal case of lust.

"These guys, they're all bad and aggressive as shit, and everybody wets themselves when they walk by, and then they meet some girl and suddenly they're not über-alphas; they are just misunderstood little boys who want to talk about their feelings."

"Is there a point to this dissertation?"

He faced me. "I can't be that. If that's what she wants, then I shouldn't even bother."

I sighed. "Do you have a costume kink? French maid, nurse . . ."

"Catholic school girl."

Bingo. "You wouldn't mind Andrea wearing a Catholic school uniform, would you?"

"No, I wouldn't." His eyes glazed over and he slipped off to some faraway place.

I snapped my fingers. "Raphael! Focus."

He blinked at me.

"I'm guessing—and this is just a wild stab in the dark—that Andrea might not mind if once in a while you dressed up as a pirate. But I wouldn't advise holding her relatives for ransom nookie. She might shoot you in the head. Several times. With silver bullets."

An understanding crept into Raphael's eyes. "I see."

"While we're on the subject, maybe you can clear something up for me as well. Suppose there is an alpha male. Suppose he decides he likes a female. How would he go about . . ." Courting, wooing? What was the right word here?

"Getting into her pants?" Raphael suggested.

"Yes. That."

He leaned back. "Well, you have to understand that boudas aren't jackals, and jackals aren't rats, and rats aren't wolves. Everybody has their own little quirks. But basically it's about proving that you're clever and capable enough and can provide for her and defend her and your cubs, should there be any."

"Does it involve breaking and entering?"

A little smile stretched Raphael's lips. "I see His Majesty made a move. Has he asked you to make him dinner yet?"

I growled. "This isn't about me and Curran."

He laughed softly. "Basically, yes. It's all about breaking and entering. The way the Pack is set up, all land belongs to the Pack as a whole. There is a bit of land around the meeting place of each clan that's traditionally held as that clan's exclusive domain, like those four square miles around

Bouda House. It's mostly a courtesy so the clan could meet in private. There is no clan territory and no individual territory, so your house becomes your territory. When you're pursuing a female, you're trying to prove that you're clever enough to get in and out of her territory."

"Aha."

"Like I said, people get really elaborate with it. It's a point of pride. And every clan has their own traditions. Rats are all about food. When Robert, the rat alpha, was trying to get Thomas to notice him, he stuffed his mattress with M&M'S. Direct, but it worked. They've been together for twelve years now. Wolves are all about class and propriety. Let's take Jennifer, the wolf alpha. She has all of those sisters—I think there are six of them altogether—and they meet twice a week for tea. They're English. She happened to mention to one of her friends that her dishes were all chipped and mismatched and she needed a new set. Daniel was courting her at the time. Wolves got that perfect memory thing. Apparently he broke into her house and replaced all of her dishes with an antique set in mint condition. She came home, opened the cabinets, and found everything exactly the way she had arranged it, every cup, every plate, nothing even an inch out of place. Except everything was brand new. She had a cup and a plate in the sink, and he even replaced those and filled them with water exactly the way he found them."

Raphael shrugged. "I thought it was a bit dry myself, but wolf girls raved about it for years. So classy and elegant and so sublime . . ." He rolled his eyes.

I couldn't resist. "What do boudas do?"

"We try to be funny." His eyes sparkled. "My mom had to go out of town, and while she was gone, my dad glued all of her furniture to the ceiling."

I pictured Aunt B walking into her house and finding all of her furniture upside down on the ceiling. Oh God. I couldn't help grinning. "What did your mom think about that?"

"She was pissed about the cat."

I stared at him. "Your dad . . . ?"

"Oh no." Raphael shook his head. "No, he didn't glue the cat to the ceiling—that would be cruel. But she had this wire-cage cat carrier, and he glued that to the ceiling and stuffed the cat into it."

I saw where it was going, but it was too good to interrupt and I tried to hold the laughter in.

"The cat got pissed off and peed all over the place, and because the carrier was upside down, it went straight through the bars. The ceiling fan was on at the time, and the draft made the pee into a sort of mist . . ."

I lost it and doubled over.

Raphael was grinning. "He tried to clean it up, but it got all over the carpet. It was a slight miscalculation on my dad's part. He wasn't a cat person, you see."

"That's hard to beat," I finally managed.

"Yeah."

"Are you going to do something for Andrea?"

His face took on a sly look. "I've been thinking about it. It would have to be really good."

I finally got the last laughter out of my system. "What do cats do?"

Raphael shook his head. "Cats are weird. There is no telling."

We lapsed into silence.

"So what did Curran do?" he asked finally.

I gave him the look designed to communicate the threat of certain and immediate death.

He shrugged it off. "Tell me. You owe me for coming with you on this trip. I could get hauled before Curran for aiding you and the cat."

"I never said I was helping Jim."

Raphael spread his arms. "Come on. I'm not an idiot. So what did the Beast Lord do?"

"This doesn't go any further. I mean it."

He nodded.

"He's been breaking into my place and watching me sleep."

A frown troubled Raphael's handsome face. "A bit straightforward. I wouldn't expect Curran to pull something elaborate, but that's too basic even for him. Has he done anything odd? Rearrange anything?"

"No."

The frown deepened.

I tapped my fingers on the wheel. "The whole point of the exercise seems to be letting the woman know you're coming into her territory and escaping unharmed."

Raphael nodded.

"I don't think Curran was ever planning on my finding out he was watching me. It just sort of slipped out. So what is the point of being clever if you don't let the woman know you're clever?"

"I don't know." Raphael looked at me helplessly. "I don't have a clue what's going through his head."

That made two of us.

CHAPTER 22

———◆———

THE WORLD CONSTRICTED. PRESSURE GRIPPED THE car, squeezing my body like a sponge. For a moment I felt like my atoms had edged together closer than the laws of physics would allow and then the ley line spat us out. The car rolled to a gentle stop, right past a dark-haired woman holding two black horses. I got out. Friesians. All about sixteen hands tall, huge, black, with flowing, wavy manes and long feathers of satiny midnight hair along their fetlocks. The knight horses. Powerful, beautiful, and impressive as hell. Thank you, Jim.

"Are those for us?"

The woman eyed me with open suspicion. "Name?"

"Kate Daniels."

"Then they're for you. This is Marcus and that over there is Bathsheba."

"I'll take the mare," Raphael said.

"Be careful with my babies."

"We're riding two miles down to the school and coming right back," I promised. "I'll have them back to you in an hour."

"Whole."

"In perfect health."

We mounted. The woman looked me over, studied Raphael, and snorted. "I should've brought a camera. A picture would've been a hell of a promotion."

Except it wouldn't have worked during magic, but I was too polite to point that out.

We trotted down to the path. Marcus proved ridiculously easy to handle, attuned to the most minute cues almost as if he was anticipating me. If I ever lost my mind and purchased a horse, I knew which one I would be getting.

In a few minutes we sighted the school. From horseback, the complex resembled a fortress, an octagon enclosed by an eight-foot wall complete with an arched entrance and a portcullis. A couple of guards patrolled the wall, and they didn't hesitate to level hunting bows at us. A sentry at the gates checked out my ID for a good twenty seconds—being dressed in black, riding black horses, and carrying black weapons had its drawbacks. Finally he nodded. "We're expecting you. Your girl is at the far end of the yard, to the left." He waved us through.

I urged Marcus on and he obliged, building to a thunderous canter. We pounded around the main building, my cloak dramatically flaring. A group of about twenty children stood a respectable distance from the striped disks of archery targets propped up near the wall. Four aimed their bows at the targets, while the rest waited in somewhat orderly fashion around an enormous elm tree under the gaze of a large man in chain mail and a small dark woman. Citlalli, the counselor. Perfect.

The kids sighted us and went very still. I scanned the crowd and saw a blond-haired girl, still too small and too thin for her thirteen years. There was my kiddo. Standing off by herself in the back.

We drew even with the group. Marcus danced under me, unhappy his run was brought short. I tried to look suitably lethal. Raphael glowered next to me. A hungry ruby sheen rolled over his eyes. The boys went pale. The girl-children valiantly tried to keep from swooning.

Julie finally woke up out of her stupor and elbowed her way to me.

I fixed her with my hard stare. She flinched.

"Knife," I ordered.

She reached into her clothes and produced one of my black throwing daggers. God damn it. I had counted them the other day and I could've sworn they were all there. I prayed for Marcus to stand still, took the dagger from her fingers, whipped about in the saddle, and threw it, all in a single quick motion. The dagger sliced into the elm's bark, sinking halfway in. Somebody gasped.

"You can have it back when you graduate."

Julie caught on. "Yes, ma'am."

She called me "ma'am." I waited for the sky to split and belch forth the four horsemen of the Apocalypse, but for some reason they failed to appear.

"It has come to my attention that you're talking."

"I'm sorry, ma'am."

"Do I have to remind you that you signed a nondisclosure agreement with the Order?"

Julie's face was the definition of remorse.

"It was your choice to attend this school. If I find out that you're divulging classified information again, I will pull you out and stick you into the Order's Academy faster than you can blink. Am I clear?"

"Yes, ma'am." Julie snapped to attention.

"You're coming with me."

"Should I get my things?"

"No, we have no time. The Pack requires immediate assistance." Derek required immediate assistance.

This was Raphael's cue to swing down from his saddle, which he accomplished with breathtaking grace. He came up to Julie and inclined his head in a nod that felt more like a shallow bow. "Julie. The Beast Lord inquires if you're well."

Julie favored him with a very polite bow. "I am. Please give His Lordship my thanks for his consideration."

"You can thank him yourself. He will be most pleased to see you."

Raphael leaned down, offering her his palm. Julie didn't miss a beat. She stepped onto his hand and let him hoist her up onto Marcus behind me. Her skinny arms locked around my waist.

Raphael took a short running start and leapt onto his horse, hands-free. We swung our mounts and took off. We cleared the gates, roared down the path and around the bend, out of sight of the walls, and slowed to a brisk walk.

"That was the coolest thing ever," Julie said breathlessly.

"It should up your street cred. But you're on your own from now on. I can't magically appear and overwhelm your classmates with toughness every time somebody is being a jerk. Now if somebody asks you about what happened, you very seriously tell them that you can't speak about it. People can't stand it when someone knows something they don't. It will drive them nuts."

She hugged me. "Thanks."

"I really do need your help."

"What's wrong?"

"Derek is in trouble."

"No," Julie whispered and hugged me tighter.

CHAPTER 23

JULIE CRIED. SHE KNELT BY DEREK'S MANGLED body and cried, silent tears rolling down her cheeks. I waited next to her. She needed to cry it out. It hurt to look at him and she had to get through it, or she wouldn't be able to help.

After about five minutes Julie stirred and swiped the back of her hand under her nose. I handed her a handkerchief. She wiped her eyes, blew her nose, and nodded. "Okay."

Jim and Doolittle approached from the doorway. I sensed others in the gloom, watching, Raphael being one of them. I had explained to him that aiding and abetting my sorry butt would land him into scalding water, but he'd just grinned and followed me and Julie all the way to the house. He and Jim had spoken for a couple of minutes and then he'd been allowed inside.

Jim crouched next to Julie and opened a small cookie tin. Two pale yellow shards lay inside on white gauze, one from the four-armed corpse which Dali had stumbled on,

and the other from Saiman's victim. Doolittle had found
the second shard during the autopsy, stuck in the Reaper's
arm. He and Jim tried to explain to me what the body reverted to after they took it out, but I couldn't quite wrap
my mind around it. Apparently, neither could they, because
they stuck it into a body bag, locked it in some room in
the basement, and strongly discouraged me from going to
see it.

Julie picked up the shard and concentrated, her gaze
fixed on the sharp sliver of yellow stone. She looked at it
for a long moment, dropped it into the tin, and looked at the
body.

"Here." Her slender finger pointed at Derek's mangled
thigh.

A scalpel flashed in Doolittle's dark fingers. He made a
neat incision, pulled it open with his fingers, and dipped
artery forceps into the cut. I held my breath.

He pulled the forceps free. A bloody shard gleamed under the harsh light of the lamp.

"Thank you, Jesus." Doolittle dropped the shard into the
tin.

It's over. Finally.

"Here." Julie pointed to Derek's left side.

Doolittle hesitated.

"Cut here." The pale finger touched Derek's ribs.

The doctor cut again. Another shard joined the first.

"Here." The finger pointed to the center of Derek's
chest, where the black burn scar crossed his pectorals.

Fuck, how many of those things did they stick into him?

Doolittle cut. "Nothing."

"Deeper," Julie said.

Dark blood gushed from the cut.

I flinched.

An eternity later Doolittle said, "Here it is." I heard the
quiet sound of the shard falling into the tin.

"Are there more?" Doolittle asked.

"No," Julie answered.

I looked up. Nothing had changed. Derek lay unmoving. "What now?"

"Now we wait," Doolittle said.

I SAT IN DARKNESS, IN A LOW CHAIR, WATCHING Derek's body. It had been three hours since Doolittle had removed the shards. Derek hadn't moved. His body showed no change.

In the room across the hallway Doolittle slept in a La-Z-Boy, his face haggard and worn-out even in his sleep. He'd stayed awake for two days straight, trying to keep Derek alive, but it was feeling helpless that finally did him in. For the first hour after Julie had found the shards, we waited on the edges of our seats. Then hope slowly turned into depression. I watched it take its toll on Doolittle until finally he abandoned his vigil and retreated into the room. I had checked on him on the way to the bathroom: he was slumped in his chair, sunken deep into a dream.

Julie appeared in the doorway, carrying two mugs. She approached, handed one cup to me, and sat by my feet. I sipped from the mug. Hot tea, with lemon. I had taught her how to make it properly. Apparently, it stuck.

"Why the cage?" she said, pointing to the hole in the floor, where the silver and steel bars glinted weakly. "I almost walked into it."

"It's a loup cage. Every shapeshifter safe house has one, just in case." If Derek went loup, Jim and Doolittle wanted to contain him quickly. It wasn't a thought I cared to contemplate. And certainly not a thought I cared to discuss with Julie.

"How did you meet?" she asked softly.

"Hm?"

"Derek and you. How did you meet?"

I didn't really want to talk about it. Still, it was better than wallowing in my despair. "I was looking for Greg's killer. The Order had given me the last file my guardian was working on, and I had retraced his steps, trying to find

out why he was killed. The file led me to the Pack. I didn't
realize this at the time, but Greg had worked very closely
with the Pack. There was a feeling of mutual trust between
him and the shapeshifters. But they didn't know anything
about me and I didn't know anything about them. I only
knew that Greg had been torn to pieces by somebody's
claws."

I took a swallow of my tea. "I had access to Jim—we
had worked together in the Guild—and Jim told Curran
about my investigation. Curran decided to find out what I
knew and had Jim arrange to meet me. In Unicorn Lane of
all places. It didn't go well."

Julie snorted quietly. "Big surprise."

"Yeah. Now when I look back at it, I realize it was a
test. His Furry Majesty was trying to gauge what I was
made of and I showed him." I shrugged. "Live and learn."
So many problems could've been avoided if I hadn't
crouched down in the darkness and called out, "Here, kitty,
kitty, kitty."

"What happened next?"

"Eventually the Pack invited me to one of their gather-
ings to discuss things in greater detail. You've seen how
they treat outsiders. Bite first, apologize later. They brought
me to their Keep in the middle of the night and led me underground to this huge room. I stepped inside and found
half a thousand shapeshifters and they weren't happy to see
me."

"Were you scared?"

"I was scared I'd blow it. I realized by this point that if I
couldn't get the Pack to work with me, I'd make things a
lot harder for myself. I had gone from a no-name merc to
making arrangements with the head of the People and the
Beast Lord, and I was seriously outclassed. I wasn't used
to that."

"I know what you mean," Julie murmured. "You try
your best and only make yourself feel stupid. Everybody
seems to know some sort of secret that you don't and that
makes them better than you."

I reached over and petted her wispy hair. "The school's that bad, huh?"

"Sometimes. It's okay usually. But there are mean people and they do nasty things, and if you call them on it, they make it seem like you just don't get it." She squeezed her hands into tight fists and said through clenched teeth, "They make me so mad. If we were on the street, I'd punch them. But if I do punch them, that will just mean I can't win by their dumb rules."

"Well, then you know exactly how I felt." I could do the punching. Punching was easy. It was the clever banter and dealing in convoluted half-truths and almost-lies that made me want to jump out of my skin.

"So what did you do?"

"I made my way down through the room, and this group of young shapeshifters barred my way and started making lots of noise. I knew Curran had put them up to it to see what I would do. One of them reached out and touched me, and I took him over with a power word and made him guard me against the rest."

"Derek," Julie guessed.

"Yep. And then it turned into this huge complicated deal, because Curran thought I was challenging him by taking his wolf . . ." I waved my hand. "In the end, Derek swore a blood oath to protect me so Curran wouldn't have to kill him. He's released from the oath now, but you remember how he is. He decided he's responsible for me and I feel responsible for his ass—"

With a hoarse scream, Derek jerked upright and ripped the IV tubes from his arms.

"Get Doolittle!" I lunged to the tank.

Gnarled hands gripped me. Deranged eyes flared white from the mangled face. He clawed at me, crushing my arms, agonizing screams ripping from him.

"Safe," I yelled into his ear. "It's okay, it's okay . . ."

His skin bulged, ready to rip. The dark slash of his mouth gaped open. "Hurrrts! Hurts, it hurts!"

And then Doolittle was there with a syringe and Raphael's long fingers clenched Derek's wrists, pushing pressure points to make him let go, but Derek hung on to me with desperate ferocity. The pull of his arms jerked me off my feet and dragged me into the vat. He clung to my shoulders, gouging my skin.

"Hurts!"

"Get her out!" Doolittle sank the needle into Derek's arm with no effect. "The pain's too much! He's going loup!"

Raphael wrestled Derek's arms, trying to separate him from me, but Derek just held on tighter. Doolittle dropped the syringe and grabbed Derek's left wrist. Fangs cut through Derek's disfigured lips.

"Get her out!" Doolittle screamed.

Someone thrust a piece of bloody meat into Derek's mouth. He released me and clutched on to the meat, shredding it. Bloody juice and flesh flew everywhere. I got the hell out of the vat.

On the other side of the tank, Jim dangled another raw rib eye before Derek. Derek snapped it from his fingers and ripped into it in a frenzy.

Jim's melodious voice was sweet like a lullaby. "Eat, wolf. Eat. Safe now. That's it. Eat. Leave the madness behind."

The terrible battered thing that was Derek snarled and stabbed the meat into its mouth. The eerie, juicy sounds of a predator feeding filled the room. I shook the green crap off my arms and caught sight of Julie in the doorway, pale like a wraith, eyes fixed on Derek.

Jim pushed her out of the way, stepped out of the room, and carried in a trough filled with hamburger meat. He set the trough on the floor. Derek went down on all fours. His broken legs gave out and he crashed face-first into the meat. I marched to the door and took Julie by the shoulder.

She tugged my hand off. "No."

"We don't need to see this."

In the corner Doolittle swung a heavy leather case onto the table and popped it open. Metal blades gleamed in a neat row.

"But . . ."

"No."

I pushed her out of the room. Raphael closed the door behind us and helped me carry screaming Julie away.

THE KITCHEN CABINETS CONTAINED WOODEN jars identified by handwritten adhesive labels. The jar labeled SUGAR had flour in it. The jar labeled FLOUR held an enormous amount of chili powder, which made me sneeze. The jar labeled CHILI PEPPER contained a Smith & Wesson M&P 45. I growled. I had fallen asleep next to Julie on the couch and woken up five hours later, unable to form rational thoughts because my head pounded.

"Looking for something?" Dali came up from the hallway.

"No, I'm dancing the can-can." Ask a dumb question . . .

Dali blinked at me. "Would you mind making coffee while you're dancing? I smell it on the bottom shelf, either first or second jar on the left."

I opened the first jar and looked inside. Coffee. The label said BORAX.

"What's up with the labels?"

Dali shrugged. "You're in the house of a cat whose job is to spy. He thinks he's clever. I'd be careful with the silverware drawer. There might be a bomb in it."

I extracted a small pot and set about boiling coffee.

"How's Derek?"

"I don't know. The door's still closed. They've been in there for hours."

The coffee foamed up. I held it away from the fire, put it back, and let it foam a second time. Dali got the cups. "I found out more about the jewel."

I poured coffee into her mug. Dali watched me do it. "I always spill half of it," she said. "Mine always runs down the side of the pot."

Manual dexterity—just about the only thing I was good at. "So what about the jewel?"

"A couple of old texts say that Rudra Mani has the power to calm beasts and take away the suffering of man."

A deeper meaning hidden in the description: the power to suppress a shapeshifter's animal nature and keep him locked in his humanity. "Does it? Take the suffering away, I mean?"

Dali looked into her coffee. "Having a shard in you is like having part of you cut off. It's a terrible feeling. I would prefer to be killed."

So would I in the same situation. It was akin to surrendering my magic. I hated the man who'd given it to me. Aspects of it repulsed me and I refused them. But it was a part of me. With it, I felt whole for better or for worse. Using magic made me the person I was born to be. Keeping people from being themselves drove them insane.

"Rudra is a one of Shiva's names," Dali said. "It means 'strict' or 'uncompromising.' "

How fitting. That was what the shapeshifters were, a compromise between beast and man. The gem forced them to become one or the other. I had been thinking about this on the way to the house, while riding the ley line. By then I had grown too numb to worry about Derek—I had described his condition for Julie and it had been like opening an old wound. At first there'd been the sharp slash of pain of a scab being ripped off, and then I'd bled, and the wound had gone numb.

I thought about the Order instead. About Ted and his true believer's inability to compromise. Ted wanted humans to remain human no matter the cost.

A dark storm gathered on the horizon of my mind, with Rudra Mani firmly in its center.

"Does the name 'Sultan of Death' sound familiar to you?" I asked.

Dali paused, considering, and shook her head. "I have no clue who that is."

That reminded me—I still hadn't checked on the analyses of the molten silver the rakshasas had poured onto Derek's face. The magic had fallen while I was asleep. I pulled the phone to me. Dial tone. Finally. The phone was one of those erratic devices that sometimes worked during magic. Most people had no idea how it worked. To them, it was almost magic, and sometimes magic waves shared that view.

I punched in Andrea's home number. She answered on the second ring. "Hey."

"Hey."

"I've got your results right here," she said. Not a hint of humor in her voice. "It's not silver. It's electrum."

Electrum, a naturally occurring alloy of silver and gold with a pinch of copper thrown in, was incredibly potent magically. It was also extremely toxic to shapeshifters.

"You don't rank high enough to know the rest, so they won't tell you," Andrea said, "but I do. This particular alloy is very old and very poisonous to shapeshifters. You know how high my silver tolerance is. I can't even hold it, Kate. Do you remember the agreement we made during the flare?"

"Yes." We had agreed that I would never reveal to the Order that she was a beastkin and she would never reveal that I knew enough specific information about Roland to induce a collective seizure in the entire Order.

"There is only one person who has access to this alloy in a large quantity. The composition is very specific. It's—"

"About fifty-five percent gold, forty-five percent silver, three percent copper, and the rest is random crap."

"Yes."

Samos electrum, from the coins struck on a small Greek island in the North Aegean Sea in 600 BC. My heart dropped. Logic had lost and my unreasonable paranoia had triumphed.

"I guess you know what that means, then," she said.

"Yes. Thank you," I said.

"Be careful."

I hung up.

Roland. Only he had a large supply of the ancient Samos electrum. No doubt he meant for it to be used sparingly, perhaps as bullets or stakes, but instead the rakshasas had melted the lot of it just so they could pour it on Derek's face. Dumb.

Roland was the Sultan of Death. If I continued to oppose the rakshasas, I would come into a confrontation with his agents. I would be discovered.

"Are you alright?" Dali asked.

"Never better," I said.

A hot anger swept through me. If I was discovered, I would fight him to the end with everything I had, just like my mother had. I was fucking tired of paranoia and panic. It was an irrational, totally idiotic thought, and I reveled in it.

Jim came up the stairs. "He's up and talking."

I rushed down, abandoning my coffee.

CHAPTER 24

HE SAT ON THE BED, HIS LEGS COVERED BY A BLUE sheet. He was human and his color had returned to its normal skin tone. His hair was still dark brown. And that was about all that remained of the former Derek.

His face had lost its perfect symmetry. Its lines, so sharply defined before, had thickened and grown harsher. His features gained a rough hardness, and from the top of his mouth to his hairline, his face seemed slightly uneven, as if the shattered bones of his skull didn't quite mesh. Before if he walked into a rough bar, someone would whistle and tell him he was too pretty. Now people would stare into their drinks and whisper to one another, "Here's a guy who's been through some bad shit."

He looked up. Dark velvet eyes regarded me. Usually a hint of sly humor hid there behind the solemn composure of a Pack wolf. It was gone now.

"Hi, Kate."

His lips moved but it took me a second to connect the low, raspy voice with Derek's mouth.

"Damaged vocal cords?" I asked.

He nodded.

"It's permanent," Doolittle said softly. He stepped out of the room and closed the door. It was me and Derek now.

I perched on the side of the bed. "You sound like you kill people for a living," I told him.

"I look like it, too." He smiled. The effect was chilling.

"Is there a spot on you that's safe to punch?"

"Depends on who'll be doing the punching."

"Me."

Derek winced. "Then no."

"Are you sure? I have a lot of baggage to release from the past couple of days." My voice was breaking. I struggled for control.

"Positive."

All of my guilt, all of my worry, all the anxiety and pain and regret, everything I had carefully packaged and stuffed away into the deepest recesses of myself so I could function, all of it swelled into an unbearable pressure. I fought to contain it, but it was like trying to hold back the tide. A hint of relief was all it took. The flood burst through my defenses and drowned me.

My spine turned to wet cotton. I clamped my arms to my sides, trying to hold myself rigid and keep myself from slumping over. A hard, hot clump blocked my throat. My heart thudded. It hurt, it really hurt, and I didn't even understand where the pain emanated from. I just knew I hurt all over. Cold and burning up at the same time, I had to clench my teeth to keep them from chattering.

"Kate?" Derek's alarmed voice demanded my attention. If only I could speak, I'd be okay.

I wished I could cry or something; I needed, desperately wanted, a release, but my eyes were dry and that pressure remained locked in me, battering me with pain.

Derek pushed from the pillow toward me. He'd gone pale, his new face rigid like a mask. "I'm sorry."

He put his forehead against my hair, his arms around my shoulders. I hung suspended in my own painful world, like a speck in a storm.

"You can't do this to me again." My voice sounded rusty, as though it hadn't been used in years. "You can't show me you're in trouble but not let me help. Not let me do anything."

"I won't," he promised.

"I can't deal with the guilt."

"I promise, I won't."

Everyone I dared to care about died, violently and in pain. My mother died putting a knife into Roland's eye, because he wanted to kill me. She was stolen from me before I had a chance to remember her. My dad died in his bed. I didn't even know how or why. He had sent me on a training run, three days in the wilderness, just me and a knife. The smell had hit me ten yards from the front door. I found him in his bed. He was bloated. His skin had blistered and fluids had leaked from his body. He'd disemboweled himself—the sword was still clamped in his hand. I was fifteen.

Greg died on assignment. We'd had a fight a few weeks before his death and we didn't part on good terms. He was ripped to pieces, his body shredded as if it had gone through a cheese grater.

Bran was stabbed through the back. He was almost immortal, and still he died, in my arms. I so desperately tried to keep him alive, I nearly brought him into undeath.

It was as if Death stalked me, like a cruel and cowardly enemy, taunting me, eating away at the edges of my world by stealing those I cared about. It didn't just kill; it obliterated. Every time I got distracted, it would snatch another friend from me and destroy him.

Derek had fit that pattern to a T. A part of me had known with absolute certainty that he would die just like the others. I had imagined it so vividly, I could picture myself standing over his corpse.

Explaining all this would be tedious and painful. "I thought you would die," I said simply.

"I did, too. I'm sorry."

We sat for a long time. Finally when the storm inside me calmed, I stirred, and Derek let go and turned away, hiding his face. When he looked back at me, he'd put his Pack wolf composure back on.

"Some hard-asses we are."

"Yeah. We're tough," he said with a grimace.

"Tell me about the girl."

"Her name's Olivia," he said. "Livie. I met her at the Games. She'd slip away once the bouts started and we'd talk. She's young. Her parents have money. They love her, but she was unhappy."

"Poor little rich girl?"

He nodded. "Livie never knew her real dad. Her mom married her stepdad when she was two. She said her mom dressed her up like a little doll. They both treated her like she was a golden child. Like she was special. And then she grew up and realized she was pretty but not that special: not that bright, not that talented, not gifted with magic. She told me she'd make up stories about her dad being some magic prince."

"She wanted very much to be more than what she was?" I guessed.

Derek nodded.

It was hard to grow up believing yourself to be a star and smash headfirst into the realization that only your parents thought you were one.

"She got herself a 'special' rich boyfriend. She didn't even like him that much, but he treated her like she was walking on clouds, just like her mom. He brought her to the Games and they ran into the Reapers. The Reapers recognized her. Jim said you know about rakshasas. Well, they told her she was half. If she joined them, they'd let her go through this rite to unlock her powers. She would be able to change shapes like them and to fly. There was one catch: once she started the rites, she couldn't stop."

A sick feeling claimed my stomach. "Did she agree?"

"She did." Derek grimaced. "She said she wanted to go back to the clubs where all her friends hung out and show off her new powers."

"That's shallow and stupid."

He nodded. "I know."

"Did she complete the rite?"

"Not yet. It's long, takes several weeks. They started her on small stuff. Killing some animals. At first she liked it a little. I could tell by the way she told me—she was excited, proud of herself. She thought she was hard-core. But it got real bad in a hurry."

"How bad?"

"They made her do some really sick shit." Derek shrugged. "Some of it might have been for a purpose, but some . . . They made her torture other rakshasas who needed punishment. I don't know if the rites were actually meant to unlock anything. I think they just got off on watching her pervert herself. She decided she couldn't take it anymore."

"Only there's no way out," I said.

"Yeah. She asked me for help. I told her I'd help her, but alone I wouldn't be enough. It would have to be a trade for the Pack to be involved. She agreed to tell us everything about the rakshasas and the Diamond. She said some mysterious guy made a deal with them. They're supposed to get the Wolf Diamond and use it against the Pack. She'd tell us all about it if we got her out." He sighed. "Most of the rest you already know. I went to Jim with it, and he said no and cut me off. I went to Saiman to steal the tickets, gave you the note, arranged for the transport, and headed to the spot to pick her up. When I got there, they were waiting for me. At least I put up a good fight."

"Was she there?"

He nodded.

"What did she do?"

"She watched," he said.

"Didn't try to help? Didn't protest?"

He shook his head.

"Tell me about the beating."

"They jumped me, four on one. I had two shards in me with the first punch. Then there was more of them. Cesare, the big one with tattoos, supervised it. His ink slides off his body and twists into snakes with several heads. When they bite, it burns like ice. Not much to tell. I fought. I lost. It hurt."

Cesare was going to die.

"You're going after the girl?" I asked, even though I knew the answer.

"As soon as I'm strong enough. Shouldn't be long now. Doc says that the virus in my body was suppressed but it still multiplied while the shards were embedded. Now I'm healing at a record rate. I'll be on my feet in a few hours."

"You understand that she doesn't love you?" I kept my voice calm.

"I know that." He swallowed. "For the final rite, she has to eat a human child. She'll do it because she is weak and then there will be no turning back."

"If your roles were reversed, she wouldn't do the same for you. She's using you."

"It doesn't matter what she does. It only matters what I do."

He quoted me. Nice. Hard to argue with your own words.

I dreaded what I had to say next, but it needed to be said. "Rescuing her won't resurrect your sisters."

He winced. "I was weak back then. I couldn't do anything. I tried, but I couldn't. I'm stronger now."

And there it was. Four years of being trapped in a house with a loup father who raped, tortured, and ate his children one by one, with Derek powerless to do anything about it. He saw his sisters in Livie's face. He couldn't let go any more than I could let go of my blood debts. He would persist until the rakshasas killed him.

THE INVALID DECIDED HE WANTED TO BE MOBILE and I lent him my shoulder. Together we managed the trip to the kitchen, where Jim, Dali, Doolittle, and Raphael were eating little chocolate cookies. Dali was nursing another cup of coffee next to Jim.

Across the table, Raphael was playing with a steak knife. The good doctor on his right looked like a man who'd run to Marathon and then was told he had to run back. He saw Derek and his eyes bulged. "So help me God, I shall have to kill you myself, boy. What are you doing out of bed?"

Derek grinned. Dali winced. Doolittle's eyes bulged a bit more. Jim remained stoic and Raphael just smiled.

I deposited Derek into a chair. "Why is it that you always gather in the kitchen?"

Dali shrugged. "That's where the food is."

Jim glanced at me. "We must get the Diamond."

"Agreed. The Diamond is too dangerous to the Pack. The rakshasas intend to use it as a weapon against you." I stole a cookie from the stash. "We have to get the Diamond. And Cesare's head."

They looked at me.

"Why the head?" Doolittle asked.

"Because it's easy to carry and I can torture it for a long time." And I didn't just say it out loud, did I? I checked their faces. Yep, I did.

"How do you torture a head?" Dali asked.

"You resurrect it and make it relive its death."

Jim cleared his throat. "We can't steal the Diamond and we can't buy it."

"The only way to get it is through the Games," Raphael said. Apparently Jim had brought him up to speed.

"You got something in mind?" Jim asked me.

"The tournament begins the day after tomorrow. It's a team event. We get Saiman to enter us into it."

"What makes you think he'll do it?" Jim asked.

"The question is, how did the shards get from the gem to the rakshasas? Somebody is helping them. Somebody with access to the stone. Saiman hates them. They threatened him, attacked him, and embarrassed him by killing his minotaur."

Dali came to life. "He had a minotaur?"

"Yep. He dragged him here all the way from Greece and Mart nuked him in ten seconds flat. Saiman hates the Reapers." I smiled. "But he can't really do that much to them. Once he finds out that somebody provided the Reapers with shards, he'll be livid. We offer him two things: a chance to go against the Reapers in the Pit, and an opportunity to find out who within the House is aiding them and why. He won't pass it up."

"Okay," Jim said. I realized he had already worked through it in his head. Why exactly was he using me for his mouthpiece?

"What about Livie?" Derek asked.

"They are very arrogant." I glanced to Dali for confirmation. She nodded. "Once they recognize you, chances are they will surmise we have entered the tournament to rescue her and will bring Livie out to taunt us. That's our only shot at her, because there is no way we could storm their flying barn and survive."

"They should be too overconfident to pass it up," Dali said.

"Once we go in, there is no turning back," Jim said. "It's the Reapers inside and Curran outside. If you're going to back out, now is the only time you can do it."

The kitchen fell silent. They mulled it over.

Jim reached behind him and handed me the phone from the counter. I dialed Saiman's number. He picked up immediately. It took me less than a minute to outline my proposal.

Ominous silence claimed the other end of the phone.

"How sure are you of this?" he said finally.

"I'm in possession of five shards and two corpses," I told him. "You're welcome to examine them if you wish. Can you get us into the Games?"

"This is rather short notice," Saiman said. "But yes. I can. Provided I go as Stone."

"Done," I said.

"You'll need seven fighters."

I made writing motions. Everybody except the doctor looked for a pencil.

"I've never seen such a collection of idiots in my whole life." Doolittle shook his head. "If you participate in this lunacy, y'all will get yourselves killed. Then don't come crying to me."

Now that would be a neat trick.

Dali handed me a pencil. No paper materialized and I scribbled on the tablecloth.

"Stratego, Stone, Sling, Swordmaster, Shield, Shiv, and Spell. They must all be at the Games by tonight at nine p.m. We'll be sequestered for the duration of the Games. Once you enter, there is no going back, Kate. You don't get to change your mind and go home. You fight until you can't continue."

"Understood."

"You need a name."

I covered the receiver for a moment. "We need a team name."

"Hunters," Raphael said.

"Valiant Knights of the Fur," Dali said.

"Justice Group," Jim said. "Since Justice League is taken."

"Fools." Doolittle shook his head.

"Fools," I said into the receiver.

"Fools?" Saiman asked.

"Yes."

"It will be arranged, then. The crew?"

"We'll have a doctor," I said.

"No, you won't!" Doolittle declared.

"Very good," Saiman's tone was brisk. "Remember, every member of the team must be there by nine. Don't be late."

I hung up.

Jim looked at the list. "The freak is Stone. Kate, you'll take Swordmaster. Derek?"

"Shield," Derek said. "Defensive fighter."

"Will you be able to fight in two days' time?"

He smiled. Dali winced again and said, "You have to stop doing that."

"You should take Stratego," I told Jim. "You have the most experience."

That left us with three.

Raphael's knife touched the list. "Shiv," he said. "Fast fighter."

"Are you sure?" I glanced at Raphael.

"If the lot of you survives, Curran will flay the skin off your backs," Doolittle said.

"That's what I always love about you, Doctor." Raphael grinned. "You're a cup-halfway-full kind of guy. All flowers and sunshine."

"He isn't joking, Raphael. You don't have to do this." I looked at him.

Raphael's smile got wider. "I'm a bouda, Kate. I've got no principles and no honor, but you scratch one of our own, and I'll kill you."

"I'm touched," Derek quipped. "I didn't know you cared."

"About you? I don't give a fuck." Raphael looked slightly deranged. "No, I care about her. They tried to kill her in a parking lot."

"Since when am I beloved by boudas?"

"Since you drove one of us through the flare so she wouldn't die," Raphael said. "Nobody would do that for us. Not even the other clans. Ask the cat."

Jim didn't say anything.

"I'll take Shiv." Raphael tapped the list again. "Andrea will take Sling. Don't argue, Kate. She'll shoot us both if we keep her out."

"Andrea is a knight of the Order," I said. "I don't think she can compete."

"Neither can any of us," Raphael countered and reached for the phone.

"That leaves Spell," Jim said.

We stared at it. Spell. Obviously a magic user. "Any of your crew?"

Jim shook his head.

"You should ask him where his crew is." Doolittle's face wrinkled in disgust. "Go on. Tell her."

Jim didn't look like he wanted to tell me anything.

"Where is Brenna?"

"On the roof, keeping a lookout," Jim said,

"And the rest?" Come to think of it, I hadn't seen any of them since we came out of Unicorn.

"Apparently there is a band of loups near Augusta." Doolittle leveled an outraged glare at Jim. "I've been listening to it on the radio. The city's on the verge of panic. Odd loups these. Mellow. Although they apparently performed shocking acts of animal mutilation within plain view of the farmhouse, the farmer's family slept through the whole thing. Curiously, no humans were harmed."

I almost laughed. No loup would attack livestock if human prey was available. They craved human flesh.

"They're creating a diversion," Jim said.

Raphael halted his conversation with Andrea to emit a short, distinctly hyena guff. "That's the best plan you could come up with?"

"Apparently he thinks that Curran's a moron." Doolittle shook his head.

"I'll take Spell," Dali said.

The kitchen was suddenly silent.

"I can do it. I was taught."

"No," Jim said.

"You have nobody else." Dali's jaw took on a stubborn tilt. "I'm not a fragile flower. I can do this."

"What do you do?" I asked.

She drew herself to her full height. "I curse."

"This isn't a game. You can die in that Arena," Jim snarled.

"I'm not playing," Dali snarled back.

Brenna burst through the door. "Curran!"

Oh shit.

Everybody jumped to their feet. "How close?" Jim growled.

"Two blocks, coming fast. He's heading straight for us."

"Back door! Now!" Jim ordered. "Kate—"

I shook my head. "Take Derek and go. He can't get you out of the Arena. I'll delay him. Go!"

Jim swiped Derek into his arms like a child and took off. The rest followed, including Doolittle. They galloped down the stairs, right past Julie, who stumbled to the hallway, her face looking like she had slept on it. I grabbed her by the shoulder. "Get out the back door and hide someplace close until you see me come out."

She took off without a word. That was my kid.

I FINISHED ARRANGING THE BLANKET AND A PIL-low on the floor to make it look like someone had slept there. I stepped away to admire my handiwork. Good enough. I took out Slayer and backed away. About a foot from the blanket should do it . . .

The door burst off its hinges and flew into the room, revealing Curran. His teeth were bared in a snarl and his eyes were feral. He was wearing the Pack's trademark sweatpants and a T-shirt. Bad. Very bad. Sweatpants meant he expected to change shape. Curran in a warrior form was my ultimate nightmare.

Curran bared his fangs. "Kate."

"Took you long enough."

"Where are they?"

I arched my eyebrow. "Why would I tell you?"

"Kate, don't make me force you to answer." The muscles in his thigh tensed, straining the fabric of his sweatpants.

"What happened to your seduction plan? Or are you man enough to come close only when you've kicked my sword under my bed, where I can't reach it?"

He cleared the room in a single leap. I jumped up and kicked him in midair as hard as I could. My foot collided with his chest. Like kicking a brick wall. He dropped on the makeshift bed. The blanket gave and he crashed down into the loup cage sunken deep into the floor.

I slammed the top frame shut. The complex lock clicked closed and I slid the thick bars in place, locking it down.

Curran ripped apart the blanket. His face was pure rage. He grasped the bars and recoiled.

I sat on the edge of the floor and rubbed my leg. It had gone numb from kicking him. I'd have to thank Julie for this idea. She'd almost fallen into the cage twice.

He snarled and clasped the bars. I had to give it to Curran—he lasted a full five seconds. The bars bent under the pressure but held. Made to withstand the fury of an insane shapeshifter, the cage had enough silver to burn the skin off a shapeshifter's hands. When Curran let go, gray stripes of flesh marked his palms.

Curran cursed. "It won't hold me."

No doubt. Good that it wasn't meant to hold him, only to delay him. The feeling still hadn't returned into my leg.

Gold flared in Curran's eyes. His voice became a bestial growl. "Unlock it."

The force in his eyes was so intense, I thought my heart would stop. "No."

"Kate! Release me."

"Not a chance."

"When I get out, I'll make you regret this."

I frowned. "When you get out, I'll be in the Arena of the Midnight Games, probably on my way to becoming a fresh corpse. I'll be regretting a whole lot of things, but you in this cage won't be one of them."

Curran stepped back. The rage vanished from his face. He simply quashed it, pulling calm composure on like a helmet. It had never failed to terrify me before, and it did so now.

"Very well." He sat cross-legged on the floor of the cage. "You haven't run off so you want to talk. I will hear your explanation now."

"Really, Your Majesty? So good of you to condescend. I'll try to use small words and go slow."

"You're wasting my time. I know Jim betrayed me and you're covering for him. This is your chance to dazzle me with your brilliance or baffle me with your bullshit. You won't get another. When I get out, I won't be in the mood to listen."

"Jim didn't betray you. He worships the ground you walk on. They all do and I don't understand why. It's the great mystery of the universe. But nobody betrayed you. They did it to spare you."

I unloaded. I told him the whole story. He said nothing. He just sat and listened to me, emotionless and arctic.

"Are you finished?" he asked at the end.

"Yes."

"So let me make sure I understood you. My chief of security deliberately and knowingly disobeyed my first law, because he thought he knew better than me, dragged one of my best people into it, and got him permanently disfigured, beaten, and nearly killed. And he didn't tell me?"

The lion roar vibrated in his voice.

"Then he convinced you to cover up for his insubordination, and together you attacked a group of mythological killers, aggravating the conflict between them and my Pack instead of repairing the damage. And now he and three others are going to willfully and knowingly break my law again, flaunting it before thousands of people, so there is absolutely no possible way I can sweep it under the rug, even if I had the slightest inclination to do so, which I don't. Have I gotten it right?"

"Well, yes, it sounds bad when you say it like that."

He leaned back and took a deep breath, exhaling slowly. If the cage fell apart at this point, overwhelmed by his fury, I wouldn't be surprised.

"Curran, the gem is dangerous. I think that Roland is the Sultan of Death, and if I'm right, that means you've grown too powerful to be ignored. He will keep trying to eliminate you. The Wolf Diamond is trouble in the hands of the rakshasas, but it would be even more trouble in the hands of the People or the Order. Rakshasas aren't too bright. Roland is a genius. And it's not just him. If the Order got their hands on it, they would try to duplicate its magic and then inoculate your people with it. It's a key to genocide against your kind."

"And you care why?"

"Because I don't want to see you hurt. Any of you. My best friend is beastkin. They will plug a shard into her in a minute. Andrea might not like her animal side, she might reject it, but the choice to do so should be hers."

Pushing the words out was like trying to carry a rock the size of a house up a mountain. "I should've come to you. I would have if we hadn't found a cure. Anyway, I'm sorry. I tried to help my friends. I don't have many and ... you should've seen Derek. I thought he was dying. I could actually picture myself burying his corpse. You'd have to kill him if he'd turned loup and ... I didn't want to see you hurt." I turned away. "Julie will let you out of the cage in one hour."

He didn't say anything as I left the room. He just sat in the cage, his eyes blazing with towering wrath.

Outside Julie emerged from her hiding spot between the buildings and ran up to me.

"The Beast Lord is locked in a loup cage upstairs. Here is the key." I handed her the big steel key. "Put it into the keyhole, do a quarter turn, then release the top bar, so you can swing the top open. Curran knows how to open one; he'll guide you through it. Wait one hour before you let him out. This is very important, Julie. Don't go near him before then, because he'll talk you into opening the cage. Okay?"

She nodded.

"Once you're done, if he lets you get away, call this number." I handed her a piece of paper. "That's Aunt B's phone. Explain that you are alone. Someone will come and pick you up."

"I want to come with you."

"I know. I'm sorry, but you can't. It's not a good place and I might not get out of there in one piece." I hugged her. "One hour."

"One hour," she agreed.

I went to get a horse stabled in the lot. Too late I realized that Curran had found us before the three days were up. Oh well. I seriously doubted he would call in the bet. Not after our last encounter. And if he did and I somehow managed to survive this mess, serving a dinner to him naked would be the least of my problems.

CHAPTER 25

———◆———

I HAD TO WAIT IN THE LOBBY WHILE RENE PRE-
tended to find my name on the roster of fighters. "Fools,"
she said, flipping through the pages. "Is that a description
of your team's intelligence or your need to amuse?"

"It's our motto."

"Hmmm. . . ." She pretended to leaf through paperwork.

"You like screwing with me, don't you?"

She offered me a mordant smile. "Just doing my job
properly. Like you told me."

She'd keep me waiting for a while.

I should've kissed Curran before I left. What did I have
to lose anyway?

It wasn't even real. The thing between me and Curran.
It wasn't real. I deluded myself. I had this aching need to
be loved and it was screwing with my head. Sometimes,
when you crave certain feelings, you'll trick yourself into
thinking the other person is something other than what
he appears. I'd played that game with Crest and gotten
burned for my trouble. No, thank you. To Curran, I offered
nothing more than a willing body and a sense of satisfac-

tion in having won. That was reality, cold and ugly and inescapable.

Rene's hand went to her sword. I turned.

The dark-haired swordsman I had met on the observation deck during my first visit to the Games with Saiman strode through the door. Same gray leather. Same dark cloak that put me in mind of a warrior-monk. Same supple grace. Two men accompanied him, wearing identical cloaks. The first was young and blond. A long scar sliced his neck. His dark eyes had the alertness of a trained killer. The second man was older and harder. I looked into his eyes. His stare made me want to take a step back.

Nick.

The knight-crusader. The Order prized accountability and public exposure, but some things were too ugly, too dark, even for the knights. When one of those shadowy problems reared its head, the Order threw a crusader at it. The crusader did the job and left town.

The Red Stalker who killed my guardian had been such a problem. It had required Nick's involvement. Now he looked at me like he'd never seen me before. I did my best to do the same.

Whatever Nick was up to, he was obviously undercover.

The swordsman saw me. "Have we met before, my lady?"

His voice was low and gentle. He talked like a well-fed wolf in a good mood. I smiled at him. "If we'd met, you'd know I'm not a lady."

His eyes narrowed. "And yet you seem familiar somehow. I can't shed the feeling I have seen you before. Perhaps we could speak someplace privately—"

"You don't have to speak to him," Rene cut in. Her color had gone pale. She swallowed. Scared, I realized. She was scared and she wasn't used to dealing with it.

"Remember our arrangement. You're welcome to observe and that's it. We aren't a training ground for you. If you want to contact fighters outside the Arena, it's your business. Don't recruit them here. Especially in front of me."

"Are you a fighter, my lady?"

And we're back to the "lady" again. "Occasionally."

"She's on a team and you're holding up her processing."
Rene stared at him.

The man glanced at her. The command in his glare was
unmistakable. Rene went white as a sheet but stood her
ground. He smiled amicably, bowed to us, and went on, the
blond and Nick behind him.

Rene stared after him with undisguised hatred.

"What's his name?" I asked Rene.

"Bastard," Rene murmured, scanning the papers. "He
also goes by Hugh d'Ambray."

The world fell apart.

Hugh d'Ambray. Preceptor of the Order of Iron Dogs.
My adoptive father, Voron's, best pupil and successor. Hugh
d'Ambray, Roland's Warlord.

It couldn't be a coincidence. Everyone knew Roland
would eventually seek to expand his territory. Right now he
held an area that cut diagonally through Iowa to North Da-
kota. Voron had explained it to me: it was land that nobody
wanted, where Roland could sit and build up his forces
without presenting enough of a threat to warrant an inva-
sion. Eventually, when his forces grew numerous, he would
spread east or west.

I tried to think like Roland. I was raised by Voron, damn
it. I should be able to slide into Roland's head. What did he
want in Atlanta?

The Pack. Of course. Over the past year, the Pack had
grown in size. It was now the second largest in North
America. If I were Roland, I would seek to eliminate it
now, before it grew any stronger. He didn't wish to involve
the People, his cohorts, because their actions would be
tracked back to him. No, he hired rakshasas instead. Rakshasas were dumb and vicious. He could use them like a
club to clobber the Pack. They wouldn't win, but the Pack
would be weakened. And his Warlord was here to make
sure things went smoothly.

Hugh d'Ambray would watch me in the Pit. He might

recognize my technique. He would report to Roland, who would put two and two together and come looking for me.

The doors were right behind me. Fifteen steps and I would be out of the building. A minute and I would be on my horse, riding into the night. I could vanish and they would never find me.

And abandon the six people who counted on me to watch their back.

Walking away was so easy. I looked up.

"You look like your house burned down," Rene observed.

"Just reflecting on the fact that when the Universe punches you in the teeth, it never just lets you fall down. It kicks you in the ribs a couple of times and dumps mud on your head."

"If you're lucky, it's mud. Sign here." Rene stuck a form in a clipboard in front of me. "Waives all responsibility for your death in the Pit."

I signed. Within two minutes I was weaving my way through the bottom level, accompanied by a somber Red Guard. The worry sat like a ball of ice in the pit of my stomach. I had no trouble finding the right room—I heard Andrea's voice. "Sling?"

"It's just a figure of speech," Raphael said.

I ducked into the room and saw her before a table. Firearms covered the table's surface: her two prized SIG-Sauers, a couple of Colts, Beretta, Smith & Wesson . . . She had enough weapons to hold off a small army. Raphael watched her from the bench, his face an odd meld of awe and worry.

Andrea saw me and grinned. "You know what they can do with their sling? They can stick it up their asses!"

I tried to sound smart. "Well, technically it's more of a ranged weapon, Andrea . . ."

"Screw you! I'm not going out there with a little rag and a pebble."

Raphael looked a little scared.

I crossed the room to stow my gear on the shelves. The

double doors to the bedroom were wide open and I saw Derek in one of the bunks reading a book. Doolittle hovered next to him, with a concerned look that would've done a mother hen proud.

"He's hovering," Derek said.

"I'm not hovering," Doolittle grumbled.

Derek looked at me.

"You're definitely hovering," I said. "So you decided to join us after all? I thought you said we were all fools."

"No fool like an old fool . . ." Derek murmured.

Doolittle made a long, pissed-off sound, like the growl of a bear—if the bear was about a foot tall.

"Badger!" I smiled. It fit him.

Derek rolled his eyes. "What, you just now figured it out? It's not like you can miss the musk . . ."

"Now that was uncalled for." Doolittle shook his head. "Ungrateful wretch."

I pulled a blanket and a pillow from an unclaimed bunk and took myself to an empty corner.

"What's wrong with the bed?" Derek asked.

"I don't sleep well with others." I fixed my bed on the floor. "No, I take it back; I sleep well. I just might wake up with my sword in your gut. Of course, if it is you, I'd probably roll over and go back to dreamland."

Jim came into the room, approached the beds, tensed, and hopped onto the top bunk from the floor. From there he had an excellent view of the room.

"Where is Dali?" I asked him.

"In the hot tub." Jim shrugged, his face tainted with feline disgust. "There is one adjacent to the locker room. If there is an inch of running water, she'll crawl into it. Tigers."

"I didn't know jaguars minded water." I had seen him swim before. He seemed to enjoy it.

"I don't mind swimming if there are fish or frogs involved."

Jaguar logic for you. "Everyone made it?"

"Except for the freak."

Knowing Saiman, he probably had to hire extra help to carry all his clothes.

Dali entered the room, modestly wrapped in a towel, which she immediately dropped to wave at me, and began to dress.

Derek raised his head, suddenly alert. "Incoming. Several people."

Rene appeared in the doorway. "Your owner sends his apologies. It seems your original Stone won't be joining you, but Durand sent in a substitute." She stepped aside. "In you go."

A familiar figure blocked the doorway. My feet froze to the floor.

"Play nice," Rene said and departed.

Funereal silence descended upon the room. Nobody moved.

"All right," Curran said. "Let's talk."

He took Raphael by his arm, dragging him off the bench like he was a day-old kitten. He swiped naked Dali with his other hand, brought them both to the bedroom, and shut the doors behind him.

ANDREA SAT DOWN ON THE BENCH, FACING THE door. She put one SIG-Sauer on each side. Her face wore a grim expression.

"If he injures Raphael, I'm going to shoot him. Just letting you know."

"You changed your mind about Raphael?"

"I'm still deciding," she said. "And I'm not going to let the Beast Lord take it from me by crippling him."

"Aim for the nuts," I advised and left.

I wandered through the hallway to the Gold Gate. The huge chamber of the Arena lay empty. Nothing but me and the sand.

I crossed the floor to the wire door and stepped into the Pit. The sand lay placid. In my dreams it was always splattered with blood, but now it was clean and yellow. I crouched, picked up a handful, and let it slide through my fingers. Strange how it was cold.

The grains of sand fell in a feathery curtain. Memories came. Heat. The taste of blood in my mouth. Flesh sliced, bright red. Dead eyes staring into the sky. Blinding sun. The roar of the crowd. Pain—left shoulder, a werejaguar's bite, side—a spear thrust, right calf—the razor-sharp tail of a quick reptilian monster for which I had no name . . .

"Like greeting an old friend, no?"

I turned to see an older man looking at me through the wire of the fence. Hard lines creased his face, worn and tanned to leather by years spent in the sun. His face was wide. His black hair, pulled back and gathered at the nape of his neck, was liberally salted with gray. He looked familiar.

"Hardly a friend," I told him.

Mart emerged from the Midnight Gate. He crossed the floor, silent like a shadow, in his black suit, and sailed into the air, landing effortlessly on the fence. The man hadn't heard him.

"Have you fought here before?" His voice was tinted with a light sprinkling of French.

I shook my head.

"Where, then?"

Where hadn't I? I chose the first one. "*Hoyo de Sangre.* A long time ago."

Mart watched me. He had an odd look on his face. It was definitely predatory, but there was a hint of something else to his expression, something disturbing and almost wistful.

"Ahh." The man nodded. "Ghastly place. Do not worry. The sand is the same everywhere."

I smiled. "Here it's cold."

He nodded again. "That is true. But it will make little difference. Once you hear them clamor"—he gazed at the empty seats—"you will remember. How long has it been?"

"Twelve years."

His eyebrows crept up. "Twelve? Surely not. You are far

too young and too beautiful . . ." His voice faltered. *"Mon Dieu, je me souviens de toi. Petite Tueuse . . ."*

He took a step back, as if the fence between us had grown red-hot, and walked away.

I looked at Mart. "Hey, Goldilocks. Where's your tattooed friend? He and I have a date."

He just looked at me.

"You don't say much, do you?" I pulled Slayer out and ran it between my fingers. He watched the sword.

The fence was too high. Even if I made a running jump, I still couldn't leap high enough for a good strike.

"Scaring the competition?"

I went six inches into the air and about two feet to my left, away from the voice, and saw Curran standing by the fence.

Throwing a handful of sand at him would only hammer home the point. I hadn't heard him move at all. No man of his size should be that quiet, but he snuck around like a ghost. How long he had been standing there was anybody's guess.

"Do I scare you or are you just jumpy?"

I scowled at him. "Perhaps the sound of your voice repulses me. It's an instinctual response."

"And he doesn't trigger your instincts?"

Mart smiled.

"He and I have a rendezvous in the sand. I don't have to do anything about him till then."

Curran scrutinized Mart's face. "I can't figure out if he wants to kill you or screw you."

"I'll be glad to make the choice for him."

Curran looked back at me. "Why is it you always attract creeps?"

"You tell me." Ha! Walked right into that one, yes, he did.

Mart leapt off the fence and vanished into the Midnight Gate.

I headed in the opposite direction, to the Gold. Curran stepped up and opened the fence door for me. I halted. That was a bit unexpected. Men didn't open the door for me.

"What is it?"

"I'm trying to decide if it's a trap."

"Get out of there," he growled.

"Are you going to pounce on me?"

"Do you want me to pounce on you?"

I wisely decided not to ponder that question. The answer could've been scary.

I went through the door. He pushed the door shut and caught up with me.

"Are we busted? Did you make them pack up and go home?"

"You're definitely busted. And no. I'm fighting with you."

I stopped and looked at him.

"With us? In the Pit?"

"Yes. Not good enough for you? Would you prefer Saiman?"

Mmm, Beast Lord the God Killer versus the hysterical Frost Giant. Was that even a choice?

"But what about Andorf and the first law?"

"What about Andorf?" he asked.

"Did you really take him down at fifteen years old?" I just blurted it out.

"Yes."

No smart follow-up came to mind. We turned the corner, and I saw Cesare at the end of the hallway.

I stopped. I wanted Cesare so bad I could taste his blood on my lips. Curran looked at me.

"He supervised Derek's beating," I said softly.

Curran's eyes went gold.

If we went after him now, we'd be disqualified. Oh, but we both wanted to kill him. Very, very much.

Cesare turned, saw us, and stumbled. For a moment he froze, caught like a deer in the headlights, and then he ducked into a room.

I turned and went into our quarters. Curran didn't follow.

Andrea greeted me with a wave. She sat on a bench, a variety of strange mechanical parts, which no doubt combined into a deadly firearm, spread before her on a white towel. I sat next to her.

"Where is everybody?"

"Hiding," she said. "Except for Doolittle. He was excused from the chewing-out due to having been kidnapped. He's napping now like he doesn't have a care in the world. I got to hear all sorts of interesting stuff through the door."

"Give."

She shot me a sly smile. "First, I got to listen to Jim's 'it's all my fault; I did it all by myself' speech. Then I got to listen to Derek's 'it's all my fault and I did it all by myself' speech. Then Curran promised that the next person who wanted to be a martyr would get to be one. Then Raphael made a very growling speech about how he was here for a blood debt. It was his right to have restitution for the injury caused to the friend of the boudas; it was in the damn clan charter on such and such page. And if Curran wanted to have an issue with it, they could take it outside. It was terribly dramatic and ridiculous. I loved it."

I could actually picture Curran sitting there, his hand on his forehead above his closed eyes, growling quietly in his throat.

"Then Dali told him that she was sick and tired of being treated like she was made out of glass and she wanted blood and to kick ass."

That would do him in. "So what did he say?"

"He didn't say anything for about a minute and then he chewed them out. He told Derek that he'd been irresponsible with Livie's life, and that if he was going to rescue somebody, the least he could do is to have a workable plan, instead of a poorly thought-out mess that backfired and broke just about every Pack law and got his face smashed in. He told Dali that if she wanted to be taken seriously, she had to accept responsibility for her own actions instead of pretending to be weak and helpless every time she got in trouble and that this was definitely not the venue to prove one's toughness. Apparently he didn't think her behavior was cute when she was fifteen and he's not inclined to tolerate it now that she's twenty-eight."

I was cracking up.

"He told Raphael that the blood debt overrode Pack law only in cases of murder or life-threatening injury and quoted the page of the clan charter and the section number where that could be found. He said that frivolous challenges to the alpha also violated Pack law and were punishable by isolation. It was an awesome smackdown. They had no asses left when he was done."

Andrea began snapping the gun parts together. "Then he sentenced the three of them and himself to eight weeks of hard labor, building the north wing addition to the Keep, and dismissed them. They ran out of there like their hair was on fire."

"He sentenced himself?"

"He's broken Pack law by participating in our silliness, apparently."

That's Beast Lord for you. "And Jim?"

"Oh, he got a special chewing-out after everybody else was dismissed. It was a very quiet and angry conversation, and I didn't hear most of it. I heard the end, though—he got three months of Keep building. Also, when he opened the door to leave, Curran told him very casually that if Jim wanted to pick fights with his future mate, he was welcome to do so, but he should keep in mind that Curran wouldn't come and rescue him when you beat his ass. You should've seen Jim's face."

"His what?"

"His mate. M-A-T-E."

I cursed.

Andrea grinned. "I thought that would make your day. And now you're stuck with him in here for three days and you get to fight together in the Arena. It's so romantic. Like a honeymoon."

Once again my mental conditioning came in handy. I didn't strangle her on the spot.

Raphael chose this moment to walk into the room. "The Reaper bout is about to start. Curran said to tell you that your creep's going to fight."

CHAPTER 26

THE ROWS OF SEATS, EMPTY AN HOUR BEFORE, were filled to capacity. Individuals in their own lives, here the spectators melded into a single entity, a loud, furious, excitable beast with a thousand throats. The night was young and the beast was fickle and bloodthirsty.

Someone, probably Jim or Derek, had found a narrow access staircase that connected the second and third floors. Recessed deeply into the wall to the left of the Gold Gate, it lay steeped in shadows and was practically invisible to the crowd concentrating on the brightly lit Gold Gate and the Pit itself.

I squeezed through the door behind Raphael and Andrea, who sat nicely next to each other. Everyone was there, except Doolittle. I perched on the top step, the cement cold under my butt.

The Reapers fielded only two fighters against the rival team's four. The first was Mart. The second was a woman: small, curvy, sensuous, with a waterfall of dark hair falling down her back. She looked so much like Olivia she could have been her sister. Derek saw her and tensed.

Facing them were the four members of the opposing team. The first was a huge Asian man, solid and thick like a brick. He had to be their Stone. Behind him stood Sling, a lean, dark-skinned archer armed with a bow and a belt filled with knives and darts. At least thirty arrows protruded from the sand in front of him, ready to be grabbed. To the left their Swordmaster waited, a young white man with blond hair who apparently thought he was Japanese: he wore the traditional dark blue kimono and lighter blue hakama garment with a pleated skirt over it. He carried a katana—no surprise there. The last was a woman, a mage, judging by her position in the very back. A wise choice, given the magic was up.

The gong sounded.

The archer fired. The arrow sliced the air and fell harmlessly into the sand as Mart dodged in a blur. The archer drew and fired again, with preternatural quickness. Mart dodged left, right, left, his sword held passively by his side. They thought they had him pinned. Not bloody likely.

The Stone advanced, surprisingly light on his feet. Behind him the female mage began to work something complicated, waving her arms through the air.

The Swordmaster charged the Reaper woman.

She leaned back, her arms flung out like the wings of a bird about to take flight. Mart made no move to assist her.

Ten feet from her the Swordmaster drew his blade in a flash. Should've waited . . .

The woman's bottom jaw unhinged and dropped down. Magic lashed my senses, hard and searing hot. The woman strained and vomited a dark cloud into the swordsman's face. The cloud swarmed and clamped on to the swordsman. He staggered, his charge aborted in midstep. A faint buzz echoed through the Pit.

"Bees?" I guessed.

"Wasps," Derek said.

The swordsman screamed and spun in place.

Mart charged across the sand, a trail of arrows pinning his shadow to the sand, and thrust straight into the Stone's gut. The man folded.

The swarm plaguing the swordsman split in half. The new swarm snapped to the archer like a black lasso. He ran.

As the Stone crumbled, the female mage jerked her arms. A cone of fire struck from her fingers, twisting like a horizontal tornado. Mart leapt into the air. She swung the cone up, but not fast enough. He landed on her, hammering a hard kick into the side of her neck. The impact knocked her off her feet, but not before I saw her head snap to the side.

"Broken neck," Andrea said.

The swarm caught the archer. He veered left and ran straight into Mart's sword. Mart cut him down with two short, precise strokes and walked over to the swordsman, who was still bellowing like a stuck pig. The Reaper watched him flail for a long moment, as if puzzled, then ended it in a single cut. The swarm vanished. The swordsman's head rolled on the sand.

The crowd roared in delight.

The shapeshifters next to me didn't make a sound.

"HERE IS HOW IT WORKS," JIM SAID SOFTLY, WHILE the cleaners loaded the bodies onto stretchers and raked the sand for stray body parts. "There are four fights in all. First, the qualifying bout, then second tier, third tier, and the championship fight. Only the championship fight has the entire team. The rest give us a choice. We can field one to four people for each fight. If we field four and lose all, we are automatically disqualified as 'unable to continue.'"

He paused to let it sink in. Apparently he'd been busy acquiring the information: he actually had a clipboard with notes written on a legal pad, as if he were coaching a base-ball team.

"Despite this rule, most teams field four. Fielding three is risky." He looked down the steps at Curran.

Curran shrugged. "It's your game."

So Jim retained Stratego. That was big of His Majesty.

"We break into two teams," Jim said. "Three and four."

So far, so good.

"This will minimize our risk of being eliminated and will permit us to rest between the fights."

Made total sense.

"Raphael, Andrea, Derek, and I will be in group one, and Curran, Kate, and Dali in group two."

Full break. "You want me to fight with him? On the same team?"

"Yes."

Suddenly I had an urgent need to run away screaming. "Why?"

"Derek, Raphael, and I have similar fighting styles. We move across the field. Andrea is a mobile range fighter. She can shoot and move at the same time. Dali can't," Jim said.

"I do shodo magic," Dali said. "I curse through calligraphy. I have to write the curse out on a piece of paper and I can't move while I do it. One smudge, and I might kill the lot of us."

Oh good.

"But don't worry." Dali waved her arms. "It's so precise, it usually doesn't work at all."

Better and better.

"Raphael and I aren't good defensive fighters," Jim said. "And Derek isn't up to speed yet. I have to put Dali behind Curran, because he's the strongest defense we have. He'll need a strong offense and you're the best offensive fighter I have."

Somehow that didn't sound like a compliment.

"Also the three of us have undergone similar training," Jim said. "We know what to expect from each other and we work well as a team."

He didn't think I could function in a team. Fair enough.

"Group two will take the qualifying bout and the third tier. The qualifying bout should give you little trouble and third-tier fighters shouldn't be that fresh. Group one will take the second-tier bout. We will come out together for the championship fight."

Jim flipped a page on his legal pad. "You're going up

against the Red Demons this afternoon. From what I've heard, they will be fielding a werebison, a swordsman, and some type of odd creature as their mage. You will have magic for the fight. They try to schedule the bouts during the magic waves, because magic makes for a better show. Try to appear sloppy and incompetent. The weaker you look, the more our opponents will underestimate the team, and the easier time we will all have. My lord, no claws. Kate, no magic. You'll need to win, but just barely."

He looked at his notes again and said, "About the murder law. Doesn't apply in the Pit."

Curran said nothing. Jim had just given the shapeshifters permission to kill without accountability with Curran's silence to reinforce it. Just as well. Gladiators died. That was the reality. We had to be there. The rest had volunteered. And given a chance, every member of the opposing team would murder any one of us without a second thought.

THE SAND CRUNCHED UNDER MY FOOT. I COULD already taste it on my tongue. The memories conjured heat and sunshine. I shook them off and looked across the Pit.

In the far end, three people waited for us. The swordsman, tall and carrying a hand-and-a-half sword. The werebison, shaggy with dark brown fur, towering, angry. His breadth was enormous, the shoulders packed with hard, heavy muscle, the chest like a barrel. He wore a chain mail hauberk but no pants. His legs terminated in black hooves. A dense mane of coarse hair crowned the back of his neck. His features were a meld of bull and human, but where the minotaur's face had been a cohesive whole, the shapeshifter's skull was a jumble of mismatched parts.

Behind them reared a nightmarish creature. Its lower body was python, dark brown with creamy swirls of scales. Near the abdomen, the scales became so fine, they glittered, stretching tight over a human upper body, complete with a pair of tiny breasts and a female face that looked like it belonged to a fifteen-year-old. She looked at us with emerald-green eyes. Her skull was bald and a hood of flesh spread from her head, resembling that of a king cobra.

A lamia. Great.

The lamia swayed gently, as if listening to music only she could hear. Old magic emanated from her, ancient and ice-cold. It picked up the sand and rolled it in feathery curves to caress her scales before sliding back to the Pit.

Behind me, Dali shivered. She stood in the sand with a clipboard, an ink pen, and a piece of thin rice paper cut into inch-wide strips.

I eyed the swordsman. Weak and sloppy. Okay, I could do that.

The crowd waited above us. The hum of conversation, the clearing of throats, and the sound of a thousand simultaneous breaths blended into a low hum. I scanned the seats and saw Saiman on his balcony. Aunt B, Raphael's mother, sat on his left, and Mahon, the Bear of Atlanta and the Pack's executioner, occupied the chair to his right. Sitting between the alphas of Clan Bouda and Clan Heavy. No wonder Saiman had been persuaded to give up his spot to Curran.

Behind Aunt B, I saw a familiar pale head. Couldn't be. The blond head moved and I saw Julie's face. Oh yes, it could.

"You bribed my kid!"

"We reached a business arrangement," he said. "She wanted to see you fight and I wanted to know when, where, and how you were getting into the Games."

Julie gave me a big, nervous smile and a little wave.

Just wait until I get out of here, I mouthed. We were going to have a little talk about following orders.

"I know what the problem is." Curran pulled his shoulders back and flexed, warming up a little. I stole a glance. He had decided to fight in jeans and an old black T-shirt, from which he'd torn the sleeves. Probably his workout shirt.

His biceps were carved, the muscle defined and built by

countless exertions, neither too bulky nor too lean. Perfect. Kissing him might make me guilty of catastrophically bad judgment, but at least nobody could fault my taste. The trick was not to kiss him again. Once could be an accident; twice was trouble.

"You said something?" I arched an eyebrow at him. Nonchalance—best camouflage for drooling. Both the werebison and the swordsman looked ready to charge: the muscles of their legs tense, leaning forward slightly on their toes. They seemed to be terribly sure that we would stay in one place and wait for them.

Curran was looking at their legs, too. They must be expecting a distraction from the lamia. She sat cocooned in magic, holding on with both hands as it strained on its leash.

"I said, I know why you're afraid to fight with me."

"And why is that?" If he flexed again, I'd have to implement emergency measures. Maybe I could kick some sand at him or something. Hard to look hot brushing sand out of your eyes.

"You want me."

Oh boy.

"You can't resist my subtle charm, so you're afraid you're going to make a spectacle out of yourself."

"You know what? Don't talk to me."

The gong boomed.

Memories smashed into me: heat, sand, fear.

The lamia's magic snapped like a striking cobra. I jumped up and to the left, just in time to avoid the pit in the sand that yawned open beneath my feet.

The Swordmaster was on me like white on rice. He charged in and struck in a textbook thrust of wrath, a powerful diagonal thrust delivered from the right and angled down. I jerked back. His blade whistled past me, and I grabbed his leather and smashed my forehead into his face. *There you go. Sloppy.*

Red drenched my face. The swordsman's eyes rolled back in his head and he fell.

Not good.

I turned in time to see the werebison arrive. It took him a moment to build up his speed, but as he ran now, massive, huge, blowing air from his misshapen nose, he seemed unstoppable.

Curran watched him come with a slightly bored expression. At the last moment, he stepped aside and stuck his foot out. The shapeshifter tripped and Curran helped him down by pushing none too gently on the back of his neck. The werebison flipped onto the sand, hitting the ground like a fallen skyscraper. He shuddered once and lay still, his neck bent in an unnatural angle.

He must've broken his neck in the fall. His chest was still moving. At least he didn't die.

Curran stared at him, perplexed.

Dali barked a sharp command in a language I didn't understand and tossed a piece of rice paper into the air. There was a quiet plop and the paper vanished.

We looked at the lamia expectantly. Nothing. She waved her arms, gathering magic for something nasty.

I guess the spell was a bust.

A spark of bright magenta shone above the lamia's head. It flared into glowing red jaws with demonic needle-teeth. The jaws chomped the lamia—neck, elbows, waist—and vanished. There was a loud crunch and the lamia twisted: her head turned backward, snapping her neck, her elbows protruded from the front of her arms, and she bent to the side like a flower with a broken stem.

I turned slowly and stared at Dali. She shrugged. "I guess it worked. What?"

The crowd went wild.

Jim waited for us at the Gold Gate. His teeth were bared. "What happened to barely winning?"

"You said sloppy! Look, I didn't even use my sword; I hit him with my head, like a moron."

"A man with a sword attacked you and you disarmed him and knocked him out cold in under two seconds." He turned to Curran.

The Beast Lord shrugged. "It's not my fault that he didn't know how to fall."

Jim's gaze slid from Curran to Dali. "What the hell was that?"

"Crimson Jaws of Death."

"And were you planning on letting me know that you can turn people's elbows backward?"

"I told you I did curses."

"You said they don't work!"

"I said they don't *always* work. This one worked apparently." Dali wrinkled her forehead. "It's not like I ever get to use them against live opponents anyway. It was an accident."

Jim looked at us. The clipboard snapped in his hands. He turned around and very deliberately walked away.

"I think we hurt his feelings." Dali looked at his retreating back, sighed, and went after him.

Curran looked at me. "What the hell was I supposed to do, catch the werebison as he was falling?"

BACK IN THE ROOM I GRABBED A CHANGE OF clothes and showered. When I returned, dinner had been brought in by the Red Guard: beef stew with fresh bread. Raphael had vanished right after dinner, and the shapeshifters invited me to play poker.

They killed me. Apparently I was made of tells: they could hear my heartbeat and smelled the changes in my sweat, and counted the number of times I blinked, and knew what cards I had before I looked at them. If it had been strip poker, I would've had to give them the skin off my back. I finally gave up and went back to my bed to read one of Doolittle's paperbacks, since he was otherwise occupied. The good doctor turned out to be a card fiend. Once in a while, I glanced at them. The six shapeshifters sat like statues, faces showing nothing, barely lifting their cards to steal supernaturally fast glances. It felt weird to fall asleep with someone else there, but there was something almost hypnotic about their absolute stillness that lulled me into sleep.

I dreamed that Curran and I killed a dinosaur and then had sex in the dirt.

AT ABOUT NINE, CURRAN, DALI, AND I MADE OUR way to the Gold Gate to see Andrea, Raphael, Jim, and Derek take on the Killers.

The magic was up. Andrea grinned as she passed me by. She carried her SIG-Sauers in hip holsters and a crossbow in her hands. With the magic up, the guns wouldn't fire, but she must've wanted to be prepared for the shift.

Jim and Derek carried nothing and wore identical gray sweatpants. Raphael carried two tactical knives, both with oxide finish that made the blades Teflon-black. The knife in his left was shaped like a tanto. The blade in his right was double-edged and slightly leaf-shaped: narrow at the handle, it widened before coming to a razor-sharp point. Raphael wore black boots, fitted black leather pants that molded to him with heart-shattering results, and nothing else.

As he passed me, he leaned to Curran and handed him a paper fan folded from some sort of flyer.

Curran looked at the fan. "What?"

"An emergency precaution, Your Majesty. In case the lady faints."

Curran just stared at him.

Raphael strode toward the Pit, turned, flexed a bit, and winked at me.

"Give me that," I told Curran. "I need to fan myself."

"No, you don't."

We took off to the stairs for the better view. When the three of us settled on the staircase, Andrea was drawing her crossbow in a businesslike fashion. The three shapeshifters spread out in front of her.

Across the expanse of sand, the Killers waited in a two-by-two formation.

The Killers gave off a distinctly Japanese flair. Their

Stone, a huge, towering monstrosity, had to weigh close to four hundred pounds. Dark indigo, he stood eight feet tall, with arms like tree trunks. A big, round gut protruded above his kilt, as though he'd swallowed a cannon ball. Two horns curved from the coarse mane of dark hair dripping from his skull, and two matching sabertooth-like tusks protruded from his lower jaw. His brutish, thick-featured face communicated simple rage, and the huge iron club in his hand signified his willingness to let it loose. An oni, a Japanese ogre.

Next to him crouched a beast bearing a striking resemblance to the stone statues guarding the entrances to Chinese temples. Thick and powerfully muscled, it stared at the crowd with bulging eyes brimming with intelligence. Its flanks were dark red, its mane short and curled in ruby ringlets. It sniffed the air and shook its disproportionately huge head. Its maw gaped open, wide, wider, until its head split nearly in half. Lights glinted from brilliant white fangs. A Fu Lion.

Behind him a thin-lipped redheaded woman in a white shirt and flaring black pants held a yumi, a two-meter-tall, slender, traditional Japanese bow. By her side stood an Asian man with striking, pale green eyes.

The archer began drawing her yumi bow. She stood with her feet wide apart, the left side of her body facing the target—Raphael. She raised the bow above her head and lowered it slowly, drawing as it came down, wider and wider, until the straight line of the arrow crossed just under her cheekbone.

A silver spark ignited at the tip of the arrow and ran down the shaft, flaring into white lightning.

Across the sand Andrea waited, with her crossbow down at her side. Raphael casually twirled the knife in his right hand, turning it into a metal blur.

I leaned forward, elbows on my knees, hands braided into a single fist.

"They aren't children," Curran said to me. "They know what they're doing."

It made no difference to me. I would rather walk a hundred times into the Pit than see one of them die in there.

The gong struck.

The archer fired.

Andrea snapped the crossbow up and fired without aiming. In the same blink Raphael slid out of the way of the fiery arrow, as fluidly as if his joints were made of water, and struck it down with his knife. Pieces of the arrow fell to the sand, sizzling with magic.

The archer's head snapped. The crossbow bolt sprouted precisely between her eyes. Her mouth gaped open in a black O and she toppled back like a log.

The man next to her closed his eyes and fell back. His body never touched the sand. Thin strands of magic caught and cloaked him, knitting into a gossamer web, cradling his body like a hammock. His face turned placid. He appeared asleep.

The Fu Lion roared, sounding more like a pissed-off wolverine than a feline. Plumes of reddish smoke billowed from its mouth. It charged.

It covered the distance to our line in three great bounds, each strike of its clawed feet shaking the sand like the blow of a huge sledgehammer. Derek lunged into its path, ripping the sweatpants from his body. Skin split on his back, spilling fur. Muscle and bone boiled and a seven-foot-tall werewolf grasped the Fu Lion's head. The nightmare and the lion collided, raising a spray of sand into the air. The impact pushed Derek across the sand. Derek dug his lupine feet into the sand, grinding the lion's charge to a dead halt. Sinewy muscle played along his long back under the patchy fur.

The Fu Lion jerked his head, trying to shake off the half-beast, half-man. Derek thrust his claws into the creature's massive neck. To the left Jim became a jaguar in an explosion of flesh and golden fur.

The Fu Lion reared, trying to claw. The moment it exposed its gut, Raphael and the werejaguar darted to it. Knives and claws flashed and the slippery clumps of the beast's innards tumbled out in a whoosh of blood. Derek tore his claws free and leapt aside. The Fu Lion swayed and fell.

The shapeshifters rose from his corpse, silent. Derek's eyes glowed amber, while Jim's were pools of green.

"Jim improved his warrior form," Curran said. "Interesting."

Behind the shapeshifters Andrea loaded the crossbow and fired. The crossbow spat bolts, one after another. Three shafts punctured the oni's chest, but the ogre just bellowed and brushed them off the massive shield of flesh he called his torso.

Andrea landed a shot to the forehead. The bolt bounced off the ogre's skull.

Magic grew behind the oni, blooming like a flower around the sleeping man. Long, translucent strands snaked past the oni's legs, like pale ribbons.

"Bad," Dali murmured behind me. "Bad, bad, bad . . ."

The strands knotted together. Light flashed and a creature spilled forth. Ten feet tall, it resembled a human crouching on frog legs. It squatted in the sand, leaning on abnormally long forelimbs, the magic ribbons binding its back and legs to the sleeping mage. A second set of forearms sprouted from its elbows, terminating in long, slender fingers tipped with narrow claws. A huge maw gaped where its face would have been, a black funnel turned inward. Its hide shimmered with a metallic sheen, as if the creature were spun from silver wool.

The Arena fell silent.

The shapeshifters backed up. Andrea reloaded and sent a bolt into the creature's maw. It vanished and emerged from the aberration's back. The oni danced behind it, stomping the sand.

The creature reared slightly, its sallow chest expanded, and it belched a glittering, silvery cloud.

Fine metal needles rained into the sand. One grazed Jim and he snarled. Silver.

The shapeshifters retreated. The monster kept a steady stream of metal vomit, and began crawling forward, slowly, ponderously, chasing them back to the fence.

The cloud caught Derek, slicing through his torso. He jerked as if burned, and leapt away.

"Take out the sleeper," I murmured.

Jim barked a short order, barely audible behind the hiss of needles slicing the sand. Derek ducked left, while Raphael darted right, trying to flank the creature. A second mouth bloomed in the side of the creature's chest and the new flood of needles cut Raphael short.

I clenched my sword. Curran watched with no expression, like a rock.

Another command. Raphael and Jim fell back, while Derek backed away slowly, just out of the monster's reach. The two shapeshifters grasped Andrea's legs and heaved. She flew straight up, squeezing off a single shot.

The bolt punched through the sleeper's chest, emerging through his back. He awoke with a startled scream and clawed at the shaft. The threads of translucent magic ribbons ripped and he crashed into the sand. The ribbons shrank, breaking from the monster's skin, leaving deep black gaps as they tore. The gaps grew, and the creature began to melt. It whipped about and backhanded the oni out of the way. The blue brute crashed into the fence. The silver aberration crawled to the sleeper, dragging itself faster and faster across the sand. Its back and hips were gone, melted into nothing, and yet it continued to crawl. In a moment it loomed above the flailing human, bent down, and gulped him in a single swallow. The mage's screeches died and the beast vanished.

The crowd exploded. A hundred mouths screamed at once. To the left some hoarse male voice yelled, "Goooooooal!" at the top of his lungs.

The oni stumbled to his feet and met three shapeshifters. It was short and brutal.

I opened the door and took off down to the gate. Curran and Dali caught up with me.

A few moments later the four trotted to us, covered in blood and caked with sand. Andrea ran through the gates and hugged me. "Did you see that?"

"That was a hell of a shot."

"Into the infirmary," Doolittle ordered briskly. "Quickly, before the silver sets in."

They passed us. Jim glanced at Curran. The Beast Lord nodded very slightly.

Derek and Raphael were the last through the door. The boy wonder limped badly. He looked up at Curran, stiff.

"Good," Curran said.

Derek drew himself straight. A small, proud light played in his eyes. He limped past us, trying not to lean on Raphael.

FIVE FEET FROM THE DOORS, ANDREA FELL. ONE moment she was smiling and the next she dropped like a log. Raphael released Derek and I caught him just as Raphael scooped Andrea off the floor.

"Silver poisoning," Doolittle snapped. "Bring her in."

Andrea gasped. "It burns."

I had dealt with shapeshifters damaged by silver before. It was an ugly, terrible thing. And I had gotten Andrea into it.

Raphael carried Andrea to the side room, where Doolittle had set up shop, and slid her onto a metal table.

Andrea shuddered. Spots appeared on her skin like a developing photograph. Her fingers elongated, growing claws.

"Hold on." Raphael reached for her leather vest.

"No."

"Don't be ridiculous," he snarled.

She clamped his hands. "No!" Her eyes went wild.

"Now young lady . . ." Doolittle said soothingly.

"No!"

Her back arched. She convulsed and yelped, her voice vibrating with pain. She was changing and she didn't want anyone to see.

"We need privacy," I said. "Please."

"Let's go." Suddenly Derek's weight was gone from me. Curran picked him up and strode to the back room. Dali and Jim followed. Raphael remained, pale as a sheet, holding Andrea in his arms.

She snarled in a hoarse voice.

"It's all right," I told her. "Just me, the doctor, and Raphael. They are gone."

"I want him to go," she gasped. "Please."

"You're convulsing. I can't hold you still because you're too strong, and the doctor will be too busy."

"Cut her clothes," Doolittle ordered briskly.

"No. No, no . . ." Andrea began to cry.

Raphael pulled her to him, his arms around her, her back to his chest. "It's all right," he whispered. "It's all right. It will be fine."

In less than a minute I had her nude. Ugly spots of gray peppered her torso. She must've gotten a head-on blast of the needles. Andrea shuddered again, tremors spreading from her chest to her legs. She yelped in pain.

"Don't fight the change," Doolittle said softly, opening a leather case with gleaming instruments. "Let it take you."

"I can't."

"Of course you can," I told her.

"No!" she snarled through clenched teeth.

"You aren't going to die because you're too embarrassed by your hyena freckles. I've already seen you in your natural form and Doolittle doesn't care. He's seen it all before. Right, Doctor?"

"Oh, the stories I could tell." Doolittle chuckled. "This is nothing. A minor thing." His face said otherwise, but Andrea couldn't see it. "We'll have you up and running in no time."

"And Raphael thinks you're sexy in your true form. He's a pervert, remember? Come on, Andrea. You can do it."

Raphael cradled her. "Change, sweetheart. You can do it. Just let the body take over."

The gray spots widened. She clenched my hand in hers, nearly crushing my fingers.

"Change, Andrea. You still owe me lunch, you know."

"No, I don't," she ground out.

"Yes, you do. You and Raphael ran out on me and I had to pick up the tab. If you die on me, it will be hard to collect and I'm too cheap to get stuck with the bill. Let's go."

Andrea's head jerked back, slamming into Raphael's chest. She cried out. Flesh flowed along her frame, reshaping, molding into a new body, a lean, long-legged creature covered in short fur. Her face flowed into a mix of human and hyena. Unlike the bouda shapeshifters, whose form too often was a horrific mishmash of mismatched parts, Andrea was a proportional, beautiful, elegant being. Too bad she didn't see herself that way.

Doolittle probed her abdomen with the fingers of his left hand, a scalpel in his right. "Now when I cut, you push. Nice and easy, just like you trained."

"Trained?" Andrea choked.

"The silver-extraction training," Doolittle told her.

"I haven't trained!"

Of course she hadn't trained. She pretended she wasn't a shapeshifter. "She doesn't know how," I told him.

Andrea convulsed. Raphael clamped her still. His face had gone bloodless.

"The silver burns. Your flesh tries to shrink from it and it burrows deeper and deeper into your body. You must fight it," Doolittle said. "It goes against all your instincts, but when I cut, you must strain and push against it to force it out of your body."

"I can't," Andrea gasped.

"You can," Raphael told her. "Everyone learns how to do it. Children are trained to do it. You're a knight of the Order. You can push a fucking needle out of your body. Stop crying and feeling sorry for yourself."

"I hate you," she snarled.

Doolittle positioned the scalpel above the largest gray spot. "Ready?"

He sliced without waiting for an answer. Black blood gushed from the wound. Andrea crushed my hand, screamed, straining, and a silver needle slid onto her stomach.

Doolittle swiped the silver-fouled blood from her skin with gauze. "Good girl. Very good. Now we do it again."

WHEN IT WAS DONE, RAPHAEL CARRIED ANDREA to the shower, murmuring soothing endearments into her ear. My part in it was finished. I went to the bedroom to find Dali slicing Derek's back to get out the needles. Unlike Andrea, Derek had training and his progress was much faster. He joked while Dali cut him, mangling the words with his monstrous jaws, snarled with a pretended rage, and dramatically promised to "kirrrl youraaalll for this!" Curran chuckled. Dali was giggling. Even Jim smiled, for once lingering in the room instead of watching the fights.

I couldn't stay. I wanted to be alone, by myself. *I should go and watch the fights instead.* Some other people dying for the sake of the greedy crowd. That would fix me right up. There was nowhere else I could go.

It wasn't until I was out in the hallway that the aftershock of the fight hit me. Little painful sparks danced along my skin and melted first into relief, then into electric anxiety.

At the far end of the hallway a woman in a flowing sari was heading toward me between two Red Guards. She carried an ornate metal box.

I retreated to our quarters and blocked the doorway.

The woman and the guards stopped before me. She smiled at me. "A gift. For the man with the shattered face."

I took the box. "I'll be sure that he gets it."

She smiled wider.

"That's a beautiful skin you're wearing," I told her. "I'm sure its owner screamed very loud before you killed her for it."

The Guards reached for their weapons.

"You will scream too, when I take yours," she said.

I smiled back at her. "I'll cut your heart out and make you eat it. Or you can save me the trouble and swallow your tongue like your scaled friend."

Her smile got sharper. She inclined her head and took off. The Guards escorting her followed, relieved.

I brought the box into the bedroom and explained where it came from.

Derek reached over and opened it without a word. Inside lay a wealth of human hair. He scooped it with his claws and lifted it out. No blood. Just dark hair, gathered into a horse tail and chopped off. His upper lip rose, revealing his fangs. Livie's hair.

"Was this done to disfigure her?" I asked.

Dali shook her head. "Widows cut their hair. They're taunting him. If she's his bride, then he's as good as dead."

CHAPTER 27

———◦◦◦———

I AWOKE AROUND FIVE. GYM, STRETCH, LIGHT workout, shower, breakfast. Routine. Except for all us monsters gathered around the table. The shapeshifters loved to eat. It was a wonder the table didn't break under all the food they had requested.

"These grits are terrible." Doolittle grimaced and dropped another dollop of butter into his bowl.

Dali licked her spoon. "The cook must be a blind man with two left hands."

"How can you ruin grits—that's what I want to know?" Raphael shrugged. "They're barely edible when fixed properly."

"I'll tell your mother you said that," Doolittle told him.

"The corn bread is a brick." Jim took the yellow square and knocked on the table with it. "The sausage is like paper."

"Maybe they're hoping to starve us," Andrea quipped.

"More like they're fixing to give us a hell of a stomach-ache." Curran loaded more bacon on his plate.

For people who frequently turned into animals and ate their prey raw, they sure were a choosy lot.

"Kate makes good sausage," Jim said.

Six pairs of eyes stared at me. *Thank you, Mr. Wonderful. Just what I needed.*

"Oh yeah." Andrea snapped her fingers. "The links? The ones we had the beginning of the month? I didn't know you made those. I thought they were bought. They were so good." Her smile was positively cherubic. Of all the times not to be able to shoot laser beams out of my eyes . . .

"What do you put into your sausage, Kate?" Raphael wanted to know, giving me a perfectly innocent look.

Werejaguars with big mouths with a pinch of werehyena thrown in. "Venison and rabbit."

"That sounds like some fine sausage," Doolittle said. "Will you share the recipe?"

"Sure."

"I had no idea you were a sausage expert," Curran said with a completely straight face.

Die, die, die, die. . . .

Even Derek cracked a smile. Raphael put his head down on the table and jerked a little.

"Is he choking?" Dali asked, wrinkling her forehead.

"No, he just needs a moment," Curran said. "Young bouda males. Easily excitable."

"Who are we fighting today?" I asked, wishing I could brain him with something heavy.

"Rouge Rogues," Jim said.

"That's a joke, right?" Andrea's eyebrows crept up.

Jim shook his head. "No. Led by a Frenchman. He calls himself Cyclone. A bad bunch."

"The Frenchman knows me," I said.

Jim's gaze fixed on me. "How well?"

"Well enough," Curran said. "He's scared of her."

"Did he ever see you fighting?" Andrea asked.

"Yes. A long time ago."

"How long?" Jim asked. "How well does he know how you fight?"

If he tried to take me out of this fight, I'd rip him to

shreds. "It was twelve years ago in Peru. I seriously doubt he remembers the finer points of my swordwork."

"What were you doing in Peru?" Raphael asked.

"Fighting in *Hoyo de Sangre.*" I watched it sink in. Yes, I was thirteen. No, I didn't want to talk about it. "As I said, it's irrelevant. He's a professional gladiator. He tours from arena to arena, drawn by prizes. He's a strong air mage and he favors basic powerful spells. He'll likely try an air lock or a hold. What else does he have on his team?"

Jim looked as if he'd bitten a lemon. "Assuming they will bring their best, he's got a troll as their Stone, a golem Swordmaster, and a vampire Shiv. A very old vampire."

"How old?" I asked.

"Olathe old," Jim said.

Inwardly I cringed. Olathe, Roland's former concubine, had used ancient vampires so old, they had to have become undead before the Shift, the first magic wave, when technically they weren't supposed to have existed. A vampire was an abomination in progress. The older a vampire grew, the more pronounced were the changes the *Immortuus* pathogen inflicted onto its once-human body and the more dangerous it became.

"The golem is silver," Jim said. "Sprouts blades in weird places. Preternaturally fast. Can't be cut; can't be pierced. The troll's hide is also nearly impossible to penetrate. I saw a spear bounce off. It worries me."

It would worry anybody. The vampire alone, even if the other three were paper cutouts, would give me a pause. As it was, the lineup was nearly impossible to beat. The vamp was deadly and wickedly fast. With two extra fighters and a mage, keeping the vamp from Dali would be nearly impossible.

Olathe had gotten her vampires from Roland's stable when she had fled him. Where did Cyclone get an ancient vampire, especially with the People's Warlord sitting right there in the stands?

I could crush the vamp's mind, but not without giving myself away.

"I can take the bloodsucker," Dali said. "If the magic is up."

Jim grimaced. "This isn't a regular vampire. You've never seen one like that. It's *old*."

She shook her head. "The older, the better. But it will take everything I got. I can do it once and that's it. Then I'll need a nap."

I looked at Dali. If she took out the vamp, they would lock on her. Four to three, lousy odds, especially with an air mage in the mix. There was a way I could make her safe. It would be a foolish and reckless move under normal circumstances. But with d'Ambray watching, it qualified as mind-numbingly stupid.

If she failed, she had no protection against the vampire. It would tear into her and I would hear her scream.

"If you can take out the bloodsucker, I'll make you safe for the rest of the fight, provided the magic holds."

"How?"

"Blood ward. It locks all magic out, including your own. You cast the curse and jump into the ward. Once you step into it, it will keep you locked in. You won't be able to exit without my help. But nobody else will be able to enter."

Dali bit her lip. "What if it doesn't work?"

"You just have to trust me."

She considered it for a long moment. "Okay."

Jim shook his head. "Consider taking a fourth."

"No," Curran and I said at the same time. I didn't want any more friends on my conscience.

Doolittle sighed.

I rose. "This will take a bit of practice."

THE VAMPIRE CROUCHED BY CYCLONE, OOZING necromantic magic. Jim was right. This one was *old*. No sign of it ever walking upright remained. It waited on all fours, like a dog that had somehow sprouted humanoid limbs tipped with stiletto claws. The last lingering echoes of its humanity had faded long ago. It had become a *thing*, so revoltingly alien and frightening it sent shivers down my spine.

Not an ounce of fat remained on its frame. Its thick skin clung so tightly to its steel-cable muscles that it resembled wax poured over an anatomy model made by a demented sculptor. Sharp bone protuberations broke the skin along its spine, creating a jagged ridge. Its nose was missing, and not even a slit remained. Massive, lipless jaws jutted from its sickening face, revealing a forest of fangs embedded in crimson gums. A thick horn protruded from the back of its deformed skull. Its eyes glowed dark hungry red, like rubies thrust into the skull of a demon.

I found the sharp, painful light of its mind and waited in the shadows. If Dali failed, I would crush it, whether it gave me away or not.

Next to it rose a troll. A hulking creature, he stood almost nine feet tall. His skin was dark brown, uneven, and gnarled, interrupted by patches of rougher brown. A single adjective came to mind: thick. Thick tree-trunk legs, ending in flat, round stumps of elephantine feet. Thick midsection with a round stomach that looked too hard to be termed "gut." Thick chest. Massively broad shoulders slabbed with thick muscle. Thick neck, bigger than my thigh. Thick, round head resembling a stump with a flat face. Eyes sunken deep into dark sockets, a stunted Persian cat nose, and a narrow slash of a mouth. Two tusks protruded from his lower jaw, stretching his mouth into a smirk. He looked as though he'd been carved out of a gargantuan tree trunk and allowed to petrify. Screw the spear; he'd break a chain saw.

On the far left a man waited. He was young and dark-skinned, his skull clean shaven. He had the build of a gymnast, wore nothing, and carried two identical swords. I'd never seen any quite like them. Bastard children of a scimitar and a katana, they had the narrow slickness of the Japanese blade and a slight curve with a flare at the point inherited from the Arabic sword. Three feet long and an inch and a half at the narrowest, the blades were both lively and devastating.

As we entered the Arena, the man changed. A pale sheen coated his strong features. His shape expanded with gray thickness. Armor formed on his shoulders: a textured pauldron on his left shoulder, a thinner one on his right. Huge wrist guards clamped his forearms. A wide metal belt sheathed his loins, dripping down a narrow metal cloth to protect his testicles. His body glistened with moisture and dried in an instant, snapping into sleek gray smoothness. Everything but his eyes was metal. The silver golem.

The swords pointed in my direction. Just what I needed: a tin man on steroids. Wandering around looking for a heart and singing merrily just didn't do it for the young and ambitious metal turks nowadays. This dude wanted my heart, still beating and bloody, carved freshly from my chest.

We paused on the edge of the sand. The magic was in full swing. Dali swallowed.

I carried Slayer and a tactical sword I had stolen from the Pack's armory during the flare. I handed the tactical sword to Curran. "Hold it for a second, please?" He took it and I sliced the back of my hand with Slayer. A nice, shallow cut. The blood swelled in red drops. Dali winced and turned away. I let the blood run down the blade's edge. My father and Greg both were screaming in their graves. I drew a two-foot-wide circle in the sand, leaving a narrow opening, pulled out a piece of gauze, and squeezed my hand, saturating the gauze until it dripped.

I handed the gauze to Dali. She put it onto her clipboard and stood in front of the circle's opening. It would take her a second and a single step back to enter the blood ward.

I slapped a piece of med tape onto the cut. "Just like we practiced. Do what you have to do with the vampire. If it works, or if it doesn't, step back into the circle and use the gauze to seal it. Do you understand?"

"Yes."

"Obey her," Curran said quietly.

Dali swallowed. "Yes, my lord."

We headed to the front.

The vamp would be drawn to fresh blood. Especially my

blood. The navigator would feel the draw and send it after Dali. That left us facing the troll and the golem. As long as they stood, Cyclone was safe.

"Choices, choices," I murmured.

We stood side by side. "We take the troll," Curran said.

"Yes."

Once the vampire got ahold of Dali's magic and hopefully not of Dali herself, the golem would strike at her, trying to take her out. If she did everything right, he'd fail, which would give us a few seconds for a tête-à-tête with the troll.

The troll grinned.

"Keep smiling, pretty boy." I swung the swords, warming up my wrists.

Curran was eyeing the golem. The damned thing was silver.

"The golem is mine. Don't screw with my shit."

"In this Pit, everything is mine," he said.

The sound of the gong was like my heart exploding.

Magic sliced from Cyclone. The air accreted around me and clamped me down like a wet blanket, growing heavier, compressing, squeezing ... The air lock. I froze. Across from me, Curran stood still like a statue, a small smile curving his lips. He recognized the spell as well.

The vamp flew across the sand.

The golem ran toward me.

A hard, cold blade of magic ripped through us. Somewhere in the stands a hoarse scream announced a Master of the Dead losing a vampire. Go, Dali.

The air clamped me like shackles and froze, fixing me in a death hold. Good enough.

Curran exploded into warrior form. A seven-and-a-half-foot-tall nightmare rose in his place: layered with muscle, dark gray, stripes like streaks of smoke against a velvet pelt. This time, instead of the awful meld of human and lion, a lion head sat on his shoulders, complete with enormous jaws. Only Curran could do this: keep most of his body in one shape while turning a part into another.

I launched myself into the air. The air lock shattered with a sound like torn paper. It was designed to restrain a panicking victim. The more you struggled, the harder it held you. But let it settle and you could shatter it with sudden movement.

The golem veered left, heading for Dali instead. Cyclone stumbled, momentarily woozy from having his spell broken.

The troll was on us. I darted close, under the troll's gut. Wood or no wood, he walked, which meant his knees bent. I thrust my swords between his legs and sliced the backs of his knees. He didn't go down but he grabbed for me. *That's right—look at me, you overgrown log.*

A sick stench of decomposition spread through the Arena. My eyes watered.

The demonic monstrosity that was Curran landed on the troll's back. The awful lion jaws gaped wide and clamped on to the troll's thick neck. White teeth flashed, bit, sliding between the cervical vertebrae, and sliced the spinal cord like scissors. The troll's head drooped to the side, dark blood bubbling gently to stain his shoulders. Curran grabbed the skull and tore the head from the neck. His face snapped into the horrible chimera of half human, half-lion, and he hurled the troll's head at Cyclone.

The mage made no move to dodge. He just stared, stunned. The head smashed into him, taking him off his feet. He fell limp. I whipped about.

Dali slumped inside the ward, her hands crossed protectively over her head. Her face and shoulder were wet with blood, tracing the long rip in her shirt. But the wound had already sealed.

The golem struck at her, his blades a whirl of metal, and bounced from the ward, each hit sending a pulse of burgundy through the spell. A pile of putrid flesh sagged next to Dali with a small rectangle of rice paper stuck to its top. A lonely kanji character glowed pale blue from the paper.

She'd done it. She'd taken out the vampire.

"You okay?" I shouted to her, too late remembering that she couldn't hear me.

She raised her head, saw me, and held out her thumb.

"Hey, tincan boy!" I barked. "Bring it!"

The golem turned, raising a cloud of sand into the air, and charged me. I waited with my swords raised.

He lunged. The blade slid by my cheek, fanning my skin. He *was* preternaturally fast. But it wasn't my first time. I matched his speed.

Strike, strike, strike.

I blocked him every time, letting his blades glance off mine. A familiar welcome warmth spread through my body. My muscles became pliant, my movements easy. He was fast and well trained, but I was fast too and trained better.

The blades became a whirl. I laughed and kept blocking. *You want to go there? Fine. Let's go.*

My only chance lay in tiring him out. It was hard to put a blade into a man's eye. Unfortunately, that was the only part of himself he'd left human.

Minutes flew by, sliced to shreds by the cascade of gleaming blades. The crowd had gone so quiet, only the ringing pulse of our swords breached the silence. He couldn't keep this up indefinitely and I was just warming up.

Curran loomed behind the golem. The glance cost me— a well-placed thrust sliced my left shoulder.

"No!" I barked.

Curran clamped the golem in a bear hug, trying to crush his throat. Silver flowed and metal spikes punched from the golem's back into Curran's chest, impaling him.

Curran roared in agony.

The sound shook the Pit. Pain and thunder rolled and combined, nearly bringing me to my knees. In the crowd people screamed and covered their ears.

Gray streaks slid through Curran, eating up his fur. The idiot just held on tighter. The golem spun, his movement slowed slightly, his spikes still protruding through Curran's back . . .

The universe shrank to Curran and his pain. I had to break him free. Nothing else mattered.

I attacked, leaving a slight opening on the left side. The golem committed. He thrust, throwing himself into a lunge. I didn't try to block. The slender blade sliced between my ribs. Ice pierced me, followed by a sharp, painful heat.

I plunged Slayer's blade into his left eye.

It slid perfectly into a sheath of flesh. I buried it deep, putting all my strength behind it. A one-in-a-hundred kind of strike.

The golem's mouth gaped. His silver skin shook, draining from his body, and as it drained, a scream was born in the depths of his throat, at first weak, but growing stronger. Finally it burst forth in a howl of pain and surprise.

Curran broke off, snapping the spikes.

The last smudges of silver drained from the golem's skin. He toppled to his knees. I put my foot onto his shoulder and pulled my blade out. He fell facedown. I walked off, across the sand, and thrust my hand through the blood ward.

It solidified around my hand in a flash of red. For a moment a translucent red column enclosed Dali, and then it shattered, melting into nothing. I grabbed her and hauled her out of there. Behind us Curran staggered to his feet.

The crowd erupted. God damn harpies. I turned on my foot, stared at them, and yelled, "Fuck you all!"

They just cheered louder.

I marched out of the Pit.

At the gates, Jim took one look at my face and moved out of my way.

I stomped into our quarters, straight into Doolittle's makeshift hospital. Curran followed me, slapping the door closed. I whirled around. The beast melted and Curran stood before me in his human form. Black spots peppered his chest where the spikes had pierced his flesh.

I stared at him for a second and smashed my fist into his midsection, right over the solar plexus. He grunted.

Doolittle took off.

"What the fuck is wrong with you?" I looked for something heavy to hit him with, but the room was mostly empty. There were surgical instruments but no heavy, blunt objects capable of causing the kind of pain I wanted.

He straightened.

"He was silver!" I snarled in his face. "I had it under control. What was going through your head? Here's a toxic silver golem; I think I'll jump on his back! That's a damn good idea!"

He scooped me up and suddenly I was pressed against his chest. "Were you worried about me?"

"No, I'm ranting for fun, because I'm a disagreeable bitch!"

He smiled.

"You're a moron!" I told him.

He just looked at me. Happy golden lights danced in his eyes. I'd learned exactly what those sparks meant. Fury fled, replaced by alarm.

"Kiss me and I'll kill you," I warned.

"It might be worth it," he said softly.

If he held me a moment longer, I'd lose it and kiss him first. I was so damn happy he was alive.

When drowning, grasp at anything in reach. Even a straw will do. "My side is bleeding, Your Majesty."

He released me and called for Doolittle.

DOOLITTLE CHANTED THE WOUNDS CLOSED, fussed, pricked my legs with hot needles, and declared my responses normal. "A glancing wound. Does it hurt?"

"No," I lied.

He sighed, wearing the patient expression of a martyr. "Why do I bother?"

"I don't know. Would it help if I cried like a baby?"

He shook his head. "On second thought, keep your composure."

The spots on Curran's chest were growing. I pointed to him.

Doolittle handed me the scalpel. "I need to see to Dali. She's in shock."

Funny. She didn't seem to be in shock when I saw her.

Doolittle left in a very determined fashion. I stared at the scalpel. Curran sat on the floor and presented me with his huge muscled back. Oh boy.

"Just do it," he said. "Or are you going to faint?"

"Settle down, Princess. It's not my first time."

I put my fingers on the first spot. The muscle under my fingertips was hot and swollen. I pressed down, defining the target area the way I was taught, and sliced. He strained. Black blood poured from the wound and a chunk of silver surfaced. I grabbed it with forceps and plucked it free. Three quarters of an inch wide and two inches long. Shit. Enough silver to make an average shapeshifter violently sick. How many spikes did he have in him?

I dropped it into a metal tray, wiped the blood from his back, and went to the next one as fast as I could.

Slice, pull, wipe. Over and over.

He growled once, quietly.

"Almost done," I murmured.

"Who taught you to do this?" he asked.

"A wererat."

"Do I know him?"

"Her. She died a long time ago. She liked my father."

Nine spikes.

His wounds were closing, the muscle and skin knitting together. I rose, wet a towel, and cleaned his back. He leaned back a little, prolonging contact with my fingers.

I wanted to run my hand up his back. Instead I forced myself up, rinsed the towel, and tossed it into the bin Doolittle had set out.

"Good to go," I told him and walked away before I did something seriously stupid.

CHAPTER 28

IT WAS LATE. I SAT IN THE HOT TUB, SUNKEN DEEP in a windowless room. Moisture beaded on the ceiling and weak electric lamps provided hazy illumination. The jets didn't work with or without magic.

My whole body ached. My side, my arms, my back. The golem had dished out a lot of punishment.

I contemplated emerging from the hot tub. My feet were wrinkled and I was really warm. But that would mean going back into the bedroom. We had made it to the championship fight and the Red Guards kept a very tight watch on us now. The only way out of our rooms was through a first-class interrogation and with a huge escort. Even now, as I sat here, a couple of Red Guards lingered outside the door.

A pale, sweaty Corona bottle invaded my field of vision. It was clamped in a hand attached to a muscular arm with pale blond hair.

"Peace offering," Curran said.

Did I hear him come in? No.

I took the beer. He paused on the other side of the tub.

He was wearing a white gym towel. "I'm about to take the towel off and hop in," he said. "Fair warning."

There are times in life when shrugging takes nearly all of your will. "I've seen you naked."

"Didn't want you to run away screaming or anything."

"You flatter yourself."

He took the towel off.

I hadn't exactly forgotten what he looked like without clothes. I just didn't remember it being quite so tempting. He was built with survival in mind: strong but flexible, defined but hardly slender. You could bounce a quarter from his abs.

Curran stepped into the tub. He was obviously in no hurry.

It was like walking on a high bridge: don't look down. Definitely not below his waist . . . Oh my.

He sank into the hot water near me. I remembered to breathe. "How's your back?"

"It's fine," he said. "Thanks."

"Don't mention it." It had to be sore.

"Does your side hurt?"

"No."

His smile told me he knew we were both full of it.

I drank a bit of my beer, barely tasting it. Having him at the other end of the hot tub was like standing face-to-face with a hungry tiger with no fence between us. Or rather a hungry lion with very large teeth.

"Are you going to sack Jim?" I tried to sound casual.

"No," the lion said.

Exhaling in relief was completely out of the question—he'd hear it.

Curran stretched, spreading the breadth of his massive shoulders against the tub wall. "I concede that if I was paying attention, I would have nipped this in the bud. It never should have gotten to this point."

"How so?"

"Jim took over security eight months before the Red Stalker appeared. The upir was his first big test. He blew it.

We all did. Then there was Bran. Bran stole the surveys three times, waltzed in and out of the Keep, attacked you while you were in our custody, and took out a survey crew, Jim included. Jim considers it a personal failure."

"The guy teleported. How the hell are you supposed to guard against someone who pops in and out of existence?"

Curran shifted along the tub wall, sinking a little deeper into the water. "Had I known how hard Jim took it, I would've pointed it out to him. You remember when he tried to use you as bait?"

"I remember wanting to punch him in the mouth."

"It was the first sign of trouble. His priorities had shifted to 'win at any cost.' I thought it was odd at the time, but crazy shit kept happening and I let it slip. He became paranoid. All security chiefs are paranoid, but Jim took it further than most. He began to obsess with preventing future threats, and when Derek screwed up and got his face bashed in, it pushed Jim over the edge. He couldn't handle being responsible for Derek's death and for my having to kill the kid. He had to fix it at any cost. Basically, there was a problem and I missed it. And he sure as hell didn't bring it up."

Dear Beast Lord, as your chief of security, I must warn you that I have deep-seated inadequacy issues . . . Yeah, hell would sprout roses first.

"I can't keep up with everyone all the time," Curran said. "And Jim's the one who never went nuts on me. It was his time, I guess. So to answer your question fully, there's no reason to demote him. He has a talent for his job and he's doing reasonably well considering what he's up against. If I sack him, I'll have to replace him with somebody who has less experience and will screw up more. This is a lesson. Three months of dragging giant rocks around will help him get the stress out of his system."

We sat quietly. I sipped my beer, feeling a bit fuzzy. Funny how six months sober had turned me into a lightweight. Curran rested the back of his head on the edge of the hot tub and closed his eyes. I stared at the way his face

looked, etched against the darkness of the wall. He really
was a handsome bastard. Poised like this, he seemed very
human. Nobody to impress. Nobody to command. Just him,
in the hot water, tired, hurting, stealing a few precious moments of rest, and so irresistibly erotic. Well, that last one
came out of nowhere. It was the beer. Had to be.

Despite all his growling and threats, his arrogance, I
liked being next to him. He made me feel safe. It was a
bizarre emotion. I was never safe.

I closed my eyes. That seemed like the only reasonable
way out of the situation. If I couldn't see him, I couldn't
drool over him.

"So you didn't want to see me hurt?" he said. His voice
was deceptively smooth and soft, the deep, throaty, sly purr
of a giant cat who wanted something. Admitting that I took
his well-being into consideration might have been a fatal
mistake.

"I didn't want you to have to kill Derek."

"And if he had gone loup?"

"I would have taken care of it."

"How exactly were you planning on pushing Jim aside?
He was the highest alpha. The duty was his."

"I pulled rank," I told him. "I declared that since you
had accepted the Order's assistance, I outranked everybody."

He laughed. "And they believed you?"

"Yep. I also glared menacingly for added effect. Unfortunately, I can't make my eyes glow the way yours do."

"Like this?" He breathed in my ear.

My eyes snapped open. He stood inches away, anchored
on the tub floor, his arms leaning on the tub wall on each
side of me. His eyes were molten gold, but it wasn't the
hard, lethal glow of an alpha stare. This gold was warm and
enticing, touched with a hint of longing.

"Don't make me break this bottle over your head," I
whispered.

"You won't." He grinned. "You don't want to see me
hurt."

We lunged for each other at the same time and collided, crazy with need and starving for a taste. Warnings and alarms wailed in my mind, but I shut them down. Screw it. I wanted him.

He found my mouth. The thrust of his tongue against mine made my head spin. He tasted like heaven. I kissed him back, nipping, licking, melting against him. It felt so good . . . His lips traced a fiery line from my mouth to the corner of my jaw and down my neck. My whole body sang in warm liquid triumph. His voice was a ragged whisper in my ear. "Only if you want to . . . Say no, and I'll stop."

"No," I whispered to see if he would do it.

Curran pulled back. His eyes were pure need, raw and barely under control. He swallowed. "Okay."

It was the most erotic thing I had ever seen. I reached for him and slid my hand up his chest, feeling the taut muscle.

He caught my hand and kissed my palm gently. Heated, tightly controlled want shone in his eyes. I pulled my fingers free, pushed from the wall, and kissed his throat just under the jaw. This was bliss. There was no hope for me.

He growled, closing his eyes. "What are you doing?"

"Pulling on Death's whiskers," I murmured, letting my tongue play over his skin, rough with stubble. He smelled divine, clean and male. My hands slid up his biceps. His muscles tensed under the light pressure of my fingers. He was trying very, very hard to stand still and I almost laughed. All those times when he'd called me "baby" . . . Revenge was sweet.

"Is that a yes or a no?" he asked.

I slid against him and nipped his bottom lip.

"I'll take it as a yes." The steel muscles of his arms flexed under my hands. He grabbed me, hoisted me up onto him, and kissed me, thrusting into my mouth with his tongue in a hot, slick rhythm, greedy and eager. I threw my arms around his neck. His right hand grasped my hair; his left cupped my butt and pushed me closer against him, his erection a hard, hot length across my lap.

Finally—

"Let me in," Derek growled at the door.

Go away.

The guard said something. Curran's hand found my breast and caressed the nipple, sending an electric shock through my skin, threatening to melt me . . .

"Yes," Derek snarled. "I'm a member of the damn team. Ask them."

"Curran," I whispered. "Curran!"

He snarled and kept going. The door swung open.

I hit him on the back of the neck. He submerged. *Help. I've drowned the Beast Lord.*

Derek strode to the edge of the tub. Curran surfaced at the other wall. His face wore a snarl. "What is it?"

"The Reaper woman brought another box. This one had a hand in it. Not Livie's, doesn't smell like her, but a woman's hand. Smells about two days old, maybe more. They must've iced it."

I closed my eyes and let the reality sink in. Somewhere a woman was missing a hand. Her body was probably eaten. Revulsion squirmed through me, followed by indignant rage.

"Turn the hand over to the Red Guard. There's nothing we can do about it until tomorrow," Curran said.

Derek left.

Curran watched me from the other end of the tub, the water separating us like a battlefield. His eyes were still glowing like molten honey backlit from within. I had to get a grip. To him it was a contest of wills. He said he'd have me, I said he wouldn't, and he wanted to win at any cost.

"You missed your chance. I'm not coming anywhere near you, so you might as well turn your headlights off."

He moved toward me.

"No." I'd sunk a lot of steel into that "no." He stopped.

"You wanted me," he said.

Lying would only give him greater satisfaction. I had to keep him on the other end of the tub or I would throw myself at him again. "Yes, I did."

"What happened?"

"I remembered who I am and who you are."

"And who am I? Enlighten me."

"You're the man who likes to play games and hates losing. And I'm the idiot who keeps forgetting that. Turn around, so I can get out, please." And he almost had me, too.

He sprawled against the tub wall in a leisurely fashion, showing absolutely no indication of moving.

"Fine." Let's get this over with. I crouched on the bench and rose quickly. The water came to my midthigh.

A rough noise emanated from him. It sounded almost like a groan.

I climbed out of the tub, grabbed my towel, wrapped it around myself, and left. No more tubs for me. Not for a long, long time.

CHAPTER 29

———————

I AWOKE EARLY. TOO EARLY—THE CLOCK ON THE wall said three thirty. I lay with my eyes open for a few minutes and finally rose, swiped Slayer, and snuck out of the bedroom to the outer door. Derek perched on a chair by the doorway. He looked at me with yellow eyes.

"Where are the Guards?" I murmured.

He shrugged. "Must be a shift change. They sat by the door for the last six hours and then got up and left."

"How long have they been gone?"

"Three minutes."

Could be a shift change. I doubted the Reapers would try anything funny.

The curse of the Wolf Diamond guaranteed they would try to win it. Mart's goal was the gem, since he had to have it to attack the Pack. The rakshasas didn't seem to like even odds. They preferred to have an advantage, and without the Wolf Diamond, the shapeshifters would wipe the floor with them.

I felt reasonably confident about tomorrow's fights.

True, Mart's speed was ungodly and their magic was nothing to spit at, but our team was well-balanced and the shapeshifters fought like an oiled machine. Even when the Reapers entered the Pit as a team, they broke the fights into individual duels.

"I'll be back," I said.

"Where are you going?"

I told him the truth. "I want to see the Pit."

He nodded.

I snuck through the hallway and headed to the Pit. I just wanted to run my hand through the sand and settle my memories, then I would be able to sleep. The fastest way to the sand lay through the gym. I just had to cross it and I'd come out next to the Gold Gate.

I ducked inside and jogged barefoot across the floor. Another moment and I was out of the gates into the Pit. The covers hiding enormous skylights in the roof had been removed in preparation for the championship fight. Moonlight sifted on the sand.

By the Pit, bathed in the gauze shroud of moonrays, Hugh d'Ambray, flanked by Nick and the young fighter, handed a wrapped item to Mart and Cesare.

Ice rolled down my spine. I stopped. The item was long and looked like a sword wrapped in canvas. So that was where the Guards went. He bought them off to make the exchange.

Hugh was no fool. He had seen the fights and he realized we had a decent chance of winning tomorrow. He had decided to even the odds. That would be no ordinary sword.

Cesare's upper lip wrinkled in a grimace. Mart flashed his teeth at me and the two Reapers melted into the darkness. Hugh d'Ambray looked at me and I looked back at him.

"It's not surprising that Roland would ally with the rakshasas. They're an ancient race, dependent on magic. They respect his power," I said. "It's not surprising he would use them to weaken the Pack. They're vicious and sly but not too bright. If they win, they'll make a much weaker enemy than the shapeshifters. If they lose, the Pack will be bloodied anyway. However, having Hugh d'Ambray pay off the Guards and slink about in the night like a thief to provide the rakshasas with a weapon just before the final fight, that I find surprising. That feels almost like cheating. How very unsavory."

He strode to me with a short nod. "Walk with me."

I had to find out what he gave them. Our survival depended on it. I walked next to him. Nick and the other fighter fell behind a few steps. We began making a circle around the fence.

"I like the way you move. Where have we met before?"

"Just out of curiosity, what did you give them?"

"A sword," he said.

Duh. "It would have to be something very valuable. They view weapons as toys. They melted all of your precious electrum so they could pour it onto the face of one shapeshifter."

The corners of Hugh's mouth twitched. He caught the expression and froze it before it could bloom into a grimace, but I saw it. Score one for me.

"So this sword must be very special. Something they probably shouldn't be trusted with, something that would tip the odds in their favor tomorrow. Is it one of Roland's personal weapons?"

"I liked what you did with the golem," he said. "Fast, precise, economical. Good technique."

"Was it Scourge you gave them?"

The sword he'd given them had a wide blade. It could've been Scourge, although I really hoped it wasn't. Scourge unleashed the kind of magic that decimated armies. No, it had to be something else. A sword that could be used short range with some precision.

"If you hadn't allied with the wrong side, I could've used you," he said.

"Thank you for not insulting me with an offer."

"You're welcome. I do regret that you'll die tomorrow."

"And that fact matters to you why?"

He shrugged. "It's a waste of talent."

Here he stood, my father's replacement. Voron had trained him, as he had trained me, although he didn't get Hugh from birth. Hugh was ten when he started. He was a master swordsman. My father told me he had never seen a more talented fighter. I supposed the acknowledgment of my skill by him was a compliment.

"Why do you serve him?" I asked.

A faint veneer of puzzlement overlaid his features.

I really wanted to know. Voron took him in. Voron made him who he was. Roland's magic only kept him young—he had the body and face of a man barely older than me, but he had to be close to fifty. He wouldn't age. None of Roland's top cadre felt time. It was his gift to those who served him. But surely, that alone wasn't enough.

"He's stronger than me. I haven't found anyone else who could best me." Hugh studied me. "How often do you take orders from those who are weaker, dumber, and more inept than you?"

My pride stung. "I do so because I choose to."

"Why not choose to serve a stronger master?"

"Because his vision is warped and I don't believe in it."

"His vision is that of a better world."

"A better world bought with atrocities will be rotten at the core."

"Perhaps," Hugh said.

I looked into his eyes. "There won't be a tower above Atlanta as long as I live."

"How fortunate for our cause that your life will end to-morrow." Hugh smiled. He thought me ridiculous and so he should.

"Would you spar with me?" he asked. "We have time. I was generous with the Guards."

The offer tempted me. Hugh was an innate swordsman, a one-in-a-million fighter. Sparring with him would be as close as I could ever come to sparring with Voron once again. But I had a bout to fight. Injuring me would play into his hands rather nicely. "I don't have time to give you a lesson." Chew on that.

I walked away.

"I wonder how fast you are," he said to my back.

The blond swordsman struck at me from behind. I dropped under the blur that was his lunge and thrust low, driving Slayer into the gut, from the side up. The saber punctured the stomach with a loud pop and slid deep, all the way into the pressurized aorta. It took all of my skill to execute the thrust. Hugh had gotten my goat after all.

I pushed the blond off my sword. Slayer's blade emerged, coated in scarlet. He sagged to the floor. Inside him, the blood geysered out of the aorta. A normal human would be dead already. But the blond too had the benefit of Roland's magic. It would take him a minute or two to die.

I looked at Hugh. His face betrayed nothing, but his eyes widened. I knew exactly what was going through his head. It was the same thing that went through my mind when I saw a feat of expert bladework: could I have done that?

Our eyes met. The same thought zinged between us, like an electric charge: one day we would have to meet sword to sword. But it wouldn't be today, because tomorrow I had to fight the Reapers. I had to break it off.

"You threw him away. Sloppy, Hugh."

He took a step back. Too late I realized I'd used Voron's favorite rebuke. It had just rolled off my tongue. Shit.

I left. They didn't follow me.

IN THE MORNING THE SHAPESHIFTERS MEDI-tated. Then we practiced in the gym. Jim had given us a short briefing. "The Reapers fight like samurai: one on one. There are no tactics involved. It just breaks down into individual fights. They like flash, but they are efficient."

We all had a job to do. Mine was simple: Mart. I didn't want Mart. I wanted Cesare. But Jim's strategy made sense and I was going to follow it. I'd get a chance against Cesare. I wanted to kill him entirely too much to be denied.

But none of the tactics, none of the strategy, mattered until I knew what sort of blade Hugh had given to the Reapers. He had had ample opportunity to transfer the blade to the rakshasas before last night. He knew they wouldn't be able to resist using the sword, and he didn't want its power known until today.

Roland had made several weapons. All were devastating. Just thinking on it made me grit my teeth. He must've given Hugh the order to assure the rakshasas win at any cost. I wondered if it grated on Hugh.

At two minutes till noon we lined up and marched into the Pit. Sunshine poured on us through the skylights. The shapeshifters came out in warrior form, Raphael included, with Curran in the lead. Andrea carried a crossbow and enough firearms to take on a small country. Not satisfied with her own carrying capacity, she had loaded Dali with spare ammo.

We crossed the floor of the Arena and stepped onto the sand.

Across from us seven Reapers stood in two rows. My gaze skipped over them and fastened on Mart in the center. His sword was sheathed. Damn it. *What is it? What did he give you?*

I surveyed the rest. Cesare on Mart's left. The huge rakshasa, still wearing his human skin, carried two khandas: heavy, three-foot-long double-edged swords. I'd handled khandas before; not my cup of tea: too heavy and oddly sharpened.

On Mart's right stood the rakshasa's Stone. Ten feet tall and thick, he had the head of a small elephant, complete with wide fans of ears, but instead of a dark hide, his body had the sickly yellow tint of a man stricken with jaundice. A chain mail hauberk of yellow metal suspiciously resembling gold hung from his shoulders. I guessed even elephants liked to go into battle color-coordinated.

On the elephant's shoulder perched a slender creature:

hairless, dark red like raw liver, its bony limbs tipped with black claws. It resembled a lemur the size of a short human. Two vast wings spread from its shoulders. His arms held two brutal talwars: short, wide swords.

The second line of Reapers consisted of three fighters. The first was the woman who'd delivered the hair to me. The second was a humanoid thing with four arms, clothed in a reptilian skin of mottled green and brown. The third was Livie.

The reptilian thing was abnormally slender, green, and armed with two bows. Livie had a straight sword and looked scared to death. Her head had been shaved bald. It brought my rage back with crystal clarity. Sure, what she did was stupid and weak. But she was no fighter. They had no right to bring her into this. She didn't deserve it.

Livie met my gaze. Her eyes brimmed with tears.

They had hunted us like meat. They'd hurt Derek. They'd broken his bones, poured molten electrum on his face, tortured him, and laughed. They killed shapeshifters and forced young girls into the Pit. Their existence was an injustice. They deserved to die. And I would enjoy this. *Dear God, I will enjoy this.*

The magic was in full swing. The crowd waited, electric with anticipation. A smile blazed across Mart's face. His blade was still sheathed.

Curran shifted his clawed feet in the sand next to me.

Above us on the balcony, Sophia, the producer, held up an enormous yellow stone. Luminescent, lemon yellow, shaped like a tear, it shone and played in her hands like a living current of gold, capturing the light and tossing it back in a dazzling display of fire.

Sophia raised it above her head—her arms quaked with strain—and shouted. "Let the Games begin!"

The rakshasas' mage weaved her arms through the air.

I swung my two swords, Slayer in my right hand and the tactical blade in my left.

Mart reached for his sheath, clamped it, and slid the blade free, tossing the sheath onto the sand.

A wide blade stared at me, red like the finest ruby.

Everything slowed to a crawl, and in the ensuing still-ness, my heartbeat boomed through me, impossibly loud. The Scarlet Star. One of Roland's hellish personal weap-ons, a sword he had forged over five years out of his own blood. It had the power to fire thirteen bursts of magic. Like enchanted saw blades, they would lock onto their targets, slice through anything in their path, and cleave their objec-tive in half. They couldn't be dodged. They couldn't be blocked. The blade itself couldn't be broken by an ordinary weapon. Even Curran couldn't snap it.

We would die instantly. Curran might survive long enough to be torn apart by the rakshasas.

I couldn't let him die.

I whipped about, slow as if underwater, and saw him looking back at me with gray eyes from a monster's face.

What do I do? How can I keep him alive?

It will be okay, Curran mouthed, but I couldn't hear him, all sound blocked by my panic.

I turned back. Mart gripped the sword with both hands. The red blade glistened, as if wet with blood. I had to de-stroy it, because if he completed a strike, all of us would die.

Blood. It was forged out of Roland's blood, the same blood that now coursed through my veins. There might be a way to destroy the blade after all. If I could take possession of the sword.

The gong boomed. The world leapt back to its normal speed.

I charged.

Mart began to raise the sword for an overhead strike.

I had never run so fast in my life. The sand blurred. The blade point loomed before me, rising. I grasped the crimson blade and shoved it into my stomach.

It hurt. My blood drenched the red substance of the sword. Mart stared at me, stunned. I grasped Mart's hand and pushed the sword deeper into me. The point broke through my back. Deeper. All the way to the hilt.

The blade sat inside me, a wedge of hot agony. My blood coated the metal, forging a link with Roland's. Around me the shapeshifters crashed into the rakshasas. I whispered a power word. *"Hessaad." Mine.*

Magic surged inward from the surface of my skin, from the tips of my fingers and toes, and locked onto the sword. The blade sparked, sending jolts of pain through me. It felt as though a clump of barbed wire were being drawn through my gut. I clawed on to reality, trying not to pass out. The Arena reeled, spinning in a calico whirlpool, and through the smudge of faces, I saw Hugh d'Ambray on his feet, staring at me as if he had seen a demon.

My biological father's blood reacted with mine and recognized it. The sword was mine. It would obey. *Now.*

"Ud," I whispered. *Die.* The power word that never worked. To will something to die, one must first have complete possession of it.

Magic tore from me. The sword buckled in my body, like a living creature, vibrating, striving to break free. Agony flooded me in a brilliant burst. I screamed.

The sword shattered. Pieces of the blade floated to the ground in a fine red powder. Inside my body the part of the sword that had been in me disintegrated into dust and mixed with my blood, spreading through my body. Roland's blood, scalding me as if my insides had been dropped into boiling oil. So much power . . .

The fire melted my legs. I fell down onto the sand. The inferno inside me was cooking me alive, wringing tears from my eyes. I tried to move, but my muscles refused to obey. Every cell of my body was on fire.

The whole thing had taken five, six seconds from start to finish, enough time to impale myself on the blade and utter two words. Hugh had been right—I would die today. But the unbreakable sword was shattered and Curran would live. And so would the rest of them. Not bad for five seconds of work.

A horrible roar shook the Arena. I jerked my head. Curran had seen me fall and charged over to me. The ele-

phant thundered to intercept him, and Curran disemboweled him with one strike, leaping past him. *No need to
hurry, Your Majesty. It's too late for me anyway.*

Mart dropped the useless hilt and grabbed me, his eyes
brimming with fury. Curran lunged for me.

But Mart shot straight up like an arrow. Curran's clawed
hand caught empty sand. He'd missed me by half a second.

Wind fanned my face as Mart flew up. It felt like the afterlife, but I wasn't dead yet. One doesn't feel pain in the
afterlife, and I hurt. Dear God, I hurt.

We soared above the Arena's sand, floating in the shaft
of golden sunlight stabbing through the nearest skylight. I
saw that only three rakshasas had made it alive from the
Pit's sand: Mart, Cesare, and Livie, locked in the crook of
Cesare's arm.

Tiny flecks of skin broke free from Mart's cheek, hovering in the light. He breathed, and his entire being fractured
into a thousand pieces, streaming upward like myriad but-
terflies taking flight to vanish in the glow, revealing a new
creature. He was tall, his shoulders broad, his waist and
hips narrow. Skin the color of amber stretched taut over
refined muscle. Black hair streamed from his head down to
his waist. His eyes were piercing cobalt blue, two sharp
sapphires on a beautiful face tainted with arrogance and
predatory glee.

Mart no longer needed his human skin.

He clamped me to him and I saw Sophia on the balcony,
clutching at the Wolf Diamond. We streaked to her and
stopped at her eye level.

"Gift me the jewel," Cesare ordered and held out his
hand. The curse of the stone had been weighed against the
Fools, and the Fools had won. Mart would rather risk the
anger of the Wolf Diamond than the shapeshifters' down
below.

Sophia swallowed.

"Don't," I said.

Below us the Arena roared with indignant screams.

"Gift me the jewel, woman." The tattooed snakes rose from Cesare's skin and hissed.

Sophia's long, pale fingers let go. The golden tear of the Wolf Diamond fell and landed in Cesare's huge palm. "It's yours," she said.

You moron.

The rakshasas flew up. The skylight blocked us. Mart's hand flashed and the heavy glass shattered into a glittering cascade of shards. We pushed through it and then we were flying above the city.

I LAY IN A GOLDEN CAGE IN A PUDDLE OF MY blood. It soaked my hair, my cheek, my clothes. I breathed it in, its scent and magic cloaking me. I could feel the blood around me the way I felt my limbs or my fingers. It had left my body but we remained connected. I had always sensed magic in my blood, but I'd never felt it, not like this.

Inside my stomach, tiny flecks of power smoldered, the remnants of Roland's sword. My body was absorbing them slowly, one by one. His blood mixed with my own, releasing its power, and anchored me to life and pain. I didn't move, conserving what little strength and magic I had left. I chanted, barely moving my lips, trying to push my body into regeneration. It didn't obey very well, but I kept trying. I wouldn't give up and just die.

At least the pain had dimmed enough for my eyes to stop watering.

High above me a golden ceiling stretched, shrouded in shadow. Tall walls defined a cavernous chamber, their carved glitter flowing seamlessly into the tiled floor layered with vivid velvet and silk pillows. Nataraja, the People's head honcho in Atlanta, had tried to furnish his room just like this. But his chamber atop the People's Casino paled in comparison to this room. All of Nataraja's wealth wouldn't have bought a single panel of these golden walls.

I wondered if he had gotten his interior-decorating ideas

from visiting a vimana. The People's association with rakshasas must have gone pretty far back.

Just beyond me, the Wolf Diamond shone on a narrow
metal pedestal. The two trophies of the rakshasas' might:
me and the gem. *Where is your curse now, you dumb rock?*

A steady hum underscored my thoughts. The propellers
of the vimana. I had lost consciousness during the flight.
When I came to, we had landed on the balcony of the flying
palace sitting aground in the lush jungle, and Mart had
tossed me into the cage. Now I lay there, neither alive nor
dead, suspended three feet above the floor in a cage like
some sort of canary.

Mart sat among the pillows below. He'd traded his cat
burglar suit for a turquoise flowing garment that left his
shoulders and arms bare. Three women fluttered over him,
like brightly colored hummingbirds. One washed his feet.
One brushed his hair. One held his drink. Other rakshasas
sat along the wall, a respectable distance from him, a mot-
ley crew of monstrous and human bodies in jewel-toned
cloth. Some came and others went through the arched entrances puncturing the walls.

Mart stared at me, his blue eyes two merciless gem-
stones, pushed the women aside, and strode to the cage. I
stopped chanting and just lay there, like a rag doll. I had
enough strength left for one lunge. The second he opened
that door, I'd break his neck. His finger twitched and Livie
came into my view. Her face was a pale smudge next to the
amber of Mart's skin.

Mart spoke, lilting words interspersed with harsh
sounds.

"He says that if you live, you'll serve him. If you die,
they will eat the meat off your bones."

If they ate me, they would become more powerful. I had
no idea how I could prevent it. Here's wishing for a power
word of spontaneous combustion . . .

Mart spoke again, his gaze boring into me.

"He wants to know if you understand what he said."

I had to survive now. He left me no choice.

"Do you understand?"

Arrogant asshole. A tiny ripple pulsed through the puddle of my blood. Neither of them noticed it.

My voice was a raspy whisper. That was all I could manage. "First I'll kill Cesare. Then I'll kill him."

Livie hesitated.

"Tell him."

A single sharp word snapped from Mart's lips. Livie jerked, as if whipped, and translated.

Mart smiled, baring perfect teeth, and strode back to his place.

I lay still, inhaling the vapors rising from my blood. My vision blurred, clearing for a few moments, then dissolved back into a foggy mess. The only reality that remained was the steady pain in my stomach, the blood spread out before me, and my silent chants.

A hulking shape appeared on the edge of the room and grew as it approached. Cesare. Still in his human shape. The snakes rose from his body, hissing, tangling with one another. He carried a golden goblet.

He paused by my bars and said something to Mart.

He was going to drink my blood. It would make him stronger. My blood would nourish the creature who had tried to murder Derek. *I don't think so.*

Cesare thrust his hand through the bars, and scooped my blood into the goblet. Bastard. Anger built inside me, straining. My fingers trembled.

A thin line of magic stretched between me and the blood in the cup. I still felt it. The blood was still a part of me.

He tipped the goblet to his lips.

No. Mine.

Rage snapped inside me, and I sank it into the blood, commanding it to move as if it were a limb. It obeyed.

Cesare's eyes bulged. He clawed at the gush of red that had suddenly become solid in his mouth, moaning like his tongue had been cut out. *That's right, you fucking sonovabitch.* I shot more power into the blood. It hurt, but I didn't care.

Sharp red needles burst out of Cesare's face, puncturing his left eye, his lips, his nose, and his throat. He screamed, his ruined eye draining in a gush.

Payback for Derek. Enjoy, *zaraza*.

I liquefied the blood. One more time. The needles withdrew and then burst out from his face again. Cesare writhed, howling, ripping chunks from his face. Rakshasas ran; someone screamed. I hated to cut this short. I wanted to make it last like what he had done to Derek, but they wouldn't let me keep it up. I liquefied the blood again, spiked it, twisted it in sharp bursts, melted it again, and finally hammered magic into it. A blade of blood shot out of Cesare's throat. It turned, neatly painting a crimson collar around his neck. I let the blood go and it turned to black dust, its magic exhausted.

Roland had the power to solidify and control his blood. Now I had learned it, too. I didn't know if it was the boost of having his blood sword dissolve inside me or if it was my anger, but I had the talent now and had spent every iota of it making Cesare suffer.

Cesare's head rolled off his shoulders. A small gush of blood gurgled at the base of his spinal column. His body toppled back. He fell with a thunderous crash and behind him I saw Mart. He said something to Livie and laughed. She licked her lips and translated. "He says you've proven useful already."

TIME DRIPPED BY, SLOWLY, SO VERY SLOWLY. RAK-shasas drifted through the room. I silently chanted, encouraging my body to heal, my chapped, bloody lips whispering the words over and over, but the strong current of magic inside me had shrunk to a mere trickle. It sat there weak and useless like a soggy tissue and refused to respond. Still, I tried.

Cold fingers touched my hand. I focused and saw Livie, her eyes huge as she bent to me. Tears wet her cheeks. "I'm sorry," she whispered. "I'm so sorry I got all of you into this."

"Don't be. It's not your fault."

A grimace skewed her face. She slid a small piece of metal into my palm.

Someone snarled. Livie dashed from the cage. I looked at the metal she'd given me. A knife.

She was trying to help me. When I did go, I wouldn't be completely alone.

DARKNESS ENCROACHED ON THE EDGE OF MY VIsion. It grew slowly but steadily from the corners. The pain had receded behind a wall of numbness. Still there, still present, but no longer murderously sharp. I was dying.

I waited for my life to flash before my eyes, but it didn't. I just stared at the cavernous chamber, gleaming with metallic luster, and watched the fire flare and fracture within the depths of the Wolf Diamond. My lips moved softly, still shaping regeneration chants. By all rights, I should have been dead already. My stubbornness and Roland's blood had kept me alive this long. But eventually my will would fade and I would fade with it.

I always thought my life would end in a battle or maybe with a chance strike on some dark street. But not like this. Not in a gold cage to be served as a meal to a bunch of monsters.

But Curran would live and so would Derek, and Andrea, and Jim . . . Given a choice, I would change nothing. I just wished . . . I wished I had more time.

The darkness grew again. Maybe it was time to surrender. I was so very tired of hurting.

A commotion broke out among the rakshasas. They darted back and forth. Mart rose from his pillows and began barking orders. A group of rakshasas dashed through the arched door, brandishing bizarre weapons. My weak heart hammered faster.

It couldn't be.

More rakshasas ran and then I heard it, the low, rolling roar like distant thunder laced with rage.

Curran.

I was hallucinating. He couldn't be there. I heard the pulse of propellers. We were still flying through the air.

The terrifying lion roar shook the vimana again, closer this time.

A wave of rakshasas flooded back into the chamber, bristling with weapons. A mangled body flew through one of the arched entrances. Livie sprinted to me and hid behind my cage.

The tide of monsters rallied and charged the entrance. They crashed against the doorway, struggled, and pulled back, bloodied. Curran burst into the chamber.

He wore the warrior form. Huge, gray fur stained with blood, he roared again, and the rakshasas shrank from the sound of his anger. He tore through them as if they were toy soldiers. Howls rang through the chamber as limbs were ripped, bones broken, and blood fountained in a pressurized spray.

He came for me. I couldn't believe it.

He came for me. Into a flying palace full of thousands of armed rakshasas in the middle of a magic jungle. *Oh, you stupid, stupid idiot man.* What was the God damn point of saving him only to watch him throw his life away?

Behind Curran an enormous beast charged into the room. Shaggy with dark fur, a huge muzzle gaping black, the beast roared and rammed the crowd. Giant paws swiped, crushing skulls. Mahon, the Bear of Atlanta.

A hellish creature thrust into the gap made by Mahon. She was corded with muscle, sandy brown and covered with spots. Her hands were armed with black claws. Fangs jutted out of her round jaws. She was grotesque and mind-numbingly terrifying. The beast howled and broke into an eerie hyena cackle. Every hair on the back of my neck stood on end.

Curran ripped his way to me. Cuts and wounds dotted his frame. He bled, but kept going, unstoppable in his fury and still roaring. His roar slapped your senses like a clap of thunder, shaking you to your very core. The rakshasas were too many. His only chance lay in panicking them into flight, but even panic wouldn't last long—sooner or later they would do the math and figure out that a couple hundred to three were pretty good odds, but as long as he kept blasting them with his roar and throwing them around, they couldn't think properly.

Mart thrust himself between my cage and Curran, his sword in his hands. The rest of the rakshasas pulled back, but Curran barely noticed. He lunged at Mart.

Blades flashed, impossibly fast. Mart spun out of the way and sliced deep into Curran's back. The Beast Lord whipped about, oblivious to pain, and raked his claws across Mart, ripping his robes. Red blood swelled on Mart's golden skin. They collided. Swords struck, claws rent, teeth snapped. Mart sank his short blade into Curran's side. Curran growled in pain, wrenched free, dropped down, and swiped his leg under Mart, knocking him off his feet. Mart leapt straight up off the floor, both swords in his hands, and met Curran halfway. Dumb-ass move. The Beast Lord hammered a punch into Mart's face. The rakshasa flew across the chamber, slid across the floor, and rolled to his feet. Curran chased him.

Mart spun like a dervish. His blades became a lethal whirlwind. Curran lunged into them, cuts blooming across his pelt, and grabbed at Mart. The rakshasa leapt straight up, soaring above the crowd.

Curran tensed. The monstrous muscles on his tree-trunk legs contracted like steel springs. He launched himself into the air. His claws caught Mart in midleap, hooking his leg. Mart struggled up, but Curran hung on, ripping chunks out of the rakshasa's flesh as he climbed up his body. The warped leonine mouth gaped and Curran bit Mart's side. They dropped like a stone and crashed to the floor a few feet from me. Mart slid free, slick with his own blood. His gaze fastened on the Wolf Diamond, still sitting on its pedestal. He lunged for it. His bloodied fingers grasped the topaz. He backed away and bumped into my cage.

I thrust through the bars and stabbed Livie's knife into

the base of his throat, between his left shoulder and the column of his neck. The puddle of my blood shivered, obedient to my will, and bit into his back with a hundred spikes.

The gem slipped out of his fingers.

I locked my arms on his neck, trying to choke him out, but I didn't have the strength.

Curran swept the Wolf Diamond off the floor, clamped his huge left hand onto Mart's shoulder, and smashed the topaz into Mart's face.

The rakshasa screamed.

Curran pounded him, hammering the gemstone into Mart again and again. Blood flew. The blows crushed Mart's perfection into bloody pulp. The sword fell from his fingers. Curran struck for the last time and ripped him from the cage, snapping my blood spikes, which dissipated into black dust. He twisted Mart's neck, snapping the spinal column, and shook the lifeless body at the crowd of rakshasas with a deafening roar.

They fled. They streamed out of the chamber through the arched doors, trampling one another in their hurry to get away.

Curran wrenched the cage bars apart.

"You suicidal moron," I rasped. "What are you doing here?"

"Repaying the favor," he snarled.

He pulled me out of the cage and saw the wound in my stomach. His half-form face jerked. He pressed me against his chest. "Stay with me."

"Where would I . . . go, Your Majesty?" My head was spinning.

Behind us the taller of the nightmarish beasts swept the petrified Livie from behind the cage. "It's all right," the monster told her, clamping her with one hand and holding the Wolf Diamond with the other. "Aunt B's got you."

At the opposite end of the chamber someone was fighting the current of fleeing rakshasas. A sword flashed and I recognized Hugh d'Ambray, with Nick at his heels. He saw us and shouted something.

"What is he doing here?" Curran growled.

"He's Roland's Warlord. He's here for me." He was here for the woman who had broken his master's blade.

"Tough luck. You're mine." Curran turned and ran, carrying me off. Hugh screamed, but the current of fleeing rakshasas pushed him out of the chamber.

I lay cradled in Curran's arms as he ran through the vimana. Others joined us, tall, furry shapes. I could no longer distinguish the different faces. I just rested in his arms, nearly blind, every jolt sending more pain stinging up my spine. Soft darkness tried to engulf me.

"Stay with me, baby."

"I will."

It was a dream or a nightmare, I could no longer decide. But somehow I stayed with him all the way, even as the vimana careened, even as we leapt out of it and saw it crash behind us into the green hills. I stayed with him all during the mad run through the jungle. The last things I remembered were stone ruins and Doolittle's face.

EPILOGUE

⬤——

I DREAMT OF CURRAN SNARLING, "FIX HER!" AND
Doolittle saying that he wasn't a god and there was only so
much he could do. I dreamt of Julie crying by my bed, of
Jim sitting near, of Andrea telling me some frustratingly
complicated story . . . The noises blended in my head until
finally I could stand it no longer. "Would all of you just be
quiet? Please."

I blinked and saw Curran's face.

"Hey," he said.

"Hey." I smiled. There he was, alive. I was alive. "I was
telling the people in my head to shut up."

"They have medication for that."

"I probably can't afford it."

He caressed my cheek.

"You came for me," I whispered.

"Always," he told me.

"You're a damn idiot. Trying to throw your life away?"

"Just staying sharp. Keeping you safe keeps me in
shape."

He leaned in and kissed me softly on the lips. I reached for him and he hugged me to him and held on for a long moment. I closed my eyes, smiling at the simple pleasure of his skin on mine. And then my arms grew too heavy. Gently he put me back on my pillow and walked away. I curled under my blanket, warm and safe and so perfectly happy, and fell asleep again.

THE TORTURE BEGAN IN THE MORNING WITH Doolittle holding up three fingers to my face. "How many fingers?"

"Eleven."

"Thank God," he said. "I was beginning to worry."

"Where is His Fussiness?"

"He left last night."

I struggled with a ball of emotions: regret at not seeing him, relief he was gone, happiness he was well enough to walk. There truly was no hope for me.

Doolittle sighed. "Shall I tell you the usual? Where you are, how you are, and in what manner you have gotten here?"

I looked at Doolittle. "Doc, we've got to stop meeting like this."

A sour grimace wrinkled his face. "You're preaching to the choir."

Jim was my first visitor of the day, right after I'd been poked, pierced with needles, had my temperature taken, and generally been driven to the point of wishing I had not woken up for a few more days. Jim came in and quietly sat by me, very much the Pack's chief of security rather than my surly occasional partner. He looked at me with a solemn expression and said, "We'll take care of you."

"Thank you." I couldn't take any more care at the moment. Doolittle's ministrations had nearly done me in.

Jim gave this strange little nod and left. Weirded the hell out of me.

Next came Julie, who crawled in my bed and lay there with a deeply mournful face while I chewed her out for letting Curran out of the cage early.

While she sat there, nodding to my lecture, Derek arrived.

"How's Livie?"

"She left," he said. "She thanked me, but she couldn't stay."

"I'm sorry," I told him.

"I'm not," Julie said.

"I didn't expect her to stay," Derek said. His face was a stone mask and his voice was devoid of all emotion. Despite everything I had said, he must've believed she loved him.

"I was her way out, nothing more. I'm okay with that. Besides, things have changed . . ." He pointed to his face.

Julie scrambled off the bed. "For your information, I don't care!"

She took off. Derek looked at me. "Don't care about what?"

My kid had a giant crush on my teenage werewolf side-kick. Why me? Why? What did I ever do to anybody?

I squirmed into my bed and pulled the covers up to my chin. "Your face, Derek. She doesn't care what you look like. You go sort it out yourself."

Then I slept, and when I woke up, Andrea came in and shooed Doolittle out. She pulled up the chair and looked at me.

"Where am I and how have I gotten here?" I asked. Doolittle had offered to clue me in, but I knew I'd get a lecture-free version from her.

"You're in Jim's safe house," she said. "After rakshasas grabbed you, Curran went nuts. He pulled all of the shapeshifters out of the Arena—"

"There were more than us, Mahon, and Aunt B?"

"Yes, they were in the crowd. He thought the rakshasas might go for a big finish. Don't interrupt. We followed Jim through Unicorn Lane into the jungle, chased after the vimana until it landed—the damn thing lands every couple of hours, I guess to rest its propellers or something. We stormed in. There was a fight. I don't know what happened next. I was with the group that broke its engine. The next time I saw Curran, you were in his arms and you looked like shit."

"Okay." That was pretty much what I had figured.

Andrea fixed me with a hard stare and lowered her voice. "You shattered the Scarlet Star."

Crap. I didn't think she'd recognize the sword. "Eh?"

"Give me some damn credit. I'm this close to getting my Master at Arms, Firearm." Andrea wrinkled her face. "I've had all of my security briefings already. If it wasn't for Ted, I would already be a ranked knight. I know what that sword was capable of."

"Did you tell the rest of them?"

"Yes, I did." She didn't seem a bit sorry about it. "I told them how it worked and that if it wasn't for you, we'd be on the rakshasas' dining table."

"I wish you hadn't done that."

She made a short cutting motion with her hand. "That's beside the point. You broke it to pieces. It was forged out of Roland's blood and you smeared it with yours and *broke* it. I'm not stupid, Kate. Please, don't ever think that I'm stupid."

She had put two and two together. Only a blood relation would be able to disintegrate Roland's sword.

"Daughter?" she asked.

It's not exactly like I could lie. "Yep."

Her face turned a shade paler. "I thought he refused to have children."

"He made an exception in my mother's case."

"Is she still alive?"

"He killed her."

Andrea rubbed her face. "Does Curran know?"

"Nobody knows," I told her. *You're my best friend. The only one I have. Please, please don't force me to kill you. I can't do it.*

She took a deep breath. "Okay," she said. "It's good that nobody knows. Probably best we keep it that way."

I remembered to breathe.

"THIS IS RIDICULOUS," I GRUMBLED.

"Quiet, you!" Andrea slid the key into the lock and opened the door to her apartment. "You'll stay with me. It's just for a couple of days. I promised Doolittle to watch over you for a weekend. I'm supposed to keep you from 'storming any castles.'"

It was that or spend another forty-eight hours in Doolittle's care. He was the best medmage I had ever had the honor to deal with. He was a kind and caring person, a far better human being than me. But the longer you stayed in his care, the more pronounced his mother hen tendencies became. He would spoon feed me if I let him. Staying at Andrea's was the lesser of two evils.

"I still say you should have taken the flowers," she told me, walking through the apartment.

"They were from Saiman." Saiman, true to his modus operandi, had sent me white roses with a thank-you card, left on the doorstep of Jim's safe house, the location of which Saiman wasn't supposed to know. Jim nearly had an apoplexy when he saw it. The card told me that Sophia, the show's producer, had confessed to providing the shards of the Wolf Diamond to the rakshasas. She apparently employed several dummy bettors and had placed large sums on the rakshasas from the start, when they were an unknown commodity and the odds were against them. Saiman didn't mention what had become of her. Knowing him, nothing pleasant.

Andrea looked into her living room and froze. She stood still like a statue with her mouth hanging open. The bag slipped off her shoulder and crashed to the floor.

A huge thing hung suspended from the ceiling of Andrea's living room. It wasn't quite a chandelier and not quite a mobile; it was a thin, seven-feet-tall, giant metal . . .

something, a warped Christmas tree–like construction, made of brass wire and crowned with the works of Lorna Sterling, books one through eight, perched in a fanlike fashion at the very top. Below the books, several levels of wire branches radiated under all angles supporting dozens of delicate crystal ornaments suspended from tiny golden chains and twinkling softly when they bumped. Each ornament was decorated with a small ribbon and each contained a piece of fabric: white, pastel pink, blue . . .

As if in a dream, Andrea reached over and plucked one of the ornaments off the tree. It popped open in her hand. She plucked the peach fabric out, unrolled it, and held up a thong.

I blinked.

She stared, speechless, and shook the thong at me, her eyes opened wide like saucers.

"I'm going to go now," I said and escaped. Doolittle would never know.

At least I knew where Raphael had vanished during the Midnight Games.

I rode a Pack's horse to my apartment. I didn't fall off her, which required a heroic effort of will on my part. The lack of adoring crowds, ready to greet me with flowers and medals at my door, was sadly disappointing.

I stopped by the super for the new key, climbed to my apartment, and studied my new lock. Big, metal, and shiny. Not a scratch on it. Even the key itself had a bizarre groove carved into it, which made the whole setup supposedly completely burglar proof. *Pick that, Your Majesty.*

I unlocked the door, stepped inside, and shut it behind me. I kicked my shoes off, wincing at the hint of ache in my stomach. It would take a long time before it healed completely. At least I no longer bled.

Tension fled from me. Tomorrow I would worry about Hugh d'Ambray and Andrea and Roland, but now I was simply happy. Aaahh. Home. My place, my smells, my familiar rug under my feet, my kitchen, my Curran in the kitchen chair . . . Wait a damn minute.

"You!" I looked at the lock; I looked at him. So much for the burglar-proof door.

He calmly finished writing something on a piece of paper, got up, and came toward me. My heart shot into overdrive. Little golden sparks laughed in his gray eyes. He handed me the piece of paper and smiled. "Can't wait."

I just stared like an idiot.

He inhaled my scent, opened the door, and left. I looked at the paper.

I'll be busy for the next eight weeks, so let's set this for November 15th.

MENU

I want lamb or venison steak. Baked potatoes with honey butter. Corn on the cob. Rolls. And apple pie, like the one you made before. I really liked it. I want it with ice cream.

You owe me one naked dinner, but I'm not a complete beast, so you can wear a bra and panties if you so wish. The blue ones with the bow will do.

Curran,
Beast Lord of Atlanta

ACKNOWLEDGMENTS

Telling this story wouldn't have been possible without my editor, Anne Sowards. Thank you, as always, for your advice, guidance, and endless patience. I'm very fortunate to work with you, and I deeply appreciate your help and your friendship.

Thank you to my wonderful agent, Nancy Yost, for being a zealous advocate of my work and for having the patience of a saint and rescuing me time and time again.

Thank you to Cam Dufty, Ace's editorial assistant, for fielding numerous, and sometimes unreasonable, requests for help.

A huge thank you to Michelle Kasper, the production editor, and Andromeda Macri, the assistant production editor, who made sure the manuscript became a book. Thank you to cover designer Annette Fiore DeFex and artist Chad Michael Ward for the spectacular cover.

Several people have read this book and were kind enough to offer an opinion on it. They are Bianca Bradley, Brian Kell, Brooke Nelissen, Elizabeth Hull, Heather Fagan, Jeaniene Frost (who threatened me with a posse), Jennifer Lampe and Jill Myles, Leslie Schlotman, Melissa Rian, Melissa Sawmiller, Meljean Brook, Reece Notley, Shannon Crowley, Stacy Cooper, and Vernieda Vergara (who wasn't mad about Dali). Thank you so much, guys! You've made the book better.

Finally, thank you to the readers! You make it all worthwhile.

Ilona Andrews is the pseudonym of the husband-and-wife writing team of Ilona and Gordon Andrews. They live in the Smoky Mountains with their daughters and write bestselling books together.

Visit Ilona's website at www.ilona-andrews.com